Wharton's N

HARDSCRABBLE BOOKS—Fiction of New England

Chris Bohjalian, *Water Witches*

Ernest Hebert, *The Dogs of March*

Ernest Hebert, *Live Free or Die*

W. D. Wetherell, *The Wisest Man in America*

Edith Wharton (Barbara A. White, ed.), *Wharton's New England: Seven Stories and* Ethan Frome

Thomas Williams, *The Hair of Harold Roux*

Edith Wharton

WHARTON'S
NEW ENGLAND

Seven Stories and *Ethan Frome*

EDITED BY

Barbara A. White

UNIVERSITY OF NEW HAMPSHIRE

University Press of New England / Hanover and London

UNIVERSITY PRESS OF NEW ENGLAND
publishes books under its own imprint and is the publisher for
Brandeis University Press, Brown University Press, Dartmouth
College, Middlebury College Press, University of New Hampshire,
University of Rhode Island, Tufts University, University of
Vermont, Wesleyan University Press, and Salzburg Seminar.

UNIVERSITY OF NEW HAMPSHIRE
Published by University Press of New England, Hanover, NH 03755
© 1995 by the Trustees of the University of New Hampshire
All rights reserved
Printed in the United States of America   5   4   3   2   1

Library of Congress Cataloging-in-Publication Data
Wharton, Edith, 1862–1937.
   Wharton's New England : seven stories and Ethan Frome /
Edith Wharton ; edited by Barbara A. White.
     p.   cm. — (Hardscrabble books)
   ISBN 0–87451–715–x (pbk.)
     1. New England—Social life and customs—Fiction. I. White,
Barbara Anne. II. Wharton, Edith, 1862–1937. Ethan Frome.
III. Title. IV. Title: New England. V. Series.
PS3545.H16A6   1995
813'.52—dc20   94–42882

Contents

Introduction

In her autobiography, *A Backward Glance* (1934), Edith Wharton tells us that her colonial ancestors lived first in Massachusetts. But they soon "transferred their activities to the easier-going New York, where people seem from the outset to have been more interested in making money and acquiring property than in Predestination and witch-burning."[1] By the time Edith was born in 1862 her family fortunes had long been amassed, and she would grow up to become a leading chronicler of monied and propertied New York. Indeed, after she died in 1937, many critics would consider "old New York" her proper subject and the novels that describe it, *The House of Mirth* (1905) and the Pulitzer Prize–winning *The Age of Innocence* (1920), her most enduring fictions.

But a part of Edith Wharton was always fascinated by the land of predestination and witch-burning that her ancestors fled. She set a surprising amount of her work in New England, from the stories that began her writing career to the novella that gained lasting fame, *Ethan Frome* (1911), a wintery tale of "Starkfield," Massachusetts. Recently the excellent but long neglected *Summer* (1917) has been recognized as a worthy companion piece to *Ethan Frome*, Wharton's "hot Ethan," as she called it.[2] Both *Ethan Frome* and *Summer* are set in the Berkshires near Lenox, Massachusetts, where Edith and her husband Teddy built an elegant house, the Mount. Chafing from the restrictions of her life as a society matron in New York, Edith considered the Mount "my first real home" (*BG*, 125); she describes it lyrically in *A Backward Glance*, recalling visits by Henry James and other friends.

Wharton used the western Massachusetts setting not only for *Ethan Frome* and *Summer* but also for a novel, *The Fruit of the Tree* (1907), and in numerous short stories throughout her career. Long after the Mount was sold, the Whartons divorced, and Edith living out her life in Paris, Starkfield would appear in "Bewitched" (1925). The last story Wharton sent to her publishers before her death was "All Souls'" (1937), another New England witch tale, and she left a number of unpublished fragments with New England settings. A full quarter of Wharton's eighty-five published short stories are set in New England. Of these, three stories, "The Angel at the Grave" (1901), "Xingu" (1911), and "All Souls'" (all in this volume), are rated among her very best.

That Wharton felt considerably attached to her New England body of work is shown by the fierceness with which she defended it from attack. Although most reviewers praised her treatment of New England, some thought her settings too bleak—as in *Ethan Frome* and the short story "The Pretext" (1908); others found mistakes, as in her depiction of factories in *The Fruit of the Tree*.[3] Wharton seldom responded to negative reviews, but she was stung by criticisms that she was an outsider who knew nothing of New England. While she quietly corrected the errors, she loudly attributed reviewers' complaints to their desire to avoid dark truths and approach New England as "seen through the rose-colored spectacles of my predecessors, Mary Wilkins [Freeman] and Sarah Orne Jewett" (*BG*, 293). In three articles and her autobiography, Wharton insisted on her firsthand knowledge of the region and the "accuracy of 'atmosphere'" in her works (*BG*, 296).

Wharton was certainly correct about her familiarity with New England. She had summered in the region since childhood in her parents' Newport, Rhode Island, mansion, and as an adolescent she made visits to Bar Harbor, Maine, where she met her lifelong friend Walter Berry. The man she chose to marry was a Bostonian and Harvard graduate; in fact, all the men closest to her—her husband Teddy, Berry, her lover Morton Fullerton, and her art critic friend Bernard Berenson—were Harvard grads, however cosmopolitan and European-oriented they seemed. After her marriage Wharton bought and refurbished a house in Newport, which she named Land's End as it looked out to sea. She became acquainted with Boston through visits to her in-laws, and Teddy's mother also had a summer house in Lenox, Massachusetts. It was thus that Edith found a way to escape the humid climate and (in her view) anti-intellectualism of Newport.

In the eyes of some, Lenox was simply Newport in the mountains.

It had become a fashionable resort for the nouveau riche, who lived in million dollar "cottages" and built castles with a hundred rooms. With some of these socialites Wharton would not be very popular. Her friend D. B. Updike, founder of the Merrymount Press in Boston, recalled that her neighbors "were sometimes made uncomfortable by the suspicion—by no means unfounded—that Mrs. Wharton was ironically amusing at their expense. I remember one evening in particular when she returned from a dinner remarking, 'The XYZ's have decided, they tell me, to have books in the library.'"[4] Once when a dowager was showing off her house and gushed, "I call this my Louis Quinze room," Wharton reportedly replied, "*Why*, my dear?" (Lewis, 148).

But in spite of the XYZ types, Wharton found fewer of Newport's social "inanities," as she put it, in Lenox (Lewis, 123), and she was intrigued by its literary past. Both Hawthorne and Melville had tramped through the Berkshires and described the area in their works, and one of America's pioneer novelists, Catharine Maria Sedgwick (1789–1867), hailed from nearby Stockbridge. Although Wharton tended to distance herself from her female forerunners, as shown in her remarks on Jewett and Wilkins Freeman, she used Sedgwick's life as a source for an unfinished novel, "The Keys of Heaven," which was set in a town called "Slowbridge."

Wharton spent every summer from 1899 through 1908 in Lenox; in her words, "There for over ten years I lived and gardened and wrote contentedly" (*BG*, 125). The Mount, the home she designed and built to her specifications, was completed in 1902. Although not as costly and ostentatious as the neighboring abodes, it still dwarfed Henry James's description—"a delicate French chateau mirrored in a Massachusetts pond."[5] The Mount, which still stands today and can be visited, is an imposing four-story white stucco building with enough space to house a dozen servants. From the living and dining rooms of the ground floor, French doors lead to a terrace that once overlooked Wharton's profuse flower gardens. To many visitors the gardens were more impressive than the house. Wharton regularly won prizes for her flowers and once confided, "I'm a better landscape gardener than novelist, and this place, every line of which is my own work, far surpasses the House of Mirth" (*Letters*, 242).

Wharton was not exactly a "summer visitor" and the Mount a summer home, for she usually spent half the year in Lenox, from June to December (and the other half in New York and Europe). She also participated in village activities, such as rearranging the Lenox Library and serving on the Village Improvement and the Flower Show committees. In ten years she spent a good deal of time in the area, and it was not her choice to leave it. But the Mount became a casualty of the Whartons' marital difficulties: Teddy refused to help manage the estate unless Edith retained him as her trustee; this she declined to do because he had embezzled some of her money to set up a mistress. Thus in 1911 the property was sold, and Edith removed permanently to Europe. Although she felt a "great ache" for the Mount, she was not to see Lenox again except as she re-created it in her fiction (*Letters*, 277).

While living at the Mount, Wharton's pattern was to write in the mornings and spend the afternoons gardening, walking, doing village committee work, or hosting an endless stream of visitors. Most important for her writing was her habit of entertaining visitors with rides through the Berkshires, in the early years by horseback or carriage and later, when the Whartons had acquired an American car, by automobile. Henry James spoke fondly of these auto rides, and Wharton's biographer notes that "as they drove slowly through the little New England villages, Edith regaled the fascinated James with reports that had reached her about the dark unsuspected life—the sexual violence, even the incest—that went on behind the bleak walls of the farmhouses" (Lewis, 140). James was not the only friend with whom Wharton shared her interest in her less wealthy, year-round neighbors. D. B. Updike recalled one windy afternoon when they drove past "a battered two-story house, unpainted, with a neglected dooryard tenanted by hens and chickens, and a few bedraggled children sitting on the stone steps. 'It is about a place like that,' said Mrs. Wharton, 'that I mean to write a story. Only last week I went to the village meeting-house in Lenox and sat there for an hour alone, trying to think what such lives would be, and some day I shall write a story about it'" (Lubbock, 23).

Eventually she would write more than one story. These leisurely rides through the New England countryside (the speed limit was twenty miles per hour and the car often broke down) seem to have deeply inspired Wharton. While her fiction based in Newport tends to be brittle social comedy, and except for the description of Newport in *The Age of Innocence* inferior to her other work, her Lenox observations stimulated her imagination and remained vivid in her mind. Wharton toured with Updike in 1905, but she composed *Ethan Frome* with "the greatest joy and the fullest ease" in 1911 and as late as 1916 wrote *Summer* "at a high pitch of creative joy, but amid a thousand interruptions, and while the rest of my being was steeped in the tragic realities of the war; yet I do not remember ever visualizing with more intensity the inner scene, or the creatures peopling it" (*BG*, 293, 356).

From Wharton's perspective, her auto trips through the Berkshires, and even as far away as Boston, New Hampshire, and Maine, only proved her knowledge of New England. One could, however, take another view of Edith Wharton and guest being chauffeured through the countryside in her luxurious car while they peered at the rustics, trying to envision the inside of a dilapidated farmhouse. This is the pose of the outsider. It could easily be argued that even if Wharton resided in New England, her class status kept her from truly knowing it: she was perhaps an aristocrat gone slumming and her New England "a seasonal landscape through which one drove with Henry James."[6] Wharton was bound to make mistakes, however much she researched local customs and events, and recent critics have found an increasing number of "errors" in Wharton's work. It has been said of *Ethan Frome,* for instance, that Ethan should deliver boards instead of logs, shouldn't shave before he milks the cows, wouldn't waste time coasting downhill, and would never have allowed Mattie to attend a church dance, if there had been such things.

Of course, for every critic who complains that Wharton was an Episcopalian and failed to understand rural Christianity, there are several for whom the dance at the church glows in the imagination. It is important to ask whether Wharton had the desire or intent to portray New England in the thorough, balanced manner of the so-called "local colorist." Rather, she seems to have used New England settings for her own more Hawthornean purposes, as symbolic means of exploring favorite subjects, such as the absence of high culture in modern life, the permeation of the present by the past, and the claustrophobia of female experience. Wharton's New England fiction is most easily characterized by what it is *not* about, not like *The House of Mirth* and *The Age of Innocence* primarily about marriage and divorce, the dishonesty of the socioeconomic system, the power of society to mold individual lives, the turning of women into beautiful objects. With the exception of some Newport stories, it is less socially dense than her other work, more inclined to the probing of psyches than the dissection of manners.

Wharton's New England fiction has a wide range, however, running the gamut from light comedy to horror. One tale in this volume is a witty satire that makes fun of cultural pretensions ("Xingu"). Others treat the New England past and Puritan legacy in critical but complex ways ("The Lamp of Psyche," "The Angel at the Grave," and "The Pretext"). Finally, in the chilling *Ethan Frome* and her New England ghost stories ("The Triumph of Night," "Bewitched," and "All Souls'"), Wharton undertakes to scare us; she uses barren settings and cold and snow imagery to create haunting tales shadowed by isolation, crime, and incest. What holds this wide-ranging body of work together are the themes that Wharton sometimes wrote about in her other work but associated most strongly with New England: poverty and decay, moral intolerance ("witch-burning"), cultural emptiness, and oppression by the past.

Poverty and decay are the hallmarks of Wharton's New England. She was clearly less interested in the mansions of her peers than the unpainted farmhouses with bedraggled children on the steps. In her early work the poverty often seems exaggerated, as in "Friends" (1900), one of her first stories set in New England. The heroine's friend lives in a shabby hovel in coastal Sailport while she struggles to support a "crippled" brother and "slatternly" sister.[7] The town is described as a sort of wasteland—the streets are full of dust and garbage, and even "the patches of ground between the houses are not gardens, but waste spaces strewn with nameless refuse" (1:197). Wharton's emphatic opening line, "Sailport is an ugly town" (1:197), recalls her comment that she sought to avoid the rose-colored glasses of her forerunners. One can detect a strong anxiety of influence at work, as Wharton was clearly influenced by Sarah Orne Jewett and Mary Wilkins Freeman, even if she can only acknowledge them in a backhanded way. At the beginning of her career Wharton feared being pigeonholed as a "woman writer" or "local colorist," and along with such male authors as Theodore Dreiser and Stephen Crane, she wanted to announce her departure from the genteel, or rose-colored, tradition in American letters. Thus the exaggerated grimness of Sailport. An early version of the story was in fact rejected for being too negative, and Wharton had to promise her publisher to tone down "the *squalid* part" (*Letters*, 32).

Wharton's portrayal of a decaying New England was realistic to some extent, however. The region's population was shifting westward and into large cities, leaving behind empty farms; the once great seafaring centers, such as Portsmouth, New Hampshire, lost their power and riches. At the time Wharton began to publish, Boston had already been supplanted by New York as the literary center of the country. Young people made their way in the world by moving out of New England. Thus Wharton could accurately have an old-timer say of Ethan Frome: "Guess he's been in Starkfield too many winters. Most of the smart ones get away." Only Frome's obligation to care for his invalid parents, and later his wife, keeps him from abandoning his "stark field" for greener pastures. At the end of "Friends" the young heroine follows the path of Wharton's ancestors and moves to New York; there is no doubt that this is supposed to be a happy ending.

As her career progressed, Wharton was less insistent about describing New England as a rubbish heap, but the New England–New York contrast appears in many early tales. Generally the comparison is not very favorable to New England. Although in her life Wharton often felt she was escaping her native city for a relatively quiet and beautiful New England, she strikes a different balance in her fiction. It follows the same pattern as her autobiographical statement about her ancestors: New York is making money and having fun; New England is being poor and burning witches.

In "The Lamp of Psyche" (1895), Wharton's first really distinguished New England tale, the contrast is central. Delia Corbett lives blissfully in Paris with her cosmopolitan husband who grew up in New York. Delia, however, has been raised by her Bostonian aunt, a high-minded Puritan engaged in "the unsmiling pursuit of Purposes." When Delia and her husband visit Boston, Delia fears her pleasure-loving husband and "incurably serious" aunt will hate each other; instead they get along, but Delia herself changes her mind about her "perfect" mate. Typically, Wharton never tells us whether or not he stayed home from the Civil War out of cowardice, as Delia assumes; in any case he cannot survive being viewed in Boston light. Although Delia thought she had successfully rejected her New England background, her aunt's foolish "moral enthusiasms," she cannot actually do so. Like the mythical Psyche, she is compelled to shine a lamp on her lover and be disillusioned. She cannot escape her past, a familiar Wharton refrain, or her personal civil war between Boston and New York. Fortunately, Wharton maintains a light touch throughout the story, and the New York–Boston contrast has amusing overtones that are absent from the more heavy-handed "Friends." Even Delia's disillusionment does not have to be viewed as a tragedy, Wharton suggests, for the transmutation of her "passionate worship" to "tolerant affection" may be a necessary sign of growth and maturity.

The moral intolerance or, at the least, moral fervor that Wharton presents as part of Delia's legacy appears in some form in all her New England works. As late as 1937, the year of her death, Wharton stated that "the Bostonian gentleman of the old school who said that his wife always made it a moral issue whether the mutton should be roast or boiled, summed up very happily the relation of Boston to the universe" (2:878). In certain stories the oppressive morality has to do directly with the New England past and the high moral seriousness with which it is sometimes regarded. "The Angel at the Grave," one of Wharton's finest tales, shows the protagonist struggling with the burden of a famous Transcendentalist grandfather. Paulina devotes her life to keeping up the home and memory of Orestes Anson (whose name recalls Orestes Brownson, a friend of Emerson). She even rejects a suitor because he refuses to take the Anson heritage seriously, behaving "with the innocent profanity of infants sporting on a tomb."

Paulina was based on a real-life New Englander, Wharton's friend Sally Norton, who gave up marriage to assist her father, Charles Eliot Norton. A professor of fine arts at Harvard and a friend of Henry James, Charles Eliot Norton allowed Wharton the use of his extensive library, and some of the most memorable Lenox motor trips were taken to visit him and Sally at Ashfield, forty miles from the Mount. Although both Nortons encouraged Wharton's writing career, she must have noted with amusement that Charles Eliot criticized any of her heroines who committed adultery, and Sally greeted _Summer_ with absolute "puritanical recoil" (Lewis, 398). When her father lay dying, Sally wrote to ask if she might have done better by him; Wharton replied a trifle impatiently, "Alas, I should like to get up in the housetops and cry to all who come after us: 'Take [i.e., seize] your own life, every one of you'" (_Letters_, 163).

The suitor Sally relinquished to care for her father was an Englishman, but in "The Angel at the Grave" he hails from New York, an "outskirt which survived in Paulina's geography only because Dr. Anson had gone there once or twice to lecture." Although Paulina is tempted by the offer to marry and move to New York, an "emanation from the walls of the House" prevents her. Eventually the House, always capitalized, becomes a prison, and Paulina joins Wharton's other claustrophobic heroines: "it seemed to her that she had been walled alive into a tomb hung with the effigies of dead ideas. She felt a desperate longing to escape into the outer air." If the story ended here, we might consider Paulina an unlucky version of Wharton's earlier New Englanders, one who has missed the boat to New York. Instead, the news that before Anson became a Transcendentalist he had made a major scientific discovery, identifying a species of fish that formed an evolutionary link, means his reputation will be revived and Paulina can share in the work.

Has Paulina, then, really wasted her life? From the beginning Wharton allows for alternative interpretations, showing that Paulina loves her work and, like Mary Wilkins Freeman's New England nun in the story with that title, has no trouble giving up her suitor to preserve it. The event that changes the House into a prison is not the loss of her beau but the rejection of her manuscript. The restoration of communication at the end of the story and the promise that she can publish her biography lift the prison walls.

As is often the case in her best work, Wharton maintains a double perspective throughout. The story may be read as a satire of "cloudy" New England philosophies or the burden of past doctrines in general; why waste time at the grave keeping watch over dead ideas? On the other hand, the past must be come to terms with, and only the angel at the grave's vigilance permits any continuity in individual consciousness or public tradition. The same doubleness prevails in one of Wharton's last New England stories, "Duration" (1936). In this farce two Bostonians are being lionized for having reached their hundredth birthdays. Only in New England, Wharton suggests, would such an absurdity occur, that is, would longevity be worshiped solely for itself. On the other hand, it is "duration" that allows the centenarians to take revenge on their families for having ignored them all their lives. In a typical Wharton joke, one of the hundred-year-old characters is named Syngleton Perch, and so the prehistoric fish of "An Angel at the Grave" pops up years later in another story.

The New England past casts a darker shadow in one of Wharton's

most underrated tales, "The Pretext." The action takes place in Wentworth, an elm-shaded university town that is less ugly than Sailport
but snobbish and pretentious—it "sits in judgment" on the world.
Wharton satirizes the town's air of moral superiority, especially in
light of the dullness that has imprisoned her heroine, Margaret Ransom. After a lifetime of dutifully attending meetings of the Wentworth Higher Thought Club and being married to the dry university
lawyer, Margaret comes alive when she falls in love with a visiting
Englishman. The story begins as she "springs" upstairs to her mirror
after a talk with Guy Dawnish, the much younger man she and her
husband have befriended during his stay in New England. Although
Margaret sees thinning hair and a lined face, if she steps back from
the mirror the lingering pink from her blush disguises the wrinkles
and if she lets her hair down . . . "but was it right to try to make one's
hair look thicker and wavier than it really was?"

Wharton has fun contrasting Margaret's new sensual awareness
with the remnants of her "rigid New England ancestry." Even her
looking glass is a "cramped eagle-topped mirror above her plain prim
dressing table." Naturally it has an unflattering surface, for that is
the only kind of "meager concession to the weakness of the flesh"
allowed by puritanical Wentworth. The familiar New England–New
York contrast enters this story when Margaret's husband interrupts
her revery at the mirror. He thinks her hair looks messy, much like
the Brant girl's: "The Brant girl was their horror—the horror of all
right-thinking Wentworth; a laced, whale-boned, frizzle-headed,
high-heeled daughter of iniquity, who came—from New York, of
course—on long disturbing tumultuous visits to a Wentworth aunt."
Margaret is shocked at the very idea of looking "New Yorky" like
the Brant girl.

Margaret's New England background governs her behavior even
during her "one hour of life," as she thinks of it, her farewell meeting
with Guy on the banks of the campus river. Here in a wonderful scene
Margaret's guilt and fear prevent her from listening to what Guy
wants to tell her; she "said to herself that, whatever he was saying,
she must not hear it." She is thus prepared for letting Guy's English
relative, who cannot imagine a young man loving a middle-aged
housewife, convince her that Guy has used her as a "pretext" to hide
another relationship. The story ends at the opposite extreme from
"An Angel at the Grave" when Margaret drags herself upstairs to her

mirror; trying to "clear her eyes of all illusions," she finds "no trace of youth." But Margaret's sight is affected, of course, by her Puritan mirror, and people cannot clear their eyes of all illusions. Ironically, Margaret lets the town of Wentworth win and opts for disillusion, the one illusion that dries up her hidden pool of happiness.

Margaret Ransom's Wentworth bears a strong resemblance to Hillbridge, the university town Wharton created for several satires of moral, intellectual, and artistic pretensions. Hillbridge, which seems to be Cambridge moved to western Massachusetts, has the pretty elm-lined streets of Wentworth, but its attractions too are on the surface. As a Wharton character notes, "'Appearances' still ruled . . . where didn't they, in the university world, and more especially in New England?"[8] In the case of Hillbridge, Wharton is concerned with both its appearance of moral superiority and its pretense to a "broad and up-to-date culture" ("Xingu"). The town is actually the breeding ground of an inferior, deadening popular culture, as in the stories "The Pelican" (1898) and "The Descent of Man" (1904). In one early New England story, "April Showers" (1900), popular culture is likened to sewer gas—"doesn't smell bad, and infects the system without your knowing it" (1:190). Apparently Wharton never departed from her view that "this grim New England country, for all its beauty, gives nothing to compensate for the complete mental starvation."[9]

In the artist story "The Recovery" (1901), this mental starvation almost ruins the career of the painter Keniston. He becomes complacent about his art after being deified by the critics and professors of Hillbridge. To them, he "ran neck and neck with the President of the University, a prehistoric relic who had known Emerson, and who was still sent about the country in cotton wool to open educational institutions with a toothless oration on Brook Farm" (1:259). So much for the cultural heritage of New England. Keniston's "recovery" as an artist does not begin until he tours the Louvre and discovers that his paintings are sewer gas, inferior to the work of the "masters." All this seems a bit snobbish, and "The Recovery" typifies Wharton's Hillbridge stories in its high earnestness about art.

"Xingu" is a happy exception. Wharton still portrays Hillbridge as a cultural desert, but the story's wit and relative lightheartedness elevate it above her other Hillbridge tales. The story's well-known first line sets the pace: "Mrs. Ballinger is one of the ladies who pursue Culture in bands, as though it were dangerous to meet alone." When

Mrs. Ballinger's lunch club, composed of like-minded "huntresses of erudition," entertains a visiting novelist, new member Mrs. Roby rescues the lagging conversation by introducing Xingu. Everyone pretends to know what Xingu is, and Wharton showers the reader with puns until Xingu is finally exposed as a river in Brazil. Part of the joke applies directly to what Wharton saw as New England moralism. The club members are shocked that Mrs. Roby reads for amusement ("hardly what I look for in my choice of books"), and they obligingly misinterpret her warning that ladies would find it dangerous to trace the source of Xingu; it is readily assumed that something "indelicate" may be involved.

The Hillbridge ladies are not entirely to blame for their "parched minds" (which would naturally be attracted to the river Xingu), and Wharton's satire is not mean spirited. She even includes herself and her friends, as the arrogant novelist Osric Dane seems to be a mixture of Henry James and Wharton herself. Dane has just written _The Wings of Death_, an obscure work that recalls Wharton's least favorite James novel, _The Wings of the Dove_. But Dane resembles Wharton more than James in her determinism and extreme pessimism. Always capable of making fun of herself, Wharton describes Dane's novel in terms reminiscent of reviewers' criticism of her New England works as too negative. In her writing Dane has captured "the dark hopelessness of it all" by using "the wonderful tone-scheme of black on black."

Black on black could describe _Ethan Frome_ and Wharton's New England ghost stories, where there is little comic relief. In _Ethan Frome_ the protagonist is overcome by the same dark features Wharton attributes to New England in her earlier short stories: grinding poverty, cultural emptiness, and the oppression of a Puritan past. Ethan Frome's poverty, in the form of his "barren farm and failing saw-mill," keeps him from realizing his dream of leaving Starkfield for a larger place. Even before he falls in love with Mattie Silver and yearns for the money to take her away, "he had always wanted to be an engineer, and to live in towns, where there were lectures and big libraries." Starkfield lacks even the consolation of a visiting Osric Dane. Ethan's situation, Wharton indicates, is made particularly painful by the denial of his intellectual aspirations. Before his father's death he had studied engineering at a college in Worcester. Now he expresses "resentment" at his ignorance of scientific advances. Ethan has a great sensitivity to the quiet and beauty of his environment, but like Wharton herself he cannot tolerate the "mental starvation." As much as she loved the Mount, we recall, she could not stay there all year. "I am wretched at being in town," she would tell Sally Norton. "Oh, to live in the country all the year round" (Lewis, 161). But then she would have missed the "mental refreshment" she found in New York and Europe (*Letters*, 104).

Of course it is not only Ethan's poverty that traps him in Starkfield but also his moral scruples. He left college to care for his invalid mother and missed selling the farm and moving to a larger town because of Zeena's illness early in their marriage. As he contemplates going West with Mattie, he recalls that "he was a poor man, the husband of a sickly woman, whom his desertion would leave alone and destitute; and even if he had had the heart to desert her he could have done so only by deceiving two kindly people who had pitied him." The latter are Mr. and Mrs. Hale, from whom Ethan considers borrowing money but rejects the idea because he would be taking advantage of their sympathy in order "to obtain money from them on false pretenses." Here Ethan seems to be making it a moral issue whether the mutton should be roasted or boiled. Although Wharton clearly wants us to admire Ethan's basic honesty and sense of responsibility for others (his positive New England traits), his refusal to budge an inch in relation to the Hales makes him a "prisoner for life."

In Ethan's family graveyard stands a memorial to his ancestors, "ETHAN FROME AND ENDURANCE HIS WIFE, WHO DWELLED TOGETHER IN PEACE FOR FIFTY YEARS." The living Ethan wonders, in a bit of foreshadowing, whether the same epitaph will be written over him and Zeena. Everything repeats itself. It is no accident that Zeena originally came to the Fromes, as Ethan's cousin, to nurse his mother; then Mattie, Zeena's cousin, came to nurse Zeena. Several times the women seem to Ethan to eerily change places, as when Mattie replaces Zeena on the threshold, repeating the previous evening, and Zeena's face "supersedes" Mattie's in the rocking chair. If the Starkfield women are interchangeable, we are prepared for the ghastly tableau at the end where the fresh and childlike Mattie has turned into Zeena. Mattie is now "witch-like," and critic Elizabeth Ammons has effectively interpreted *Ethan Frome* as a fairy tale in which poverty and isolation turn women into witches (and the men who stay, she might have added, into silent martyrs).[10] The past bears down on the present and links Endurance Frome, with her Puritan name, to Ethan's mother, to Zeena, to Mattie. What seems so grim is not Ethan's or any one character's individual tragedy but the unbroken chain of want and despair.

Fittingly, *Ethan Frome* takes place in winter (in its French version it was known as *L'hiver*). The ubiquitous snow makes the New England farmhouses even more isolated, and the chain of despair seems frozen into place. Wharton, who ranks with the greatest writers in her creation of setting and atmosphere, uses snow and cold to brilliant effect in creating a frightening, voidlike atmosphere. The narrator and Ethan are caught in one storm, for instance, in which the snow falls "straight and steadily from a sky without wind, in a soft universal diffusion. . . . It seemed to be a part of the thickening darkness, to be the winter night itself descending on us layer by layer." The colors of *Ethan Frome* are black and white, with the blank scary white of Herman Melville's Moby Dick and only a touch of color provided by Mattie's cheeks and the red pickle dish.

Wharton's snowy settings are organic and not just decorative. The snow becomes an agent in Ethan's unfolding story: it delays him in getting the glue for the broken pickle dish and leads inexorably to the sledding accident. Just as Ethan's maimed body is paralleled in his house, his emotions are mirrored in the frozen landscape. As the narrator describes him, "He seemed a part of the mute melancholy landscape, an incarnation of its frozen woe, with all that was warm and sentient in him fast bound below the surface." The snow is such a "smothering medium" that Ethan has buried his feelings, memories, and perhaps his will. He used to be able to remember his trip to Florida and in winter call up the sight of the sunlit landscape, "but now it's all snowed under." Ethan, "by nature grave and inarticulate," as Wharton tended to see New Englanders, finally lapses into silence in the same way that his mother stopped talking in her last years and Zeena eventually "fell silent." The silence seems to be that of the grave. No wonder Ethan "looks as if he was dead." The novella ends with Mrs. Hale's statement, "I don't see's there's much difference between the Fromes up at the farm and the Fromes down in the graveyard."

·   ·   ·

This blurring of the lines between the living and the dead became characteristic of Wharton's New England work after *Ethan Frome*. She had started writing ghost stories, having published two in 1910, the year before *Ethan*. Her best New England tales would now fall into the ghost-story genre, and the most notable of these are set in "mute melancholy landscapes" of snow and cold. In her first New England ghost story, "The Triumph of Night" (1914), a snowstorm literally attacks the protagonist. George Faxon is "exposed to the full assault of nightfall and winter. The blast that swept him came off New Hampshire snowfields and ice-hung forests. It seemed to have traversed interminable leagues of frozen silence, filling them with the same cold roar and sharpening its edge against the same bitter black-and-white landscape." Yet the snow is pure in comparison with the fetid atmosphere of the house where Faxon takes refuge. This home of a noted businessman and philanthropist is warm and opulent, filled with hothouse flowers, but reflects the corruption of its owner, who kills his nephew for his money.

Faxon's immediate "nervous collapse" and his failure to expose the businessman's evil intent are hard to account for. True, he is a stranger and the person least likely to be believed; as Wharton puts it in somewhat overwrought language, "*he,* the one weaponless and defenseless spectator, the one whom none of the others would believe or understand if he attempted to reveal what he knew—*he* alone had been singled out as the victim of this dreadful initiation!" But Faxon does not even try to speak out and prevent the murder. Only months later when partially recovered from his breakdown does he question his behavior. The experience has destroyed him, it is implied at the end, for now "a great trail of darkness lay on everything. He had looked too deep down into the abyss."

In another New England story, "The Young Gentlemen" (1926), the revelation of an evil hidden beneath the surface leads to the pro-tagonist's suicide. Waldo Cranch (Waldo suggesting Ralph Waldo Emerson again and Cranch meaning cancer or canker) has twin sons, dwarfs, whom he has hidden away for thirty years in a wing of his house in coastal Harpledon. The discovery of the "young gentlemen" drives Waldo to kill himself: "He rushed out and died sooner than have them seen" (2:398). As in the case of "The Triumph of Night," Waldo's extreme reaction is not explained. Is the revelation of secrets so terrible that it must lead to immediate death or permanent "ner-

vous collapse"? In "The Young Gentlemen" even the first-person narrator, a friend of Waldo's, breaks down when the dwarfs are revealed.
He flees to Boston and explains that he has "never yet had the courage
to go down to Harpledon and see them" (2:402). Geographically, it
should be "up" to Harpledon, for Harpledon is supposed to be north
of Boston. Psychologically, "down" seems accurate, as the narrator
resembles George Faxon in his panicky flight from the "abyss" of his
unconscious.

One possible explanation of the terror of "going down to see
them" has to do with the hint of incest in Wharton's late New
England stories. Wharton had long seen incest as a prominent feature
of New England life and would titillate her Lenox guests with spec-
ulations about what went on inside the dilapidated houses they drove
by. She notes in her autobiography that when she lived there, "the
snow-bound villages of Western Massachusetts were still grim places,
morally and physically: insanity, incest and slow mental and moral
starvation were hidden away behind the paintless wooden house-
fronts . . . or in the isolated farm-houses" (*BG*, 293–94). In *Ethan
Frome* Wharton makes Ethan and Zeena cousins and portrays the
relationship between Ethan and Mattie in father-daughter terms.
Mattie, with her "slim young throat" and "brown wrist no bigger
than a child's," is consistently described as childlike, and the older
Ethan acts like a father as he picks her up from dances with partners
her own age and teaches her about the constellations. Still, the suggestion of incest is less pronounced than the other items on Wharton's
list, such as "slow mental and moral starvation." Incest plays a much
greater role in *Summer,* the companion piece to *Ethan Frome* that
was published in 1917. The heroine of this novel actually marries her
foster father, who may have been her real father. At any rate, he
adopted her when she was a child and first tried to seduce her in her
early adolescence. (It was *Summer* that shocked Wharton's puritanical friend Sally Norton.) Unknown to Sally, Wharton was writing
around the same time as *Summer* her outline and pornographic fragment of "Beatrice Palmato," the story of an incest victim who com-
mits suicide when her secret is revealed.

After *Summer* and "Beatrice Palmato," incest-related situations
and motifs appear over and over in Wharton's stories—the existence
of a terrible secret in the past, the simultaneous impossibility of the
secret either staying buried or coming to light, the revelation of a

secret leading to breakdown and immobility, and the connection of the secret with the hidden corruption of a patriarch. This corruption is often accompanied by the complicity of a woman, though not in "The Triumph of Night" and "The Young Gentlemen." The incest motifs in Wharton's work are exactly those most frequently reported by survivors of incest. Of course Wharton's preoccupation with guilty secrets involving fathers' hidden corruption does not necessarily mean that she herself was an incest victim. It is certainly suggestive, however, when considered together with the unexplained coolness of her relationship with her parents and the persistent occurrence of incest themes and bizarre father-daughter relationships in her writing.[11]

Whether or not Wharton was herself an incest victim, the "shadow of incest," as Alan Henry Rose calls it, lies over her work. The later New England tales are well characterized by Rose, a significant exception to the critics who have disparaged Wharton's handling of the region. Rose contends that Wharton's view of New England as a cultural emptiness freed her imagination "to range in a manner not duplicated in her cluttered urban world" and to capture a "sense of void." He lists as the components of her New England theme a barren setting, a helpless protagonist, and a shadow of incest over all.[12] Although Rose does not explain the whys of this configuration, there is no question that the features he names are present.

In "Bewitched" (1925), Wharton's first New England story after "The Triumph of Night," the barren setting is again a snowstorm. The story takes place near the isolated Starkfield of *Ethan Frome* and is permeated with the same cold and snow imagery and the same creepy death-in-life atmosphere. In fact, many elements of *Ethan Frome* reappear: the repression of emotions connected with icy cold; the passive characters driven mad or turned into witches, either by their isolation or the cramped Puritan past that seems to bear down on them. Prudence Rutledge, whose first name recalls her Puritan forebears and who literally lives atop the ruins of an early settlement, has a text over her mantelpiece reading "The Soul That Sinneth It Shall Die."

The shadow of incest in "Bewitched" is cast by the significantly named "Brand" family, which has been founded on incest or near-incest—the community feels Brand should not have married his cousin. But the couple has two "handsome" daughters, and all seems well until the Brand women begin mysteriously dying, just like the Palmato women in Wharton's outline for her incest story. (Interestingly, the Brand family has the same family constellation—authoritarian father, meek mother, rebellious older daughter, naive younger daughter.) Mrs. Brand simply "pined away and died"; Ora, after a conflict with her father when he refuses to let her marry, "wasted away"; and the "ignorant" Venny is apparently killed by her father. Wharton portrays Sylvester Brand as violent and alcoholic. He is "animal and primitive," "savage and morose," and has a "rough bullying power." The only character strong enough to deal with him is the avenging Mrs. Rutledge, and indeed these two are the antagonists in the story. Prudence Rutledge avenges not only her husband's bewitching but also, it is implied, the crime of incest. She is hardly the most pleasant of avengers, as she seems more dead than alive and reminds the narrator of his mad aunt who freed a canary from its cage by strangling it. The revenge of Mrs. Rutledge destroys the victim as well as the perpetrator, recalling Mary Wilkins Freeman's "Old Woman Magoun" (1909); in this story the supposed "rose-coloured spectacles" of Wharton's predecessor envision a woman who poisons her beloved granddaughter to protect her from incest.

The women in "Bewitched" who have been somehow "killed" by Mr. Brand and lie dead or alive in their freezing tombs resemble the victims of Mr. Jones, the ghost who bears Wharton's father's name in her story with that title. As a ghost, Mr. Jones guards the "secret past" (2:181); when alive he had been the jailor of his employer's deaf and dumb wife, who looks out from her portrait "dumbly, inexpressively, in a stare of frozen beauty" (2:606). This woman, whose only name is that on a monument, "Also His Wife," reminds the narrator of generations of silenced women buried so completely in the house that "they must hardly have known when they passed from their beds to their graves" (2:599).

Such a fate threatens Sara Clayburn in Wharton's last story, the highly acclaimed "All Souls'." Mrs. Clayburn's Connecticut estate, Whitegates, suggests the cemetery, as did the fluted urns on Prudence Rutledge's fenceposts. But here we are given not just a connection between all the killed women and incest but a symbolic reenactment of the abuse. On All Souls' Eve Mrs. Clayburn's servants disappear, perhaps to lead the local witches' coven, and a snowstorm disables the electricity, heat, and telephone. Mrs. Clayburn has broken her ankle and is left alone in her cold, empty house (body/consciousness/ grave), wounded and in pain. She feels "she must find out what was happening belowstairs—or had happened" and thus limps around the house. As she approaches the kitchen, which might be considered the female center of the house, she hears a low, emphatic male voice (that turns out to be coming from a portable radio) and fears she has betrayed her presence: "But to her astonishment the voice went on speaking. It was as though neither the speaker nor his listeners had heard her. The invisible stranger spoke so low that she could not make out what he was saying, but the tone was passionately earnest, almost threatening. The next moment she realized that he was speaking in a foreign language, a language unknown to her."

One-way communication, low and secretive, passionate and threatening, and in a language foreign to the victim, is a perfect paradigm for child sexual abuse. Sara Clayburn may seem a dowager in pearls, but she is really, as her cousin calls her, "a frightened child." As she finds the radio, Mrs. Clayburn enacts the incest victim's typical struggle between needing to know and being afraid to and reacts like most Wharton characters who see ghosts, fainting in terror. Although "her memory of what next happened remained indistinct," she drags herself from the ground floor up to her own room, where "apparently, she fell across the threshold, again unconscious . . ." (Wharton's ellipses). Thus, while others are off at a coven enjoying themselves sexually (it is implied), Sara Clayburn's sole human intercourse has been violation at her center by a male foreigner who can only speak his own needs and cannot hear hers.

The aftermath is also much like sexual abuse, as Mrs. Clayburn feels that a "tissue of lies was being woven about her." The other members of the household claim her experience never took place, and the doctor feels "embarrassed at being drawn into an unintelligible controversy with which he had no time to deal." They reduce Mrs. Clayburn to the status of a child, like George Faxon, "the one whom none of the others would believe or understand." Mrs. Clayburn is expected to remain silent about the lost thirty-six hours. The outer manifestation of the "tissue of lies" to be wrapped around her life is the snowstorm that covers the house, "muffling the outer world in layers on layers of thick white velvet, and intensifying the silence within. . . . Silence—more silence! It seemed to be piling itself up like the snow on the roof and in the gutters. Silence. How many people that she knew had any idea what silence was—and how loud it sounded when you really listened to it?"

Of course silence, and the importance of breaking it, is a major theme of incest survivors, who describe having once been "frozen in their terrorized silence."[13] As we have seen, Wharton often associates repression and death-in-life with freezing cold; even in more realistic stories like "The Pretext" she refers to the "frozen lives" of Margaret's ancestors. Few of Wharton's women ever escape their frozen silence, but Mrs. Clayburn, her last heroine, finally cuts through the tissue of lies. As the silence "folded down on her like a pall," Mrs. Clayburn's greatest fear was that "no one will ever know what has happened here. Even I shan't know." She summons the strength to overcome this fear and manages to tell her writer cousin, a modern "angel at the grave," who believes her and narrates the story.

We could easily predict the cousin's place of residence, and indeed Mrs. Clayburn flees to New York at the end of the story, never returning to Whitegates. Thus Wharton's last story ends in exactly the same way as her early "Friends." The Connecticut of "All Souls'" is just as bleak as Sailport and, as something of a graveyard, considerably more frightening. Wharton explains that All Souls' Eve is "the night when the dead can walk," and for her, New England seems to be the *place* where the dead walk, where the repressed comes to light. It is interesting that Wharton's New England stories have a greater number of female narrators and reflectors than her other tales, and more of the stories focus directly on female experience. Perhaps Wharton associated New England with her deepest self; she seems to have projected onto New England aspects of herself that she most feared: repression, coldness, inarticulateness, mental starvation, and even lack of high culture (when compared to the international "masters").

At any rate, the New England work seems "bewitched," written more by the frightened child than the sophisticated realist who dissected the social life of old New York. One can find the witty woman of the world in "Xingu" and some of the other comedies and satires, but readers who seek the realist may be disappointed. Wharton's New England settings range from the garbage dumps of Sailport to the ash heaps of North Ashmore to the empty desert of the unfortunate Hillbridge (in one of her last stories, "Permanent Wave," a character says "the grave was a circus compared with . . . a New England university town"; 2:792–93). Taken as a rounded portrait of New England, these wastelands are obviously simplistic and "unfair"; critics of Wharton's portrayal could also point to excesses in her view of the dreaded Midwest, which is pilloried in descriptions of "Apex City" and "Euphoria." Yet however short Wharton may fall as a chronicler of living New Englanders, her dark-colored spectacles helped her sound the depths and create powerful symbolic landscapes that claim our attention.

Notes

1. Edith Wharton, *A Backward Glance* (New York: D. Appleton-Century, 1934), 9; hereafter cited in the text as *BG*.

2. *The Letters of Edith Wharton*, ed. R. W. B. Lewis and Nancy Lewis (New York: Charles Scribner's Sons, 1988), 385; hereafter cited in the text as *Letters*.

3. The setting of "The Pretext" is discussed in an anonymous review, "Short Stories by Mrs. Wharton," *New York Times Saturday Review*, Oct. 3, 1908, 541. For mistakes in *The Fruit of the Tree*, see R. W. B. Lewis, *Edith Wharton: A Biography* (New York: Harper and Row, 1975), 181; hereafter cited in the text as Lewis. See also Elizabeth Shepley Sergeant, "Idealized New England," *New Republic*, May 8, 1915, 20–21.

4. Percy Lubbock, *Portrait of Edith Wharton* (New York: D. Appleton-Century, 1947), 17; subsequent references are noted in the text.

5. *The Letters of Henry James*, ed. Leon Edel (Cambridge: Belknap Press, 1984), 4:325.

6. Bernard DeVoto, "Introduction," in *Ethan Frome* (New York: Scribner's, 1938), viii. See also Nancy R. Leach, "New England in the Stories of Edith Wharton," *New England Quarterly* 30 (Mar. 1957): 96; and Abigail Ann Hamblen, "Edith Wharton in New England," *New England Quarterly* 38 (June 1965): 240. Hamblen accuses Wharton of showing "contemptuous pity" for the poor.

7. "Friends," in *The Collected Short Stories of Edith Wharton*, ed. R. W. B. Lewis (New York: Charles Scribner's Sons, 1968), 1:200. This collection is hereafter cited in the text by the volume and page number only.

8. "The Day of the Funeral" (2:670). The rule of appearances is also the main theme of "Joy in the House," where the heroine lives in a "stifling atmosphere . . . of smoothing over and ignoring and dissembling" (2:271).

9. Quoted in Blake Nevius, *Edith Wharton's "Ethan Frome": The Story with Sources and Commentary* (New York: Charles Scribner's Sons, 1968), 2.

10. Elizabeth Ammons, *Edith Wharton's Argument with America* (Athens: University of Georgia Press, 1980), 59–77.

11. For description of the "post-incest syndrome," see E. Sue Blume, *Secret Survivors: Uncovering Incest and Its Aftereffects in Women* (New York: John Wiley, 1990); Judith Lewis Herman, *Father-Daughter Incest* (Cambridge: Harvard University Press, 1981); and Diana E. H. Russell, *The Secret Trauma: Incest in the Lives of Girls and Women* (New York: Basic Books, 1986). The "Beatrice Palmato" outline and fragment, found in Wharton's papers, are published in Lewis, 544–48. Two recent books suggest that Wharton may have been sexually abused by her father: David Holbrook, *Edith Wharton and the Unsatisfactory Man* (New York: St. Martin's Press, 1991); and Barbara A. White, *Edith Wharton: A Study of the Short Fiction* (New York: Twayne, 1991).

12. Alan Henry Rose, " 'Such Depths of Sad Initiation': Edith Wharton and New England," *New England Quarterly* 50 (Sept. 1977): 424.

13. Toni A. H. McNaron and Yarrow Morgan, eds., *Voices in the Night: Women Speaking about Incest* (Pittsburgh: Cleis Press, 1982), 11.

New England Works by Edith Wharton

A. Published Short Stories Set in New England

The stories are listed in chronological order by publication date.

"The Lamp of Psyche." *Scribner's* 18 (Oct. 1895): 418–28.
"The Pelican." *Scribner's* 24 (Nov. 1898): 620–29.
"The Twilight of the God." In *The Greater Inclination*. New York: Scribner's, 1899.
"A Coward." In *The Greater Inclination*. New York: Scribner's, 1899.
"April Showers." *Youth's Companion* 74 (18 Jan. 1900): 25–28.
"Friends." *Youth's Companion* 74 (23 Aug. 1900): 405–6; (30 Aug. 1900): 417–18.
"The Line of Least Resistance." *Lippincott's* 66 (Oct. 1900): 559–70.
"The Angel at the Grave." *Scribner's* 29 (Feb. 1901): 158–66.
"The Recovery." *Harper's* 102 (Feb. 1901): 468–77.
"The Descent of Man." *Scribner's* 35 (March 1904): 313–22.
"The Introducers." *Ainslee's* 16 (Dec. 1905): 139–48; (Jan. 1906): 61–67.
"The Pretext." *Scribner's* 44 (Aug. 1908): 173–87.
"Xingu." *Scribner's* 50 (Dec. 1911): 684–96.
"The Triumph of Night." *Scribner's* 56 (Aug. 1914): 149–62.
"Bewitched." *Pictorial Review* 26 (Mar. 1925): 14–16.
"The Young Gentlemen." *Pictorial Review* 27 (Feb. 1926): 29–30, 84–91.
"Joy in the House." *Nash's Pall Mall* 90 (Dec. 1932): 6–9, 72–75.
"The Day of the Funeral." *Woman's Home Companion* 60 (Jan. 1933): 7–8; (Feb. 1933): 15–16 (under title "In a Day").
"Permanent Wave." *Redbook* 64 (Apr. 1935): 20–23 (under title "Poor Old Vincent").
"Duration." In *The World Over*. New York: Appleton-Century, 1936.
"All Souls'." In *Ghosts*. New York: Appleton-Century, 1937.

B. Other Works

FICTION

The Fruit of the Tree. New York: Scribner's, 1907.
Ethan Frome. New York: Scribner's, 1911.
Summer. New York: D. Appleton, 1917.

NONFICTION

"Introduction." In *Ethan Frome*, v–x. New York: Scribner's, 1922.
"The Writing of *Ethan Frome*." *Colophon* 11 (Sept. 1932), n.p.
"Foreword." In Owen Davis and Donald Davis, *Ethan Frome: A Dramatization of Edith Wharton's Novel*, vii–viii. New York: Scribner's, 1936.

UNPUBLISHED FRAGMENTS

"Cruise of the Fleetwig," 20 pp.
"A Granted Prayer," 13 pp.
"The Keys of Heaven," 6 pp.
"Mother Earth," 25 pp.
"New England," 67 pp.

Wharton's New England

THE LAMP OF PSYCHE

(1895)

Wharton composed "The Lamp of Psyche" in 1893 when still a fledgling author. She reveals some uncertainty in setting up the situation and establishing the point of view; the narrator discusses the heroine's "foibles" directly with the reader and even apologizes for Delia's having been infatuated with Corbett before her first husband died. A manuscript of this story shows that before Wharton settled on third-person narration, she experimented with a first-person narrator who would put forth his discoveries about Delia much in the manner of Ethan Frome.

But the story was "the best of her works to date," as Wharton's biographer notes (Lewis, 70). She probably failed to include it in her first collection of short stories not because of quality but because it reflected too clearly her own marriage, another volatile Boston–New York combination. Wharton characters commonly become disillusioned with previously admired lovers, and the title "The Lamp of Psyche" directly reflects this theme. The mythical Psyche, having been forbidden to look at her lover Cupid, lost him after she took a lamp and examined him while he slept.

Wharton's reference to the myth of Psyche suggests that Delia's easy dismissal of her New England background, of her aunt's morality and the "rarefied atmosphere of philanthropy and reform," is only on the surface. Actually the New England in Delia needed to shine the lamp on her husband, to bring him to Boston to be tested and found wanting.

DELIA CORBETT was too happy; her happiness frightened her. Not on theological grounds, however; she was sure that people had a right to be happy; but she was equally sure that it was a right seldom recognized by destiny. And her happiness almost touched the confines of pain—it bordered on that sharp ecstasy which she had known, through one sleepless night after another, when what had now become a reality had haunted her as an unattainable longing.

Delia Corbett was not in the habit of using what the French call *gros mots* in the rendering of her own emotions; she took herself, as a rule, rather flippantly, with a dash of contemptuous pity. But she felt that she had now entered upon a phase of existence wherein it became her to pay herself an almost reverential regard. Love had set his golden crown upon her forehead, and the awe of the office allotted her subdued her doubting heart. To her had been given the one portion denied to all other women on earth, the immense, the unapproachable privilege of becoming Laurence Corbett's wife.

Here she burst out laughing at the sound of her own thoughts, and rising from her seat walked across the drawing room and looked at herself in the mirror above the mantelpiece. She was past thirty and had never been very pretty; but she knew herself to be capable of loving her husband better and pleasing him longer than any other woman in the world. She was not afraid of rivals; he and she had seen each other's souls.

She turned away, smiling carelessly at her insignificant reflection, and went back to her armchair near the balcony. The room in which she sat was very beautiful; it pleased Corbett to make all his surroundings beautiful. It was the drawing room of his hotel in Paris, and the balcony near which his wife sat overlooked a small bosky garden framed in ivied walls, with a mouldering terra-cotta statue in the center of its cup-shaped lawn. They had now been married some two months and, after traveling for several weeks, had both desired to return to Paris; Corbett because he was really happier there than elsewhere, Delia because she passionately longed to enter as a wife the house where she had so often come and gone as a guest. How she used to find herself dreaming in the midst of one of Corbett's delightful dinners (to which she and her husband were continually being summoned) of a day when she might sit at the same table, but facing its master, a day when no carriage should wait to whirl her away from the brightly lit porte-cochère, and when, after the guests had gone, he and she should be left alone in his library and she might sit down beside him and put her hand in his! The high-minded reader may infer from this that I am presenting him, in the person of Delia Corbett, with a heroine whom he would not like his wife to meet; but how many of us could face each other in the calm consciousness of moral rectitude if our inmost desire were not hidden under a convenient garb of lawful observance?

Delia Corbett, as Delia Benson, had been a very good wife to her first husband; some people (Corbett among them) had even thought her laxly tolerant of "poor Benson's" weaknesses. But then she knew her own; and it is admitted that nothing goes so far toward making us blink the foibles of others as the wish to have them extend a like mercy to ourselves. Not that Delia's foibles were of a tangible nature; they belonged to the order which escapes analysis by the coarse process of our social standards. Perhaps their very immateriality, the consciousness that she could never be brought to book for them before any human tribunal, made her the more restive under their weight; for she was of a nature to prefer buying her happiness to stealing it. But her rising scruples were perpetually being allayed by some fresh indiscretion of Benson's, to which she submitted with an undeviating amiability which flung her into the opposite extreme of wondering if she didn't really influence him to do wrong—if she mightn't help him to do better. All these psychological subtleties exerted, however, no influence over her conduct which, since the day of her marriage, had been a model of delicate circumspection. It was only necessary to look at Benson to see that the most eager reformer could have done little to improve him. In the first place he must have encountered the initial difficulty, most disheartening to reformers, of making his neophyte distinguish between right and wrong. Undoubtedly it was within the measure even of Benson's primitive perceptions to recognize that some actions were permissible and others were not; but his sole means of classifying them was to try both, and then deny having committed those of which his wife disapproved. Delia had once owned a poodle who greatly desired to sleep on a white fur rug which she destined to other uses. She and the poodle disagreed on the subject, and the latter, though submitting to her authority (when reinforced by a whip), could never be made to see the justice of her demand, and consequently (as the rug frequently revealed) never missed an opportunity of evading it when her back was turned. Her husband often reminded her of the poodle, and, not having a whip or its moral equivalent to control him with, she had long since resigned herself to seeing him smudge the whiteness of her early illusions. The worst of it was that her resignation was such a cheap virtue. She had to be perpetually rousing herself to a sense of Benson's enormities; through the ever-lengthening perspective of her indifference they looked as small as the details of a landscape seen through the wrong end of a telescope. Now and then she tried to remind herself that she had married him for love; but she was well aware that the sentiment she had once entertained for him had nothing in common with the state of mind which the words now represented to her; and this naturally diminished the force of the argument. She had married him at nineteen, because he had beautiful blue eyes and always wore a gardenia in his coat; really, as far as she could remember, these considerations had been the determining factors in her choice. Delia as a child (her parents were since dead) had been a much-indulged daughter, with a liberal allowance of pocket-money, and permission to spend it unquestioned and unadvised. Subsequently, she used sometimes to look, in a critical humor, at the various articles which she had purchased in her teens; futile chains and lockets, valueless china knickknacks, and poor engravings of sentimental pictures. These, as a chastisement to her taste, she religiously preserved; and they often made her think of Benson. No one, she could not but reflect, would have blamed her if, with the acquirement of a fuller discrimination, she had thrown them all out of the window and replaced them by some object of permanent merit; but she was expected not only to keep Benson for life, but to conceal the fact that her taste had long since discarded him.

It could hardly be expected that a woman who reasoned so dispassionately about her mistakes should attempt to deceive herself about her preferences. Corbett personified all those finer amenities of mind and manners which may convert the mere act of being into a beneficent career; to Delia he seemed the most admirable man she had ever met, and she would have thought it disloyal to her best aspirations not to admire him. But she did not attempt to palliate her warmer feeling under the mask of a plausible esteem; she knew that she loved him, and scorned to disavow that also. So well, however, did she keep her secret that Corbett himself never suspected it, until her husband's death freed her from the obligation of concealment. Then, indeed, she gloried in its confession; and after two years of widowhood, and more than two months of marriage, she was still under the spell of that moment of exquisite avowal.

She was reliving it now, as she often did in the rare hours which separated her from her husband; when presently she heard his step on the stairs, and started up with the blush of eighteen. As she walked across the room to meet him she asked herself perversely (she was given to such obliqueness of self-scrutiny) if to a dispassionate eye he would appear as complete, as supremely well-equipped as she beheld him, or if she walked in a cloud of delusion, dense as the god-concealing mist of Homer. But whenever she put this question to herself, Corbett's appearance instantly relegated it to the limbo of solved enigmas; he was so obviously admirable that she wondered that people didn't stop her in the street to attest her good fortune.

As he came forward now, his renewal of satisfaction was so strong in her that she felt an impulse to seize him and assure herself of his reality; he was so perilously like the phantasms of joy which had mocked her dissatisfied past. But his coat sleeve was convincingly tangible; and, pinching it, she felt the muscles beneath.

"What—all alone?" he said, smiling back her welcome.

"No, I wasn't—I was with you!" she exclaimed; then fearing to appear fatuous, added, with a slight shrug, "Don't be alarmed—it won't last."

"That's what frightens me," he answered, gravely.

"Precisely," she laughed; "and I shall take good care not to reassure you!"

They stood face to face for a moment, reading in each other's eyes the completeness of their communion; then he broke the silence by saying, "By the way, I'd forgotten; here's a letter for you."

She took it unregardingly, her eyes still deep in his; but as her glance turned to the envelope she uttered a note of pleasure.

"Oh, how nice—it's from your only rival!"

"Your Aunt Mary?"

She nodded. "I haven't heard from her in a month—and I'm afraid I haven't written to her either. You don't know how many beneficent intentions of mine you divert from their proper channels."

"But your Aunt Mary has had you all your life—I've only had you two months," he objected.

Delia was still contemplating the letter with a smile. "Dear thing!" she murmured. "I wonder when I shall see her?"

"Write and ask her to come and spend the winter with us."

"What—and leave Boston, and her kindergartens, and associated charities, and symphony concerts, and debating clubs? You don't know Aunt Mary!"

"No, I don't. It seems so incongruous that you should adore such a bundle of pedantries."

"I forgive that, because you've never seen her. How I wish you could!"

He stood looking down at her with the all-promising smile of the happy lover. "Well, if she won't come to us we'll go to her."

"Laurence—and leave this!"

"It will keep—we'll come back to it. My dear girl, don't beam so; you make me feel as if you hadn't been happy until now."

"No—but it's your thinking of it!"

"I'll do more than think; I'll act; I'll take you to Boston to see your Aunt Mary."

"Oh, Laurence, you'd hate doing it."

"Not doing it together."

She laid her hand for a moment on his. "What a difference that does make in things!" she said, as she broke the seal of the letter.

"Well, I'll leave you to commune with Aunt Mary. When you've done, come and find me in the library."

Delia sat down joyfully to the perusal of her letter, but as her eye traveled over the closely-written pages her gratified expression turned to one of growing concern; and presently, thrusting it back into the envelope, she followed her husband to the library. It was a charming room and singularly indicative, to her fancy, of its occupant's character; the expanse of harmonious bindings, the fruity bloom of Renaissance bronzes, and the imprisoned sunlight of two or three old pictures fitly epitomizing the delicate ramifications of her husband's taste. But now her glance lingered less appreciatively than usual on the warm tones and fine lines which formed so expressive a background for Corbett's fastidious figure.

"Aunt Mary has been ill—I'm afraid she's been seriously ill," she announced as he rose to receive her. "She fell in coming downstairs from one of her tenement house inspections, and it brought on water on the knee. She's been laid up ever since—some three or four weeks now. I'm afraid it's rather bad at her age; and I don't know how she will resign herself to keeping quiet."

"I'm very sorry," said Corbett, sympathetically; "but water on the knee isn't dangerous, you know."

"No—but the doctor says she mustn't go out for weeks and weeks; and that will drive her mad. She'll think the universe has come to a standstill."

"She'll find it hasn't," suggested Corbett, with a smile which took the edge from his comment.

"Ah, but such discoveries hurt—especially if one makes them late in life!"

Corbett stood looking affectionately at his wife.

"How long is it," he asked, "since you have seen your Aunt Mary?"

"I think it must be two years. Yes, just two years; you know I went home on business after—" She stopped; they never alluded to her first marriage.

Corbett took her hand. "Well," he declared, glancing rather wistfully at the Paris Bordone above the mantelpiece, "we'll sail next month and pay her a little visit."

II

Corbett was really making an immense concession in going to America at that season; he disliked the prospect at all times, but just as his hotel in Paris had reopened its luxurious arms to him for the winter, the thought of departure was peculiarly distasteful. Delia knew it, and winced under the enormity of the sacrifice which he had imposed upon himself; but he bore the burden so lightly, and so smilingly derided her impulse to magnify the heroism of his conduct, that she gradually yielded to the undisturbed enjoyment of her anticipation. She was really very glad to be returning to Boston as Corbett's wife; her occasional appearances there as Mrs. Benson had been so eminently unsatisfactory to herself and her relatives that she naturally desired to efface them by so triumphal a reentry. She had passed so great a part of her own life in Europe that she viewed with a secret leniency Corbett's indifference to his native land; but though she did not mind his not caring for his country she was intensely anxious that his country should care for him. He was a New Yorker, and entirely unknown, save by name, to her little circle of friends and relatives in Boston; but she reflected, with tranquil satisfaction, that, if he were cosmopolitan enough for Fifth Avenue, he was also cultured enough for Beacon Street. She was not so confident of his being altruistic enough for Aunt Mary; but Aunt Mary's appreciations covered so wide a range that there seemed small doubt of his coming under the head of one of her manifold enthusiasms.

Altogether Delia's anticipations grew steadily rosier with the approach to Sandy Hook; and to her confident eye the Statue of Liberty, as they passed under it in the red brilliance of a winter sunrise, seemed to look down upon Corbett with her Aunt Mary's most approving smile.

Delia's Aunt Mary—known from the Back Bay to the South End as Mrs. Mason Hayne—had been the chief formative influence of her niece's youth. Delia, after the death of her parents, had even spent two years under Mrs. Hayne's roof, in direct contrast with all her apostolic ardors, her inflammatory zeal for righteousness in everything from baking powder to municipal government; and though the girl never felt any inclination to interpret her aunt's influence in action, it was potent in modifying her judgment of herself and others. Her parents had been incurably frivolous, Mrs. Hayne was incurably serious, and Delia, by some unconscious powers of selection, tended to frivolity of conduct, corrected by seriousness of thought. She would have shrunk from the life of unadorned activity, the unsmiling pursuit of Purposes with a capital letter, to which Mrs. Hayne's energies were dedicated; but it lent relief to her enjoyment of the purposeless to measure her own conduct by her aunt's utilitarian standards. This curious sympathy with aims so at variance with her own ideals would hardly have been possible to Delia had Mrs. Hayne been a narrow

enthusiast without visual range beyond the blinders of her own vo-
cation; it was the consciousness that her aunt's perceptions included
even such obvious inutility as hers which made her so tolerant of her
aunt's usefulness. All this she had tried, on the way across the At-
lantic, to put vividly before Corbett; but she was conscious of a vague
inability on his part to adjust his conception of Mrs. Hayne to his
wife's view of her; and Delia could only count on her aunt's abound-
ing personality to correct the one-sidedness of his impression.

Mrs. Hayne lived in a wide brick house on Mount Vernon Street,
which had belonged to her parents and grandparents, and from which
she had never thought of moving. Thither, on the evening of their
arrival in Boston, the Corbetts were driven from the Providence Station. Mrs. Hayne had written to her niece that Cyrus would meet
them with a "hack"; Cyrus was a sable factotum designated in Mrs.
Hayne's vocabulary as a "chore man." When the train entered the
station he was, in fact, conspicuous on the platform, his smile shining
like an open piano, while he proclaimed with abundant gesture the
proximity of "de hack," and Delia, descending from the train into
his dusky embrace, found herself guiltily wishing that he could have
been omitted from the function of their arrival. She could not help
wondering what her husband's valet would think of him. The valet
was to be lodged at a hotel: Corbett himself had suggested that his
presence might disturb the routine of Mrs. Hayne's household, a view
in which Delia had eagerly acquiesced. There was, however, no possibility of dissembling Cyrus, and under the valet's depreciatory eye
the Corbetts suffered him to precede them to the livery stable landau,
with blue shades and a confidentially disposed driver, which awaited
them outside the station.

During the drive to Mount Vernon Street Delia was silent; but as
they approached her aunt's swell-fronted domicile she said, hurriedly,
"You won't like the house."

Corbett laughed. "It's the inmate I've come to see," he com-
mented.

"Oh, I'm not afraid of her," Delia almost too confidently rejoined.

The parlormaid who admitted them to the hall (a discouraging
hall, with a large-patterned oilcloth and buff walls stenciled with a
Greek border) informed them that Mrs. Hayne was above; and as-
cending to the next floor they found her genial figure, supported on
crutches, awaiting them at the drawing room door. Mrs. Hayne was

a tall, stoutish woman, whose bland expanse of feature was accentuated by a pair of gray eyes of such surpassing penetration that Delia often accused her of answering people's thoughts before they had finished thinking them. These eyes, through the close fold of Delia's embrace, pierced instantly to Corbett, and never had that accomplished gentleman been more conscious of being called upon to present his credentials. But there was no reservation in the uncritical warmth of Mrs. Hayne's welcome, and it was obvious that she was unaffectedly happy in their coming.

She led them into the drawing room, still clinging to Delia, and Corbett, as he followed, understood why his wife had said that he would not like the house. One saw at a glance that Mrs. Hayne had never had time to think of her house or her dress. Both were scrupulously neat, but her gown might have been an unaltered one of her mother's, and her drawing room wore the same appearance of contented archaism. There was a sufficient number of armchairs, and the tables (mostly marble-topped) were redeemed from monotony by their freight of books; but it had not occurred to Mrs. Hayne to substitute logs for hard coal in her fireplace, nor to replace by more personal works of art the smoky expanses of canvas "after" Raphael and Murillo which lurched heavily forward from the walls. She had even preserved the knotty antimacassars on her high-backed armchairs, and Corbett, who was growing bald, resignedly reflected that during his stay in Mount Vernon Street he should not be able to indulge in any lounging.

III

Delia held back for three days the question which burned her lips; then, following her husband upstairs after an evening during which Mrs. Hayne had proved herself especially comprehensive (even questioning Corbett upon the tendencies of modern French art), she let escape the imminent "Well?"

"She's charming," Corbett returned, with the fine smile which always seemed like a delicate criticism.

"Really?"

"Really, Delia. Do you think me so narrow that I can't value such a character as your aunt's simply because it's cast in different lines from mine? I once told you that she must be a bundle of pedantries, and you prophesied that my first sight of her would correct that impression. You were right; she's a bundle of extraordinary vitalities. I never saw a woman more thoroughly alive; and that's the great secret of living—to be thoroughly alive."

"I knew it; I knew it!" his wife exclaimed. "Two such people couldn't help liking each other."

"Oh, I should think she might very well help liking me."

"She doesn't; she admires you immensely; but why?"

"Well, I don't precisely fit into any of her ideals, and the worst part of having ideals is that people who don't fit into them have to be discarded."

"Aunt Mary doesn't discard anybody," Delia interpolated.

"Her heart may not, but I fancy her judgment does."

"But she doesn't exactly fit into any of your ideals, and yet you like her," his wife persisted.

"I haven't any ideals," Corbett lightly responded. "*Je prends mon bien où je le trouve*; and I find a great deal in your Aunt Mary."

Delia did not ask Mrs. Hayne what she thought of her husband; she was sure that, in due time, her aunt would deliver her verdict; it was impossible for her to leave anyone unclassified. Perhaps, too, there was a latent cowardice in Delia's reticence; an unacknowledged dread lest Mrs. Hayne should range Corbett among the intermediate types.

After a day or two of mutual inspection and adjustment the three lives under Mrs. Hayne's roof lapsed into their separate routines. Mrs. Hayne once more set in motion the complicated machinery of her own existence (rendered more intricate by the accident of her lameness), and Corbett and his wife began to dine out and return the visits of their friends. There were, however, some hours which Corbett devoted to the club or to the frequentation of the public libraries, and these Delia gave to her aunt, driving with Mrs. Hayne from one committee meeting to another, writing business letters at her dictation, or reading aloud to her the reports of the various philanthropic, educational, or political institutions in which she was interested. She had been conscious on her arrival of a certain aloofness from her aunt's militant activities; but within a week she was swept back into the strong current of Mrs. Hayne's existence. It was like stepping from a gondola to an ocean steamer; at first she was dazed by the throb of the screw and the rush of parting waters, but gradually she felt herself infected by the exhilaration of getting to a fixed place in the shortest possible time. She could make sufficient allowance for the versatility of her moods to know that, a few weeks after her return to Paris, all that seemed most strenuous in Mrs. Hayne's occupations would fade to unreality; but that did not defend her from the strong spell of the moment. In its light her own life seemed vacuous, her husband's aims trivial as the subtleties of Chinese ivory carving; and she wondered if he walked in the same revealing flash.

Some three weeks after the arrival of the Corbetts in Mount Vernon Street, it became manifest that Mrs. Hayne had overtaxed her strength and must return for an undetermined period to her lounge. The life of restricted activity to which this necessity condemned her left her an occasional hour of leisure when there seemed no more letters to be dictated, no more reports to be read; and Corbett, always sure to do the right thing, was at hand to speed such unoccupied moments with the ready charm of his talk.

One day when, after sitting with her for some time, he departed to the club, Mrs. Hayne, turning to Delia, who came in to replace him, said, emphatically, "My dear, he's delightful."

"Oh, Aunt Mary, so are you!" burst gratefully from Mrs. Corbett.

Mrs. Hayne smiled. "Have you suspended your judgment of me until now?" she asked.

"No; but your liking each other seems to complete you both."

"Really, Delia, your husband couldn't have put that more gracefully. But sit down and tell me about him."

"Tell you about him?" repeated Delia, thinking of the voluminous letters in which she had enumerated to Mrs. Hayne the sum of her husband's merits.

"Yes," Mrs. Hayne continued, cutting, as she talked, the pages of a report on state lunatic asylums; "for instance, you've never told me why so charming an American has condemned America to the hard fate of being obliged to get on without him."

"You and he will never agree on that point, Aunt Mary," said Mrs. Corbett, coloring.

"Never mind; I rather like listening to reasons that I know beforehand I'm bound to disagree with; it saves so much mental effort. And besides, how can you tell? I'm very uncertain."

"You are very broad-minded, but you'll never understand his just having drifted into it. Any definite reason would seem to you better than that."

"Ah—he drifted into it?"

"Well, yes. You know his sister, who married the Comte de Vitrey and went to live in Paris, was very unhappy after her marriage; and when Laurence's mother died there was no one left to look after her; and so Laurence went abroad in order to be near her. After a few years Monsieur de Vitrey died too; but by that time Laurence didn't care to come back."

"Well," said Mrs. Hayne, "I see nothing shocking in that. Your husband can gratify his tastes much more easily in Europe than in America; and, after all, that is what we're all secretly striving to do. I'm sure if there were more lunatic asylums and poorhouses and hospitals in Europe than there are here I should be very much inclined to go and live there myself."

Delia laughed. "I knew you would like Laurence," she said, with a wisdom bred of the event.

"Of course I like him; he's a liberal education. It's very interesting to study the determining motives in such a man's career. How old is your husband, Delia?"

"Laurence is fifty-two."

"And when did he go abroad to look after his sister?"

"Let me see—when he was about twenty-eight; it was in 1867, I think."

"And before that he had lived in America?"

"Yes, the greater part of the time."

"Then of course he was in the war?" Mrs. Hayne continued, laying down her pamphlet. "You've never told me about that. Did he see any active service?"

As she spoke Delia grew pale; for a moment she sat looking blankly at her aunt.

"I don't think he was in the war at all," she said at length in a low tone.

Mrs. Hayne stared at her. "Oh, you must be mistaken," she said, decidedly. "Why shouldn't he have been in the war? What else could he have been doing?"

Mrs. Corbett was silent. All the men of her family, all the men of her friends' families, had fought in the war; Mrs. Hayne's husband had been killed at Bull Run, and one of Delia's cousins at Gettysburg.

Ever since she could remember it had been regarded as a matter of course by those about her that every man of her husband's generation who was neither lame, halt, nor blind should have fought in the war. Husbands had left their wives, fathers their children, young men their sweethearts, in answer to that summons; and those who had been deaf to it she had never heard designated by any name but one.

But all that had happened long ago; for years it had ceased to be a part of her consciousness. She had forgotten about the war; about her uncle who fell at Bull Run, and her cousin who was killed at Gettysburg. Now, of a sudden, it all came back to her, and she asked herself the question which her aunt had just put to her—why had her husband not been in the war? What else could he have been doing?

But the very word, as she repeated it, struck her as incongruous; Corbett was a man who never did anything. His elaborate intellectual processes bore no flower of result; he simply *was*—but had she not hitherto found that sufficient? She rose from her seat, turning away from Mrs. Hayne.

"I really don't know," she said, coldly. "I never asked him."

IV

Two weeks later the Corbetts returned to Europe. Corbett had really been charmed with his visit, and had in fact shown a marked inclination to outstay the date originally fixed for their departure. But Delia was firm; she did not wish to remain in Boston. She acknowledged that she was sorry to leave her Aunt Mary; but she wanted to get home.

"You turncoat!" Corbett said, laughing. "Two months ago you reserved that sacred designation for Boston."

"One can't tell where it is until one tries," she answered, vaguely.

"You mean that you don't want to come back and live in Boston?"

"Oh, no—no!"

"Very well. But pray take note of the fact that I'm very sorry to leave. Under your Aunt Mary's tutelage I'm becoming a passionate patriot."

Delia turned away in silence. She was counting the moments which led to their departure. She longed with an unreasoning intensity to get away from it all; from the dreary house in Mount Vernon Street, with its stenciled hall and hideous drawing room, its monotonous food served in unappetizing profusion; from the rarefied atmosphere of philanthropy and reform which she had once found so invigorating; and most of all from the reproval of her aunt's altruistic activities. The recollection of her husband's delightful house in Paris, so framed for a noble leisure, seemed to mock the aesthetic barrenness of Mrs. Hayne's environment. Delia thought tenderly of the mellow bindings, the deep-piled rugs, the pictures, bronzes, and tapestries; of the "first nights" at the Français, the eagerly discussed *conférences* on art or literature, the dreaming hours in galleries and museums, and all the delicate enjoyments of the life to which she was returning. It would be like passing from a hospital ward to a flower-filled drawing room; how could her husband linger on the threshold?

Corbett, who observed her attentively, noticed that a change had come over her during the last two weeks of their stay in Mount Vernon Street. He wondered uneasily if she were capricious; a man who has formed his own habits upon principles of the finest selection does not care to think that he has married a capricious woman. Then he reflected that the love of Paris is an insidious disease, breaking out when its victim least looks for it, and concluded that Delia was suffering from some such unexpected attack.

Delia certainly was suffering. Ever since Mrs. Hayne had asked her that innocent question—"Why shouldn't your husband have been in the war?"—she had been repeating it to herself day and night with the monotonous iteration of a monomaniac. Whenever Corbett came into the room, with that air of giving the simplest act its due value which made episodes of his entrances, she was tempted to cry out to him—"Why weren't you in the war?" When she heard him, at a dinner, point one of his polished epigrams, or smilingly demolish the syllogism of an antagonist, her pride in his achievement was chilled by the question—"Why wasn't he in the war?" When she saw him in the street, give a coin to a crossing sweeper, or lift his hat ceremoniously to one of Mrs. Hayne's maidservants (he was always considerate of poor people and servants) her approval winced under the reminder—"Why wasn't he in the war?" And when they were alone together, all through the spell of his talk and the exquisite pervasion of his presence ran the embittering undercurrent, "Why wasn't he in the war?"

At times she hated herself for the thought; it seemed a disloyalty to life's best gift. After all, what did it matter now? The war was over and forgotten; it was what the newspapers call "a dead issue." And why should any act of her husband's youth affect their present happiness together? Whatever he might once have been, he was perfect now; admirable in every relation of life; kind, generous, upright; a loyal friend, an accomplished gentleman, and, above all, the man she loved. Yes—but why had he not been in the war? And so began again the reiterant torment of the question. It rose up and lay down with her; it watched with her through sleepless nights, and followed her into the street; it mocked her from the eyes of strangers, and she dreaded lest her husband should read it in her own. In her saner moments she told herself that she was under the influence of a passing mood, which would vanish at the contact of her wonted life in Paris. She had become overstrung in the high air of Mrs. Hayne's moral enthusiasms; all she needed was to descend again to regions of more temperate virtue. This thought increased her impatience to be gone; and the days seemed interminable which divided her from departure.

The return to Paris, however, did not yield the hoped-for alleviation. The question was still with her, clamoring for a reply, and reinforced, with separation, by the increasing fear of her aunt's unspoken verdict. That shrewd woman had never again alluded to the subject of her brief colloquy with Delia; up to the moment of his farewell she had been unreservedly cordial to Corbett; but she was not the woman to palter with her convictions.

Delia knew what she must think; she knew what name, in the old days, Corbett would have gone by in her aunt's uncompromising circle.

Then came a flash of resistance—the heart's instinct of self-preservation. After all, what did she herself know of her husband's reasons for not being in the war? What right had she to set down to cowardice a course which might have been enforced by necessity, or dictated by unimpeachable motives? Why should she not put to him the question which she was perpetually asking herself? And not having done so, how dared she condemn him unheard?

A month or more passed in that torturing indecision. Corbett had returned with fresh zest to his accustomed way of life, weaned, by his first glimpse of the Champs Élysées, from his factitious enthusiasm for Boston. He and his wife entertained their friends delightfully, and frequented all the "first nights" and "private views" of the season, and Corbett continued to bring back knowing "bits" from the Hotel Drouot, and rare books from the quays; never had he appeared more cultivated, more decorative and enviable; people agreed that Delia Benson had been uncommonly clever to catch him.

One afternoon he returned later than usual from the club, and finding his wife alone in the drawing room, begged her for a cup of tea. Delia reflected, in complying, that she had never seen him look better; his fifty-two years sat upon him like a finish which made youth appear crude, and his voice, as he recounted his afternoon's doings, had the intimate inflections reserved for her ear.

"By the way," he said presently, as he set down his teacup, "I had almost forgotten that I've brought you a present—something I picked up in a little shop in the Rue Bonaparte. Oh, don't look too expectant; it's not a *chef-d'oeuvre*; on the contrary, it's about as bad as it can be. But you'll see presently why I bought it."

As he spoke he drew a small, flat parcel from the breast pocket of his impeccable frock coat and handed it to his wife.

Delia, loosening the paper which wrapped it, discovered within an oval frame studded with pearls and containing the crudely executed miniature of an unknown young man in the uniform of a United States cavalry officer. She glanced inquiringly at Corbett.

"Turn it over," he said.

She did so, and on the back, beneath two unfamiliar initials, read the brief inscription:

"Fell at Chancellorsville, May 3, 1863."

The blood rushed to her face as she stood gazing at the words.

"You see now why I bought it?" Corbett continued. "All the pieties of one's youth seemed to protest against leaving it in the clutches of a Jew pawnbroker in the Rue Bonaparte. It's awfully bad, isn't it?— but some poor soul might be glad to think that it had passed again into the possession of fellow countrymen." He took it back from her, bending to examine it critically. "What a daub!" he murmured. "I wonder who he was? Do you suppose that by taking a little trouble one might find out and restore it to his people?"

"I don't know—I dare say," she murmured, absently.

He looked up at the sound of her voice. "What's the matter, Delia? Don't you feel well?" he asked.

"Oh, yes. I was only thinking"—she took the miniature from his hand. "It was kind of you, Laurence, to buy this—it was like you."

"Thanks for the latter clause," he returned, smiling.

Delia stood staring at the vivid flesh tints of the young man who had fallen at Chancellorsville.

"You weren't very strong at his age, were you, Laurence? Weren't you often ill?" she asked.

Corbett gave her a surprised glance. "Not that I'm aware of," he said, "I had the measles at twelve, but since then I've been unromantically robust."

"And you—you were in America until you came abroad to be with your sister?"

"Yes—barring a trip of a few weeks in Europe."

Delia looked again at the miniature; then she fixed her eyes upon her husband's.

"Then why weren't you in the war?" she said.

Corbett answered her gaze for a moment; then his lids dropped, and he shifted his position slightly.

"Really," he said, with a smile, "I don't think I know."

They were the very words which she had used in answering her aunt.

"You don't know?" she repeated, the question leaping out like an electric shock. "What do you mean when you say that you don't know?"

"Well—it all happened some time ago," he answered, still smiling, "and the truth is that I've completely forgotten the excellent reasons that I doubtless had at the time for remaining at home."

"Reasons for remaining at home? But there were none; every man of your age went to the war; no one stayed at home who wasn't lame, or blind, or deaf, or ill, or—" Her face blazed, her voice broke passionately.

Corbett looked at her with rising amazement.

"Or—?" he said.

"Or a coward," she flashed out. The miniature dropped from her hands, falling loudly on the polished floor.

The two confronted each other in silence; Corbett was very pale.

"I've told you," he said, at length, "That I was neither lame, deaf, blind, nor ill. Your classification is so simple that it will be easy for you to draw your own conclusion."

And very quietly, with that admirable air which always put him in the right, he walked out of the room. Delia, left alone, bent down and picked up the miniature; its protecting crystal had been broken by the fall. She pressed it close to her and burst into tears.

An hour later, of course, she went to ask her husband's forgiveness. As a woman of sense she could do no less; and her conduct had been so absurd that it was the more obviously pardonable. Corbett, as he kissed her hand, assured her that he had known it was only nervousness; and after dinner, during which he made himself exceptionally agreeable, he proposed their ending the evening at the Palais Royal, where a new play was being given.

Delia had undoubtedly behaved like a fool, and was prepared to do meet penance for her folly by submitting to the gentle sarcasm of her husband's pardon; but when the episode was over, and she realized that she had asked her question and received her answer, she knew that she had passed a milestone in her existence. Corbett was perfectly charming; it was inevitable that he should go on being charming to the end of the chapter. It was equally inevitable that she should go on being in love with him; but her love had undergone a modification which the years were not to efface.

Formerly he had been to her like an unexplored country, full of bewitching surprises and recurrent revelations of wonder and beauty; now she had measured and mapped him, and knew beforehand the direction of every path she trod. His answer to her question had given her the clue to the labyrinth; knowing what he had once done, it seemed quite simple to forecast his future conduct. For that long-past action was still a part of his actual being; he had not outlived or disowned it; he had not even seen that it needed defending.

Her ideal of him was shivered like the crystal above the miniature of the warrior of Chancellorsville. She had the crystal replaced by a piece of clear glass which (as the jeweler pointed out to her) cost much less and looked equally well; and for the passionate worship which she had paid her husband she substituted a tolerant affection which possessed precisely the same advantages.

THE ANGEL AT THE GRAVE

(1901)

By the time she published "The Angel at the Grave," Wharton was
an accomplished writer. The story, which ranks among her best, is
based on the life of her friend Sara "Sally" Norton, daughter of
Charles Eliot Norton, Harvard professor and cultural critic. Like
Paulina in the story, Sally rejected a chance to marry (in this case an
Englishman) and stayed home to tend her father and, after his death,
edit his papers.

But if Sally/Paulina is "walled alive into a tomb," the story is also
a comedy. Colored throughout by Wharton's most sparkling wit, it
pokes fun at the New England past. The name of Paulina's grandfather, Orestes Anson, recalls a friend of Ralph Waldo Emerson, and
Wharton plays with Emersonian rhetoric in mocking the high moral
seriousness of Paulina's inheritance. She uses terms such as "necessity," "destiny," and "predestination" and gets in as many titles of
Emerson essays as possible—"Nature," "Compensation," and "Fate."

The working of fate turns out to be a serious theme in the story.
Although the ending has been criticized as "at once unexpected and
not quite persuasive" (Lewis, 99), it seems fitting that a story about
fate would end unexpectedly. Paulina, who was "designed" to spend
her womanhood guarding the Anson heritage, is simply being affected by another turn of the wheel of fortune. Moreover, Wharton
prepares the reader by emphasizing the "nourishment" Paulina re-
ceives from her work; only if we view marriage as the only happy
ending do we assume that Paulina necessarily made the wrong choice
in rejecting her suitor.

THE HOUSE stood a few yards back from the elm-shaded village street, in that semipublicity sometimes cited as a democratic protest against old world standards of domestic exclusiveness. This candid exposure to the public eye is more probably a result of the gregariousness which, in the New England bosom, oddly coexists with a shrinking from direct social contact; most of the inmates of such houses preferring that furtive intercourse which is the result of observation through shuttered windows and a categorical acquaintance with the neighboring clothes-lines. The House, however, faced its public with a difference. For sixty years it had written itself with a capital letter, had self-consciously squared itself in the eye of an admiring nation. The most searching inroads of village intimacy hardly counted in a household that opened on the universe; and a lady whose doorbell was at any moment liable to be rung by visitors from London or Vienna was not likely to flutter upstairs when she observed a neighbor "stepping over."

The solitary inmate of the Anson House owed this induration of the social texture to the most conspicuous accident in her annals: the fact that she was the only granddaughter of the great Orestes Anson. She had been born, as it were, into a museum, and cradled in a glass case with a label; the first foundations of her consciousness being built on the rock of her grandfather's celebrity. To a little girl who acquires her earliest knowledge of literature through a *Reader* embellished with fragments of her ancestor's prose, that personage necessarily fills an heroic space in the foreground of life. To communicate with one's past through the impressive medium of print, to have, as it were, a footing in every library in the country, and an acknowledged kinship with that world-diffused clan, the descendants of the great, was to be pledged to a standard of manners that amazingly simplified the lesser relations of life. The village street on which Paulina Anson's youth looked out led to all the capitals of Europe; and over the roads of intercommunication unseen caravans bore back to the elm-shaded House the tribute of an admiring world.

Fate seemed to have taken a direct share in fitting Paulina for her part as the custodian of this historic dwelling. It had long been secretly regarded as a "visitation" by the great man's family that he had left no son and that his daughters were not "intellectual." The ladies themselves were the first to lament their deficiency, to own that nature had denied them the gift of making the most of their opportunities. A profound veneration for their parent and an unswerving faith in his doctrines had not amended their congenital incapacity to understand what he had written. Laura, who had her moments of mute rebellion against destiny, had sometimes thought how much easier it would have been if their progenitor had been a poet; for she could recite, with feeling, portions of *The Culprit Fay* and of the poems of Mrs. Hemans; and Phoebe, who was more conspicuous for memory than imagination, kept an album filled with "selections." But the great man was a philosopher; and to both daughters respiration was difficult on the cloudy heights of metaphysic. The situation would have been intolerable but for the fact that, while Phoebe and Laura were still at school, their father's fame had passed from the open ground of conjecture to the chill privacy of certitude. Dr. Anson had in fact achieved one of those anticipated immortalities not uncommon at a time when people were apt to base their literary judgments on their emotions, and when to affect plain food and despise England went a long way toward establishing a man's intellectual preeminence. Thus, when the daughters were called on to strike a filial attitude about their parent's pedestal, there was little to do but to pose gracefully and point upward; and there are spines to which the immobility of worship is not a strain. A legend had by this time crystallized about the great Orestes, and it was of more immediate interest to the public to hear what brand of tea he drank, and whether he took off his boots in the hall, than to rouse the drowsy echo of his dialectic. A great man never draws so near his public as when it has become unnecessary to read his books and is still interesting to know what he eats for breakfast.

As recorders of their parent's domestic habits, as pious scavengers of his wastepaper basket, the Misses Anson were unexcelled. They always had an interested anecdote to impart to the literary pilgrim, and the tact with which, in later years, they intervened between the public and the growing inaccessibility of its idol, sent away many an enthusiast satisfied to have touched the veil before the sanctuary. Still it was felt, especially by old Mrs. Anson, who survived her husband for some years, that Phoebe and Laura were not worthy of their privileges. There had been a third daughter so unworthy of hers that she had married a distant cousin, who had taken her to live in a new Western community where the *Works of Orestes Anson* had not yet become a part of the civic consciousness; but of this daughter little was said, and she was tacitly understood to be excluded from the family heritage of fame. In time, however, it appeared that the traditional penny with which she had been cut off had been invested to unexpected advantage; and the interest on it, when she died, returned to the Anson House in the shape of a granddaughter who was at once felt to be what Mrs. Anson called a "compensation." It was Mrs. Anson's firm belief that the remotest operations of nature were governed by the centripetal force of her husband's greatness and that Paulina's exceptional intelligence could be explained only on the ground that she was designed to act as the guardian of the family temple.

The House, by the time Paulina came to live in it, had already acquired the publicity of a place of worship; not the perfumed chapel of a romantic idolatry but the cold clean empty meetinghouse of ethical enthusiasms. The ladies lived on its outskirts, as it were, in cells that left the central fane undisturbed. The very position of the furniture had come to have a ritual significance: the sparse ornaments were the offerings of kindred intellects, the steel engravings by Raphael Morghen marked the Via Sacra of a European tour, and the black walnut desk with its bronze inkstand modeled on the Pantheon was the altar of this bleak temple of thought.

To a child compact of enthusiasms, and accustomed to pasture them on the scanty herbage of a new social soil, the atmosphere of the old house was full of floating nourishment. In the compressed perspective of Paulina's outlook it stood for a monument of ruined civilizations, and its white portico opened on legendary distances. Its very aspect was impressive to eyes that had first surveyed life from the jigsaw "residence" of a raw-edged Western town. The high-ceilinged rooms, with their paneled walls, their polished mahogany, their portraits of triple-stocked ancestors and of ringleted "females" in crayon, furnished the child with the historic scenery against which a young imagination constructs its vision of the past. To other eyes the cold spotless thinly-furnished interior might have suggested the shuttered mind of a maiden lady who associates fresh air and sunlight with dust and discoloration; but it is the eye which supplies the coloring matter, and Paulina's brimmed with the richest hues.

Nevertheless, the House did not immediately dominate her. She had her confused outreachings toward other centers of sensation, her vague intuition of a heliocentric system; but the attraction of habit, the steady pressure of example, gradually fixed her roving allegiance and she bent her neck to the yoke. Vanity had a share in her subjugation; for it had early been discovered that she was the only person in the family who could read her grandfather's works. The fact that she had perused them with delight at an age when (even presupposing a metaphysical bias) it was impossible for her to understand them, seemed to her aunts and grandmother sure evidence of predestination. Paulina was to be the interpreter of the oracle, and the philosophic fumes so vertiginous to meaner minds would throw her into the needed condition of clairvoyance. Nothing could have been more genuine than the emotion on which this theory was based. Paulina, in fact, delighted in her grandfather's writings. His sonorous periods, his mystic vocabulary, his bold flights into the rarefied air of the abstract, were thrilling to a fancy unhampered by the need of definitions. This purely verbal pleasure was supplemented later by the excitement of gathering up crumbs of meaning from the rhetorical board. What could have been more stimulating than to construct the theory of a girlish world out of the fragments of this Titanic cosmogony? Before Paulina's opinions had reached the stage when ossification sets in their form was fatally predetermined.

The fact that Dr. Anson had died and that his apotheosis had taken place before his young priestess' induction to the temple, made her ministrations easier and more inspiring. There were no little personal traits—such as the great man's manner of helping himself to salt, or the guttural cluck that started the wheels of speech—to distract the eye of young veneration from the central fact of his divinity. A man whom one knows only through a crayon portrait and a dozen yellowing tomes on free will and intuition is at least secure from the belittling effects of intimacy.

Paulina thus grew up in a world readjusted to the fact of her grandfather's greatness; and as each organism draws from its surroundings the kind of nourishment most needful to its growth, so from this somewhat colorless conception she absorbed warmth, brightness and variety. Paulina was the type of woman who transmutes thought into sensation and nurses a theory in her bosom like a child.

In due course Mrs. Anson "passed away"—no one died in the Anson vocabulary—and Paulina became more than ever the foremost figure of the commemorative group. Laura and Phoebe, content to leave their father's glory in more competent hands, placidly lapsed into needlework and fiction, and their niece stepped into immediate prominence as the chief "authority" on the great man. Historians who were "getting up" the period wrote to consult her and to borrow documents; ladies with inexplicable yearnings begged for an interpretation of phrases which had "influenced" them, but which they had not quite understood; critics applied to her to verify some doubtful citation or to decide some disputed point in chronology; and the great tide of thought and investigation kept up a continuous murmur on the quiet shores of her life.

An explorer of another kind disembarked there one day in the shape of a young man to whom Paulina was primarily a kissable girl, with an afterthought in the shape of a grandfather. From the outset it had been impossible to fix Hewlett Winsloe's attention on Dr. Anson. The young man behaved with the innocent profanity of infants sporting on a tomb. His excuse was that he came from New York, a Cimmerian outskirt which survived in Paulina's geography only because Dr. Anson had gone there once or twice to lecture. The curious thing was that she should have thought it worth-while to find excuses for young Winsloe. The fact that she did so had not escaped the attention of the village; but people, after a gasp of awe, said it was the most natural thing in the world that a girl like Paulina Anson should think of marrying. It would certainly seem a little odd to see a man in the House, but young Winsloe would of course understand that the Doctor's books were not to be disturbed, and that he must go down to the orchard to smoke. The village had barely framed this *modus vivendi* when it was convulsed by the announcement that young Winsloe declined to live in the House on any terms. Hang going down to the orchard to smoke! He meant to take his wife to New York. The village drew its breath and watched.

Did Persephone, snatched from the warm fields of Enna, peer half-consentingly down the abyss that opened at her feet? Paulina, it must be owned, hung a moment over the black gulf of temptation. She would have found it easy to cope with a deliberate disregard of her grandfather's rights; but young Winsloe's unconsciousness of that shadowy claim was as much a natural function as the falling of leaves on a grave. His love was an embodiment of the perpetual renewal which to some tender spirits seems a crueler process than decay.

On women of Paulina's mold this piety toward implicit demands, toward the ghosts of dead duties walking unappeased among usurping passions, has a stronger hold than any tangible bond. People said that she gave up young Winsloe because her aunts disapproved of her leaving them; but such disapproval as reached her was an emanation from the walls of the House, from the bare desk, the faded portraits, the dozen yellowing tomes that no hand but hers ever lifted from the shelf.

II

After that the house possessed her. As if conscious of its victory, it imposed a conqueror's claim. It had once been suggested that she should write a life of her grandfather, and the task from which she had shrunk as from a too-oppressive privilege now shaped itself into a justification of her course. In a burst of filial pantheism she tried to lose herself in the vast ancestral consciousness. Her one refuge from scepticism was a blind faith in the magnitude and the endurance of the idea to which she had sacrificed her life, and with a passionate instinct of self-preservation she labored to fortify her position.

The preparations for the *Life* led her through byways that the most scrupulous of the previous biographers had left unexplored. She accumulated her material with a blind animal patience unconscious of fortuitous risks. The years stretched before her like some vast blank page spread out to receive the record of her toil; and she had a mystic conviction that she would not die till her work was accomplished.

The aunts, sustained by no such high purpose, withdrew in turn to their respective divisions of the Anson "plot," and Paulina remained alone with her task. She was forty when the book was completed. She had traveled little in her life, and it had become more and more difficult to her to leave the House even for a day; but the dread of entrusting her document to a strange hand made her decide to carry it herself to the publisher. On the way to Boston she had a sudden vision of the loneliness to which this last parting condemned her. All her youth, all her dreams, all her renunciations lay in that neat bundle on her knee. It was not so much her grandfather's life as her own that she had written; and the knowledge that it would come back to her in all the glorification of print was no more help than, to a mother's grief, the assurance that the lad she must part with will return with epaulets.

She had naturally addressed herself to the firm which had published her grandfather's works. Its founder, a personal friend of the philosopher's, had survived the Olympian group of which he had been a subordinate member, long enough to bestow his octogenarian approval on Paulina's pious undertaking. But he had died soon afterward; and Miss Anson found herself confronted by his grandson, a person with a brisk commercial view of his trade, who was said to have put "new blood" into the firm.

This gentleman listened attentively, fingering her manuscript as though literature were a tactile substance; then, with a confidential twist of his revolving chair, he emitted the verdict: "We ought to have had this ten years sooner."

Miss Anson took the words as an allusion to the repressed avidity of her readers. "It has been a long time for the public to wait," she solemnly assented.

The publisher smiled. "They haven't waited," he said.

She looked at him strangely. "Haven't waited?"

"No—they've gone off; taken another train. Literature's like a big railway station now, you know: there's a train starting every minute. People are not going to hang around the waiting room. If they can't get to a place when they want to they go somewhere else."

The application of this parable cost Miss Anson several minutes of throbbing silence. At length she said: "Then I am to understand that the public is no longer interested in—in my grandfather?" She felt as though heaven must blast the lips that risked such a conjecture.

"Well, it's this way. He's a name still, of course. People don't exactly want to be caught not knowing who he is; but they don't want to spend two dollars finding out, when they can look him up for nothing in any biographical dictionary."

Miss Anson's world reeled. She felt herself adrift among mysterious forces, and no more thought of prolonging the discussion than of opposing an earthquake with argument. She went home carrying the manuscript like a wounded thing. On the return journey she found herself traveling straight toward a fact that had lurked for months in the background of her life, and that now seemed to await her on the very threshold: the fact that fewer visitors came to the House. She owned to herself that for the last four or five years the number had steadily diminished. Engrossed in her work, she had noted the change only to feel thankful that she had fewer interruptions. There had been a time when, at the traveling season, the bell rang continuously, and the ladies of the House lived in a chronic state of "best silks" and expectancy. It would have been impossible then to carry on any consecutive work; and she now saw that the silence which had gathered round her task had been the hush of death.

Not of *his* death! The very walls cried out against the implication. It was the world's enthusiasm, the world's faith, the world's loyalty that had died. A corrupt generation that had turned aside to worship the brazen serpent. Her heart yearned with a prophetic passion over the lost sheep straying in the wilderness. But all great glories had their interlunar period; and in due time her grandfather would once more flash full-orbed upon a darkling world.

The few friends to whom she confided her adventure reminded her with tender indignation that there were other publishers less subject to the fluctuations of the market; but much as she had braved for her grandfather she could not again brave that particular probation. She found herself, in fact, incapable of any immediate effort. She had lost her way in a labyrinth of conjecture where her worst dread was that she might put her hand upon the clue.

She locked up the manuscript and sat down to wait. If a pilgrim had come just then the priestess would have fallen on his neck; but she continued to celebrate her rites alone. It was a double solitude; for she had always thought a great deal more of the people who came to see the House than of the people who came to see her. She fancied that the neighbors kept a keen eye on the path to the House; and there were days when the figure of a stranger strolling past the gate seemed to focus upon her the scorching sympathies of the village. For a time she thought of traveling; of going to Europe, or even to Boston; but to leave the House now would have seemed like deserting her post.

Gradually her scattered energies centered themselves in the fierce resolve to understand what had happened. She was not the woman to
live long in an unmapped country or to accept as final her private
interpretation of phenomena. Like a traveler in unfamiliar regions she
began to store for future guidance the minutest natural signs. Un-
flinchingly she noted the accumulating symptoms of indifference that
marked her grandfather's descent toward posterity. She passed from
the heights on which he had been grouped with the sages of his day
to the lower level where he had come to be "the friend of Emerson,"
"the correspondent of Hawthorne," or (later still) "the Dr. Anson"
mentioned in their letters. The change had taken place as slowly and
imperceptibly as a natural process. She could not say that any ruthless
hand had stripped the leaves from the tree: it was simply that, among
the evergreen glories of his group, her grandfather's had proved
deciduous.

She had still to ask herself why. If the decay had been a natural
process, was it not the very pledge of renewal? It was easier to find
such arguments than to be convinced by them. Again and again she
tried to drug her solicitude with analogies; but at last she saw that
such expedients were but the expression of a growing incredulity. The
best way of proving her faith in her grandfather was not to be afraid
of his critics. She had no notion where these shadowy antagonists
lurked; for she had never heard of the great man's doctrine being
directly combated. Oblique assaults there must have been, however,
Parthian shots at the giant that none dared face; and she thirsted to
close with such assailants. The difficulty was to find them. She began
by rereading the *Works*; thence she passed to the writers of the same
school, those whose rhetoric bloomed perennial in *First Readers* from
which her grandfather's prose had long since faded. Amid that clamor
of far-off enthusiasms she detected no controversial note. The little
knot of Olympians held their views in common with an early Christian promiscuity. They were continually proclaiming their admiration for each other, the public joining as chorus in this guileless
antiphon of praise; and she discovered no traitor in their midst.

What then had happened? Was it simply that the main current of
thought had set another way? Then why did the others survive? Why
were they still marked down as tributaries to the philosophic stream?
This question carried her still farther afield, and she pressed on with
the passion of a champion whose reluctance to know the worst might

be construed into a doubt of his cause. At length—slowly but inevitably—an explanation shaped itself. Death had overtaken the doctrines about which her grandfather had draped his cloudy rhetoric.
They had disintegrated and been reabsorbed, adding their little pile
to the dust drifted about the mute lips of the Sphinx. The great man's
contemporaries had survived not by reason of what they taught, but
of what they were; and he, who had been the mere mask through
which they mouthed their lesson, the instrument on which their tune
was played, lay buried deep among the obsolete tools of thought.

The discovery came to Paulina suddenly. She looked up one evening from her reading and it stood before her like a ghost. It had
entered her life with stealthy steps, creeping close before she was
aware of it. She sat in the library, among the carefully-tended books
and portraits; and it seemed to her that she had been walled alive into
a tomb hung with the effigies of dead ideas. She felt a desperate longing to escape into the outer air, where people toiled and loved, and
living sympathies went hand in hand. It was the sense of wasted labor
that oppressed her; of two lives consumed in that ruthless process
that uses generations of effort to build a single cell. There was a
dreary parallel between her grandfather's fruitless toil and her own
unprofitable sacrifice. Each in turn had kept vigil by a corpse.

III

The bell rang—she remembered it afterward—with a loud thrilling
note. It was what they used to call the "visitor's ring"; not the tentative tinkle of a neighbor dropping in to borrow a saucepan or discuss parochial incidents, but a decisive summons from the outer
world.

Miss Anson put down her knitting and listened. She sat upstairs
now, making her rheumatism an excuse for avoiding the rooms below.
Her interests had insensibly adjusted themselves to the perspective of
her neighbors' lives, and she wondered—as the bell re-echoed—if it
could mean that Mrs. Hemingway's baby had come. Conjecture had
time to ripen into certainty, and she was limping toward the closet
where her cloak and bonnet hung, when her little maid fluttered in
with the announcement: "A gentleman to see the house."

"The *House*?"

"Yes, m'm. I don't know what he means," faltered the messenger, whose memory did not embrace the period when such announcements were a daily part of the domestic routine.

Miss Anson glanced at the proffered card. The name it bore—*Mr. George Corby*—was unknown to her, but the blood rose to her languid cheek. "Hand me my Mechlin cap, Katy," she said, trembling a little, as she laid aside her walking stick. She put her cap on before the mirror, with rapid unsteady touches. "Did you draw up the library blinds?" she breathlessly asked.

She had gradually built up a wall of commonplace between herself and her illusions, but at the first summons of the past filial passion swept away the frail barriers of expediency.

She walked downstairs so hurriedly that her stick clicked like a girlish heel; but in the hall she paused, wondering nervously if Katy had put a match to the fire. The autumn air was cold and she had the reproachful vision of a visitor with elderly ailments shivering by her inhospitable hearth. She thought instinctively of the stranger as a survivor of the days when such a visit was a part of the young enthusiast's itinerary.

The fire was unlit and the room forbiddingly cold; but the figure which, as Miss Anson entered, turned from a lingering scrutiny of the bookshelves, was that of a fresh-eyed sanguine youth clearly independent of any artificial caloric. She stood still a moment, feeling herself the victim of some anterior impression that made this robust presence an insubstantial thing; but the young man advanced with an air of genial assurance which rendered him at once more real and more reminiscent.

"Why this, you know," he exclaimed, "is simply immense!"

The words, which did not immediately present themselves as slang to Miss Anson's unaccustomed ear, echoed with an odd familiarity through the academic silence.

"The room, you know, I mean," he explained with a comprehensive gesture. "These jolly portraits, and the books—that's the old gentleman himself over the mantelpiece, I suppose?—and the elms outside, and—and the whole business. I do like a congruous background—don't you?"

His hostess was silent. No one but Hewlett Winsloe had ever spoken of her grandfather as "the old gentleman."

"It's a hundred times better than I could have hoped," her visitor continued, with a cheerful disregard of her silence. "The seclusion, the remoteness, the philosophic atmosphere—there's so little of that kind of flavor left! I should have simply hated to find that he lived over a grocery, you know. I had the deuce of a time finding out where he *did* live," he began again, after another glance of parenthetical enjoyment. "But finally I got on the trail through some old book on Brook Farm. I was bound I'd get the environment right before I did my article."

Miss Anson, by this time, had recovered sufficient self-possession to seat herself and assign a chair to her visitor.

"Do I understand," she asked slowly, following his rapid eye about the room, "that you intend to write an article about my grandfather?"

"That's what I'm here for," Mr. Corby genially responded; "that is, if you're willing to help me; for I can't get on without your help," he added with a confident smile.

There was another pause, during which Miss Anson noticed a fleck of dust on the faded leather of the writing table and a fresh spot of discoloration in the right-hand upper corner of Raphael Morghen's "Parnassus."

"Then you believe in him?" she said, looking up. She could not tell what had prompted her; the words rushed out irresistibly.

"Believe in him?" Corby cried, springing to his feet. "Believe in Orestes Anson? Why, I believe he's simply the greatest—the most stupendous—the most phenomenal figure we've got!"

The color rose to Miss Anson's brow. Her heart was beating passionately. She kept her eyes fixed on the young man's face, as though it might vanish if she looked away.

"You—you mean to say this in your article?" she asked.

"Say it? Why, the facts will say it," he exulted. "The baldest kind of a statement would make it clear. When a man is as big as that he doesn't need a pedestal!"

Miss Anson sighed. "People used to say that when I was young," she murmured. "But now—"

Her visitor stared. "When you were young? But how did they know—when the thing hung fire as it did? When the whole edition was thrown back on his hands?"

"The whole edition—what edition?" It was Miss Anson's turn to stare.

"Why, of his pamphlet—*the* pamphlet—the one thing that counts,

that survives, that makes him what he is! For heaven's sake," he trag-
ically adjured her, "don't tell me there isn't a copy of it left!"

Miss Anson was trembling slightly. "I don't think I understand
what you mean," she faltered, less bewildered by his vehemence than
by the strange sense of coming on an unexplored region of the very
heart of her dominion.

"Why, his account of the *amphioxus*, of course! You can't mean
that his family didn't know about it—that *you* don't know about it?
I came across it by the merest accident myself, in a letter of vindi-
cation that he wrote in 1830 to an old scientific paper; but I understood there were journals—early journals; there must be references
to it somewhere in the twenties. He must have been at least ten or
twelve years ahead of Yarrell; and he saw the whole significance of it,
too—he saw where it led to. As I understand it, he actually anticipated in his pamphlet Saint Hilaire's theory of the universal type, and
supported the hypothesis by describing the notochord of the *amphioxus* as a cartilaginous vertebral column. The specialists of the
day jeered at him, of course, as the specialists in Goethe's time jeered
at the plant metamorphosis. As far as I can make out, the anatomists
and zoologists were down on Dr. Anson to a man; that was why his
cowardly publishers went back on their bargain. But the pamphlet
must be here somewhere—he writes as though, in his first disappointment, he had destroyed the whole edition; but surely there must
be at least one copy left?"

His scientific jargon was as bewildering as his slang; and there
were even moments in his discourse when Miss Anson ceased to distinguish between them; but the suspense with which he continued to
gaze on her acted as a challenge to her scattered thoughts.

"The *amphioxus*," she murmured, half rising. "It's an animal,
isn't it—a fish? Yes, I think I remember." She sank back with the
inward look of one who retraces some lost line of association.

Gradually the distance cleared, the details started into life. In her
researches for the biography she had patiently followed every rami-
fication of her subject, and one of these overgrown paths now led her
back to the episode in question. The great Orestes's title of "Doctor"
had in fact not been merely the spontaneous tribute of a national admiration; he had actually studied medicine in his youth, and his di-
aries, as his granddaughter now recalled, showed that he had passed
through a brief phase of anatomical ardor before his attention was

diverted to supersensual problems. It had indeed seemed to Paulina, as she scanned those early pages, that they revealed a spontaneity, a freshness of feeling somehow absent from his later lucubrations—as though this one emotion had reached him directly, the others through some intervening medium. In the excess of her commemorative zeal she had even struggled through the unintelligible pamphlet to which a few lines in the journal had bitterly directed her. But the subject and the phraseology were alien to her and unconnected with her conception of the great man's genius; and after a hurried perusal she had averted her thoughts from the episode as from a revelation of failure. At length she rose a little unsteadily, supporting herself against the writing table. She looked hesitatingly about the room; then she drew a key from her old-fashioned reticule and unlocked a drawer beneath one of the bookcases. Young Corby watched her breathlessly. With a tremulous hand she turned over the dusty documents that seemed to fill the drawer. "Is this it?" she said, holding out a thin discolored volume.

He seized it with a gasp. "Oh, by George," he said, dropping into the nearest chair.

She stood observing him strangely as his eye devoured the moldy pages.

"Is this the only copy left?" he asked at length, looking up for a moment as a thirsty man lifts his head from his glass.

"I think it must be. I found it long ago, among some old papers that my aunts were burning up after my grandmother's death. They said it was of no use—that he'd always meant to destroy the whole edition and that I ought to respect his wishes. But it was something *he* had written; to burn it was like shutting the door against his voice—against something he had once wished to say, and that nobody had listened to. I wanted him to feel that I was always here, ready to listen, even when others hadn't thought it worth-while; and so I kept the pamphlet, meaning to carry out his wish and destroy it before my death."

Her visitor gave a groan of retrospective anguish. "And but for me—but for today—you would have?"

"I should have thought it my duty."

"Oh, by George—by George!" he repeated, subdued afresh by the inadequacy of speech.

She continued to watch him in silence. At length he jumped up and impulsively caught her by both hands.

"He's bigger and bigger!" he almost shouted. "He simply leads the field! You'll help me go to the bottom of this, won't you? We must turn out all the papers—letters, journals, memoranda. He must have made notes. He must have left some record of what led up to this. We must leave nothing unexplored. By Jove," he cried, looking up at her with his bright convincing smile, "do you know you're the grand-daughter of a Great Man?"

Her color flickered like a girl's. "Are you—sure of him?" she whispered, as though putting him on his guard against a possible betrayal of trust.

"Sure! Sure! My dear lady—" he measured her again with his quick confident glance. "Don't *you* believe in him?"

She drew back with a confused murmur. "I—used to." She had left her hands in his: their pressure seemed to send a warm current to her heart. "It ruined my life!" she cried with sudden passion. He looked at her perplexedly.

"I gave up everything," she went on wildly, "to keep *him* alive. I sacrificed myself—others—I nursed his glory in my bosom and it died—and left me—left me here alone." She paused and gathered her courage with a gasp. "Don't make the same mistake!" she warned him.

He shook his head, still smiling. "No danger of that! You're not alone, my dear lady. He's here with you—he's come back to you to-day. Don't you see what's happened? Don't you see that it's your love that has kept him alive? If you'd abandoned your post for an in-stant—let things pass into other hands—if your wonderful tenderness hadn't perpetually kept guard—this might have been—must have been—irretrievably lost." He laid his hand on the pamphlet. "And then—then he *would* have been dead!"

"Oh," she said, "don't tell me too suddenly!" And she turned away and sank into a chair.

The young man stood watching her in an awed silence. For a long time she sat motionless, with her face hidden, and he thought she must be weeping.

At length he said, almost shyly: "You'll let me come back, then? You'll help me work this thing out?"

She rose calmly and held out her hand. "I'll help you," she declared.

"I'll come tomorrow, then. Can we get to work early?"

"As early as you please."

"At eight o'clock, then," he said briskly. "You'll have the papers ready?"

"I'll have everything ready." She added with a half-playful hesitancy: "And the fire shall be lit for you."

He went out with his bright nod. She walked to the window and watched his buoyant figure hastening down the elm-shaded street. When she turned back into the empty room she looked as though youth had touched her on the lips.

THE PRETEXT

(1908)

This story has interesting biographical connections. In January 1908 Henry James wrote Wharton to relinquish his rights in "our petite donnée," the case of a young English acquaintance who had attended Harvard and fallen in love with a professor's wife, leading him to defy his family. Wharton and James had imagined a conclusion in which an English relative would visit the middle-aged wife and decide she had been used as a "pretext" (Henry James and Edith Wharton Letters: 1900–1915, ed. Lyall H. Powers [New York: Charles Scribner's Sons, 1990], 87–88).

By the time Wharton wrote the story she was embarking on an affair with a younger man, journalist Morton Fullerton. Thus she had, like her heroine Margaret Ransom, "a secret life of incommunicable joys." But Margaret's joy is more short-lived than Wharton's, because Margaret credits the relative's idea of the pretext. Critics too have assumed that Guy lied and named Margaret to protect his real lover. But why would he lie and where did he find time to see another woman while working and visiting Margaret daily? Guy's actions would make more sense if he truly loved Margaret, the only objection being the assumption that young men do not fall in love with older, ordinary-looking women. Once the possibility is admitted, we can see how Wharton undercuts the English relative, who keeps repeating, "I simply don't see."

Nor can Margaret see very clearly. In her bedroom she uses a cramped Puritan mirror that cannot properly reflect a sensual woman to whom a youth could be attracted. She accepts too soon the relative's unflattering edict and loses her joy in being loved.

MRS. RANSOM, when the front door had closed on her visitor, passed with a spring from the drawing room to a narrow hall, and thence up the narrow stairs to her bedroom.

Though slender, and still light of foot, she did not always move so quickly: hitherto, in her life, there had not been much to hurry for, save the recurring domestic tasks that compel haste without fostering elasticity; but some impetus of youth revived, communicated to her by her talk with Guy Dawnish, now found an expression in her girlish flight upstairs, her girlish impatience to bolt herself into her room with her throbs and her blushes.

Her blushes? Was she really blushing?

She approached the cramped eagle-topped mirror above her plain prim dressing table: just such a meager concession to the weakness of the flesh as every old-fashioned house in Wentworth counted among its relics. The face reflected in this unflattering surface—for even the mirrors of Wentworth erred on the side of deprecation—did not seem, at first sight, a suitable theater for the display of the tenderer emotions, and its owner blushed more deeply as the fact was forced upon her.

Her fair hair had grown too thin—it no longer quite hid the blue veins in the candid forehead that one seemed to see turned toward professorial desks, in large bare halls where a snowy winter light fell uncompromisingly on rows of "thoughtful women." Her mouth was thin, too, and a little strained; her lips were too pale; and there were lines in the corners of her eyes. It was a face which had grown middle-aged while it waited for the joys of youth.

Well—but if she could still blush? Instinctively she drew back a little, so that her scrutiny became less microscopic, and the pretty lingering pink threw a veil over her pallor, the hollows in her temples,

the faint wrinkles of inexperience about her lips and eyes. How a little color helped! It made her eyes so deep and shining. She saw now why bad women rouged . . . her redness deepened at the thought.

But suddenly she noticed for the first time that the collar of her dress was too low. It showed the shrunken lines of the throat. She rummaged feverishly in a tidy scentless drawer, and snatching out a bit of black velvet, bound it about her neck. Yes—that was better. It gave her the relief she needed. Relief—contrast—that was it! She had never had any, either in her appearance or in her setting. She was as flat as the pattern of the wallpaper—and so was her life. And all the people about her had the same look. Wentworth was the kind of place where husbands and wives gradually grew to resemble each other— one or two of her friends, she remembered, had told her lately that she and Ransom were beginning to look alike. . . .

But why had she always, so tamely, allowed her aspect to conform to her situation? Perhaps a gayer exterior would have provoked a brighter fate. Even now—she turned back to the glass, loosened her tight strands of hair, ran the fine end of the comb under them with a frizzing motion, and then disposed them, more lightly and amply, above her eager face. Yes—it was really better; it made a difference. She smiled at herself with a timid coquetry, and her lips seemed rosier as she smiled. Then she laid down the comb and the smile faded. It made a difference, certainly—but was it right to try to make one's hair look thicker and wavier than it really was? Between that and rouging the ethical line seemed almost imperceptible, and the specter of her rigid New England ancestry rose reprovingly before her. She was sure that none of her grandmothers had ever simulated a curl or encouraged a blush. A blush, indeed! What had any of them ever had to blush for in all their frozen lives? And what, in heaven's name, had she? She sat down in the stiff mahogany rocking chair beside her work table and tried to collect herself. From childhood she had been taught to "collect herself"—but never before had her small sensations and aspirations been so widely scattered, diffused over so vague and uncharted an expanse. Hitherto they had lain in neatly sorted and easily accessible bundles on the high shelves of a perfectly ordered moral consciousness. And now—now that for the first time they *needed* collecting—now that the little winged and scattered bits of self were dancing madly down the vagrant winds of fancy, she knew no spell to call them to the fold again. The best way, no doubt—if

only her bewilderment permitted—was to go back to the beginning—
the beginning, at least, of today's visit—to recapitulate, word for
word and look for look. . . .

She clasped her hands on the arms of the chair, checked its swaying
with a thrust of her foot, and fixed her eyes on the inward vision. . . .

To begin with, what had made today's visit so different from the
others? It became suddenly vivid to her that there had been many,
almost daily, others, since Guy Dawnish's coming to Wentworth.
Even the previous winter—the winter of his arrival from England—
his visits had been numerous enough to make Wentworth aware
that—very naturally—Mrs. Ransom was "looking after" the stray
young Englishman committed to her husband's care by an eminent
Q.C. whom the Ransoms had known on one of their London visits,
and with whom Ransom had since maintained professional relations.
All this was in the natural order of things, as sanctioned by the social
code of Wentworth. Every one was kind to Guy Dawnish—some
rather importunately so, as Margaret Ransom had smiled to observe—but it was recognized as fitting that she should be kindest,
since he was in a sense her property, since his people in England, by
profusely acknowledging her kindness, had given it the domestic
sanction without which, to Wentworth, any social relation between
the sexes remained unhallowed and to be viewed askance. Yes! And
even this second winter, when the visits had become so much more
frequent, so admitted a part of the day's routine, there had not been,
for anyone, a hint of surprise or of conjecture.

Mrs. Ransom smiled with a faint bitterness. She was protected by
her age, no doubt—her age and her past, and the image her mirror
gave back to her. . . .

Her door handle turned suddenly, and the bolt's resistance was
met by an impatient knock.

"Margaret!"

She started up, her brightness fading, and unbolted the door to
admit her husband.

"Why are you locked in? Why, you're not dressed yet!" he exclaimed.

It was possible for Ransom to reach his dressing room by a slight
circuit through the passage; but it was characteristic of the relentless
domesticity of their relation that he chose, as a matter of course, the
directer way through his wife's bedroom. She had never before been

disturbed by this practice, which she accepted as inevitable, but had merely adapted her own habits to it, delaying her hasty toilet till he was safe in his room, or completing it before she heard his step on the stair; since a scrupulous traditional prudery had miraculously survived this massacre of all the privacies.

"Oh, I shan't dress this evening—I shall just have some tea in the library after you've gone," she answered absently. "Your things are laid out," she added, rousing herself.

He looked surprised. "The dinner's at seven. I suppose the speeches will begin at nine. I thought you were coming to hear them."

She wavered. "I don't know. I think not. Mrs. Sperry's ill, and I've no one else to go with."

He glanced at his watch. "Why not get hold of Dawnish? Wasn't he here just now? Why didn't you ask him?"

She turned toward her dressing table and straightened the comb and brush with a nervous hand. Her husband had given her, that morning, two tickets for the ladies' gallery in Hamblin Hall, where the great public dinner of the evening was to take place—a banquet offered by the faculty of Wentworth to visitors of academic eminence—and she had meant to ask Dawnish to go with her: it had seemed the most natural thing to do, till the end of his visit came, and then, after all, she had not spoken. . . .

"It's too late now," she murmured, bending over her pincushion.

"Too late? Not if you telephone him."

Her husband came toward her, and she turned quickly to face him, lest he should suspect her of trying to avoid his eye. To what duplicity was she already committed!

Ransom laid a friendly hand on her arm: "Come along, Margaret. You know I speak for the bar." She was aware, in his voice, of a little note of surprise at his having to remind her of this.

"Oh, yes. I meant to go, of course—"

"Well, then—" He opened his dressing-room door, and caught a glimpse of the retreating housemaid's skirt. "Here's Maria now. Maria! Call up Mr. Dawnish—at Mrs. Creswell's, you know. Tell him Mrs. Ransom wants him to go with her to hear the speeches this evening—the *speeches*, you understand?—and he's to call for her at a quarter before nine."

Margaret heard the Irish "Yessir" on the stairs, and stood motionless while her husband added loudly: "And bring me some towels when you come up." Then he turned back into his wife's room.

"Why, it would be a thousand pities for Guy to miss this. He's so interested in the way we do things over here—and I don't know that he's ever heard me speak in public." Again the slight note of fatuity! Was it possible that Ransom was fatuous?

He paused in front of her, his shortsighted unobservant glance turned unexpectedly on her face.

"You're not going like that, are you?" he asked, with glaring eyeglasses.

"Like what?" she faltered, lifting a conscious hand to the velvet at her throat.

"With your hair in such a fearful mess. Have you been shampooing it? You look like the Brant girl at the end of a tennis match."

The Brant girl was their horror—the horror of all right-thinking Wentworth; a laced, whale-boned, frizzle-headed, high-heeled daughter of iniquity, who came—from New York, of course—on long disturbing tumultuous visits to a Wentworth aunt, working havoc among the freshmen, and leaving, when she departed, an angry wake of criticism that ruffled the social waters for weeks. *She,* too, had tried her hand at Guy—with ludicrous unsuccess. And now, to be compared to her—to be accused of looking "New Yorky!" Ah, there are times when husbands are obtuse; and Ransom, as he stood there, thick and yet juiceless, in his dry legal middle age, with his wiry dust-colored beard and his perpetual *pince-nez,* seemed to his wife a sudden embodiment of this traditional attribute. Not that she had ever fancied herself, a poor soul, a *"femme incomprise."* She had, on the contrary, prided herself on being understood by her husband almost as much as on her complete comprehension of him. Wentworth laid a good deal of stress on "motives"; and Margaret Ransom and her husband had dwelt in complete community of motive. It had been the proudest day of her life when, without consulting her, he had refused an offer of partnership in an eminent New York firm because he preferred the distinction of practicing in Wentworth, of being known as the legal representative of the University. Wentworth, in fact, had always been the bond between the two; they were united in their veneration for that estimable seat of learning, and in their modest yet vivid consciousness of possessing its tone. The Wentworth "tone" is unmistakable: it permeates every part of the social economy, from the coiffure of the ladies to the preparation of the food. It has its sumptuary laws as well as its curriculum of learning. It sits in judgment not only on its own townsmen but on the rest of the world— enlightening, criticizing, ostracizing a heedless universe—and nonconformity to Wentworth standards involves obliteration from Wentworth's consciousness.

In a world without traditions, without reverence, without stability, such little expiring centers of prejudice and precedent make an irresistible appeal to those instincts for which a democracy has neglected to provide. Wentworth, with its "tone," its backward references, its inflexible aversions and condemnations, its hard moral outline preserved intact against a whirling background of experiment, had been all the poetry and history of Margaret Ransom's life. Yes, what she had really esteemed in her husband was the fact of being so intense an embodiment of Wentworth; so long and closely identified, for instance, with its legal affairs, that he was almost a part of its university existence, that of course, at a college banquet, he would inevitably speak for the bar!

It was wonderful of how much consequence all this had seemed till now. . . .

II

When, punctually at ten minutes to seven, her husband had emerged from the house, Margaret Ransom remained seated in her bedroom, addressing herself anew to the difficult process of self-collection. As an aid to this endeavor, she bent forward and looked out of the window, following Ransom's figure as it receded down the elm-shaded street. He moved almost alone between the prim flowerless grass plots, the white porches, the protrusion of irrelevant shingled gables, which stamped the empty street as part of an American college town. She had always been proud of living in Hill Street, where the university people congregated, proud to associate her husband's retreating back, as he walked daily to his office, with backs literary and pedagogic, backs of which it was whispered, for the edification of duly impressed visitors: "Wait till that old boy turns—that's so-and-so."

This had been her world, a world destitute of personal experience, but filled with a rich sense of privilege and distinction, of being not as those millions were who, denied the inestimable advantage of living at Wentworth, pursued elsewhere careers foredoomed to futility.

And now—!

She rose and turned to her work table, where she had dropped, on entering, the handful of photographs that Guy Dawnish had left with her. While he sat so close, pointing out and explaining, she had hardly taken in the details; but now, on the full tones of his low young voice, they came back with redoubled distinctness. This was Guise Abbey, his uncle's place in Wiltshire, where, under his grandfather's rule, Guy's own boyhood had been spent: a long gabled Jacobean façade, many-chimneyed, ivy-draped, overhung (she felt sure) by the boughs of a venerable rookery. And in this other picture—the walled garden at Guise—that was his uncle, Lord Askern, a hale gouty-looking figure, planted robustly on the terrace, a gun on his shoulder and a couple of setters at his feet. And here was the river below the park, with Guy "punting" a girl in a flapping hat—how Margaret hated the flap that hid the girl's face! And here was the tennis court, with Guy among a jolly cross-legged group of youths in flannels, and pretty girls about the tea table under the big lime: in the center the curate handing bread and butter, and in the middle distance a footman approaching with more cups.

Margaret raised this picture closer to her eyes, puzzling, in the diminished light, over the face of the girl nearest to Guy Dawnish—bent above him in profile, while he laughingly lifted his head. No hat hid this profile, which stood out clearly against the foliage behind it.

"And who is that handsome girl?" Margaret had said, detaining the photograph as he pushed it aside, and struck by the fact that, of the whole group, he had left only this member unnamed.

"Oh, only Gwendolen Matcher—I've always known her— Look at this: the almshouses at Guise. Aren't they jolly?"

And then—without her having had the courage to ask if the girl in the punt were also Gwendolen Matcher—they passed on to photographs of his rooms at Oxford, of a cousin's studio in London—one of Lord Askern's grandsons was "artistic"—of the rose-hung cottage in Wales to which, on the old Earl's death, his daughter-in-law, Guy's mother, had retired.

Every one of the photographs opened a window on the life Margaret had been trying to picture since she had known him—a life so rich, so romantic, so packed—in the mere casual vocabulary of daily life—with historic reference and poetic allusion, that she felt almost oppressed by this distant whiff of its air. The very words he used fascinated and bewildered her. He seemed to have been born into all sorts of connections, political, historical, official, that made the Ransom situation at Wentworth as featureless at the top shelf of a dark closet. Someone in the family had "asked for the Chiltern Hundreds"—one uncle was an Elder Brother of the Trinity House—someone else was the Master of a College—someone was in command at Devonport—the Army, the Navy, the House of Commons, the House of Lords, the most venerable seats of learning, were all woven into the dense background of this young man's light unconscious talk. For the unconsciousness was unmistakable. Margaret was not without experience of the transatlantic visitor who sounds loud names and evokes reverberating connections. The poetry of Guy Dawnish's situation lay in the fact that it was so completely a part of early associations and accepted facts. Life was like that in England—in Wentworth, of course (where he had been sent, through his uncle's influence, for two years' training in the neighboring electrical works at Smedden)—in Wentworth, though "immensely jolly," it was different. The fact that he was qualifying to be an electrical engineer—with the hope of a secretaryship at the London end of the great Smedden Company—that, at best, he was returning home to a life of industrial "grind," this fact, though avowedly a bore, did not disconnect him from that brilliant pinnacled past, that many-faceted existence in which the brightest episodes of the whole body of English fiction seemed collectively reflected. Of course he would have to work—younger sons' sons almost always had to—but his uncle Askern (like Wentworth) was "immensely jolly," and Guise always open to him, and his other uncle, the Master, a capital old boy too—and in town he could always put him up with his clever aunt, Lady Caroline Duckett, who had made a "beastly marriage" and was horribly poor, but who knew everybody jolly and amusing, and had always been particularly kind to him.

It was not—and Margaret had not, even in her own thoughts, to defend herself from the imputation—it was not what Wentworth would have called the "material side" of her friend's situation that captivated her. She was austerely proof against such appeals: her enthusiasms were of all the imaginative order. What subjugated her was the unexampled prodigality with which he poured for her the same draught of tradition of which Wentworth held out its little teacupful. He besieged her with a million Wentworths in one—saying, as it were: "All these are mine for the asking—and I choose you instead!"

For this, she told herself somewhat dizzily, was what it came to—the summing up toward which her conscientious efforts at self-collection had been gradually pushing her: with all this in reach, Guy Dawnish was leaving Wentworth reluctantly.

"I *was* a bit lonely here at first—but *now*!" And again: "It will be jolly, of course, to see them all again—but there are some things one doesn't easily give up. . . ."

If he had known only Wentworth, it would have been wonderful enough that he should have chosen her out of all Wentworth—but to have known that other life, and to set her in the balance against it—poor Margaret Ransom, in whom, at the moment, nothing seemed of weight but her years! Ah, it might well produce, in nerves, and brain, and poor unpracticed pulses, a flushed tumult of sensation, the rush of a great wave of life, under which memory struggled in vain to reassert itself, to particularize again just what his last words—the very last—had been. . . .

When consciousness emerged, quivering, from this retrospective assault, it pushed Margaret Ransom—feeling herself a mere leaf in the blast—toward the writing table from which her innocent and voluminous correspondence habitually flowed. She had a letter to write now—much shorter but more difficult than any she had ever been called on to indite.

"Dear Mr. Dawnish," she began, "since telephoning you just now I have decided not—"

Maria's voice, at the door, announced that tea was in the library: "And I s'pose it's the brown silk you'll wear to the speaking?"

In the usual order of the Ransom existence, its mistress' toilet was performed unassisted; and the mere inquiry—at once friendly and deferential—projected, for Margaret, a strong light on the importance of the occasion. That she should answer "But I am not going," when the going was so manifestly part of a household solemnity about which the thoughts below stairs fluttered in proud participation; that in face of such participation she should utter a word implying indifference or hesitation—nay, revealing herself the transposed uprooted thing she had been on the verge of becoming; to do this was—well, infinitely harder than to perform the alternative act of tearing up the sheet of note paper under her reluctant pen.

Yes, she said, she would wear the brown silk. . . .

III

All the heat and glare from the long illuminated table, about which the fumes of many courses still hung in a savory fog, seemed to surge up to the ladies' gallery, and concentrate themselves in the burning cheeks of a slender figure withdrawn behind the projection of a pillar.

It never occurred to Margaret Ransom that she was sitting in the shade. She supposed that the full light of the chandeliers was beating on her face—and there were moments when it seemed as though all the heads about the great horseshoe below, bald, shaggy, sleek, close-thatched, or thinly latticed, were equipped with an additional pair of eyes, set at an angle which enabled them to rake her face as relentlessly as the electric burners.

In the lull after a speech, the gallery was fluttering with the rustle of programs consulted, and Mrs. Sheff (the Brant girl's aunt) leaned forward to say enthusiastically: "And now we're to hear Mr. Ransom!"

A louder buzz rose from the table, and the heads (without relaxing their upward vigilance) seemed to merge and flow together, like an attentive flood, toward the upper end of the horseshoe, where all the threads of Margaret Ransom's consciousness were suddenly drawn into what seemed a small speck, no more—a black speck that rose, hung in air, dissolved into gyrating gestures, became distended, enormous, preponderant—became her husband "speaking."

"It's the heat—" Margaret gasped, pressing her handkerchief to her whitening lips, and finding just strength enough left to push back farther into the shadow.

She felt a touch on her arm. "It *is* horrible—shall we go?" a voice suggested; and, "Yes, yes, let us go," she whispered, feeling, with a great throb of relief, *that* to be the only possible, the only conceivable, solution. To sit and listen to her husband *now*—how could she ever have thought she could survive it? Luckily, under the lingering hubbub from below, his opening words were inaudible, and she had only to run the gauntlet of sympathetic feminine glances, shot after her between waving fans and programs, as, guided by Guy Dawnish, she managed to reach the door. It was really so hot that even Mrs. Sheff was not much surprised—till long afterward. . . .

The winding staircase was empty, half dark and blessedly silent. In a committee room below Dawnish found the inevitable water jug, and filled a glass for her, while she leaned back, confronted only by a frowning college President in an emblazoned frame. The academic frown descended on her like an anathema when she rose and followed her companion out of the building.

Hamblin Hall stands at the end of the long green campus with its sextuple line of elms—the boast and singularity of Wentworth. A pale spring moon, rising above the dome of the University Library, at the opposite end of the elm walk, diffused a pearly mildness in the sky, melted to thin haze the shadows of the trees, and turned to golden yellow the lights of the college windows. Against this soft suffusion of light the Library cupola assumed a Bramantesque grace, the white steeple of the Congregational church became a campanile topped by a winged spirit, and the scant porticoes of the older halls the colonnades of classic temples.

"This is better—" Dawnish said, as they passed down the steps and under the shadow of the elms.

They moved on a little way in silence before he began again: "You're too tired to walk. Let us sit down a few minutes."

Her feet, in truth, were leaden, and not far off a group of park benches, encircling the pedestal of a patriot in bronze, invited them to rest. But Dawnish was guiding her toward a lateral path which bent, through shrubberies, toward a strip of turf between two buildings.

"It will be cooler by the river," he said, moving on without waiting for a possible protest. None came: it seemed easier, for the moment, to let herself be led without any conventional feint of resistance. And besides, there was nothing wrong about *this*—the wrong would have been in sitting up there in the glare, pretending to listen to her husband, a dutiful wife among her kind. . . .

The path descended, as both knew, to the chosen, the inimitable spot of Wentworth: that fugitive curve of the river, where, before hurrying on to glut the brutal industries of South Wentworth and Smedden, it simulated for a few hundred yards the leisurely pace of an ancient university stream, with willows on its banks and a stretch of turf extending from the grounds of Hamblin Hall to the boat-houses at the farther bend. Here, too, were benches beneath the willows, and so close to the river that the voice of its gliding softened and filled out the reverberating silence between Margaret and her companion, and made her feel that she knew why he had brought her there.

"Do you feel better?" he asked gently, as he sat down beside her.

"Oh, yes. I only needed a little air."

"I'm so glad you did. Of course the speeches were tremendously interesting—but I prefer this. What a good night!"

"Yes."

There was a pause, which now, after all, the soothing accompaniment of the river seemed hardly sufficient to fill.

"I wonder what time it is. I ought to be going home," Margaret began at length.

"Oh, it's not late. They'll be at it for hours in there—yet."

She made a faint inarticulate sound. She wanted to say: "No—Robert's speech was to be the last—" but she could not bring herself to pronounce Ransom's name, and at the moment no other way of refuting her companion's statement occurred to her.

The young man leaned back luxuriously, reassured by her silence.

"You see it's my last chance—and I want to make the most of it."

"Your last chance?" How stupid of her to repeat his words on that cooing note of interrogation! It was just such a lead as the Brant girl might have given him.

"To be with you—like this. I haven't had so many. And there's less than a week left."

She attempted to laugh. "Perhaps it will sound longer if you call it five days."

The flatness of that, again! And she knew there were people who called her intelligent. Fortunately he did not seem to notice it; but her laugh continued to sound in her own ears—the coquettish chirp of middle age! She decided that if he spoke again—if he *said anything*—she would make no further effort at evasion: she would take it directly, seriously, frankly—she would not be doubly disloyal.

"Besides," he continued, throwing his arm along the back of the bench, and turning toward her so that his face was like a dusky bas-relief with a silver rim—"Besides, there's something I've been wanting to tell you."

The sound of the river seemed to cease altogether: the whole world became silent.

Margaret had trusted her inspiration farther than it appeared likely to carry her. Again she could think of nothing happier than to repeat, on the same witless note of interrogation: "To tell me?"

"You only."

The constraint, the difficulty, seemed to be on his side now: she divined it by the renewed shifting of his attitude—he was capable, usually, of such fine intervals of immobility—and by a confusion in his utterance that set her own voice throbbing in her throat.

"You've been so perfect to me," he began again. "It's not my fault if you've made me feel that you would understand everything—make allowances for everything—see just how a man may have held out, and fought against a thing—as long as he had the strength. . . . This may be my only chance; and I can't go away without telling you."

He had turned from her now, and was staring at the river, so that his profile was projected against the moonlight in all its beautiful young dejection.

There was a slight pause, as though he waited for her to speak; then she leaned forward and laid her hand on his.

"If I have really been—if I have done for you even the least part of what you say . . . what you imagine . . . will you do for me, now, just one thing in return?"

He sat motionless, as if fearing to frighten away the shy touch on his hand, and she left it there, conscious of her gesture only as part of the high ritual of their farewell.

"What do you want me to do?" he asked in a low tone.

"*Not* to tell me!" she breathed on a deep note of entreaty.

"*Not* to tell you—?"

"Anything—*anything*—just to leave our . . . our friendship . . . as it has been—as—as a painter, if a friend asked him, might leave a picture—not quite finished, perhaps, . . . but all the more exquisite. . . ."

She felt the hand under hers slip away, recover itself, and seek her own, which had flashed out of reach in the same instant—felt the start that swept him round on her as if he had been caught and turned about by the shoulders.

"You—*you*—?" he stammered, in a strange voice full of fear and tenderness; but she held fast, so centered in her inexorable resolve that she was hardly conscious of the effect her words might be producing.

"Don't you see," she hurried on, "don't you *feel* how much safer it is—yes, I'm willing to put it so!—how much safer to leave everything undisturbed . . . just as . . . as it has grown of itself . . . without trying to say: 'It's this or that' . . . ? It's what we each choose to call it to ourselves, after all, isn't it? Don't let us try to find a name that . . . that we should both agree upon . . . we probably shouldn't succeed." She laughed abruptly. "And ghosts vanish when one names them!" she ended with a break in her voice.

When she ceased her heart was beating so violently that there was a rush in her ears like the noise of the river after rain, and she did not immediately make out what he was answering. But as she recovered her lucidity she said to herself that, whatever he was saying, she must not hear it; and she began to speak again, half playfully, half appealingly, with an eloquence of entreaty, an ingenuity in argument, of which she had never dreamed herself capable. And then, suddenly, strangling hands seemed to reach up from her heart to her throat, and she had to stop.

Her companion remained motionless. He had not tried to regain her hand, and his eyes were away from her, on the river. But his nearness had become something formidable and exquisite—something she had never before imagined. A flush of guilt swept over her—vague reminiscences of French novels and of opera plots. This was what such women felt, then . . . this was "shame." . . . Phrases of the newspaper and the pulpit danced before her. . . . She dared not speak, and his silence began to frighten her. Had ever a heart beat so wildly before in Wentworth?

He turned at last, and taking her two hands, quite simply, kissed them one after the other.

"I shall never forget—" he said in a confused voice, unlike his own.

A return of strength enabled her to rise, and even to let her eyes meet his for a moment.

"Thank you," she said, simply also.

She turned away from the bench, regaining the path that led back to the college buildings, and he walked beside her in silence. When they reached the elm walk it was dotted with dispersing groups. The "speaking" was at an end, and Hamblin Hall had poured its audience out into the moonlight. Margaret felt a rush of relief, followed by a receding wave of regret. She had the distant sensation that her hour— her one hour—was over.

One of the groups just ahead broke up as they approached, and projected Ransom's solid bulk against the moonlight.

"My husband," she said hastening forward; and she never afterward forgot the look of his back—heavy, round-shouldered, yet a little pompous—in a badly-fitting overcoat that stood out at the neck and hid his collar. She had never before noticed how he dressed.

IV

They met again, inevitably, before Dawnish left; but the thing she feared did not happen—he did not try to see her alone.

It even became clear to her, in looking back, that he had deliberately avoided doing so; and this seemed merely an added proof of his "understanding," of that deep undefinable communion that set them alone in an empty world, as if on a peak above the clouds.

The five days passed in a flash; and when the last one came, it brought to Margaret Ransom an hour of weakness, of profound disorganization, when old barriers fell, old convictions faded—when to be alone with him for a moment became, after all, the one craving of her heart. She knew he was coming that afternoon to say "good-bye"—and she knew also that Ransom was to be away at South Wentworth. She waited alone in her pale little drawing room, with its scant kakemonos, its one or two chilly reproductions from the antique, its slippery Chippendale chairs. At length the bell rang, and her world became a rosy cloud—through which she presently discerned the austere form of Mrs. Sperry, wife of the Professor of Paleontology, who had come to talk over with her the next winter's program for the Higher Thought Club. They debated the question for an hour, and when Mrs. Sperry departed Margaret had a confused impression that the course was to deal with the influence of the First Crusade on the development of European architecture—but the sentient part of her knew only that Dawnish had not come.

He "bobbed in," as he would have put it, after dinner—having, it appeared, run across Ransom early in the day, and learned that the latter would be absent till evening. Margaret was in the study with her husband when the door opened and Dawnish stood there. Ransom—who had not had time to dress—was seated at his desk, a pile of shabby law books at his elbow, the light from a hanging lamp falling on his grayish stubble of hair, his sallow forehead and spectacled eyes. Dawnish, towering higher than usual against the shadows of the room, and refined by his unusual pallor, hung a moment on the threshold, then came in, explaining himself profusely—laughing, accepting a cigar, letting Ransom push an armchair forward—a Dawnish she had never seen, ill at ease, ejaculatory, yet somehow more mature, more obscurely in command of himself.

Margaret drew back, seating herself in the shade, in such a way that she saw her husband's head first, and beyond it their visitor's, relieved against the dusk of the bookshelves. Her heart was still—she felt no throbbing in her throat or temples: all her life seemed concentrated in the hand that lay on her knee, the hand he would touch when they said good-bye.

Afterward her heart rang all the changes, and there was a mood in which she reproached herself for cowardice—for having deliberately missed her one moment with him, the moment in which she might have sounded the depths of life, for joy or anguish. But that mood was fleeting and infrequent. In quieter hours she blushed for it—she even trembled to think that he might have guessed such a regret in her. It seemed to convict her of a lack of fineness that he should have had, in his youth and his power, a tenderer, surer sense of the peril of a rash touch—should have handled the case so much more delicately.

At first her days were fire and the nights long solemn vigils. Her thoughts were no longer vulgarized and defaced by any notion of "guilt." She was ashamed now of her shame. What had happened was as much outside the sphere of her marriage as some transaction in a star. It had simply given her a secret life of incommunicable joys, as if all the wasted springs of her youth had been stored in some hidden pool, and she could return there now to bathe in them.

After that there came a phase of loneliness, through which the life about her loomed phantasmal and remote. She thought the dead must feel thus, repeating the vain gestures of the living beside some Stygian shore. She wondered if any other woman had lived to whom *nothing had ever happened*? And then his first letter came. . . .

It was a charming letter—a perfect letter. The little touch of awkwardness and constraint under its boyish spontaneity told her more than whole pages of eloquence. He spoke of their friendship—of their good days together. . . . Ransom, chancing to come in while she read, noticed the foreign stamps; and she was able to hand him the letter, saying gaily: "There's a message for you," and knowing all the while that *her* message was safe in her heart.

On the days when the letters came the outlines of things grew indistinct, and she could never afterward remember what she had done or how the business of life had been carried on. It was always a surprise when she found dinner on the table as usual, and Ransom seated opposite to her, running over the evening paper.

But though Dawnish continued to write, with all the English loyalty to the outward observances of friendship, his communications came only at intervals of several weeks, and between them she had time to repossess herself, to regain some sort of normal contact with life. And the customary, the recurring, gradually reclaimed her, the net of habit tightened again—her daily life became real, and her one momentary escape from it an exquisite illusion. Not that she ceased to believe in the miracle that had befallen her; she still treasured the reality of her one moment beside the river. What reason was there for doubting it? She could hear the ring of truth in young Dawnish's voice: "It's not my fault if you've made me feel that you would understand everything. . . ." No! she believed in her miracle, and the belief sweetened and illumined her life; but she came to see that what was for her the transformation of her whole being might well have been, for her companion, a mere passing explosion of gratitude, of boyish good fellowship touched with the pang of leave-taking. She even reached the point of telling herself that it was "better so"; this view of the episode so defended it from the alternating extremes of self-reproach and derision, so enshrined it in a pale immortality to which she could make her secret pilgrimages without reproach.

For a long time she had not been able to pass by the bench under the willows—she even avoided the elm walk till autumn had stripped its branches. But every day, now, she noted a step toward recovery; and at last a day came when, walking along the river, she said to herself, as she approached the bench: "I used not to be able to pass here without thinking of him; *and now I am not thinking of him at all*!"

This seemed such convincing proof of her recovery that she began, as spring returned, to permit herself, now and then, a quiet session on the bench—a dedicated hour from which she went back fortified to her task.

She had not heard from her friend for six weeks or more—the intervals between his letters were growing longer. But that was "best" too, and she was not anxious, for she knew he had obtained the post he had been preparing for, and that his active life in London had begun. The thought reminded her, one mild March day, that in leaving the house she had thrust in her reticule a letter from a Wentworth friend who was abroad on a holiday. The envelope bore the London postmark, a fact showing that the lady's face was turning toward home. Margaret seated herself on her bench, and began to read the letter.

The London described was that of shops and museums—as remote as possible from the setting of Guy Dawnish's existence. But suddenly Margaret's eye fell on his name, and the page began to tremble in her hands.

"I heard such a funny thing yesterday, about your friend Mr. Dawnish. We went to a tea at Professor Bunce's (I do wish you knew the Bunces—their atmosphere is so *uplifting*), and there I met that Miss Bruce-Pringle who came out last year to take a course in histology at the Annex. Of course she asked about you and Mr. Ransom, and then she told me she had just seen Mr. Dawnish's aunt—the clever one he was always talking about, Lady Caroline something—and that they were all in a dreadful state about him. I wonder if you knew he was engaged when he went to America? He never mentioned it to *us*. She said it was not a positive engagement, but an understanding with a girl he has always been devoted to, who lives near their place in Wiltshire; and both families expected the marriage to take place as soon as he got back. It seems the girl is an heiress (you know *how low* the English ideals are compared with ours), and Miss Bruce-Pringle said his relations were perfectly delighted at his 'being provided for,' as she called it. Well, when he got back he asked the girl to release him; and she and her family were furious, and so were his people; but he holds out, and won't marry her, and won't give a reason, except that he has 'formed an unfortunate attachment.' Did you ever hear anything so peculiar? His aunt, who is quite wild about it, says it must have happened at Wentworth, because he didn't go anywhere else in America. Do you suppose it *could* have been the Brant girl? But why 'unfortunate' when everybody knows she would have jumped at him?"

Margaret folded the letter and looked out across the river. It was not the same river, but a mystic current shot with moonlight. The bare willows wove a leafy veil above her head, and beside her she felt the nearness of youth and tempestuous tenderness. It had all happened just here, on this very seat by the river—it had come to her, and passed her by, and she had not held out a hand to detain it. . . .

Well! Was it not, by that very abstention, made more deeply and ineffaceably hers? She could argue thus while she had thought the episode, on his side, a mere transient effect of propinquity; but now that she knew it had altered the whole course of his life, now that it took on substance and reality, asserted a separate existence outside of her own troubled consciousness—now it seemed almost cowardly to have missed her share in it.

She walked home in a dream. Now and then, when she passed an acquaintance, she wondered if the pain and glory were written on her face. But Mrs. Sperry, who stopped her at the corner of Maverick Street to say a word about the next meeting of the Higher Thought Club, seemed to remark no change in her.

When she reached home Ransom had not yet returned from the office, and she went straight to the library to tidy his writing table. It was part of her daily duty to bring order out of the chaos of his papers, and of late she had fastened on such small recurring tasks as some one falling over a precipice might snatch at the weak bushes in its clefts.

When she had sorted the letters she took up some pamphlets and newspapers, glancing over them to see if they were to be kept. Among the papers was a page torn from a London *Times* of the previous month. Her eye ran down its columns and suddenly a paragraph flamed out.

"We are requested to state that the marriage arranged between Mr. Guy Dawnish, son of the late Colonel the Hon. Roderick Dawnish, of Malby, Wilts, and Gwendolen, daughter of Samuel Matcher, Esq., of Armingham Towers, Wilts, will not take place."

Margaret dropped the paper and sat down, hiding her face against the stained baize of the desk. She remembered the photograph of the tennis court at Guise—she remembered the handsome girl at whom Guy Dawnish looked up, laughing. A gust of tears shook her, loosening the dry surface of conventional feeling, welling up from unsuspected depths. She was sorry—very sorry, yet so glad—so ineffably, impenitently glad.

V

There came a reaction in which she decided to write to him. She even sketched out a letter of sisterly, almost motherly, remonstrance, in which she reminded him that he "still had all his life before him." But she reflected that so, after all, had she; and that seemed to weaken the argument.

In the end she decided not to send the letter. He had never spoken to her of his engagement to Gwendolen Matcher, and his letters had contained no allusion to any sentimental disturbance in his life. She had only his few broken words, that night by the river, on which to build her theory of the case. But illuminated by the phrase "an unfortunate attachment" the theory towered up, distinct and immovable, like some high landmark by which travelers shape their course. She had been loved—extraordinarily loved. But he had chosen that she should know of it by his silence rather than by his speech. He had understood that only on those terms could their transcendent communion continue—that he must lose her to keep her. To break that silence would be like spilling a cup of water in a waste of sand. There would be nothing left for her thirst.

Her life, thenceforward, was bathed in a tranquil beauty. The days flowed by like a river beneath the moon—each ripple caught the brightness and passed it on. She began to take a renewed interest in her familiar round of duties. The tasks which had once seemed colorless and irksome had now a kind of sacrificial sweetness, a symbolic meaning into which she alone was initiated. She had been restless—had longed to travel; now she felt that she should never again care to leave Wentworth. But if her desire to wander had ceased she traveled in spirit, performing invisible pilgrimages in the footsteps of her friend. She regretted that her one short visit to England had taken her so little out of London—that her acquaintance with the landscape had been formed chiefly through the windows of a railway carriage. She threw herself into the architectural studies of the Higher Thought

Club, and distinguished herself, at the spring meetings, by her fluency, her competence, her inexhaustible curiosity on the subject of the growth of English Gothic. She ransacked the shelves of the college library, she borrowed photographs of the cathedrals, she pored over the folio pages of "The Seats of Noblemen and Gentlemen." She was like some banished princess who learns that she has inherited a domain in her own country, who knows that she will never see it, yet feels, wherever she walks, its soil beneath her feet.

May was half over, and the Higher Thought Club was to hold its last meeting, previous to the college festivities which, in early June, agreeably disorganized the social routine of Wentworth. The meeting was to take place in Margaret Ransom's drawing room, and on the day before she sat upstairs preparing for her dual duties as hostess and orator—for she had been invited to read the final paper of the course.

In order to sum up with precision her conclusions on the subject of English Gothic, she had been rereading an analysis of the structural features of the principal English cathedrals; and she was murmuring over to herself the phrase: "The longitudinal arches of Lincoln have an approximately elliptical form" when there came a knock on the door, and Maria's voice announced: "There's a lady down in the parlor."

Margaret's soul dropped from the heights of the shadowy vaulting to the dead level of an afternoon call at Wentworth.

"A lady? Did she give no name?"

Maria became confused. "She only said she was a lady—" and in reply to her mistress's look of mild surprise: "Well, ma'am, she told me so three or four times over."

Margaret laid her book down, leaving it open at the description of Lincoln, and slowly descended the stairs. As she did so, she repeated to herself: "The longitudinal arches are elliptical."

On the threshold below, she had the odd impression that her bare inanimate drawing room was brimming with life and noise—an impression produced, as she presently perceived, by the resolute forward dash—it was almost a pounce—of the one small figure restlessly measuring its length.

The dash checked itself within a yard of Margaret, and the lady—a stranger—held back long enough to stamp on her hostess a sharp impression of sallowness, leanness, keenness, before she said, in a voice that might have been addressing an unruly committee meeting: "I am Lady Caroline Duckett—a fact I found it impossible to make clear to the young woman who let me in."

A warm wave rushed up from Margaret's heart to her face. She held out both hands impulsively. "Oh, I'm so glad—I'd no idea—"

Her voice sank under her visitor's impartial scrutiny.

"I don't wonder," said the latter dryly. "I suppose she didn't mention either that my object in calling here was to see Mrs. Ransom?"

"Oh, yes—won't you sit down?" Margaret pushed a chair forward. She seated herself at a little distance, brain and heart humming with a confused interchange of signals. This dark sharp woman was his aunt—the "clever aunt" who had had such a hard life, but had always managed to keep her head above water. Margaret remembered that Guy had spoken of her kindness—perhaps she would seem kinder when they had talked together a little. Meanwhile the first impression she produced was of an amplitude out of all proportion to her somewhat scant exterior. With her small flat figure, her shabby heterogeneous dress, she was as dowdy as any Professor's wife at Wentworth; but her dowdiness (Margaret borrowed a literary analogy to define it), her dowdiness was somehow "of the center." Like the insignificant emissary of a great power, she was to be judged rather by her passports than her person.

While Margaret was receiving these impressions, Lady Caroline, with quick birdlike twists of her head, was gathering others from the pale void spaces of the drawing room. Her eyes, divided by a sharp nose like a bill, seemed to be set far enough apart to see at separate angles; but suddenly she bent both of them on Margaret.

"This *is* Mrs. Ransom's house?" she asked, with an emphasis on the verb that gave a distinct hint of unfulfilled expectations.

Margaret assented.

"Because your American houses, especially in the provincial towns, all look so remarkably alike, that I thought I might have been mistaken; and as my time is extremely limited—in fact I'm sailing on Wednesday—"

She paused long enough to let Margaret say: "I had no idea you were in America."

Lady Caroline made no attempt to take this up. "—And so much of it," she carried on her sentence, "has been wasted in talking to people I really hadn't the slightest desire to see, that you must excuse me if I go straight to the point."

Margaret felt a sudden tension of the heart. "Of course," she said, while a voice within her cried: "He's dead—he has left me a message."

There was another pause; then Lady Caroline went on with increasing asperity: "So that—in short—if I *could* see Mrs. Ransom at once—"

Margaret looked up in surprise. "I am Mrs. Ransom," she said.

The other stared a moment, with much the same look of cautious incredulity that had marked her inspection of the drawing room. Then light came to her.

"Oh, I beg your pardon. I should have said that I wished to see Mrs. *Robert* Ransom, not Mrs. Ransom. But I understood that in the States you don't make those distinctions." She paused a moment, and then went on, before Margaret could answer: "Perhaps, after all, it's as well that I should see you instead, since you're evidently one of the household—your son and his wife live with you, I suppose? Yes, on the whole, then, it's better—I shall be able to talk so much more frankly." She spoke as if, as a rule, circumstances prevented her giving rein to this prosperity. "And frankness, of course, is the only way out of this—this extremely tiresome complication. You know, I suppose, that my nephew thinks he's in love with your daughter-in-law?"

Margaret made a slight movement, but her visitor pressed on without heeding it. "Oh, don't fancy, please, that I'm pretending to take a high moral ground—though his mother does, poor dear! I can perfectly imagine that in a place like this—I've just been walking about it for two hours—a young man of Guy's age would *have* to provide himself with some sort of distraction; and he's not the kind to go in for anything objectionable. Oh, we quite allow for that—we should allow for the whole affair, if it hadn't so preposterously ended in his throwing over the girl he was engaged to, and upsetting an arrangement that affected a number of people besides himself. I understand that in the States it's different—the young people have only themselves to consider. In England—in our class, I mean—a great deal may depend on a young man's making a good match; and in Guy's case I may say that his mother and sisters (I won't include myself, though I might) have been simply stranded—thrown overboard—by his freak. You can understand how serious it is when I tell you that it's that and nothing else that has brought me all the way to America. And my first idea was to go straight to your daughter-in-law, since her influence is the only thing we can count on now, and put it to her fairly, as I'm putting it to you. But, on the whole, I dare say it's better to see you first—you might give me an idea of the line to take with her. I'm prepared to throw myself on her mercy!"

Margaret rose from her chair, outwardly rigid in proportion to her inward tremor.

"You don't understand—" she began.

Lady Caroline brushed the interruption aside. "Oh, but I do—completely! I cast no reflection on your daughter-in-law. Guy has made it quite clear to us that his attachment is—has, in short, not been rewarded. But don't you see that that's the worst of it? There'd be much more hope of his recovering if Mrs. Robert Ransom had—had—"

Margaret's voice broke from her in a cry. "I am Mrs. Robert Ransom," she said.

If Lady Caroline Duckett had hitherto given her hostess the impression of a person not easily silenced, this fact added sensibly to the effect produced by the intense stillness which now fell on her.

She sat quite motionless, her large bangled hands clasped about the meager fur boa she had unwound from her neck on entering, her rusty black veil pushed up to the edge of a "fringe" of doubtful authenticity, her thin lips parted on a gasp that seemed to sharpen itself on the edges of her teeth. So overwhelming and helpless was her silence that Margaret began to feel a motion of pity beneath her indignation—a desire at least to facilitate the excuses which must terminate their disastrous colloquy. But when Lady Caroline found voice she did not use it to excuse herself.

"You *can't* be," she said, quite simply.

"Can't be?" Margaret stammered, with a flushing cheek.

"I mean, it's some mistake. Are there *two* Mrs. Robert Ransoms in the same town? Your family arrangements are so extremely puzzling." She had a farther rush of enlightenment. "Oh, I *see*! I ought of course to have asked for Mrs. Robert Ransom *Junior*!"

The idea sent her to her feet with a haste which showed her impatience to make up for lost time.

"There is no other Mrs. Robert Ransom at Wentworth," said Margaret.

"No other—no 'Junior'? Are you *sure*?" Lady Caroline fell back into her seat again. "Then I simply don't see," she murmured.

Margaret's blush had fixed itself on her throbbing forehead. She remained standing, while her strange visitor continued to gaze at her with a perturbation in which the consciousness of indiscretion had evidently as yet no part.

"I simply don't see," she repeated.

Suddenly she sprang up, and advancing to Margaret, laid an inspired hand on her arm. "But, my dear woman, you can help us out all the same; you can help us to find out *who it is*—and you will, won't you?—because, as it's not you, you can't in the least mind what I've been saying—"

Margaret, freeing her arm from her visitor's hold, drew back a step; but Lady Caroline instantly rejoined her.

"Of course, I can see that if it *had* been, you might have been annoyed: I dare say I put the case stupidly—but I'm so bewildered by this new development—by his using you all this time as a pretext that I really don't know where to turn for light on the mystery—"

She had Margaret in her imperious grasp again, but the latter broke from her with a more resolute gesture.

"I'm afraid I have no light to give you," she began; but once more Lady Caroline caught her up.

"Oh, but do please understand me! I condemn Guy most strongly for using your name—when we all know you'd been so amazingly kind to him! I haven't a word to say in his defense—but of course the important thing now is: *who is the woman, since you're not*?"

The question rang out loudly, as if all the pale puritan corners of the room flung it back with a shudder at the speaker. In the silence that ensued Margaret felt the blood ebbing back to her heart; then she said, in a distinct and level voice: "I know nothing of the history of Mr. Dawnish."

Lady Caroline gave a stare and a gasp. Her distracted hand groped for her boa, and she began to wind it mechanically about her long neck.

"It would really be an enormous help to us—and to poor Gwendolen Matcher," she persisted pleadingly. "And you'd be doing Guy himself a good turn."

Margaret remained silent and motionless while her visitor drew on

one of the worn gloves she had pulled off to adjust her veil. Lady
Caroline gave the veil a final twitch.

"I've come a tremendously long way," she said, "and, since it isn't
you, I can't think why you won't help me. . . ."

When the door had closed on her visitor Margaret Ransom went
slowly up the stairs to her room. As she dragged her feet from one
step to another, she remembered how she had sprung up the same
steep flight after that visit of Guy Dawnish's when she had looked in
the glass and seen on her face the blush of youth.

When she reached her room she bolted the door as she had done
that day, and again looked at herself in the narrow mirror above her
dressing table. It was just a year since then—the elms were budding
again, the willows hanging their green veil above the bench by the
river. But there was no trace of youth left in her face—she saw it now
as others had doubtless always seen it. If it seemed as it did to Lady
Caroline Duckett, what look must it have worn to the fresh gaze of
young Guy Dawnish?

A pretext—she had been a pretext. He had used her name to screen
someone else—or perhaps merely to escape from a situation of which
he was weary. She did not care to conjecture what his motive had
been—everything connected with him had grown so remote and
alien. She felt no anger—only an unspeakable sadness, a sadness
which she knew would never be appeased.

She looked at herself long and steadily: she wished to clear her eyes
of all illusions. Then she turned away and took her usual seat beside
her work table. From where she sat she could look down the empty
elm-shaded street, up which, at this hour every day, she was sure to
see her husband's figure advancing. She would see it presently—she
would see it for many years to come. She had an aching vision of the
length of the years that stretched before her. Strange that one who
was not young should still, in all likelihood, have so long to live!

Nothing was changed in the setting of her life, perhaps nothing
would ever change in it. She would certainly live and die in Wentworth. And meanwhile the days would go on as usual, bringing the
usual obligations. As the word flitted through her brain she remembered that she had still to put the finishing touches to the paper she
was to read the next afternoon at the meeting of the Higher Thought
Club.

The book she had been reading lay face downward beside her, where she had left it an hour ago. She took it up, and slowly and painfully, like a child laboriously spelling out the syllables, she went on with the rest of the sentence:

"—And they spring from a level not much above that of the springing of the transverse and diagonal ribs, which are so arranged as to give a convex curve to the surface of the vaulting conoid."

XINGU

(1911)

Wharton's information about the river Xingu, a tributary of the Amazon, came from her friend Henry James. In 1911, when she wrote "Xingu" (the story was not collected until 1916 due to the intervention of the war), James was beginning his autobiography. He probably reminisced to Wharton about his brother William, who had once participated in a zoological expedition in Brazil.

In the story, Mrs. Roby exposes the intellectual pretensions of her lunch club in Hillbridge, a composite New England university town that Wharton used several times in her work. As the ladies try to impress a visiting novelist with their knowledge of Xingu (a new philosophy of some sort?), Wharton entertains the reader with a cascade of outrageous puns. The story's brilliant wit and wordplay have made it one of the most popular of Wharton's tales.

The reader might make the objection that in this story women are being ridiculed for their intellectual aspirations. But if so, Mrs. Roby is excepted and the satire rather goodnaturedly spread around. Even Henry James comes in for his share. The visiting novelist, Osric Dane, has just written The Wings of Death, a title reminiscent of James's The Wings of the Dove. Although Wharton is sometimes wrongly viewed as a "disciple" of James, she did not uniformly admire his work. Here she makes a sly reference to James's later, involved writing style when she comments that no one can figure out how The Wings of Death ends: "Osric Dane, overcome by the awful significance of her own meaning, has mercifully veiled it—perhaps even from herself."

MRS. BALLINGER is one of the ladies who pursue Culture in bands, as though it were dangerous to meet alone. To this end she had founded the Lunch Club, an association composed of herself and several other indomitable huntresses of erudition. The Lunch Club, after three or four winters of lunching and debate, had acquired such local distinction that the entertainment of distinguished strangers became one of its accepted functions; in recognition of which it duly extended to the celebrated Osric Dane, on the day of her arrival in Hillbridge, an invitation to be present at the next meeting.

The club was to meet at Mrs. Ballinger's. The other members, behind her back, were of one voice in deploring her unwillingness to cede her rights in favor of Mrs. Plinth, whose house made a more impressive setting for the entertainment of celebrities; while, as Mrs. Leveret observed, there was always the picture gallery to fall back on.

Mrs. Plinth made no secret of sharing this view. She had always regarded it as one of her obligations to entertain the Lunch Club's distinguished guests. Mrs. Plinth was almost as proud of her obligations as she was of her picture gallery; she was in fact fond of implying that the one possession implied the other, and that only a woman of her wealth could afford to live up to a standard as high as that which she had set herself. An all-round sense of duty, roughly adaptable to various ends, was, in her opinion, all that Providence exacted of the more humbly stationed; but the power which had predestined Mrs. Plinth to keep a footman clearly intended her to maintain an equally specialized staff of responsibilities. It was the more to be regretted that Mrs. Ballinger, whose obligations to society were bounded by the narrow scope of two parlormaids, should have been so tenacious of the right to entertain Osric Dane.

The question of that lady's reception had for a month past profoundly moved the members of the Lunch Club. It was not that they felt themselves unequal to the task, but that their sense of the opportunity plunged them into the agreeable uncertainty of the lady who weighs the alternatives of a well-stocked wardrobe. If such subsidiary members as Mrs. Leveret were fluttered by the thought of exchanging ideas with the author of *The Wings of Death,* no forebodings disturbed the conscious adequacy of Mrs. Plinth, Mrs. Ballinger and Miss Van Vluyck. *The Wings of Death* had, in fact, at Miss Van Vluyck's suggestion, been chosen as the subject of discussion at the last club meeting, and each member had thus been enabled to express her own opinion or to appropriate whatever sounded well in the comments of the others.

Mrs. Roby alone had abstained from profiting by the opportunity but it was now openly recognized that, as a member of the Lunch Club, Mrs. Roby was a failure. "It all comes," as Miss Van Vluyck put it, "of accepting a woman on a man's estimation." Mrs. Roby, returning to Hillbridge from a prolonged sojourn in exotic lands—the other ladies no longer took the trouble to remember where—had been heralded by the distinguished biologist, Professor Foreland, as the most agreeable woman he had ever met; and the members of the Lunch Club, impressed by an encomium that carried the weight of a diploma, and rashly assuming that the Professor's social sympathies would follow the line of his professional bent, had seized the chance of annexing a biological member. Their disillusionment was complete. At Miss Van Vluyck's first offhand mention of the pterodactyl Mrs. Roby had confusedly murmured: "I know so little about meters—" and after that painful betrayal of incompetence she had prudently withdrawn from further participation in the mental gymnastics of the club.

"I suppose she flattered him," Miss Van Vluyck summed up—"or else it's the way she does her hair."

The dimensions of Miss Van Vluyck's dining room having restricted the membership of the club to six, the nonconductiveness of one member was a serious obstacle to the exchange of ideas, and some wonder had already been expressed that Mrs. Roby should care to live, as it were, on the intellectual bounty of the others. This feeling was increased by the discovery that she had not yet read *The Wings of Death.* She owned to having heard the name of Osric Dane; but that—incredible as it appeared—was the extent of her acquaintance with the celebrated novelist. The ladies could not conceal their surprise; but Mrs. Ballinger, whose pride in the club made her wish to put even Mrs. Roby in the best possible light, gently insinuated that, though she had not had time to acquaint herself with *The Wings of Death,* she must at least be familiar with its equally remarkable predecessor, *The Supreme Instant.*

Mrs. Roby wrinkled her sunny brows in a conscientious effort of memory, as a result of which she recalled that, oh, yes, she *had* seen the book at her brother's, when she was staying with him in Brazil, and had even carried it off to read one day on a boating party; but they had all got to shying things at each other in the boat, and the book had gone overboard, so she had never had the chance—

The picture evoked by this anecdote did not increase Mrs. Roby's credit with the club, and there was a painful pause, which was broken by Mrs. Plinth's remarking: "I can understand that, with all your other pursuits, you should not find much time for reading; but I should have thought you might at least have *got up The Wings of Death* before Osric Dane's arrival.

Mrs. Roby took this rebuke good-humoredly. She had meant, she owned, to glance through the book; but she had been so absorbed in a novel of Trollope's that—

"No one reads Trollope now," Mrs. Ballinger interrupted.

Mrs. Roby looked pained. "I'm only just beginning," she confessed.

"And does he interest you?" Mrs. Plinth inquired.

"He amuses me."

"Amusement," said Mrs. Plinth, "is hardly what I look for in my choice of books."

"Oh, certainly, *The Wings of Death* is not amusing," ventured Mrs. Leveret, whose manner of putting forth an opinion was like that of an obliging salesman with a variety of other styles to submit if his first selection does not suit.

"Was it *meant* to be?" inquired Mrs. Plinth, who was fond of asking questions that she permitted no one but herself to answer. "Assuredly not."

"Assuredly not—that is what I was going to say," assented Mrs. Leveret, hastily rolling up her opinion and reaching for another. "It was meant to—to elevate."

Miss Van Vluyck adjusted her spectacles as though they were the black cap of condemnation. "I hardly see," she interposed, "how a book steeped in the bitterest pessimism can be said to elevate, however much it may instruct."

"I meant, of course, to instruct," said Mrs. Leveret, flurried by the unexpected distinction between two terms which she had supposed to be synonymous. Mrs. Leveret's enjoyment of the Lunch Club was frequently marred by such surprises; and not knowing her own value to the other ladies as a mirror for their mental complacency she was sometimes troubled by a doubt of her worthiness to join in their debates. It was only the fact of having a dull sister who thought her clever that saved her from a sense of hopeless inferiority.

"Do they get married in the end?" Mrs. Roby interposed.

"They—who?" the Lunch Club collectively exclaimed.

"Why, the girl and man. It's a novel, isn't it? I always think that's the one thing that matters. If they're parted it spoils my dinner."

Mrs. Plinth and Mrs. Ballinger exchanged scandalized glances, and the latter said: "I should hardly advise you to read *The Wings of Death* in that spirit. For my part, when there are so many books one *has* to read, I wonder how any one can find time for those that are merely amusing."

"The beautiful part of it," Laura Glyde murmured, "is surely just this—that no one can tell *how The Wings of Death* ends. Osric Dane, overcome by the awful significance of her own meaning, has mercifully veiled it—perhaps even from herself—as Apelles, in representing the sacrifice of Iphigenia, veiled the face of Agamemnon."

"What's that? Is it poetry?" whispered Mrs. Leveret to Mrs. Plinth, who, disdaining a definite reply, said coldly: "You should look it up. I always make it a point to look things up." Her tone added—"Though I might easily have it done for me by the footman."

"I was about to say," Miss Van Vluyck resumed, "that it must always be a question whether a book *can* instruct unless it elevates."

"Oh—" murmured Mrs. Leveret, now feeling herself hopelessly astray.

"I don't know," said Mrs. Ballinger, scenting in Miss Van Vluyck's tone a tendency to depreciate the coveted distinction of entertaining Osric Dane; "I don't know that such a question can seriously be raised as to a book which has attracted more attention among thoughtful people than any novel since *Robert Elsmere*."

"Oh, but don't you see," exclaimed Laura Glyde, "that it's just the dark hopelessness of it all—the wonderful tone scheme of black on black—that makes it such an artistic achievement? It reminded me when I read it of Prince Rupert's *manière noire* . . . the book is etched, not painted, yet one feels the color values so intensely. . . ."

"Who is *he*? Mrs. Leveret whispered to her neighbor. "Someone she's met abroad?"

"The wonderful part of the book," Mrs. Ballinger conceded, "is that it may be looked at from so many points of view. I hear that as a study of determinism Professor Lupton ranks it with *The Data of Ethics*."

"I'm told that Osric Dane spent ten years in preparatory studies before beginning to write it," said Mrs. Plinth. "She looks up everything—verifies everything. It has always been my principle, as you know. Nothing would induce me, now, to put aside a book before I'd finished it, just because I can buy as many more as I want."

"And what do *you* think of *The Wings of Death*? Mrs. Roby abruptly asked her.

It was the kind of question that might be termed out of order, and the ladies glanced at each other as though disclaiming any share in such a breach of discipline. They all knew there was nothing Mrs. Plinth so much disliked as being asked her opinion of a book. Books were written to read; if one read them what more could be expected? To be questioned in detail regarding the contents of a volume seemed to her as great an outrage as being searched for smuggled laces at the Custom House. The club had always respected this idiosyncrasy of Mrs. Plinth's. Such opinions as she had were imposing and substantial: her mind, like her house, was furnished with monumental "pieces" that were not meant to be disarranged; and it was one of the unwritten rules of the Lunch Club that, within her own province, each member's habits of thought should be respected. The meeting therefore closed with an increased sense, on the part of the other ladies, of Mrs. Roby's hopeless unfitness to be one of them.

II

Mrs. Leveret, on the eventful day, arrived early at Mrs. Ballinger's, her volume of *Appropriate Allusions* in her pocket.

It always flustered Mrs. Leveret to be late at the Lunch Club: she liked to collect her thoughts and gather a hint, as the others assembled, of the turn the conversation was likely to take. Today, however, she felt herself completely at a loss; and even the familiar contact of *Appropriate Allusions,* which stuck into her as she sat down, failed to give her any reassurance. It was an admirable little volume, compiled to meet all the social emergencies; so that, whether on the occasion of Anniversaries, joyful or melancholy (as the classification ran), of Banquets, social or municipal, or of Baptisms, Church of England or sectarian, its student need never be at a loss for a pertinent reference. Mrs. Leveret, though she had for years devoutly conned its pages, valued it, however, rather for its moral support than for its practical services; for though in the privacy of her own room she commanded an army of quotations, these invariably deserted her at the critical moment, and the only phrase she retained—*Canst thou draw out leviathan with a hook?*—was one she had never yet found occasion to apply.

Today she felt that even the complete mastery of the volume would hardly have insured her self-possession; for she thought it probable that, even if she *did,* in some miraculous way, remember an Allusion, it would be only to find that Osric Dane used a different volume (Mrs. Leveret was convinced that literary people always carried them), and would consequently not recognize her quotations.

Mrs. Leveret's sense of being adrift was intensified by the appearance of Mrs. Ballinger's drawing room. To a careless eye its aspect was unchanged; but those acquainted with Mrs. Ballinger's way of arranging her books would instantly have detected the marks of recent perturbation. Mrs. Ballinger's province, as a member of the Lunch Club, was the Book of the Day. On that, whatever it was, from a novel to a treatise on experimental psychology, she was confidently, authoritatively "up." What became of last year's books, or last week's even; what she did with the "subjects" she had previously professed with equal authority; no one had ever yet discovered. Her mind was an hotel where facts came and went like transient lodgers, without leaving their address behind, and frequently without paying for their board. It was Mrs. Ballinger's boast that she was "abreast with the Thought of the Day," and her pride that this advanced position should be expressed by the books on her table. These volumes, frequently renewed, and almost always damp from the press, bore names generally unfamiliar to Mrs. Leveret, and giving her, as she furtively scanned them, a disheartening glimpse of new fields of knowledge to be breathlessly traversed in Mrs. Ballinger's wake. But today a number of maturer-looking volumes were adroitly mingled with the *primeurs* of the press—Karl Marx jostled Professor Bergson, and the *Confessions of St. Augustine* lay beside the last work on "Mendelism"; so that even to Mrs. Leveret's fluttered perceptions it was clear that Mrs. Ballinger didn't in the least know what Osric Dane was likely to talk about, and had taken measures to be prepared for anything. Mrs. Leveret felt like a passenger on an ocean steamer who is told that there is no immediate danger, but that she had better put on her lifebelt.

It was a relief to be roused from these forebodings by Miss Van Vluyck's arrival.

"Well, my dear," the newcomer briskly asked her hostess, "what subjects are we to discuss today?"

Mrs. Ballinger was furtively replacing a volume of Wordsworth by a copy of Verlaine. "I hardly know," she said, somewhat nervously. "Perhaps we had better leave that to circumstances."

"Circumstances?" said Miss Van Vluyck drily. "That means, I suppose, that Laura Glyde will take the floor as usual, and we shall be deluged with literature."

Philanthropy and statistics were Miss Van Vluyck's province, and she resented any tendency to divert their guest's attention from these topics.

Mrs. Plinth at this moment appeared.

"Literature?" she protested in a tone of remonstrance. "But this is perfectly unexpected. I understood we were to talk of Osric Dane's novel."

Mrs. Ballinger winced at the discrimination, but let it pass. "We can hardly make that our chief subject—at least not *too* intentionally," she suggested. "Of course we can let our talk *drift* in that direction; but we ought to have some other topic as an introduction, and that is what I wanted to consult you about. The fact is, we know so little of Osric Dane's tastes and interests that it is difficult to make any special preparation."

"It may be difficult," said Mrs. Plinth with decision, "but it is necessary. I know what that happy-go-lucky principle leads to. As I told one of my nieces the other day, there are certain emergencies for which a lady should always be prepared. It's in shocking taste to wear

colors when one pays a visit of condolence, or a last year's dress when
there are reports that one's husband is on the wrong side of the market; and so it is with conversation. All I ask is that I should know
beforehand what is to be talked about; then I feel sure of being able
to say the proper thing.

"I quite agree with you," Mrs. Ballinger assented; "but—"

And at that instant, heralded by the fluttered parlormaid, Osric
Dane appeared upon the threshold.

Mrs. Leveret told her sister afterward that she had known at a
glance what was coming. She saw that Osric Dane was not going to
meet them halfway. That distinguished personage had indeed entered
with an air of compulsion not calculated to promote the easy exercise
of hospitality. She looked as though she were about to be photographed for a new edition of her books.

The desire to propitiate a divinity is generally in inverse ratio to
its responsiveness, and the sense of discouragement produced by Osric Dane's entrance visibly increased the Lunch Club's eagerness to
please her. Any lingering idea that she might consider herself under
an obligation to her entertainers was at once dispelled by her manner:
as Mrs. Leveret said afterward to her sister, she had a way of looking
at you that made you feel as if there was something wrong with your
hat. This evidence of greatness produced such an immediate impression on the ladies that a shudder of awe ran through them when Mrs.
Roby, as their hostess led the great personage into the dining room,
turned back to whisper to the others: "What a brute she is!"

The hour about the table did not tend to revise this verdict. It was
passed by Osric Dane in the silent deglutition of Mrs. Ballinger's
menu, and by the members of the club in the emission of tentative
platitudes which their guest seemed to swallow as perfunctorily as
the successive courses of the luncheon.

Mrs. Ballinger's reluctance to fix a topic had thrown the club into
a mental disarray which increased with the return to the drawing
room where the actual business of discussion was to open. Each lady
waited for the other to speak; and there was a general shock of disappointment when their hostess opened the conversation by the painfully commonplace inquiry: "Is this your first visit to Hillbridge?"

Even Mrs. Leveret was conscious that this was a bad beginning;
and a vague impulse of deprecation made Miss Glyde interject: "It is
a very small place indeed."

Mrs. Plinth bristled. "We have a great many representative people," she said, in the tone of one who speaks for her order.

Osric Dane turned to her. "What do they represent?" she asked.

Mrs. Plinth's constitutional dislike to being questioned was intensified by her sense of unpreparedness; and her reproachful glance
passed the question on to Mrs. Ballinger.

"Why," said that lady, glancing in turn at the other members, "as
a community I hope it is not too much to say that we stand for
culture."

"For art—" Miss Glyde interjected.

"For art and literature," Mrs. Ballinger amended.

"And for sociology, I trust," snapped Miss Van Vluyck.

"We have a standard," said Mrs. Plinth, feeling herself suddenly
secure on the vast expanse of a generalization; and Mrs. Leveret,
thinking there must be room for more than one on so broad a statement, took courage to murmur: "Oh, certainly; we have a standard."

"The object of our little club," Mrs. Ballinger continued, "is to
concentrate the highest tendencies of Hillbridge—to centralize and
focus its intellectual effort."

This was felt to be so happy that the ladies drew an almost audible
breath of relief.

"We aspire," the President went on, "to be in touch with whatever
is highest in art, literature and ethics."

Osric Dane again turned to her. "What ethics?" she asked.

A tremor of apprehension encircled the room. None of the ladies
required any preparation to pronounce on a question of morals; but
when they were called ethics it was different. The club, when fresh
from the *Encyclopedia Britannica*, the *Reader's Handbook* or Smith's
Classical Dictionary, could deal confidently with any subject; but
when taken unawares it had been known to define agnosticism as a
heresy of the Early Church and Professor Froude as a distinguished
histologist; and such minor members as Mrs. Leveret still secretly
regarded ethics as something vaguely pagan.

Even to Mrs. Ballinger, Osric Dane's question was unsettling, and
there was a general sense of gratitude when Laura Glyde leaned forward to say, with her most sympathetic accent: "You must excuse
us, Mrs. Dane, for not being able, just at present, to talk of anything
but *The Wings of Death*."

"Yes," said Miss Van Vluyck, with a sudden resolve to carry the war into the enemy's camp. "We are so anxious to know the exact purpose you had in mind in writing your wonderful book."

"You will find," Mrs. Plinth interposed, "that we are not superficial readers."

"We are eager to hear from you," Miss Van Vluyck continued, "if the pessimistic tendency of the book is an expression of your own convictions or—"

"Or merely," Miss Glyde thrust in, "a somber background brushed in to throw your figures into more vivid relief. *Are* you not primarily plastic?"

"*I* have always maintained," Mrs. Ballinger interposed, "that you represent the purely objective method—"

Osric Dane helped herself critically to coffee. "How do you define objective?" she then inquired.

There was a flurried pause before Laura Glyde intensely murmured: "In reading *you* we don't define, we feel."

Osric Dane smiled. "The cerebellum," she remarked, "is not infrequently the seat of the literary emotions." And she took a second lump of sugar.

The sting that this remark was vaguely felt to conceal was almost neutralized by the satisfaction of being addressed in such technical language.

"Ah, the cerebellum," said Miss Van Vluyck complacently. "The club took a course in psychology last winter."

"Which psychology?" asked Osric Dane.

There was an agonizing pause, during which each member of the club secretly deplored the distressing inefficiency of the others. Only Mrs. Roby went on placidly sipping her chartreuse. At last Mrs. Ballinger said with an attempt at a high tone: "Well, really, you know, it was last year that we took psychology, and this winter we have been so absorbed in—"

She broke off, nervously trying to recall some of the club's discussions; but her faculties seemed to be paralyzed by the petrifying state of Osric Dane. What *had* the club been absorbed in? Mrs. Ballinger, with a vague purpose of gaining time, repeated slowly: "We've been so intensely absorbed in—"

Mrs. Roby put down her liqueur glass and drew near the group with a smile.

"In Xingu?" she gently prompted.

A thrill ran through the other members. They exchanged confused glances, and then, with one accord, turned a gaze of mingled relief and interrogation on their rescuer. The expression of each denoted a different phase of the same emotion. Mrs. Plinth was the first to compose her features to an air of reassurance: after a moment's hasty adjustment her look almost implied that it was she who had given the word to Mrs. Ballinger.

"Xingu, of course!" exclaimed the latter with her accustomed promptness, while Miss Van Vluyck and Laura Glyde seemed to be plumbing the depths of memory, and Mrs. Leveret, feeling apprehensively for *Appropriate Allusions,* was somehow reassured by the uncomfortable pressure of its bulk against her person.

Osric Dane's change of countenance was no less striking than that of her entertainers. She too put down her coffee cup, but with a look of distinct annoyance; she too wore, for a brief moment, what Mrs. Roby afterward described as the look of feeling for something in the back of her head; and before she could dissemble these momentary signs of weakness, Mrs. Roby, turning to her with a deferential smile, had said: "And we've been so hoping that today you would tell us just what you think of it."

Osric Dane received the homage of the smile as a matter of course; but the accompanying question obviously embarrassed her, and it became clear to her observers that she was not quick at shifting her facial scenery. It was as though her countenance had so long been set in an expression of unchallenged superiority that the muscles had stiffened, and refused to obey her orders.

"Xingu—" she said, as if seeking in her turn to gain time.

Mrs. Roby continued to press her. "Knowing how engrossing the subject is, you will understand how it happens that the club has let everything else go to the wall for the moment. Since we took up Xingu I might almost say—were it not for your books—that nothing else seems to us worth remembering."

Osric Dane's stern features were darkened rather than lit up by an uneasy smile. "I am glad to hear that you make one exception," she gave out between narrowed lips.

"Oh, of course," Mrs. Roby said prettily; "but as you have shown us that—so very naturally!—you don't care to talk of your own things, we really can't let you off from telling us exactly what you think about Xingu; especially," she added, with a still more persuasive smile, "as some people say that one of your last books was saturated with it."

It was an *it*, then—the assurance sped like fire through the parched minds of the other members. In their eagerness to gain the least little clue to Xingu they almost forgot the joy of assisting at the discomfiture of Mrs. Dane.

The latter reddened nervously under her antagonist's challenge. "May I ask," she faltered out, "to which of my books you refer?"

Mrs. Roby did not falter. "That's just what I want you to tell us; because, though I was present, I didn't actually take part."

"Present at what?" Mrs. Dane took her up; and for an instant the trembling members of the Lunch Club thought that the champion Providence had raised up for them had lost a point. But Mrs. Roby explained herself gaily: "At the discussion, of course. And so we're dreadfully anxious to know just how it was that you went into the Xingu."

There was a portentous pause, a silence so big with incalculable dangers that the members with one accord checked the words on their lips, like soldiers dropping their arms to watch a single combat between their leaders. Then Mrs. Dane gave expression to their inmost dread by saying sharply: "Ah—you say *the* Xingu, do you?"

Mrs. Roby smiled undauntedly. "It *is* a shade pedantic, isn't it? Personally, I always drop the article: but I don't know how the other members feel about it."

The other members looked as though they would willingly have dispensed with this appeal to their opinion, and Mrs. Roby, after a bright glance about the group, went on: "They probably think, as I do, that nothing really matters except the thing itself—except Xingu."

No immediate reply seemed to occur to Mrs. Dane, and Mrs. Ballinger gathered courage to say: "Surely everyone must feel that about Xingu."

Mrs. Plinth came to her support with a heavy murmur of assent, and Laura Glyde sighed out emotionally: "I have known cases where it has changed a whole life."

"It has done me worlds of good," Mrs. Leveret interjected, seeming to herself to remember that she had either taken it or read it the winter before.

"Of course," Mrs. Roby admitted, "the difficulty is that one must give up so much time to it. It's very long."

"I can't imagine," said Miss Van Vluyck, "grudging the time given to such a subject."

"And deep in places," Mrs. Roby pursued; (so then it was a book!) "And it isn't easy to skip."

"I never skip," said Mrs. Plinth dogmatically.

"Ah, it's dangerous to, in Xingu. Even at the start there are places where one can't. One must just wade through."

"I should hardly call it *wading*," said Mrs. Ballinger sarcastically.

Mrs. Roby sent her a look of interest. "Ah—you always found it went swimmingly?"

Mrs. Ballinger hesitated. "Of course there are difficult passages," she conceded.

"Yes; some are not at all clear—even," Mrs. Roby added, "if one is familiar with the original."

"As I suppose you are?" Osric Dane interposed, suddenly fixing her with a look of challenge.

Mrs. Roby met it by a deprecating gesture. "Oh, it's really not difficult up to a certain point; though some of the branches are very little known, and it's almost impossible to get at the source."

"Have you ever tried?" Mrs. Plinth inquired, still distrustful of Mrs. Roby's thoroughness.

Mrs. Roby was silent for a moment; then she replied with lowered lids: "No—but a friend of mine did; a very brilliant man; and he told me it was best for women—not to. . . ."

A shudder ran around the room. Mrs. Leveret coughed so that the parlormaid, who was handing the cigarettes, should not hear; Miss Van Vluyck's face took on a nauseated expression, and Mrs. Plinth looked as if she were passing someone she did not care to bow to. But the most remarkable result of Mrs. Roby's words was the effect they produced on the Lunch Club's distinguished guest. Osric Dane's impassive features suddenly softened to an expression of the warmest human sympathy, and edging her chair toward Mrs. Roby's she asked: "Did he really? And—did you find he was right?"

Mrs. Ballinger, in whom annoyance at Mrs. Roby's unwonted assumption of prominence was beginning to displace gratitude for the aid she had rendered, could not consent to her being allowed, by such dubious means, to monopolize the attention of their guest. If Osric

Dane had not enough self-respect to resent Mrs. Roby's flippancy, at least the Lunch Club would do so in the person of its President.

Mrs. Ballinger laid her hand on Mrs. Roby's arm. "We must not forget," she said with a frigid amiability, "that absorbing as Xingu is to *us,* it may be less interesting to—"

"Oh, no, on the contrary, I assure you," Osric Dane intervened.

"—to others," Mrs. Ballinger finished firmly; "and we must not allow our little meeting to end without persuading Mrs. Dane to say a few words to us on a subject which, today, is much more present in all our thoughts. I refer, of course, to *The Wings of Death.*"

The other members, animated by various degrees of the same sentiment, and encouraged by the humanized mien of their redoubtable guest, repeated after Mrs. Ballinger: "Oh, yes, you really *must* talk to us a little about your book."

Osric Dane's expression became as bored, though not as haughty, as when her work had been previously mentioned. But before she could respond to Mrs. Ballinger's request, Mrs. Roby had risen from her seat, and was pulling down her veil over her frivolous nose.

"I'm so sorry," she said, advancing toward her hostess with outstretched hand, "but before Mrs. Dane begins I think I'd better run away. Unluckily, as you know, I haven't read her books, so I should be at a terrible disadvantage among you all, and besides, I've an engagement to play bridge."

If Mrs. Roby had simply pleaded her ignorance of Osric Dane's works as a reason for withdrawing, the Lunch Club, in view of her recent prowess, might have approved such evidence of discretion; but to couple this excuse with the brazen announcement that she was foregoing the privilege for the purpose of joining a bridge party was only one more instance of her deplorable lack of discrimination.

The ladies were disposed, however, to feel that her departure—now that she had performed the sole service she was ever likely to render them—would probably make for greater order and dignity in the impending discussion, besides relieving them of the sense of self-distrust which her presence always mysteriously produced. Mrs. Ballinger therefore restricted herself to a formal murmur of regret, and the other members were just grouping themselves comfortably about Osric Dane when the latter, to their dismay, started up from the sofa on which she had been seated.

"Oh wait—do wait, and I'll go with you!" she called out to Mrs.

Roby; and, seizing the hands of the disconcerted members, she administered a series of farewell pressures with the mechanical haste of a railway conductor punching tickets.

"I'm so sorry—I'd quite forgotten—" she flung back at them from the threshold; and as she joined Mrs. Roby, who had turned in surprise at her appeal, the other ladies had the mortification of hearing her say, in a voice which she did not take the pains to lower: "If you'll let me walk a little way with you, I should so like to ask you a few more questions about Xingu. . . ."

III

The incident had been so rapid that the door closed on the departing pair before the other members had time to understand what was happening. Then a sense of indignity put upon them by Osric Dane's unceremonious desertion began to contend with the confused feeling that they had been cheated out of their due without exactly knowing how or why.

There was a silence, during which Mrs. Ballinger, with a perfunctory hand, rearranged the skillfully grouped literature at which her distinguished guest had not so much as glanced; then Miss Van Vluyck tartly pronounced: "Well, I can't say that I consider Osric Dane's departure a great loss."

This confession crystallized the resentment of the other members, and Mrs. Leveret exclaimed: "I do believe she came on purpose to be nasty!"

It was Mrs. Plinth's private opinion that Osric Dane's attitude toward the Lunch Club might have been very different had it welcomed her in the majestic setting of the Plinth drawing rooms; but not liking to reflect on the inadequacy of Mrs. Ballinger's establishment she sought a roundabout satisfaction in deprecating her lack of foresight.

"I said from the first that we ought to have had a subject ready. It's what always happens when you're unprepared. Now if we'd only got up Xingu—"

The slowness of Mrs. Plinth's mental processes was always allowed for by the club; but this instance of it was too much for Mrs. Ballinger's equanimity.

"Xingu!" she scoffed. "Why, it was the fact of our knowing so

much more about it than she did—unprepared though we were—
that made Osric Dane so furious. I should have thought that was plain
enough to everybody!"

This retort impressed even Mrs. Plinth, and Laura Glyde, moved
by an impulse of generosity, said: "Yes, we really ought to be grateful
to Mrs. Roby for introducing the topic. It may have made Osric Dane
furious, but at least it made her civil."

"I am glad we were able to show her," added Miss Van Vluyck,
"that a broad and up-to-date culture is not confined to the great intellectual centers."

This increased the satisfaction of the other members, and they began to forget their wrath against Osric Dane in the pleasure of having
contributed to her discomfiture.

Miss Van Vluyck thoughtfully rubbed her spectacles. "What surprised me most," she continued, "was that Fanny Roby should be so
up on Xingu."

This remark threw a light chill on the company, but Mrs. Ballinger
said with an air of indulgent irony: "Mrs. Roby always has the knack
of making a little go a long way; still, we certainly owe her a debt for
happening to remember that she'd heard of Xingu." And this was
felt by the other members to be a graceful way of canceling once and
for all the club's obligation to Mrs. Roby.

Even Mrs. Leveret took courage to speed a timid shaft of irony. "I
fancy Osric Dane hardly expected to take a lesson in Xingu at Hillbridge!"

Mrs. Ballinger smiled. "When she asked me what we represented—do you remember—I wish I'd simply said we represented
Xingu!"

All the ladies laughed appreciatively at this sally, except Mrs.
Plinth, who said, after a moment's deliberation: "I'm not sure it
would have been wise to do so."

Mrs. Ballinger, who was already beginning to feel as if she had
launched at Osric Dane the retort which had just occurred to her,
turned ironically on Mrs. Plinth. "May I ask why?" she inquired.

Mrs. Plinth looked grave. "Surely," she said, "I understood from
Mrs. Roby herself that the subject was one it was as well not to go
into too deeply?"

Miss Van Vluyck rejoined with precision: "I think that applied
only to an investigation of the origin of the—of the—"; and suddenly

she found that her usually accurate memory had failed her. "It's a part of the subject I never studied myself," she concluded.

"Nor I," said Mrs. Ballinger.

Laura Glyde bent toward them with widened eyes. "And yet it seems—doesn't it—the part that is fullest of an esoteric fascination?"

"I don't know on what you base that," said Miss Van Vluyck argumentatively.

"Well, didn't you notice how intensely interested Osric Dane became as soon as she heard what the brilliant foreigner—he *was* a foreigner, wasn't he—had told Mrs. Roby about the origin—the origin of the rite—or whatever you call it?"

Mrs. Plinth looked disapproving, and Mrs. Ballinger visibly wavered. Then she said: "It may not be desirable to touch on the—on that part of the subject in general conversation; but, from the importance it evidently has to a woman of Osric Dane's distinction, I feel as if we ought not to be afraid to discuss it among ourselves—without gloves—though with closed doors, if necessary."

"I'm quite of your opinion," Miss Van Vluyck came briskly to her support; "on condition, that is, that all grossness of language is avoided."

"Oh, I'm sure we shall understand without that," Mrs. Leveret tittered; and Laura Glyde added significantly: "I fancy we can read between the lines," while Mrs. Ballinger rose to assure herself that the doors were really closed.

Mrs. Plinth had not yet given her adhesion. "I hardly see," she began, "what benefit is to be derived from investigating such peculiar customs—"

But Mrs. Ballinger's patience had reached the extreme limit of tension. "That at least," she returned; "that we shall not be placed again in the humiliating position of finding ourselves less up on our own subjects than Fanny Roby!"

Even to Mrs. Plinth this argument was conclusive. She peered furtively about the room and lowered her commanding tones to ask: "Have you got a copy?"

"A—a copy?" stammered Mrs. Ballinger. She was aware that the other members were looking at her expectantly, and that this answer was inadequate, so she supported it by asking another question. "A copy of what?"

Her companions bent their expectant gaze on Mrs. Plinth, who, in turn, appeared less sure of herself than usual. "Why, of—of—the book," she explained.

"What book?" snapped Miss Van Vluyck, almost as sharply as Osric Dane.

Mrs. Ballinger looked at Laura Glyde, whose eyes were interrogatively fixed on Mrs. Leveret. The fact of being deferred to was so new to the latter that it filled her with an insane temerity. "Why, Xingu, of course!" she exclaimed.

A profound silence followed this challenge to the resources of Mrs. Ballinger's library, and the latter, after glancing nervously toward the Books of the Day, returned with dignity: "It's not a thing one cares to leave about."

"I should think *not!*" exclaimed Mrs. Plinth.

"It *is* a book, then?" said Miss Van Vluyck.

This again threw the company into disarray, and Mrs. Ballinger, with an impatient sigh, rejoined: "Why—there *is* a book—naturally. . . ."

"Then why did Miss Glyde call it a religion?"

Laura Glyde started up. "A religion? I never—"

"Yes, you did," Miss Van Vluyck insisted; "you spoke of rites; and Mrs. Plinth said it was a custom."

Miss Glyde was evidently making a desperate effort to recall her statement; but accuracy of detail was not her strongest point. At length she began in a deep murmur: "Surely they used to do something of the kind at the Eleusinian mysteries—"

"Oh—" said Miss Van Vluyck, on the verge of disapproval; and Mrs. Plinth protested: "I understood there was to be no indelicacy!"

Mrs. Ballinger could not control her irritation. "Really, it is too bad that we should not be able to talk the matter over quietly among ourselves. Personally, I think that if one goes into Xingu at all—"

"Oh, so do I!" cried Miss Glyde.

"And I don't see how one can avoid doing so, if one wishes to keep up with the Thought of the Day—"

Mrs. Leveret uttered an exclamation of relief. "There—that's it!" she interposed.

"What's it?" the President took her up.

"Why—it's a—a Thought: I mean a philosophy."

This seemed to bring a certain relief to Mrs. Ballinger and Laura

Glyde, but Miss Van Vluyck said: "Excuse me if I tell you that you're all mistaken. Xingu happens to be a language."

"A language!" the Lunch Club cried.

"Certainly. Don't you remember Fanny Roby's saying that there were several branches, and that some were hard to trace? What could that apply to but dialects?"

Mrs. Ballinger could no longer restrain a contemptuous laugh. "Really, if the Lunch Club has reached such a pass that it has to go to Fanny Roby for instruction on a subject like Xingu, it had almost better cease to exist!"

"It's really her fault for not being clearer," Laura Glyde put in.

"Oh, clearness and Fanny Roby!" Mrs. Ballinger shrugged. "I dare say we shall find she was mistaken on almost every point."

"Why not look it up?" said Mrs. Plinth.

As a rule this recurrent suggestion of Mrs. Plinth's was ignored in the heat of the discussion, and only resorted to afterward in the privacy of each member's home. But on the present occasion the desire to ascribe their own confusion of thought to the vague and contradictory nature of Mrs. Roby's statements caused the members of the Lunch Club to utter a collective demand for a book of reference.

At this point the production of her treasured volume gave Mrs. Leveret, for a moment, the unusual experience of occupying the center front; but she was not able to hold it long, for *Appropriate Allusions* contained no mention of Xingu.

"Oh, that's not the kind of thing we want!" exclaimed Miss Van Vluyck. She cast a disparaging glance over Mrs. Ballinger's assortment of literature, and added impatiently: "Haven't you any useful books?"

"Of course I have," replied Mrs. Ballinger indignantly; "I keep them in my husband's dressing room."

From this region, after some difficulty and delay, the parlormaid produced the W–Z volume of an *Encyclopedia* and, in deference to the fact that the demand for it had come from Miss Van Vluyck, laid the ponderous tome before her.

There was a moment of painful suspense while Miss Van Vluyck rubbed her spectacles, adjusted them, and turned to Z; and a murmur of surprise when she said: "It isn't here."

"I suppose," said Mrs. Plinth, "it's not fit to be put in a book of reference."

"Oh, nonsense!" exclaimed Mrs. Ballinger. "Try X."

Miss Van Vluyck turned back through the volume, peering short-sightedly up and down the pages, till she came to a stop and remained motionless, like a dog on a point.

"Well, have you found it?" Mrs. Ballinger inquired after a considerable delay.

"Yes. I've found it," said Miss Van Vluyck in a queer voice.

Mrs. Plinth hastily interposed: "I beg you won't read it aloud if there's anything offensive."

Miss Van Vluyck, without answering, continued her silent scrutiny.

"Well, what *is* it?" exclaimed Laura Glyde excitedly.

"*Do* tell us!" urged Mrs. Leveret, feeling that she would have something awful to tell her sister.

Miss Van Vluyck pushed the volume aside and turned slowly toward the expectant group.

"It's a river."

"A *river*?"

"Yes: in Brazil. Isn't that where she's been living?"

"Who? Fanny Roby? Oh, but you must be mistaken. You've been reading the wrong thing," Mrs. Ballinger exclaimed, leaning over her to seize the volume.

"It's the only Xingu in the *Encyclopedia*; and she *has* been living in Brazil," Miss Van Vluyck persisted.

"Yes: her brother has a consulship there," Mrs. Leveret interposed.

"But it's too ridiculous! I—we—why we *all* remember studying Xingu last year—or the year before last," Mrs. Ballinger stammered.

"I thought I did when *you* said so," Laura Glyde avowed.

"*I* said so?" cried Mrs. Ballinger.

"Yes. You said it had crowded everything else out of your mind."

"Well *you* said it had changed your whole life!"

"For that matter Miss Van Vluyck said she had never grudged the time she'd given it."

Mrs. Plinth interposed: "I made clear that I knew nothing whatever of the original."

Mrs. Ballinger broke off the dispute with a groan. "Oh, what does it all matter if she's been making fools of us? I believe Miss Van Vluyck's right—she was talking of the river all the while!"

"How could she? It's too preposterous," Miss Glyde exclaimed.

"Listen." Miss Van Vluyck had repossessed herself of the *Encyclopedia,* and restored her spectacles to a nose reddened by excitement. " 'The Xingu, one of the principal rivers of Brazil, rises on the plateau of Mato Grosso, and flows in a northerly direction for a length of no less than one-thousand one-hundred and eighteen miles, entering the Amazon near the mouth of the latter river. The upper course of the Xingu is auriferous and fed by numerous branches. Its source was first discovered in 1884 by the German explorer von den Steinen, after a difficult and dangerous expedition through a region inhabited by tribes still in the Stone Age of culture.' "

The ladies received this communication in a state of stupefied silence from which Mrs. Leveret was the first to rally. "She certainly *did* speak of its having branches."

The word seemed to snap the last thread of their incredulity. "And of its great length," gasped Mrs. Ballinger.

"She said it was awfully deep, and you couldn't skip—you just had to wade through," Miss Glyde added.

The idea worked its way more slowly through Mrs. Plinth's compact resistances. "How could there be anything improper about a river?" she inquired.

"Improper?"

"Why, what she said about the source—that it was corrupt?"

"Not corrupt, but hard to get at," Laura Glyde corrected. "Someone who'd been there had told her so. I dare say it was the explorer himself—doesn't it say the expedition was dangerous?"

" 'Difficult and dangerous,' " read Miss Van Vluyck.

Mrs. Ballinger pressed her hands to her throbbing temples. "There's nothing she said that wouldn't apply to a river—to this river!" She swung about excitedly to the other members. "Why, do you remember her telling us that she hadn't read *The Supreme Instant* because she'd taken it on a boating party while she was staying with her brother, and someone had 'shied' it overboard—'shied' of course was her own expression."

The ladies breathlessly signified that the expression had not escaped them.

"Well—and then didn't she tell Osric Dane that one of her books was simply saturated with Xingu? Of course it was, if one of Mrs. Roby's rowdy friends had thrown it into the river!"

This surprising reconstruction of the scene in which they had just participated left the members of the Lunch Club inarticulate. At length, Mrs. Plinth, after visibly laboring with the problem, said in a heavy tone: "Osric Dane was taken in too."

Mrs. Leveret took courage at this. "Perhaps that's what Mrs. Roby did it for. She said Osric Dane was a brute, and she may have wanted to give her a lesson."

Miss Van Vluyck frowned. "It was hardly worth-while to do it at our expense."

"At least," said Miss Glyde with a touch of bitterness, "she succeeded in interesting her, which was more than we did."

"What chance had we?" rejoined Mrs. Ballinger. "Mrs. Roby monopolized her from the first. And *that,* I've no doubt, was her purpose—to give Osric Dane a false impression of her own standing in the club. She would hesitate at nothing to attract attention: we all know how she took in poor Professor Foreland."

"She actually makes him give bridge teas every Thursday," Mrs. Leveret piped up.

Laura Glyde struck her hands together. "Why, this is Thursday, and it's *there* she's gone, of course; and taken Osric with her!"

"And they're shrieking over us at this moment," said Mrs. Ballinger between her teeth.

This possibility seemed too preposterous to be admitted. "She would hardly dare," said Miss Van Vluyck, "confess the imposture to Osric Dane."

"I'm not so sure: I thought I saw her make a sign as she left. If she hadn't made a sign, why should Osric Dane have rushed out after her?"

"Well, you know, we'd all been telling her how wonderful Xingu was, and she said she wanted to find out more about it," Mrs. Leveret said, with a tardy impulse of justice to the absent.

This reminder, far from mitigating the wrath of the other members, gave it a stronger impetus.

"Yes—and that's exactly what they're both laughing over now," said Laura Glyde ironically.

Mrs. Plinth stood up and gathered her expensive furs about her monumental form. "I have no wish to criticize," she said; "but unless the Lunch Club can protect its members against the recurrence of such—such unbecoming scenes, I for one—"

"Oh, so do I!" agreed Miss Glyde, rising also.

Miss Van Vluyck closed the *Encyclopedia* and proceeded to button herself into her jacket. "My time is really too valuable—" she began.

"I fancy we are all of one mind," said Mrs. Ballinger, looking searchingly at Mrs. Leveret, who looked at the others.

"I always deprecate anything like a scandal—" Mrs. Plinth continued.

"She has been the cause of one today!" exclaimed Miss Glyde.

Mrs. Leveret moaned: "I don't see how she *could*!" and Miss Van Vluyck said, picking up her notebook: "Some women stop at nothing."

"—But if," Mrs. Plinth took up her argument impressively, "anything of the kind had happened in *my* house" (it never would have, her tone implied), "I should have felt that I owed it to myself either to ask for Mrs. Roby's resignation—or to offer mine."

"Oh, Mrs. Plinth—" gasped the Lunch Club.

"Fortunately for me," Mrs. Plinth continued with an awful magnanimity, "the matter was taken out of my hands by our President's decision that the right to entertain distinguished guests was a privilege vested in her office; and I think the other members will agree that, as she was alone in this opinion, she ought to be alone in deciding on the best way of effacing its—its really deplorable consequences."

A deep silence followed this outbreak of Mrs. Plinth's long-stored resentment.

"I don't see why *I* should be expected to ask her to resign—" Mrs. Ballinger at length began; but Laura Glyde turned back to remind her: "You know she made you say that you'd got on swimmingly in Xingu."

An ill-timed giggle escaped from Mrs. Leveret, and Mrs. Ballinger energetically continued "—But you needn't think for a moment that I'm afraid to!"

The door of the drawing room closed on the retreating backs of the Lunch Club, and the President of that distinguished association, seating herself at her writing table, and pushing away a copy of *The Wings of Death* to make room for her elbow, drew forth a sheet of the club's notepaper, on which she began to write: "My dear Mrs. Roby—"

ETHAN FROME

(1911)

The first version of Ethan Frome *was written in Paris around 1907 as a French-language exercise. Wanting to update her skills in French, Wharton began writing a short story for her instructor. The manuscript, which has survived, contains only the kernel of the finished work: a New England farmer named Hart falls in love with his sickly wife's niece; there is no sledding accident and no internal narrator. Several years later Wharton took up the story in English, motivated, she said, by a stay at the Mount, when a distant glimpse of Bear Mountain brought Ethan back to her memory. She worked at high intensity through the winter of 1910–11, again in Paris. Aware of the irony of her surroundings, she wrote a friend: "The scene is laid at Starkfield, Massachusetts, and the nearest cosmopolis is called Shadd's Falls. It amuses me to do that decor in the Rue de Varenne"* (Letters, 232).

This is the first of many comments Wharton made about Ethan Frome. *In discussing the reviews of the book in her foreword to a 1936 dramatization of* Ethan, *she notes that she is breaking her life-long rule of never replying to any criticism of her work. But in fact she broke the rule three times previously, in an introduction to the 1922 edition, in a 1932 article, and in her autobiography; Wharton wrote more about* Ethan Frome *than the rest of her work put together (see the list of nonfiction in "New England Works by Edith Wharton"). Her discussions treat the composition of* Ethan Frome, *including the story of its origin in French and Wharton's certainty from the beginning that it would be shorter than a novel: "It must be treated as starkly and summarily as life had always presented itself to my protagonists." Any attempt to elaborate would be foreign to the "deep-rooted reticence and inarticulateness" of the people she was trying to draw* (Nevius, 70–71).

But the main purpose of Wharton's commentary on Ethan Frome was to defend it—first and foremost from the charge that she did not know the New England countryside (see the introduction to this volume). She emphasized her ten years' residence in western Massachusetts and the authenticity of details in the novella. The sledding mishap, for instance, was based on an actual incident on Court House Hill in Lenox when a young woman crashed into a lamppost and died. Secondarily, Wharton wanted to explain the seemingly overcomplicated method of narration—her use of an internal narrator, which she traces to Balzac and Browning, and especially a narrator who gradually learns Ethan's story from different sources. She was striving for "the effect of roundness" (Nevius, 71) she could get by letting the story be seen through various eyes, Harmon Gow's and Mrs. Hale's as well as the narrator's. Modern readers might observe that the narrator still presents his own "vision" of events, that is, he includes much that he could not have been told by anyone else; how, then, is this narrator more useful than a simple omniscient narrator? Perhaps Wharton felt that the story would seem more natural and acceptable from someone closer to Ethan's status, a man and a worker in the region instead of a "grande dame." In other words, Wharton tried to bridge the gulf between Shadd's Falls and the rue de Varenne.

When Ethan Frome was published in 1911, it did not sell as many copies as Wharton had hoped, but reviewers immediately recognized its flawless technique and praised the construction and style; more than one writer compared the novella to Greek tragedy. Henry James saw "a beautiful art & tone & truth—a beautiful artful keptdownness," delighting Wharton with his first unqualified praise (Lewis, 310). The only serious objection made by anyone was to the book's unrelieved grimness. Wharton treated her characters cruelly, some readers thought, making them suffer without the final redemption of Greek tragedy. This view reached its apotheosis in Lionel Trilling's article "The Morality of Inertia," written in the 1950s, by which time Ethan Frome had become both a classic and a commercial success.

In her commentary on the book Wharton responds to the "grimness and cruelty" criticism, attributing it to readers who cannot face reality without rose-colored glasses. Wharton's vision is a dark one. If the wheel of fortune spins rather benignly in a comedy like "The

Angel at the Grave," *fate bears down bleakly and inexorably on the majority of her characters. They are bound both by their own mistakes and by larger forces beyond their control—in the case of* Ethan Frome *the poverty, isolation, and cramped culture of their birthplace.*

I HAD the story, bit by bit, from various people, and, as generally happens in such cases, each time it was a different story.

If you know Starkfield, Massachusetts, you know the post office. If you know the post office you must have seen Ethan Frome drive up to it, drop the reins on his hollow-backed bay and drag himself across the brick pavement to the white colonnade: and you must have asked who he was.

It was there that, several years ago, I saw him for the first time; and the sight pulled me up sharp. Even then he was the most striking figure in Starkfield, though he was but the ruin of a man. It was not so much his great height that marked him, for the "natives" were easily singled out by their lank longitude from the stockier foreign breed: it was the careless powerful look he had, in spite of a lameness checking each step like the jerk of a chain. There was something bleak and unapproachable in his face, and he was so stiffened and grizzled that I took him for an old man and was surprised to hear that he was not more than fifty-two. I had this from Harmon Gow, who had driven the stage from Bettsbridge to Starkfield in pre-trolley days and knew the chronicle of all the families on his line.

"He's looked that way ever since he had his smash-up; and that's twenty-four years ago come next February," Harmon threw out between reminiscent pauses.

The "smash-up" it was—I gathered from the same informant—which, besides drawing the red gash across Ethan Frome's forehead, had so shortened and warped his right side that it cost him a visible effort to take the few steps from his buggy to the post-office window. He used to drive in from his farm every day at about noon, and as that was my own hour for fetching my mail I often passed him in the porch or stood beside him while we waited on the motions of the distributing hand behind the grating. I noticed that, though he came so punctually, he seldom received anything but a copy of the *Bettsbridge Eagle,* which he put without a glance into his sagging pocket. At intervals, however, the postmaster would hand him an envelope addressed to Mrs. Zenobia—or Mrs. Zeena—Frome, and usually bearing conspicuously in the upper left-hand corner the address of some manufacturer of patent medicine and the name of his specific. These documents my neighbor would also pocket without a glance, as if too much used to them to wonder at their number and variety, and would then turn away with a silent nod to the postmaster.

Every one in Starkfield knew him and gave him a greeting tempered to his own grave mien; but his taciturnity was respected and it was only on rare occasions that one of the older men of the place detained him for a word. When this happened he would listen quietly, his blue eyes on the speaker's face, and answer in so low a tone that his words never reached me; then he would climb stiffly into his buggy, gather up the reins in his left hand and drive slowly away in the direction of his farm.

"It was a pretty bad smash-up?" I questioned Harmon, looking after Frome's retreating figure, and thinking how gallantly his lean brown head, with its shock of light hair, must have sat on his strong shoulders before they were bent out of shape.

"Wust kind," my informant assented. "More'n enough to kill most men. But the Fromes are tough. Ethan'll likely touch a hundred."

"Good God!" I exclaimed. At the moment Ethan Frome, after climbing to his seat, had leaned over to assure himself of the security of a wooden box—also with a druggist's label on it—which he had placed in the back of the buggy, and I saw his face as it probably looked when he thought himself alone. "*That* man touch a hundred? He looks as if he was dead and in hell now!"

Harmon drew a slab of tobacco from his pocket, cut off a wedge and pressed it into the leather pouch of his cheek. "Guess he's been in Starkfield too many winters. Most of the smart ones get away."

"Why didn't *he?*"

"Somebody had to stay and care for the folks. There warn't ever anybody but Ethan. Fust his father—then his mother—then his wife."

"And then the smash-up?"

Harmon chuckled sardonically. "That's so. He *had* to stay then."

"I see. And since then they've had to care for him?"

Harmon thoughtfully passed his tobacco to the other cheek. "Oh, as to that: I guess it's always Ethan done the caring."

Though Harmon Gow developed the tale as far as his mental and moral reach permitted there were perceptible gaps between his facts, and I had the sense that the deeper meaning of the story was in the gaps. But one phrase stuck in my memory and served as the nucleus about which I grouped my subsequent information: "Guess he's been in Starkfield too many winters."

Before my own time there was up I had learned to know what that meant. Yet I had come in the degenerate day of trolley, bicycle and rural delivery, when communication was easy between the scattered mountain villages, and the bigger towns in the valleys, such as Bettsbridge and Shadd's Falls, had libraries, theaters and Y.M.C.A. halls to which the youth of the hills could descend for recreation. But when winter shut down on Starkfield, and the village lay under a sheet of snow perpetually renewed from the pale skies, I began to see what life there—or rather its negation—must have been in Ethan Frome's young manhood.

I had been sent up by my employers on a job connected with the big powerhouse at Corbury Junction, and a long-drawn carpenters' strike had so delayed the work that I found myself anchored at Starkfield—the nearest habitable spot—for the best part of the winter. I chafed at first, and then, under the hypnotizing effect of routine, gradually began to find a grim satisfaction in the life. During the early part of my stay I had been struck by the contrast between the vitality of the climate and the deadness of the community. Day by day, after the December snows were over, a blazing blue sky poured down torrents of light and air on the winter landscape, which gave them back in an intenser glitter. One would have supposed that such an atmosphere must quicken the emotions as well as the blood; but it seemed to produce no change except that of retarding still more the sluggish pulse of Starkfield. When I had been there a little longer, and had seen this phase of crystal clearness followed by long stretches of sunless cold; when the storms of February had pitched their white tents about the devoted village and the wild cavalry of March winds had charged down to their support; I began to understand why Starkfield emerged from its six months' siege like a starved garrison capitulating without quarter. Twenty years earlier the means of resistance must have been far fewer, and the enemy in command of almost all the lines of access between the beleaguered villages; and, considering these things, I felt the sinister force of Harmon's phrase: "Most of the smart ones get away." But if that were the case, how could any combination of obstacles have hindered the flight of a man like Ethan Frome?

During my stay at Starkfield I lodged with a middle-aged widow colloquially known as Mrs. Ned Hale. Mrs. Hale's father had been the village lawyer of the previous generation, and "lawyer Varnum's house," where my landlady still lived with her mother, was the most considerable mansion in the village. It stood at one end of the main street, its classic portico and small-paned windows looking down a flagged path between Norway spruces to the slim white steeple of the Congregational church. It was clear that the Varnum fortunes were at the ebb, but the two women did what they could to preserve a decent dignity; and Mrs. Hale, in particular, had a certain wan refinement not out of keeping with her pale old-fashioned house.

In the "best parlor," with its black horsehair and mahogany weakly illuminated by a gurgling Carcel lamp, I listened every evening to another and more delicately shaded version of the Starkfield chronicle. It was not that Mrs. Ned Hale felt, or affected, any social superiority to the people about her; it was only that the accident of a finer sensibility and a little more education had put just enough distance between herself and her neighbors to enable her to judge them with detachment. She was not unwilling to exercise this faculty, and I had great hopes of getting from her the missing facts of Ethan Frome's story, or rather such a key to his character as should coordinate the facts I knew. Her mind was a storehouse of innocuous anecdote and any question about her acquaintances brought forth a volume of detail; but on the subject of Ethan Frome I found her unexpectedly reticent. There was no hint of disapproval in her reserve; I merely felt in her an insurmountable reluctance to speak of him or his affairs, a low "Yes, I knew them both . . . it was awful . . ." seeming to be the utmost concession that her distress could make to my curiosity.

So marked was the change in her manner, such depths of sad initiation did it imply, that, with some doubts as to my delicacy, I put the case anew to my village oracle, Harmon Gow; but got for my pains only an uncomprehending grunt.

"Ruth Varnum was always as nervous as a rat; and, come to think of it, she was the first one to see 'em after they was picked up. It happened right below lawyer Varnum's, down at the bend of the Corbury road, just round the time that Ruth got engaged to Ned Hale. The young folks was all friends, and I guess she just can't bear to talk about it. She's had troubles enough of her own."

All the dwellers in Starkfield, as in more notable communities, had had troubles enough of their own to make them comparatively indifferent to those of their neighbors; and though all conceded that Ethan Frome's had been beyond the common measure, no one gave me an explanation of the look in his face which, as I persisted in thinking, neither poverty nor physical suffering could have put there. Nevertheless, I might have contented myself with the story pieced together from these hints had it not been for the provocation of Mrs. Hale's silence, and—a little later—for the accident of personal contact with the man.

On my arrival at Starkfield, Denis Eady, the rich Irish grocer, who was the proprietor of Starkfield's nearest approach to a livery stable, had entered into an agreement to send me over daily to Corbury Flats, where I had to pick up my train for the Junction. But about the middle of the winter Eady's horses fell ill of a local epidemic. The illness spread to the other Starkfield stables and for a day or two I was put to it to find a means of transport. Then Harmon Gow suggested that Ethan Frome's bay was still on his legs and that his owner might be glad to drive me over.

I stared at the suggestion. "Ethan Frome? But I've never even spoken to him. Why on earth should he put himself out for me?"

Harmon's answer surprised me still more. "I don't know as he would; but I know he wouldn't be sorry to earn a dollar."

I had been told that Frome was poor, and that the sawmill and the arid acres of his farm yielded scarcely enough to keep his household through the winter; but I had not supposed him to be in such want as Harmon's words implied, and I expressed my wonder.

"Well, matters ain't gone any too well with him," Harmon said. "When a man's been setting round like a hulk for twenty years or more, seeing things that want doing, it eats inter him, and he loses his grit. That Frome farm was always 'bout as bare's a milkpan when the cat's been round; and you know what one of them old watermills is wuth nowadays. When Ethan could sweat over 'em both from sunup to dark he kinder choked a living out of 'em; but his folks ate up most everything, even then, and I don't see how he makes out now. Fust his father got a kick, out haying, and went soft in the brain, and gave away money like Bible texts afore he died. Then his mother got queer and dragged along for years as weak as a baby; and his wife Zeena, she's always been the greatest hand at doctoring in the county. Sickness and trouble: that's what Ethan's had his plate full up with, ever since the very first helping."

The next morning, when I looked out, I saw the hollow-backed bay between the Varnum spruces, and Ethan Frome, throwing back his worn bearskin, made room for me in the sleigh at his side. After that, for a week, he drove me over every morning to Corbury Flats, and on my return in the afternoon met me again and carried me back through the icy night to Starkfield. The distance each way was barely three miles, but the old bay's pace was slow, and even with firm snow under the runners we were nearly an hour on the way. Ethan Frome drove in silence, the reins loosely held in his left hand, his brown seamed profile, under the helmet-like peak of the cap, relieved against the banks of snow like the bronze image of a hero. He never turned his face to mine, or answered, except in monosyllables, the questions I put, or such slight pleasantries as I ventured. He seemed a part of the mute melancholy landscape, an incarnation of its frozen woe, with all that was warm and sentient in him fast bound below the surface; but there was nothing unfriendly in his silence. I simply felt that he lived in a depth of moral isolation too remote for casual access, and I had the sense that his loneliness was not merely the result of his personal plight, tragic as I guessed that to be, but had in it, as Harmon Gow had hinted, the profound accumulated cold of many Starkfield winters.

Only once or twice was the distance between us bridged for a moment; and the glimpses thus gained confirmed my desire to know more. Once I happened to speak of an engineering job I had been on the previous year in Florida, and of the contrast between the winter landscape about us and that in which I had found myself the year before; and to my surprise Frome said suddenly: "Yes: I was down there once, and for a good while afterward I could call up the sight of it in winter. But now it's all snowed under."

He said no more, and I had to guess the rest from the inflection of his voice and his sharp relapse into silence.

Another day, on getting into my train at the Flats, I missed a volume of popular science—I think it was on some recent discoveries in biochemistry—which I had carried with me to read on the way. I thought no more about it till I got into the sleigh again that evening, and saw the book in Frome's hand.

"I found it after you were gone," he said.

I put the volume into my pocket and we dropped back into our usual silence; but as we began to crawl up the long hill from Corbury Flats to the Starkfield ridge I became aware in the dusk that he had turned his face to mine.

"There are things in that book that I didn't know the first word about," he said.

I wondered less at his words than at the queer note of resentment in his voice. He was evidently surprised and slightly aggrieved at his own ignorance.

"Does that sort of thing interest you?" I asked.

"It used to."

"There are one or two rather new things in the book: there have been some big strides lately in that particular line of research." I waited a moment for an answer that did not come; then I said: "If you'd like to look the book through I'd be glad to leave it with you."

He hesitated, and I had the impression that he felt himself about to yield to a stealing tide of inertia; then, "Thank you—I'll take it," he answered shortly.

I hoped that this incident might set up some more direct communication between us. Frome was so simple and straightforward that I was sure his curiosity about the book was based on a genuine interest in its subject. Such tastes and acquirements in a man of his condition made the contrast more poignant between his outer situation and his inner needs, and I hoped that the chance of giving expression to the latter might at least unseal his lips. But something in his past history, or in his present way of living, had apparently driven him too deeply into himself for any casual impulse to draw him back to his kind. At our next meeting he made no allusion to the book, and our intercourse seemed fated to remain as negative and one-sided as if there had been no break in his reserve.

Frome had been driving me over to the Flats for about a week when one morning I looked out of my window into a thick snowfall. The height of the white waves massed against the garden fence and along the wall of the church showed that the storm must have been going on all night, and that the drifts were likely to be heavy in the open. I thought it probable that my train would be delayed; but I had to be at the powerhouse for an hour or two that afternoon, and I decided, if Frome turned up, to push through to the Flats and wait there till my train came in. I don't know why I put it in the conditional, however, for I never doubted that Frome would appear. He was not the kind of man to be turned from his business by any commotion of the elements; and at the appointed hour his sleigh glided up through the snow like a stage apparition behind thickening veils of gauze.

I was getting to know him too well to express either wonder or gratitude at his keeping his appointment; but I exclaimed in surprise as I saw him turn his horse in a direction opposite to that of the Corbury road.

"The railroad's blocked by a freight train that got stuck in a drift below the Flats," he explained, as we jogged off into the stinging whiteness.

"But look here—where are you taking me, then?"

"Straight to the Junction, by the shortest way," he answered, pointing up School House Hill with his whip.

"To the Junction—in this storm? Why, it's a good ten miles!"

"The bay'll do it if you give him time. You said you had some business there this afternoon. I'll see you get there."

He said it so quietly that I could only answer: "You're doing me the biggest kind of favor."

"That's all right," he rejoined.

Abreast of the schoolhouse the road forked, and we dipped down a lane to the left, between hemlock boughs bent inward to their trunks by the weight of the snow. I had often walked that way on Sundays, and knew that the solitary roof showing through bare branches near the bottom of the hill was that of Frome's sawmill. It looked exanimate enough, with its idle wheel looming above the black stream dashed with yellow-white spume, and its cluster of sheds sagging under their white load. Frome did not even turn his head as we drove by, and still in silence we began to mount the next slope. About a mile farther, on a road I had never traveled, we came to an orchard of starved apple trees writhing over a hillside among outcroppings of slate that nuzzled up through the snow like animals pushing out their noses to breathe. Beyond the orchard lay a field or two, their boundaries lost under drifts; and above the fields, huddled against the white immensities of land and sky, one of those lonely New England farmhouses that make the landscape lonelier.

"That's my place," said Frome, with a sideway jerk of his lame elbow; and in the distress and oppression of the scene I did not know what to answer. The snow had ceased, and a flash of watery sunlight exposed the house on the slope above us in all its plaintive ugliness. The black wraith of a deciduous creeper flapped from the porch, and the thin wooden walls, under their worn coat of paint, seemed to shiver in the wind that had risen with the ceasing of the snow.

"The house was bigger in my father's time: I had to take down the 'L,' a while back," Frome continued, checking with a twitch of the left rein the bay's evident intention of turning in through the broken-down gate.

I saw then that the unusually forlorn and stunted look of the house was partly due to the loss of what is known in New England as the "L": that long deep-roofed adjunct usually built at right angles to the main house, and connecting it, by way of storerooms and toolhouse, with the woodshed and cow-barn. Whether because of its symbolic sense, the image it presents of a life linked with the soil, and enclosing in itself the chief sources of warmth and nourishment, or whether merely because of the consolatory thought that it enables the dwellers in that harsh climate to get to their morning's work without facing the weather, it is certain that the "L" rather than the house itself seems to be the center, the actual hearthstone, of the New England farm. Perhaps this connection of ideas, which had often occurred to me in my rambles about Starkfield, caused me to hear a wistful note in Frome's words, and to see in the diminished dwelling the image of his own shrunken body.

"We're kinder side-tracked here now," he added, "but there was considerable passing before the railroad was carried through to the Flats." He roused the lagging bay with another twitch; then, as if the mere sight of the house had let me too deeply into his confidence for any farther pretence of reserve, he went on slowly: "I've always set down the worst of mother's trouble to that. When she got the rheumatism so bad she couldn't move around she used to sit up there and watch the road by the hour; and one year, when they was six months mending the Bettsbridge pike after the floods, and Harmon Gow had to bring his stage round this way, she picked up so that she used to

get down to the gate most days to see him. But after the trains begun
running nobody ever come by here to speak of, and mother never
could get it through her head what had happened, and it preyed on
her right along till she died."

As we turned into the Corbury road the snow began to fall again,
cutting off our last glimpse of the house; and Frome's silence fell with
it, letting down between us the old veil of reticence. This time the
wind did not cease with the return of the snow. Instead, it sprang up
to a gale which now and then, from a tattered sky, flung pale sweeps
of sunlight over a landscape chaotically tossed. But the bay was as
good as Frome's word, and we pushed on to the Junction through
the wild white scene.

In the afternoon the storm held off, and the clearness in the west
seemed to my inexperienced eye the pledge of a fair evening. I finished
my business as quickly as possible, and we set out for Starkfield with
a good chance of getting there for supper. But at sunset the clouds
gathered again, bringing an earlier night, and the snow began to fall
straight and steadily from a sky without wind, in a soft universal
diffusion more confusing than the gusts and eddies of the morning.
It seemed to be a part of the thickening darkness, to be the winter
night itself descending on us layer by layer.

The small ray of Frome's lantern was soon lost in this smothering
medium, in which even his sense of direction, and the bay's homing
instinct, finally ceased to serve us. Two or three times some ghostly
landmark sprang up to warn us that we were astray, and then was
sucked back into the mist; and when we finally regained our road the
old horse began to show signs of exhaustion. I felt myself to blame
for having accepted Frome's offer, and after a short discussion I persuaded him to let me get out of the sleigh and walk along through
the snow at the bay's side. In this way we struggled on for another
mile or two, and at last reached a point where Frome, peering into
what seemed to me formless night, said: "That's my gate down
yonder."

The last stretch had been the hardest part of the way. The bitter
cold and heavy going had nearly knocked the wind out of me, and I
could feel the horse's side ticking like a clock under my hand.

"Look here, Frome," I began, "there's no earthly use in your going
any farther—" but he interrupted me: "Nor you neither. There's been
about enough of this for anybody."

I understood that he was offering me a night's shelter at the farm, and without answering I turned into the gate at his side, and followed him to the barn, where I helped him to unharness and bed down the tired horse. When this was done he unhooked the lantern from the sleigh, stepped out again into the night, and called to me over his shoulder: "This way."

Far off above us a square of light trembled through the screen of snow. Staggering along in Frome's wake I floundered toward it, and in the darkness almost fell into one of the deep drifts against the front of the house. Frome scrambled up the slippery steps of the porch, digging a way through the snow with his heavily booted foot. Then he lifted his lantern, found the latch, and led the way into the house. I went after him into a low unlit passage, at the back of which a ladder-like staircase rose into obscurity. On our right a line of light marked the door of the room which had sent its ray across the night; and behind the door I heard a woman's voice droning querulously.

Frome stamped on the worn oilcloth to shake the snow from his boots, and set down his lantern on a kitchen chair which was the only piece of furniture in the hall. Then he opened the door.

"Come in," he said; and as he spoke the droning voice grew still . . .

It was that night that I found the clue to Ethan Frome, and began to put together this vision of his story . . . .
. . . .
. . . .

I

The village lay under two feet of snow, with drifts at the windy corners. In a sky of iron the points of the Dipper hung like icicles and Orion flashed his cold fires. The moon had set, but the night was so transparent that the white house-fronts between the elms looked gray against the snow, clumps of bushes made black stains on it, and the basement windows of the church sent shafts of yellow light far across the endless undulations.

Young Ethan Frome walked at a quick pace along the deserted street, past the bank and Michael Eady's new brick store and lawyer

Varnum's house with the two black Norway spruces at the gate. Opposite the Varnum gate, where the road fell away toward the Corbury valley, the church reared its slim white steeple and narrow peristyle. As the young man walked toward it the upper windows drew a black arcade along the side wall of the building, but from the lower openings, on the side where the ground sloped steeply down to the Corbury road, the light shot its long bars, illuminating many fresh furrows in the track leading to the basement door, and showing, under an adjoining shed, a line of sleighs with heavily blanketed horses.

The night was perfectly still, and the air so dry and pure that it gave little sensation of cold. The effect produced on Frome was rather of a complete absence of atmosphere, as though nothing less tenuous than ether intervened between the white earth under his feet and the metallic dome overhead. "It's like being in an exhausted receiver," he thought. Four or five years earlier he had taken a year's course at a technological college at Worcester, and dabbled in the laboratory with a friendly professor of physics; and the images supplied by that experience still cropped up, at unexpected moments, through the totally different associations of thought in which he had since been living. His father's death, and the misfortunes following it, had put a premature end to Ethan's studies; but though they had not gone far enough to be of much practical use they had fed his fancy and made him aware of huge cloudy meanings behind the daily face of things.

As he strode along through the snow the sense of such meanings glowed in his brain and mingled with the bodily flush produced by his sharp tramp. At the end of the village he passed before the darkened front of the church. He stood there a moment, breathing quickly, and looking up and down the street, in which not another figure moved. The pitch of the Corbury road, below lawyer Varnum's spruces, was the favorite coasting-ground of Starkfield, and on clear evenings the church corner rang till late with the shouts of the coasters; but tonight not a sled darkened the whiteness of the long declivity. The hush of midnight lay on the village, and all its waking life was gathered behind the church windows, from which strains of dance music flowed with the broad bands of yellow light.

The young man, skirting the side of the building, went down the slope toward the basement door. To keep out of range of the revealing rays from within he made a circuit through the untrodden snow and gradually approached the farther angle of the basement wall. Thence, still hugging the shadow, he edged his way cautiously forward to the nearest window, holding back his straight spare body and craning his neck till he got a glimpse of the room.

Seen thus, from the pure and frosty darkness in which he stood, it seemed to be seething in a mist of heat. The metal reflectors of the gas-jets sent crude waves of light against the whitewashed walls, and the iron flanks of the stove at the end of the hall looked as though they were heaving with volcanic fires. The floor was thronged with girls and young men. Down the side wall facing the window stood a row of kitchen chairs from which the older women had just risen. By this time the music had stopped, and the musicians—a fiddler, and the young lady who played the harmonium on Sundays—were hastily refreshing themselves at one corner of the supper table which aligned its devastated pie-dishes and ice-cream saucers on the platform at the end of the hall. The guests were preparing to leave, and the tide had already set toward the passage where coats and wraps were hung, when a young man with a sprightly foot and a shock of black hair shot into the middle of the floor and clapped his hands. The signal took instant effect. The musicians hurried to their instruments, the dancers—some already half-muffled for departure—fell into line down each side of the room, the older spectators slipped back to their chairs, and the lively young man, after diving about here and there in the throng, drew forth a girl who had already wound a cherry-colored "fascinator" about her head, and leading her up to the end of the floor, whirled her down its length to the bounding tune of a Virginia reel.

Frome's heart was beating fast. He had been straining for a glimpse of the dark head under the cherry-colored scarf and it vexed him that another eye should have been quicker than his. The leader of the reel, who looked as if he had Irish blood in his veins, danced well, and his partner caught his fire. As she passed down the line, her light figure swinging from hand to hand in circles of increasing swiftness, the scarf flew off her head and stood out behind her shoulders, and Frome, at each turn, caught sight of her laughing panting lips, the cloud of dark hair about her forehead, and the dark eyes which seemed the only fixed points in a maze of flying lines.

The dancers were going faster and faster, and the musicians, to keep up with them, belabored their instruments like jockeys lashing their mounts on the homestretch; yet it seemed to the young man at the window that the reel would never end. Now and then he turned his eyes from the girl's face to that of her partner, which, in the exhilaration of the dance, had taken on a look of almost impudent ownership. Denis Eady was the son of Michael Eady, the ambitious Irish grocer, whose suppleness and effrontery had given Starkfield its first notion of "smart" business methods, and whose new brick store testified to the success of the attempt. His son seemed likely to follow in his steps, and was meanwhile applying the same arts to the conquest of the Starkfield maidenhood. Hitherto Ethan Frome had been content to think him a mean fellow; but now he positively invited a horsewhipping. It was strange that the girl did not seem aware of it: that she could lift her rapt face to her dancer's, and drop her hands into his, without appearing to feel the offense of his look and touch.

Frome was in the habit of walking into Starkfield to fetch home his wife's cousin, Mattie Silver, on the rare evenings when some chance of amusement drew her to the village. It was his wife who had suggested, when the girl came to live with them, that such opportunities should be put in her way. Mattie Silver came from Stamford, and when she entered the Fromes' household to act as her cousin Zeena's aid it was thought best, as she came without pay, not to let her feel too sharp a contrast between the life she had left and the isolation of a Starkfield farm. But for this—as Frome sardonically reflected—it would hardly have occurred to Zeena to take any thought for the girl's amusement.

When his wife first proposed that they should give Mattie an occasional evening out he had inwardly demurred at having to do the extra two miles to the village and back after his hard day on the farm; but not long afterward he had reached the point of wishing that Starkfield might give all its nights to revelry.

Mattie Silver had lived under his roof for a year, and from early morning till they met at supper he had frequent chances of seeing her; but no moments in her company were comparable to those when, her arm in his, and her light step flying to keep time with his long stride, they walked back through the night to the farm. He had taken to the girl from the first day, when he had driven over to the Flats to meet her, and she had smiled and waved to him from the train, crying out "You must be Ethan!" as she jumped down with her bundles, while he reflected, looking over her slight person: "She don't look much on housework, but she ain't a fretter, anyhow." But it was not only that the coming to his house of a bit of hopeful young life was like the lighting of a fire on a cold hearth. The girl was more than the bright serviceable creature he had thought her. She had an eye to see and an ear to hear: he could show her things and tell her things, and taste the bliss of feeling that all he imparted left long reverberations and echoes he could wake at will.

It was during their night walks back to the farm that he felt most intensely the sweetness of this communion. He had always been more sensitive than the people about him to the appeal of natural beauty. His unfinished studies had given form to this sensibility and even in his unhappiest moments field and sky spoke to him with a deep and powerful persuasion. But hitherto the emotion had remained in him as a silent ache, veiling with sadness the beauty that evoked it. He did not even know whether any one else in the world felt as he did, or whether he was the sole victim of this mournful privilege. Then he learned that one other spirit had trembled with the same touch of wonder: that at his side, living under his roof and eating his bread, was a creature to whom he could say: "That's Orion down yonder; the big fellow to the right is Aldebaran, and the bunch of little ones— like bees swarming—they're the Pleiades . . ." or whom he could hold entranced before a ledge of granite thrusting up through the fern while he unrolled the huge panorama of the ice age, and the long dim stretches of succeeding time. The fact that admiration for his learning mingled with Mattie's wonder at what he taught was not the least part of his pleasure. And there were other sensations, less definable but more exquisite, which drew them together with a shock of silent joy: the cold red of sunset behind winter hills, the flight of cloud-flocks over slopes of golden stubble, or the intensely blue shadows of hemlocks on sunlit snow. When she said to him once: "It looks just as if it was painted!" it seemed to Ethan that the art of definition could go no farther, and that words had at last been found to utter his secret soul. . . .

As he stood in the darkness outside the church these memories came back with the poignancy of vanished things. Watching Mattie whirl down the floor from hand to hand he wondered how he could ever have thought that his dull talk interested her. To him, who was never gay but in her presence, her gaiety seemed plain proof of in-difference. The face she lifted to her dancers was the same which, when she saw him, always looked like a window that has caught the sunset. He even noticed two or three gestures which, in his fatuity, he had thought she kept for him: a way of throwing her head back when she was amused, as if to taste her laugh before she let it out, and a trick of sinking her lids slowly when anything charmed or moved her.

The sight made him unhappy, and his unhappiness roused his latent fears. His wife had never shown any jealousy of Mattie, but of late she had grumbled increasingly over the housework and found oblique ways of attracting attention to the girl's inefficiency. Zeena had always been what Starkfield called "sickly," and Frome had to admit that, if she were as ailing as she believed, she needed the help of a stronger arm than the one which lay so lightly in his during the night walks to the farm. Mattie had no natural turn for housekeeping, and her training had done nothing to remedy the defect. She was quick to learn, but forgetful and dreamy, and not disposed to take the matter seriously. Ethan had an idea that if she were to marry a man she was fond of the dormant instinct would wake, and her pies and biscuits become the pride of the county; but domesticity in the abstract did not interest her. At first she was so awkward that he could not help laughing at her; but she laughed with him and that made them better friends. He did his best to supplement her unskilled efforts, getting up earlier than usual to light the kitchen fire, carrying in the wood overnight, and neglecting the mill for the farm that he might help her about the house during the day. He even crept down on Saturday nights to scrub the kitchen floor after the women had gone to bed; and Zeena, one day, had surprised him at the churn and had turned away silently, with one of her queer looks.

Of late there had been other signs of her disfavor, as intangible but more disquieting. One cold winter morning, as he dressed in the dark, his candle flickering in the draught of the ill-fitting window, he had heard her speak from the bed behind him.

"The doctor don't want I should be left without anybody to do for me," she said in her flat whine.

He had supposed her to be asleep, and the sound of her voice had startled him, though she was given to abrupt explosions of speech after long intervals of secretive silence.

He turned and looked at her where she lay indistinctly outlined under the dark calico quilt, her high-boned face taking a grayish tinge from the whiteness of the pillow.

"Nobody to do for you?" he repeated.

"If you say you can't afford a hired girl when Mattie goes."

Frome turned away again, and taking up his razor stooped to catch the reflection of his stretched cheek in the blotched looking-glass above the washstand.

"Why on earth should Mattie go?"

"Well, when she gets married, I mean," his wife's drawl came from behind him.

"Oh, she'd never leave us as long as you needed her," he returned, scraping hard at his chin.

"I wouldn't ever have it said that I stood in the way of a poor girl like Mattie marrying a smart fellow like Denis Eady," Zeena answered in a tone of plaintive self-effacement.

Ethan, glaring at his face in the glass, threw his head back to draw the razor from ear to chin. His hand was steady, but the attitude was an excuse for not making an immediate reply.

"And the doctor don't want I should be left without anybody," Zeena continued. "He wanted I should speak to you about a girl he's heard about, that might come—"

Ethan laid down the razor and straightened himself with a laugh.

"Denis Eady! If that's all I guess there's no such hurry to look round for a girl."

"Well, I'd like to talk to you about it," said Zeena obstinately.

He was getting into his clothes in fumbling haste. "All right. But I haven't got the time now; I'm late as it is," he returned, holding his old silver turnip-watch to the candle.

Zeena, apparently accepting this as final, lay watching him in silence while he pulled his suspenders over his shoulders and jerked his arms into his coat; but as he went toward the door she said, suddenly and incisively: "I guess you're always late, now you shave every morning."

That thrust had frightened him more than any vague insinuations about Denis Eady. It was a fact that since Mattie Silver's coming he had taken to shaving every day; but his wife always seemed to be asleep when he left her side in the winter darkness, and he had stupidly assumed that she would not notice any change in his appearance. Once or twice in the past he had been faintly disquieted by Zenobia's way of letting things happen without seeming to remark them, and then, weeks afterward, in a casual phrase, revealing that she had all along taken her notes and drawn her inferences. Of late, however, there had been no room in his thoughts for such vague apprehensions. Zeena herself, from an oppressive reality, had faded into an insubstantial shade. All his life was lived in the sight and sound of Mattie Silver, and he could no longer conceive of its being otherwise. But now, as he stood outside the church, and saw Mattie spinning down the floor with Denis Eady, a throng of disregarded hints and menaces wove their cloud about his brain . . .

II

As the dancers poured out of the hall Frome, drawing back behind the projecting storm door, watched the segregation of the grotesquely muffled groups, in which a moving lantern ray now and then lit up a face flushed with food and dancing. The villagers, being afoot, were the first to climb the slope to the main street, while the country neighbors packed themselves more slowly into the sleighs under the shed.

"Ain't you riding, Mattie?" a woman's voice called back from the throng about the shed, and Ethan's heart gave a jump. From where he stood he could not see the persons coming out of the hall till they had advanced a few steps beyond the wooden sides of the storm door; but through its cracks he heard a clear voice answer: "Mercy no! Not on such a night."

She was there, then, close to him, only a thin board between. In another moment she would step forth into the night, and his eyes, accustomed to the obscurity, would discern her as clearly as though she stood in daylight. A wave of shyness pulled him back into the dark angle of the wall, and he stood there in silence instead of making his presence known to her. It had been one of the wonders of their intercourse that from the first, she, the quicker, finer, more expressive, instead of crushing him by the contrast, had given him something of her own ease and freedom; but now he felt as heavy and loutish as in his student days, when he had tried to "jolly" the Worcester girls at a picnic.

He hung back, and she came out alone and paused within a few yards of him. She was almost the last to leave the hall, and she stood looking uncertainly about her as if wondering why he did not show himself. Then a man's figure approached, coming so close to her that under their formless wrappings they seemed merged in one dim outline.

"Gentleman friend gone back on you? Say, Matt, that's tough! No, I wouldn't be mean enough to tell the other girls. I ain't as low-down as that." (How Frome hated his cheap banter!) "But look at here, ain't it lucky I got the old man's cutter down there waiting for us?"

Frome heard the girl's voice, gaily incredulous: "What on earth's your father's cutter doin' down there?"

'Why, waiting for me to take a ride. I got the roan colt too. I kinder knew I'd want to take a ride tonight," Eady, in his triumph, tried to put a sentimental note into his bragging voice.

The girl seemed to waver, and Frome saw her twirl the end of her scarf irresolutely about her fingers. Not for the world would he have made a sign to her, though it seemed to him that his life hung on her next gesture.

"Hold on a minute while I unhitch the colt," Denis called to her, springing toward the shed.

She stood perfectly still, looking after him, in an attitude of tranquil expectancy torturing to the hidden watcher. Frome noticed that she no longer turned her head from side to side, as though peering through the night for another figure. She let Denis Eady lead out the horse, climb into the cutter and fling back the bearskin to make room for her at his side; then, with a swift motion of flight, she turned about and darted up the slope toward the front of the church.

"Good-bye! Hope you'll have a lovely ride!" she called back to him over her shoulder.

Denis laughed, and gave the horse a cut that brought him quickly abreast of her retreating figure.

"Come along! Get in quick! It's as slippery as thunder on this turn," he cried, leaning over to reach out a hand to her.

She laughed back at him: "Good night! I'm not getting in."

By this time they had passed beyond Frome's earshot and he could only follow the shadowy pantomime of their silhouettes as they continued to move along the crest of the slope above him. He saw Eady, after a moment, jump from the cutter and go toward the girl with the reins over one arm. The other he tried to slip through hers; but she eluded him nimbly, and Frome's heart, which had swung out over a black void, trembled back to safety. A moment later he heard the jingle of departing sleigh bells and discerned a figure advancing alone toward the empty expanse of snow before the church.

In the black shade of the Varnum spruces he caught up with her and she turned with a quick "Oh!"

"Think I'd forgotten you, Matt?" he asked with sheepish glee.

She answered seriously: "I thought maybe you couldn't come back for me."

"Couldn't? What on earth could stop me?"

"I knew Zeena wasn't feeling any too good today."

"Oh, she's in bed long ago." He paused, a question struggling in him. "Then you meant to walk home all alone?"

"Oh, I ain't afraid!" she laughed.

They stood together in the gloom of the spruces, an empty world glimmering about them wide and gray under the stars. He brought his question out.

"If you thought I hadn't come, why didn't you ride back with Denis Eady?"

"Why, where *were* you? How did you know? I never saw you!"

Her wonder and his laughter ran together like spring rills in a thaw. Ethan had the sense of having done something arch and ingenious. To prolong the effect he groped for a dazzling phrase, and brought out, in a growl of rapture: "Come along."

He slipped an arm through hers, as Eady had done, and fancied it was faintly pressed against her side; but neither of them moved. It was so dark under the spruces that he could barely see the shape of her head beside his shoulder. He longed to stoop his cheek and rub it against her scarf. He would have liked to stand there with her all night in the blackness. She moved forward a step or two and then paused again above the dip of the Corbury road. Its icy slope, scored by innumerable runners, looked like a mirror scratched by travelers at an inn.

"There was a whole lot of them coasting before the moon set," she said.

"Would you like to come in and coast with them some night?" he asked.

"Oh, *would* you, Ethan? It would be lovely!"

"We'll come tomorrow if there's a moon."

She lingered, pressing closer to his side. "Ned Hale and Ruth Varnum came just as *near* running into the big elm at the bottom.

We were all sure they were killed." Her shiver ran down his arm.
"Wouldn't it have been too awful? They're so happy!"

"Oh, Ned ain't much at steering. I guess I can take you down all
right!" he said disdainfully.

He was aware that he was "talking big," like Denis Eady; but his
reaction of joy had unsteadied him, and the inflection with which she
had said of the engaged couple "They're so happy!" made the words
sound as if she had been thinking of herself and him.

"The elm *is* dangerous, though. It ought to be cut down," she
insisted.

"Would you be afraid of it, with me?"

"I told you I ain't the kind to be afraid," she tossed back, almost
indifferently; and suddenly she began to walk on with a rapid step.

These alterations of mood were the despair and joy of Ethan
Frome. The motions of her mind were as incalculable as the flit of a
bird in the branches. The fact that he had no right to show his feelings, and thus provoke the expression of hers, made him attach a
fantastic importance to every change in her look and tone. Now he
thought she understood him, and feared; now he was sure she did
not, and despaired. Tonight the pressure of accumulated misgivings
sent the scale drooping toward despair, and her indifference was the
more chilling after the flush of joy into which she had plunged him
by dismissing Denis Eady. He mounted School House Hill at her side
and walked on in silence till they reached the lane leading to the sawmill; then the need of some definite assurance grew too strong for
him.

"You'd have found me right off if you hadn't gone back to have
that last reel with Denis," he brought out awkwardly. He could not
pronounce the name without a stiffening of the muscles of his throat.

"Why, Ethan, how could I tell you were there?"

"I suppose what folks say is true," he jerked out at her, instead of
answering.

She stopped short, and he felt, in the darkness, that her face was
lifted quickly to his. "Why, what do folks say?"

"It's natural enough you should be leaving us," he floundered on,
following his thought.

"Is that what they say?" she mocked back at him; then, with a
sudden drop of her sweet treble: "You mean that Zeena—ain't suited
with me any more?" she faltered.

Their arms had slipped apart and they stood motionless, each seeking to distinguish the other's face.

"I know I ain't anything like as smart as I ought to be," she went on, while he vainly struggled for expression. "There's lots of things a hired girl could do that come awkward to me still—and I haven't got much strength in my arms. But if she'd only tell me I'd try. You know she hardly ever says anything, and sometimes I can see she ain't suited, and yet I don't know why." She turned on him with a sudden flash of indignation. "You'd ought to tell me, Ethan Frome—you'd ought to! Unless *you* want me to go too—"

Unless he wanted her to go too! The cry was balm to his raw wound. The iron heavens seemed to melt and rain down sweetness. Again he struggled for the all-expressive word, and again, his arm in hers, found only a deep "Come along."

They walked on in silence through the blackness of the hemlock-shaded lane, where Ethan's sawmill gloomed through the night, and out again into the comparative clearness of the fields. On the farther side of the hemlock belt the open country rolled away before them gray and lonely under the stars. Sometimes their way led them under the shade of an overhanging bank or through the thin obscurity of a clump of leafless trees. Here and there a farmhouse stood far back among the fields, mute and cold as a gravestone. The night was so still that they heard the frozen snow crackle under their feet. The crash of a loaded branch falling far off in the woods reverberated like a musket shot, and once a fox barked, and Mattie shrank closer to Ethan, and quickened her steps.

At length they sighted the group of larches at Ethan's gate, and as they drew near it the sense that the walk was over brought back his words.

"Then you don't want to leave us, Matt?"

He had to stoop his head to catch her stifled whisper: "Where'd I go, if I did?"

The answer sent a pang through him but the tone suffused him with joy. He forgot what else he had meant to say and pressed her against him so closely that he seemed to feel her warmth in his veins.

"You ain't crying are you, Matt?"

"No, of course I'm not," she quavered.

They turned in at the gate and passed under the shaded knoll where, enclosed in a low fence, the Frome gravestones slanted at crazy angles through the snow. Ethan looked at them curiously. For years that quiet company had mocked his restlessness, his desire for change and freedom. "We never got away—how should you?" seemed to be written on every headstone; and whenever he went in or out of his gate he thought with a shiver: "I shall just go on living here till I join them." But now all desire for change had vanished, and the sight of the little enclosure gave him a warm sense of continuance and stability.

"I guess we'll never let you go, Matt," he whispered, as though even the dead, lovers once, must conspire with him to keep her; and brushing by the graves, he thought: "We'll always go on living here together, and some day she'll lie there beside me."

He let the vision possess him as they climbed the hill to the house. He was never so happy with her as when he abandoned himself to these dreams. Halfway up the slope Mattie stumbled against some unseen obstruction and clutched his sleeve to steady herself. The wave of warmth that went through him was like the prolongation of his vision. For the first time he stole his arm about her, and she did not resist. They walked on as if they were floating on a summer stream.

Zeena always went to bed as soon as she had had her supper, and the shutterless windows of the house were dark. A dead cucumber-vine dangled from the porch like the crape streamer tied to the door for a death, and the thought flashed through Ethan's brain: "If it was there for Zeena—" Then he had a distinct sight of his wife lying in their bedroom asleep, her mouth slightly open, her false teeth in a tumbler by the bed . . .

They walked around to the back of the house, between the rigid gooseberry bushes. It was Zeena's habit, when they came back late from the village, to leave the key of the kitchen door under the mat. Ethan stood before the door, his head heavy with dreams, his arm still about Mattie. "Matt—" he began, not knowing what he meant to say.

She slipped out of his hold without speaking, and he stooped down and felt for the key.

"It's not there!" he said, straightening himself with a start.

They strained their eyes at each other through the icy darkness. Such a thing had never happened before.

"Maybe she's forgotten it," Mattie said in a tremulous whisper; but both of them knew that it was not like Zeena to forget.

"It might have fallen off into the snow," Mattie continued, after a pause during which they had stood intently listening.

"It must have been pushed off, then," he rejoined in the same tone. Another wild thought tore through him. What if tramps had been there—what if . . .

Again he listened, fancying he heard a distant sound in the house; then he felt in his pocket for a match, and kneeling down, passed its light slowly over the rough edges of snow about the doorstep.

He was still kneeling when his eyes, on a level with the lower panel of the door, caught a faint ray beneath it. Who could be stirring in that silent house? He heard a step on the stairs, and again for an instant the thought of tramps tore through him. Then the door opened and he saw his wife.

Against the dark background of the kitchen she stood up tall and angular, one hand drawing a quilted counterpane to her flat breast, while the other held a lamp. The light, on a level with her chin, drew out of the darkness her puckered throat and the projecting wrist of the hand that clutched the quilt, and deepened fantastically the hollows and prominences of her high-boned face under its ring of crimping pins. To Ethan, still in the rosy haze of his hour with Mattie, the sight came with the intense precision of the last dream before waking. He felt as if he had never before known what his wife looked like.

She drew aside without speaking, and Mattie and Ethan passed into the kitchen, which had the deadly chill of a vault after the dry cold of the night.

"Guess you forgot about us, Zeena," Ethan joked, stamping the snow from his boots.

"No. I just felt so mean I couldn't sleep."

Mattie came forward, unwinding her wraps, the color of the cherry scarf in her fresh lips and cheeks. "I'm so sorry, Zeena! Isn't there anything I can do?"

"No; there's nothing." Zeena turned away from her. "You might 'a' shook off that snow outside," she said to her husband.

She walked out of the kitchen ahead of them and pausing in the hall raised the lamp at arm's length, as if to light them up the stairs.

Ethan paused also, affecting to fumble for the peg on which he hung his coat and cap. The doors of the two bedrooms faced each other across the narrow upper landing, and tonight it was peculiarly repugnant to him that Mattie should see him follow Zeena.

"I guess I won't come up yet awhile," he said, turning as if to go back to the kitchen.

Zeena stopped short and looked at him. "For the land's sake—what you going to do down here?"

"I've got the mill accounts to go over."

She continued to stare at him, the flame of the unshaded lamp bringing out with microscopic cruelty the fretful lines of her face.

"At this time o' night? You'll ketch your death. The fire's out long ago."

Without answering he moved away toward the kitchen. As he did so his glance crossed Mattie's and he fancied that a fugitive warning gleamed through her lashes. The next moment they sank to her flushed cheeks and she began to mount the stairs ahead of Zeena.

"That's so. It *is* powerful cold down here," Ethan assented; and with lowered head he went up in his wife's wake, and followed her across the threshold of their room.

III

There was some hauling to be done at the lower end of the wood lot, and Ethan was out early the next day.

The winter morning was as clear as crystal. The sunrise burned red in a pure sky, the shadows on the rim of the woodlot were darkly blue, and beyond the white and scintillating fields patches of far-off forest hung like smoke.

It was in the early morning stillness, when his muscles were swinging to their familiar task and his lungs expanding with long draughts of mountain air, that Ethan did his clearest thinking. He and Zeena had not exchanged a word after the door of their room had closed on them. She had measured out some drops from a medicine bottle on a chair by the bed and, after swallowing them, and wrapping her head in a piece of yellow flannel, had lain down with her face turned away. Ethan undressed hurriedly and blew out the light so that he should not see her when he took his place at her side. As he lay there he could hear Mattie moving about in her room, and her candle, sending its small ray across the landing, drew a scarcely perceptible line of light under his door. He kept his eyes fixed on the light till it vanished. Then the room grew perfectly black, and not a sound was audible but Zeena's asthmatic breathing. Ethan felt confusedly that there were many things he ought to think about, but through his tingling veins and tired brain only one sensation throbbed: the warmth of Mattie's shoulder against his. Why had he not kissed her when he held her there? A few hours earlier he would not have asked himself the question. Even a few minutes earlier, when they had stood alone outside the house, he would not have dared to think of kissing her. But since he had seen her lips in the lamplight he felt that they were his.

Now, in the bright morning air, her face was still before him. It was part of the sun's red and of the pure glitter on the snow. How the girl had changed since she had come to Starkfield! He remembered what a colorless slip of a thing she had looked the day he had met her at the station. And all the first winter, how she had shivered with cold when the northerly gales shook the thin clapboards and the snow beat like hail against the loose-hung windows!

He had been afraid that she would hate the hard life, the cold and loneliness; but not a sign of discontent escaped her. Zeena took the view that Mattie was bound to make the best of Starkfield since she hadn't any other place to go to; but this did not strike Ethan as conclusive. Zeena, at any rate, did not apply the principle in her own case.

He felt all the more sorry for the girl because misfortune had, in a sense, indentured her to them. Mattie Silver was the daughter of a cousin of Zenobia Frome's, who had inflamed his clan with mingled sentiments of envy and admiration by descending from the hills to Connecticut, where he had married a Stamford girl and succeeded to her father's thriving "drug" business. Unhappily Orin Silver, a man of far-reaching aims, had died too soon to prove that the end justifies the means. His accounts revealed merely what the means had been; and these were such that it was fortunate for his wife and daughter that his books were examined only after his impressive funeral. His wife died of the disclosure, and Mattie, at twenty, was left alone to make her way on the fifty dollars obtained from the sale of her piano. For this purpose her equipment, though varied, was inadequate. She could trim a hat, make molasses candy, recite "Curfew shall not ring tonight," and play "The Lost Chord" and a pot-pourri from "Carmen." When she tried to extend the field of her activities in the direction of stenography and bookkeeping her health broke down, and six months on her feet behind the counter of a department store did not tend to restore it. Her nearest relations had been induced to place their savings in her father's hands, and though, after his death, they ungrudgingly acquitted themselves of the Christian duty of returning good for evil by giving his daughter all the advice at their disposal, they could hardly be expected to supplement it by material aid. But when Zenobia's doctor recommended her looking about for some one to help her with the housework the clan instantly saw the chance of exacting a compensation from Mattie. Zenobia, though doubtful of the girl's efficiency, was tempted by the freedom to find fault without much risk of losing her; and so Mattie came to Starkfield.

Zenobia's fault-finding was of the silent kind, but not the less penetrating for that. During the first months Ethan alternately burned with the desire to see Mattie defy her and trembled with fear of the result. Then the situation grew less strained. The pure air, and the long summer hours in the open, gave back life and elasticity to Mattie, and Zeena, with more leisure to devote to her complex ailments, grew less watchful of the girl's omissions; so that Ethan, struggling on under the burden of his barren farm and failing sawmill, could at least imagine that peace reigned in his house.

There was really, even now, no tangible evidence to the contrary; but since the previous night a vague dread had hung on his skyline. It was formed of Zeena's obstinate silence, of Mattie's sudden look of warning, of the memory of just such fleeting imperceptible signs as those which told him, on certain stainless mornings, that before night there would be rain.

His dread was so strong that, man-like, he sought to postpone certainty. The hauling was not over till midday, and as the lumber was to be delivered to Andrew Hale, the Starkfield builder, it was really easier for Ethan to send Jotham Powell, the hired man, back to the farm on foot, and drive the load down to the village himself. He had scrambled up on the logs, and was sitting astride of them, close over his shaggy grays, when, coming between him and their steaming necks, he had a vision of the warning look that Mattie had given him the night before.

"If there's going to be any trouble I want to be there," was his vague reflection, as he threw to Jotham the unexpected order to unhitch the team and lead them back to the barn.

It was a slow trudge home through the heavy fields, and when the two men entered the kitchen Mattie was lifting the coffee from the stove and Zeena was already at the table. Her husband stopped short at sight of her. Instead of her usual calico wrapper and knitted shawl she wore her best dress of brown merino, and above her thin strands of hair, which still preserved the tight undulations of the crimping pins, rose a hard perpendicular bonnet, as to which Ethan's clearest notion was that he had to pay five dollars for it at the Bettsbridge Emporium. On the floor beside her stood his old valise and a bandbox wrapped in newspapers.

"Why, where are you going, Zeena?" he exclaimed.

"I've got my shooting pains so bad that I'm going over to Betts- bridge to spend the night with Aunt Martha Pierce and see that new doctor," she answered in a matter-of-fact tone, as if she had said she was going into the storeroom to take a look at the preserves, or up to the attic to go over the blankets.

In spite of her sedentary habits such abrupt decisions were not without precedent in Zeena's history. Twice or thrice before she had suddenly packed Ethan's valise and started off to Bettsbridge, or even Springfield, to seek the advice of some new doctor, and her husband had grown to dread these expeditions because of their cost. Zeena always came back laden with expensive remedies, and her last visit to Springfield had been commemorated by her paying twenty dollars for an electric battery of which she had never been able to learn the use. But for the moment his sense of relief was so great as to preclude all other feelings. He had now no doubt that Zeena had spoken the truth in saying, the night before, that she had sat up because she felt "too mean" to sleep: her abrupt resolve to seek medical advice showed that, as usual, she was wholly absorbed in her health.

As if expecting a protest, she continued plaintively: "If you're too busy with the hauling I presume you can let Jotham Powell drive me over with the sorrel in time to ketch the train at the Flats."

Her husband hardly heard what she was saying. During the winter months there was no stage between Starkfield and Bettsbridge, and the trains which stopped at Corbury Flats were slow and infrequent. A rapid calculation showed Ethan that Zeena could not be back at the farm before the following evening. . . .

"If I'd supposed you'd 'a' made any objection to Jotham Powell's driving me over—" she began again, as though his silence had implied refusal. On the brink of departure she was always seized with a flux of words. "All I know is," she continued, "I can't go on the way I am much longer. The pains are clear away down to my ankles now, or I'd 'a' walked in to Starkfield on my own feet, sooner'n put you out, and asked Michael Eady to let me ride over on his wagon to the Flats, when he sends to meet the train that brings his groceries. I'd 'a' had two hours to wait in the station, but I'd sooner 'a' done it, even with this cold, than to have you say—"

"Of course Jotham'll drive you over," Ethan roused himself to answer. He became suddenly conscious that he was looking at Mattie while Zeena talked to him, and with an effort he turned his eyes to his wife. She sat opposite the window, and the pale light reflected from the banks of snow made her face look more than usually drawn and bloodless, sharpened the three parallel creases between ear and cheek, and drew querulous lines from her thin nose to the corners of her mouth. Though she was but seven years her husband's senior, and he was only twenty-eight, she was already an old woman.

Ethan tried to say something befitting the occasion, but there was only one thought in his mind: the fact that, for the first time since Mattie had come to live with them, Zeena was to be away for a night. He wondered if the girl were thinking of it too. . . .

He knew that Zeena must be wondering why he did not offer to drive her to the Flats and let Jotham Powell take the lumber to Starkfield, and at first he could not think of a pretext for not doing so; then he said: "I'd take you over myself, only I've got to collect the cash for the lumber."

As soon as the words were spoken he regretted them, not only because they were untrue—there being no prospect of his receiving cash payment from Hale—but also because he knew from experience the imprudence of letting Zeena think he was in funds on the eve of one of her therapeutic excursions. At the moment, however, his one desire was to avoid the long drive with her behind the ancient sorrel who never went out of a walk.

Zeena made no reply: she did not seem to hear what he had said. She had already pushed her plate aside, and was measuring out a draught from a large bottle at her elbow.

"It ain't done me a speck of good, but I guess I might as well use it up," she remarked; adding, as she pushed the empty bottle toward Mattie: "If you can get the taste out it'll do for pickles."

IV

As soon as his wife had driven off Ethan took his coat and cap from the peg. Mattie was washing up the dishes, humming one of the dance tunes of the night before. He said "So long, Matt," and she answered gaily "So long, Ethan"; and that was all.

It was warm and bright in the kitchen. The sun slanted through the south window on the girl's moving figure, on the cat dozing in a chair, and on the geraniums brought in from the doorway, where Ethan had planted them in the summer to "make a garden" for Mattie. He would have liked to linger on, watching her tidy up and then settle down to her sewing; but he wanted still more to get the hauling done and be back at the farm before night.

All the way down to the village he continued to think of his return to Mattie. The kitchen was a poor place, not "spruce" and shining as his mother had kept it in his boyhood; but it was surprising what a homelike look the mere fact of Zeena's absence gave it. And he pictured what it would be like that evening, when he and Mattie were there after supper. For the first time they would be alone together indoors, and they would sit there, one on each side of the stove, like a married couple, he in his stocking feet and smoking his pipe, she laughing and talking in that funny way she had, which was always as new to him as if he had never heard her before.

The sweetness of the picture, and the relief of knowing that his fears of "trouble" with Zeena were unfounded, sent up his spirits with a rush, and he, who was usually so silent, whistled and sang aloud as he drove through the snowy fields. There was in him a slumbering spark of sociability which the long Starkfield winters had not yet extinguished. By nature grave and inarticulate, he admired recklessness and gaiety in others and was warmed to the marrow by friendly human intercourse. At Worcester, though he had the name of keeping to himself and not being much of a hand at a good time, he had secretly gloried in being clapped on the back and hailed as "Old Ethe" or "Old Stiff"; and the cessation of such familiarities had increased the chill of his return to Starkfield.

There the silence had deepened about him year by year. Left alone, after his father's accident, to carry the burden of farm and mill, he had had no time for convivial loiterings in the village; and when his mother fell ill the loneliness of the house grew more oppressive than that of the fields. His mother had been a talker in her day, but after her "trouble" the sound of her voice was seldom heard, though she had not lost the power of speech. Sometimes, in the long winter evenings, when in desperation her son asked her why she didn't "say something," she would lift a finger and answer: "Because I'm listening"; and on stormy nights, when the loud wind was about the house, she would complain, if he spoke to her. "They're talking so out there that I can't hear you."

It was only when she drew toward her last illness, and his cousin Zenobia Pierce came over from the next valley to help him nurse her, that human speech was heard again in the house. After the mortal silence of his long imprisonment Zeena's volubility was music in his ears. He felt that he might have "gone like his mother" if the sound of a new voice had not come to steady him. Zeena seemed to understand his case at a glance. She laughed at him for not knowing the simplest sickbed duties and told him to "go right along out" and leave her to see to things. The mere fact of obeying her orders, of feeling free to go about his business again and talk with other men, restored his shaken balance and magnified his sense of what he owed her. Her efficiency shamed and dazzled him. She seemed to possess by instinct all the household wisdom that his long apprenticeship had not instilled in him. When the end came it was she who had to tell him to hitch up and go for the undertaker, and she thought it "funny" that he had not settled beforehand who was to have his mother's clothes and the sewing machine. After the funeral, when he saw her preparing to go away, he was seized with an unreasoning dread of being left alone on the farm; and before he knew what he was doing he had asked her to stay there with him. He had often thought since that it would not have happened if his mother had died in spring instead of winter . . .

When they married it was agreed that, as soon as he could straighten out the difficulties resulting from Mrs. Frome's long illness, they would sell the farm and sawmill and try their luck in a large town. Ethan's love of nature did not take the form of a taste for agriculture. He had always wanted to be an engineer, and to live in towns, where there were lectures and big libraries and "fellows doing things." A slight engineering job in Florida, put in his way during his period of study at Worcester, increased his faith in his ability as well as his eagerness to see the world; and he felt sure that, with a "smart" wife like Zeena, it would not be long before he had made himself a place in it.

Zeena's native village was slightly larger and nearer to the railway than Starkfield, and she had let her husband see from the first that life on an isolated farm was not what she had expected when she married. But purchasers were slow in coming, and while he waited for them Ethan learned the impossibility of transplanting her. She chose to look down on Starkfield, but she could not have lived in a place which looked down on her. Even Bettsbridge or Shadd's Falls would not have been sufficiently aware of her, and in the greater cities which attracted Ethan she would have suffered a complete loss of identity. And within a year of their marriage she developed the "sickliness" which had since made her notable even in a community rich in pathological instances. When she came to take care of his mother she had seemed to Ethan like the very genius of health, but he soon saw that her skill as a nurse had been acquired by the absorbed observation of her own symptoms.

Then she too fell silent. Perhaps it was the inevitable effect of life on the farm, or perhaps, as she sometimes said, it was because Ethan "never listened." The charge was not wholly unfounded. When she spoke it was only to complain, and to complain of things not in his power to remedy; and to check a tendency to impatient retort he had first formed the habit of not answering her, and finally of thinking of other things while she talked. Of late, however, since he had had reasons for observing her more closely, her silence had begun to trouble him. He recalled his mother's growing taciturnity, and wondered if Zeena were also turning "queer." Women did, he knew. Zeena, who had at her fingers' ends the pathological chart of the whole region, had cited many cases of the kind while she was nursing his mother; and he himself knew of certain lonely farmhouses in the neighborhood where stricken creatures pined, and of others where sudden tragedy had come of their presence. At times, looking at Zeena's shut face, he felt the chill of such forebodings. At other times her silence seemed deliberately assumed to conceal far-reaching intentions, mysterious conclusions drawn from suspicions and resentments impossible to guess. That supposition was even more disturbing than the other; and it was the one which had come to him the night before, when he had seen her standing in the kitchen door.

Now her departure for Bettsbridge had once more eased his mind, and all his thoughts were on the prospect of his evening with Mattie. Only one thing weighed on him, and that was his having told Zeena that he was to receive cash for the lumber. He foresaw so clearly the consequences of this imprudence that with considerable reluctance he decided to ask Andrew Hale for a small advance on his load.

When Ethan drove into Hale's yard the builder was just getting out of his sleigh.

"Hello, Ethe!" he said. "This comes handy."

Andrew Hale was a ruddy man with a big gray moustache and a stubbly double-chin unconstrained by a collar; but his scrupulously clean shirt was always fastened by a small diamond stud. This display of opulence was misleading, for though he did a fairly good business it was known that his easy-going habits and the demands of his large family frequently kept him what Starkfield called "behind." He was an old friend of Ethan's family, and his house one of the few to which Zeena occasionally went, drawn there by the fact that Mrs. Hale, in her youth, had done more "doctoring" than any other woman in Starkfield, and was still a recognized authority on symptoms and treatment.

Hale went up to the grays and patted their sweating flanks.

"Well, sir," he said, "you keep them two as if they was pets."

Ethan set about unloading the logs and when he had finished his job he pushed open the glazed door of the shed which the builder used as his office. Hale sat with his feet up on the stove, his back propped against a battered desk strewn with papers: the place, like the man, was warm, genial and untidy.

"Sit down and thaw out," he greeted Ethan.

The latter did not know how to begin, but at length he managed to bring out his request for an advance of fifty dollars. The blood rushed to his thin skin under the sting of Hale's astonishment. It was the builder's custom to pay at the end of three months, and there was no precedent between the two men for a cash settlement.

Ethan felt that if he had pleaded an urgent need Hale might have made shift to pay him; but pride, and an instinctive prudence, kept him from resorting to this argument. After his father's death it had taken time to get his head above water, and he did not want Andrew Hale, or any one else in Starkfield, to think he was going under again. Besides, he hated lying; if he wanted the money he wanted it, and it was nobody's business to ask why. He therefore made his demand with the awkwardness of a proud man who will not admit to himself that he is stooping; and he was not much surprised at Hale's refusal.

The builder refused genially, as he did everything else: he treated the matter as something in the nature of a practical joke, and wanted to know if Ethan meditating buying a grand piano or adding a "cupolo" to his house; offering, in the latter case, to give his services free of cost.

Ethan's arts were soon exhausted, and after an embarrassed pause he wished Hale good day and opened the door of the office. As he passed out the builder suddenly called after him: "See here—you ain't in a tight place, are you?"

"Not a bit," Ethan's pride retorted before his reason had time to intervene.

"Well, that's good! Because I *am*, a shade. Fact is, I was going to ask you to give me a little extra time on that payment. Business is pretty slack, to begin with, and then I'm fixing up a little house for Ned and Ruth when they're married. I'm glad to do it for 'em, but it costs." His look appealed to Ethan for sympathy. "The young people like things nice. You know how it is yourself: it's not so long ago since you fixed up your own place for Zeena."

Ethan left the grays in Hale's stable and went about some other business in the village. As he walked away the builder's last phrase lingered in his ears, and he reflected grimly that his seven years with Zeena seemed to Starkfield "not so long."

The afternoon was drawing to an end, and here and there a lighted pane spangled the cold gray dusk and made the snow look whiter. The bitter weather had driven every one indoors and Ethan had the long rural street to himself. Suddenly he heard the brisk play of sleigh bells and a cutter passed him, drawn by a free-going horse. Ethan recognized Michael Eady's roan colt, and young Denis Eady, in a handsome new fur cap, leaned forward and waved a greeting. "Hello, Ethe!" he shouted and spun on.

The cutter was going in the direction of the Frome farm, and Ethan's heart contracted as he listened to the dwindling bells. What more likely than that Denis Eady had heard of Zeena's departure for Bettsbridge, and was profiting by the opportunity to spend an hour with Mattie? Ethan was ashamed of the storm of jealousy in his breast. It seemed unworthy of the girl that his thoughts of her should be so violent.

He walked on to the church corner and entered the shade of the Varnum spruces, where he had stood with her the night before. As he passed into their gloom he saw an indistinct outline just ahead of him. At his approach it melted for an instant into two separate shapes and then conjoined again, and he heard a kiss, and a half-laughing "Oh!" provoked by the discovery of his presence. Again the outline hastily disunited and the Varnum gate slammed on one half while the other hurried on ahead of him. Ethan smiled at the discomfiture he had caused. What did it matter to Ned Hale and Ruth Varnum if they were caught kissing each other? Everybody in Starkfield knew they were engaged. It pleased Ethan to have surprised a pair of lovers on the spot where he and Mattie had stood with such a thirst for each other in their hearts; but he felt a pang at the thought that these two need not hide their happiness.

He fetched the grays from Hale's stable and started on his long climb back to the farm. The cold was less sharp than earlier in the day and a thick fleecy sky threatened snow for the morrow. Here and there a star pricked through, showing behind it a deep well of blue. In an hour or two the moon would push up over the ridge behind the farm, burn a gold-edged rent in the clouds, and then be swallowed by them. A mournful peace hung on the fields, as though they felt the relaxing grasp of the cold and stretched themselves in their long winter sleep.

Ethan's ears were alert for the jingle of sleigh bells, but not a sound broke the silence of the lonely road. As he drew near the farm he saw, through the thin screen of larches at the gate, a light twinkling in the house above him. "She's up in her room," he said to himself, "fixing herself up for supper"; and he remembered Zeena's sarcastic stare when Mattie, on the evening of her arrival, had come down to supper with smoothed hair and a ribbon at her neck.

He passed by the graves on the knoll and turned his head to glance at one of the older headstones, which had interested him deeply as a boy because it bore his name.

SACRED TO THE MEMORY OF
ETHAN FROME AND ENDURANCE HIS WIFE,
WHO DWELLED TOGETHER IN PEACE
FOR FIFTY YEARS.

He used to think that fifty years sounded like a long time to live together; but now it seemed to him that they might pass in a flash.

Then, with a sudden dart of irony, he wondered if, when their turn came, the same epitaph would be written over him and Zeena.

He opened the barn door and craned his head into the obscurity, half-fearing to discover Denis Eady's roan colt in the stall beside the sorrel. But the old horse was there alone, mumbling his crib with toothless jaws, and Ethan whistled cheerfully while he bedded down the grays and shook an extra measure of oats into their mangers. His was not a tuneful throat, but harsh melodies burst from it as he locked the barn and sprang up the hill to the house. He reached the kitchen porch and turned the door handle; but the door did not yield to his touch.

Startled at finding it locked he rattled the handle violently; then he reflected that Mattie was alone and that it was natural she should barricade herself at nightfall. He stood in the darkness expecting to hear her step. It did not come, and after vainly straining his ears he called out in a voice that shook with joy: "Hello, Matt!"

Silence answered; but in a minute or two he caught a sound on the stairs and saw a line of light about the door frame, as he had seen it the night before. So strange was the precision with which the incidents of the previous evening were repeating themselves that he half expected, when he heard the key turn, to see his wife before him on the threshold; but the door opened, and Mattie faced him.

She stood just as Zeena had stood, a lifted lamp in her hand, against the black background of the kitchen. She held the light at the same level, and it drew out with the same distinctness her slim young throat and the brown wrist no bigger than a child's. Then, striking upward, it threw a lustrous fleck on her lips, edged her eyes with velvet shade, and laid a milky whiteness above the black curve of her brows.

She wore her usual dress of darkish stuff, and there was no bow at her neck; but through her hair she had run a streak of crimson ribbon. This tribute to the unusual transformed and glorified her. She seemed to Ethan taller, fuller, more womanly in shape and motion. She stood aside, smiling silently, while he entered, and then moved away from him with something soft and flowing in her gait. She set the lamp on the table, and he saw that it was carefully laid for supper, with fresh doughnuts, stewed blueberries and his favorite pickles in a dish of gay red glass. A bright fire glowed in the stove and the cat lay stretched before it, watching the table with a drowsy eye.

Ethan was suffocated with the sense of well-being. He went out into the passage to hang up his coat and pull off his wet boots. When he came back Mattie had set the teapot on the table and the cat was rubbing itself persuasively against her ankles.

"Why, Puss! I nearly tripped over you," she cried, the laughter sparkling through her lashes.

Again Ethan felt a sudden twinge of jealousy. Could it be his coming that gave her such a kindled face?

"Well, Matt, any visitors?" he threw off, stooping down carelessly to examine the fastening of the stove.

She nodded and laughed "Yes, one," and he felt a blackness settling on his brows.

"Who was that?" he questioned, raising himself up to slant a glance at her beneath his scowl.

Her eyes danced with malice. "Why, Jotham Powell. He came in after he got back, and asked for a drop of coffee before he went down home."

The blackness lifted and light flooded Ethan's brain. "That all? Well, I hope you made out to let him have it." And after a pause he felt it right to add: "I suppose he got Zeena over to the Flats all right?"

"Oh, yes; in plenty of time."

The name threw a chill between them, and they stood a moment looking sideways at each other before Mattie said with a sly laugh: "I guess it's about time for supper."

They drew their seats up to the table, and the cat, unbidden, jumped between them into Zeena's empty chair. "Oh, Puss!" said Mattie, and they laughed again.

Ethan, a moment earlier, had felt himself on the brink of eloquence; but the mention of Zeena had paralyzed him. Mattie seemed to feel the contagion of his embarrassment, and sat with downcast lids, sipping her tea, while he feigned an insatiable appetite for doughnuts and sweet pickles. At last, after casting about for an effective opening, he took a long gulp of tea, cleared his throat, and said: "Looks as if there'd be more snow."

She feigned great interest. "Is that so? Do you suppose it'll interfere with Zeena's getting back?" She flushed red as the question escaped her, and hastily set down the cup she was lifting.

Ethan reached over for another helping of pickles. "You never can tell, this time of year, it drifts so bad on the Flats." The name had benumbed him again, and once more he felt as if Zeena were in the room between them.

"Oh, Puss, you're too greedy!" Mattie cried.

The cat, unnoticed, had crept up on muffled paws from Zeena's seat to the table, and was stealthily elongating its body in the direction of the milk jug, which stood between Ethan and Mattie. The two leaned forward at the same moment and their hands met on the handle of the jug. Mattie's hand was underneath, and Ethan kept his clasped on it a moment longer than was necessary. The cat, profiting by this unusual demonstration, tried to effect an unnoticed retreat, and in doing so backed into the pickle-dish, which fell to the floor with a crash.

Mattie, in an instant, had sprung from her chair and was down on her knees by the fragments.

"Oh, Ethan, Ethan—it's all to pieces! What will Zeena say?"

But this time his courage was up. "Well, she'll have to say it to the cat, any way!" he rejoined with a laugh, kneeling down at Mattie's side to scrape up the swimming pickles.

She lifted stricken eyes to him. "Yes, but, you see, she never meant it should be used, not even when there was company; and I had to get up on the stepladder to reach it down from the top shelf of the china closet, where she keeps it with all her best things, and of course she'll want to know why I did it—"

The case was so serious that it called forth all of Ethan's latent resolution.

"She needn't know anything about it if you keep quiet. I'll get another just like it tomorrow. Where did it come from? I'll go to Shadd's Falls for it if I have to!"

"Oh, you'll never get another even there! It was a wedding present—don't you remember? It came all the way from Philadelphia, from Zeena's aunt that married the minister. That's why she wouldn't ever use it. Oh, Ethan, Ethan, what in the world shall I do?"

She began to cry, and he felt as if every one of her tears were pouring over him like burning lead. "Don't, Matt, don't—oh, *don't!*" he implored her.

She struggled to her feet, and he rose and followed her helplessly while she spread out the pieces of glass on the kitchen dresser. It seemed to him as if the shattered fragments of their evening lay there.

"Here, give them to me," he said in a voice of sudden authority.

She drew aside, instinctively obeying his tone. "Oh, Ethan, what are you going to do?"

Without replying he gathered the pieces of glass into his broad palm and walked out of the kitchen to the passage. There he lit a candle end, opened the china closet, and, reaching his long arm up to the highest shelf, laid the pieces together with such accuracy of touch that a close inspection convinced him of the impossibility of detecting from below that the dish was broken. If he glued it together the next morning months might elapse before his wife noticed what had happened, and meanwhile he might after all be able to match the dish at Shadd's Falls or Bettsbridge. Having satisfied himself that there was no risk of immediate discovery he went back to the kitchen with a lighter step, and found Mattie disconsolately removing the last scraps of pickle from the floor.

"It's all right, Matt. Come back and finish supper," he commanded her.

Completely reassured, she shone on him through tear-hung lashes, and his soul swelled with pride as he saw how his tone subdued her. She did not even ask what he had done. Except when he was steering a big log down the mountain to his mill he had never known such a thrilling sense of mastery.

V

They finished supper, and while Mattie cleared the table Ethan went to look at the cows and then took a last turn about the house. The earth lay dark under a muffled sky and the air was so still that now and then he heard a lump of snow come thumping down from a tree far off on the edge of the woodlot.

When he returned to the kitchen Mattie had pushed up his chair to the stove and seated herself near the lamp with a bit of sewing. The scene was just as he had dreamed of it that morning. He sat down, drew his pipe from his pocket and stretched his feet to the glow. His hard day's work in the keen air made him feel at once lazy and light of mood, and he had a confused sense of being in another world, where all was warmth and harmony and time could bring no change. The only drawback to his complete well-being was the fact

that he could not see Mattie from where he sat; but he was too in-
dolent to move and after a moment he said: "Come over here and sit
by the stove."

Zeena's empty rocking chair stood facing him. Mattie rose obediently, and seated herself in it. As her young brown head detached
itself against the patchwork cushion that habitually framed his wife's
gaunt countenance, Ethan had a momentary shock. It was almost as
if the other face, the face of the superseded woman, had obliterated
that of the intruder. After a moment Mattie seemed to be affected by
the same sense of constraint. She changed her position, leaning forward to bend her head above her work, so that he saw only the fore-
shortened tip of her nose and the streak of red in her hair; then she
slipped to her feet, saying, "I can't see to sew," and went back to her
chair by the lamp.

Ethan made a pretext of getting up to replenish the stove, and when
he returned to his seat he pushed it sideways that he might get a view
of her profile and of the lamplight falling on her hands. The cat, who
had been a puzzled observer of these unusual movements, jumped up
into Zeena's chair, rolled itself into a ball, and lay watching them
with narrowed eyes.

Deep quiet sank on the room. The clock ticked above the dresser,
a piece of charred wood fell now and then in the stove, and the faint
sharp scent of the geraniums mingled with the odor of Ethan's smoke,
which began to throw a blue haze about the lamp and to hang its
grayish cobwebs in the shadowy corners of the room.

All constraint had vanished between the two, and they began to
talk easily and simply. They spoke of everyday things, of the prospect
of snow, of the next church sociable, of the loves and quarrels of
Starkfield. The commonplace nature of what they said produced in
Ethan an illusion of long-established intimacy which no outburst of
emotion could have given, and he set his imagination adrift on the
fiction that they had always spent their evenings thus and would always go on doing so . . .

"This is the night we were to have gone coasting, Matt," he said
at length, with the rich sense, as he spoke, that they could go on any
other night they chose, since they had all time before them.

She smiled back at him. "I guess you forgot!"

"No, I didn't forget; but it's as dark as Egypt outdoors. We might
go tomorrow if there's a moon."

She laughed with pleasure, her head tilted back, the lamplight sparkling on her lips and teeth. "That would be lovely, Ethan!"

He kept his eyes fixed on her, marveling at the way her face changed with each turn of their talk, like a wheat field under a summer breeze. It was intoxicating to find such magic in his clumsy words, and he longed to try new ways of using it.

"Would you be scared to go down the Corbury road with me on a night like this?" he asked.

Her cheeks burned redder. "I ain't any more scared than you are!"

"Well, *I'd* be scared, then; I wouldn't do it. That's an ugly corner down by the big elm. If a fellow didn't keep his eyes open he'd go plumb into it." He luxuriated in the sense of protection and authority which his words conveyed. To prolong and intensify the feeling he added: "I guess we're well enough here."

She let her lids sink slowly, in the way he loved. "Yes, we're well enough here," she sighed.

Her tone was so sweet that he took the pipe from his mouth and drew his chair up to the table. Leaning forward, he touched the farther end of the strip of brown stuff that she was hemming. "Say, Matt," he began with a smile, "what do you think I saw under the Varnum spruces, coming along home just now? I saw a friend of yours getting kissed."

The words had been on his tongue all the evening, but now that he had spoken them they struck him as inexpressibly vulgar and out of place.

Mattie blushed to the roots of her hair and pulled her needle rapidly twice or thrice through her work, insensibly drawing the end of it away from him. "I suppose it was Ruth and Ned," she said in a low voice, as though he had suddenly touched on something grave.

Ethan had imagined that his allusion might open the way to the accepted pleasantries, and these perhaps in turn to a harmless caress, if only a mere touch on her hand. But now he felt as if her blush had set a flaming guard about her. He supposed it was his natural awkwardness that made him feel so. He knew that most young men made nothing at all of giving a pretty girl a kiss, and he remembered that the night before, when he had put his arm about Mattie, she had not resisted. But that had been out-of-doors, under the open irresponsible night. Now, in the warm lamplit room, with all its ancient implications of conformity and order, she seemed infinitely farther away from him and more unapproachable.

To ease his constraint he said: "I suppose they'll be setting a date before long."

"Yes. I shouldn't wonder if they got married some time along in the summer." She pronounced the word *married* as if her voice caressed it. It seemed a rustling covert leading to enchanted glades. A pang shot through Ethan, and he said, twisting away from her in his chair: "It'll be your turn next, I wouldn't wonder."

She laughed a little uncertainly. "Why do you keep on saying that?"

He echoed her laugh. "I guess I do it to get used to the idea."

He drew up to the table again and she sewed on in silence, with dropped lashes, while he sat in fascinated contemplation of the way in which her hands went up and down above the strip of stuff, just as he had seen a pair of birds make short perpendicular flights over a nest they were building. At length, without turning her head or lifting her lids, she said in a low tone: "It's not because you think Zeena's got anything against me, is it?"

His former dread started up full-armed at the suggestion. "Why, what do you mean?" he stammered.

She raised distressed eyes to his, her work dropping on the table between them. "I don't know. I thought last night she seemed to have."

"I'd like to know what," he growled.

"Nobody can tell with Zeena." It was the first time they had ever spoken so openly of her attitude toward Mattie, and the repetition of the name seemed to carry it to the farther corners of the room and send it back to them in long repercussions of sound. Mattie waited, as if to give the echo time to drop, and then went on: "She hasn't said anything to *you?*"

He shook his head. "No, not a word."

She tossed the hair back from her forehead with a laugh. "I guess I'm just nervous, then. I'm not going to think about it any more."

"Oh, no—don't let's think about it, Matt!"

The sudden heat of his tone made her color mount again, not with a rush, but gradually, delicately, like the reflection of a thought stealing slowly across her heart. She sat silent, her hands clasped on her work, and it seemed to him that a warm current flowed toward him along the strip of stuff that still lay unrolled between them. Cautiously he slid his hand palm-downward along the table till his fingertips touched the end of the stuff. A faint vibration of her lashes seemed to show that she was aware of his gesture, and that it had sent a countercurrent back to her; and she let her hands lie motionless on the other end of the strip.

As they sat thus he heard a sound behind him and turned his head. The cat had jumped from Zeena's chair to dart at a mouse in the wainscot, and as a result of the sudden movement the empty chair had set up a spectral rocking.

"She'll be rocking in it herself this time tomorrow," Ethan thought. "I've been in a dream, and this is the only evening we'll ever have together." The return to reality was as painful as the return to consciousness after taking an anesthetic. His body and brain ached with indescribable weariness, and he could think of nothing to say or to do that should arrest the mad flight of the moments.

His alteration of mood seemed to have communicated itself to Mattie. She looked up at him languidly, as though her lids were weighted with sleep and it cost her an effort to raise them. Her glance fell on his hand, which now completely covered the end of her work and grasped it as if it were a part of herself. He saw a scarcely perceptible tremor cross her face, and without knowing what he did he stooped his head and kissed the bit of stuff in his hold. As his lips rested on it he felt it glide slowly from beneath them, and saw that Mattie had risen and was silently rolling up her work. She fastened it with a pin, and then, finding her thimble and scissors, put them with the roll of stuff into the box covered with fancy paper which he had once brought to her from Bettsbridge.

He stood up also, looking vaguely about the room. The clock above the dresser struck eleven.

"Is the fire all right?" she asked in a low voice.

He opened the door of the stove and poked aimlessly at the embers. When he raised himself again he saw that she was dragging toward the stove the old soapbox lined with carpet in which the cat made its bed. Then she recrossed the floor and lifted two of the geranium pots in her arms, moving them away from the cold window. He followed her and brought the other geraniums, the hyacinth bulbs in a cracked custard bowl and the German ivy trained over an old croquet hoop.

When these nightly duties were performed there was nothing left to do but to bring in the tin candlestick from the passage, light the candle and blow out the lamp. Ethan put the candlestick in Mattie's hand and she went out of the kitchen ahead of him, the light that she carried before her making her dark hair look like a drift of mist on the moon.

"Good night, Matt," he said as she put her foot on the first step of the stairs.

She turned and look at him a moment. "Good night, Ethan," she answered, and went up.

When the door of her room had closed on her he remembered that he had not even touched her hand.

VI

The next morning at breakfast Jotham Powell was between them, and Ethan tried to hide his joy under an air of exaggerated indifference, lounging back in his chair to throw scraps to the cat, growling at the weather, and not so much as offering to help Mattie when she rose to clear away the dishes.

He did not know why he was so irrationally happy, for nothing was changed in his life or hers. He had not even touched the tip of her fingers or looked her full in the eyes. But their evening together had given him a vision of what life at her side might be, and he was glad now that he had done nothing to trouble the sweetness of the picture. He had a fancy that she knew what had restrained him . . .

There was a last load of lumber to be hauled to the village, and Jotham Powell—who did not work regularly for Ethan in winter—had "come round" to help with the job. But a wet snow, melting to sleet, had fallen in the night and turned the roads to glass. There was more wet in the air and it seemed likely to both men that the weather would "milden" toward afternoon and make the going safer. Ethan therefore proposed to his assistant that they should load the sledge at the woodlot, as they had done on the previous morning, and put off the "teaming" to Starkfield till later in the day. This plan had the advantage of enabling him to send Jotham to the Flats after dinner to meet Zenobia, while he himself took the lumber down to the village.

He told Jotham to go out and harness up the grays, and for a moment he and Mattie had the kitchen to themselves. She had plunged the breakfast dishes into a tin dishpan and was bending above it with her slim arms bared to the elbow, the steam from the hot water beading her forehead and tightening her rough hair into little brown rings like the tendrils on the traveler's joy.

Ethan stood looking at her, his heart in his throat. He wanted to say: "We shall never be alone again like this." Instead, he reached down his tobacco pouch from a shelf of the dresser, put it into his pocket and said: "I guess I can make out to be home for dinner."

She answered "All right, Ethan," and he heard her singing over the dishes as he went.

As soon as the sledge was loaded he meant to send Jotham back to the farm and hurry on foot into the village to buy the glue for the pickle-dish. With ordinary luck he should have had time to carry out this plan; but everything went wrong from the start. On the way over to the woodlot one of the grays slipped on a glare of ice and cut his knee; and when they got him up again Jotham had to go back to the barn for a strip of rag to bind the cut. Then, when the loading finally began, a sleety rain was coming down once more, and the tree trunks were so slippery that it took twice as long as usual to lift them and get them in place on the sledge. It was what Jotham called a sour morning for work, and the horses, shivering and stamping under their wet blankets, seemed to like it as little as the men. It was long past the dinner hour when the job was done, and Ethan had to give up going to the village because he wanted to lead the injured horse home and wash the cut himself.

He thought that by starting out again with the lumber as soon as he had finished his dinner he might get back to the farm with the glue before Jotham and the old sorrel had had time to fetch Zenobia from the Flats; but he knew the chance was a slight one. It turned on the state of the roads and on the possible lateness of the Bettsbridge train. He remembered afterward, with a grim flash of self-derision, what importance he had attached to the weighing of these probabilities . . .

As soon as dinner was over he set out again for the woodlot, not daring to linger till Jotham Powell left. The hired man was still drying his wet feet at the stove, and Ethan could only give Mattie a quick look as he said beneath his breath: "I'll be back early."

He fancied that she nodded her comprehension; and with that scant solace he had to trudge off through the rain.

He had driven his load halfway to the village when Jotham Powell overtook him, urging the reluctant sorrel toward the Flats. "I'll have to hurry up to do it," Ethan mused, as the sleigh dropped down ahead of him over the dip of the schoolhouse hill. He worked like ten at the unloading, and when it was over hastened on to Michael Eady's for the glue. Eady and his assistant were both "down street," and young Denis, who seldom deigned to take their place, was lounging by the stove with a knot of the golden youth of Starkfield. They hailed Ethan with ironic compliments and offers of conviviality; but no one knew where to find the glue. Ethan, consumed with the longing for a last moment alone with Mattie, hung about impatiently while Denis made an ineffectual search in the obscurer corners of the store.

"Looks as if we were all sold out. But if you'll wait around till the old man comes along maybe he can put his hand on it."

"I'm obliged to you, but I'll try if I can get it down at Mrs. Homan's," Ethan answered, burning to be gone.

Denis's commercial instinct compelled him to aver on oath that what Eady's store could not produce would never be found at the widow Homan's; but Ethan, heedless of this boast, had already climbed to the sledge and was driving on to the rival establishment. Here, after considerable search, and sympathetic questions as to what he wanted it for, and whether ordinary paste flour wouldn't do as well if she couldn't find it, the widow Homan finally hunted down her solitary bottle of glue to its hiding place in a medley of cough lozenges and corset laces.

"I hope Zeena ain't broken anything she sets store by," she called after him as he turned the grays toward home.

The fitful bursts of sleet had changed into a steady rain and the horses had heavy work even without a load behind them. Once or twice, hearing sleigh bells, Ethan turned his head, fancying that Zeena and Jotham might overtake him; but the old sorrel was not in sight, and he set his face against the rain and urged on his ponderous pair.

The barn was empty when the horses turned into it and, after giving them the most perfunctory ministrations they had ever received from him, he strode up to the house and pushed open the kitchen door.

Mattie was there alone, as he had pictured her. She was bending over a pan on the stove; but at the sound of his step she turned with a start and sprang to him.

"See, here, Matt, I've got some stuff to mend the dish with! Let me get at it quick," he cried, waving the bottle in one hand while he put her lightly aside; but she did not seem to hear him.

"Oh, Ethan—Zeena's come," she said in a whisper, clutching his sleeve.

They stood and stared at each other, pale as culprits.

"But the sorrel's not in the barn!" Ethan stammered.

"Jotham Powell brought some goods over from the Flats for his wife, and he drove right on home with them," she explained.

He gazed blankly about the kitchen, which looked cold and squalid in the rainy winter twilight.

"How is she?" he asked, dropping his voice to Mattie's whisper.

She looked away from him uncertainly. "I don't know. She went right up to her room."

"She didn't say anything?"

"No."

Ethan let out his doubts in a low whistle and thrust the bottle back into his pocket. "Don't fret; I'll come down and mend it in the night," he said. He pulled on his wet coat again and went back to the barn to feed the grays.

While he was there Jotham Powell drove up with the sleigh, and when the horses had been attended to Ethan said to him: "You might as well come back up for a bite." He was not sorry to assure himself of Jotham's neutralizing presence at the supper table, for Zeena was always "nervous" after a journey. But the hired man, though seldom loth to accept a meal not included in his wages, opened his stiff jaws to answer slowly: "I'm obliged to you, but I guess I'll go along back."

Ethan looked at him in surprise. "Better come up and dry off. Looks as if there'd be something hot for supper."

Jotham's facial muscles were unmoved by this appeal and, his vocabulary being limited, he merely repeated: "I guess I'll go along back."

To Ethan there was something vaguely ominous in this stolid rejection of free food and warmth, and he wondered what had happened on the drive to nerve Jotham to such stoicism. Perhaps Zeena had failed to see the new doctor or had not liked his counsels: Ethan knew that in such cases the first person she met was likely to be held responsible for her grievance.

When he re-entered the kitchen the lamp lit up the same scene of shining comfort as on the previous evening. The table had been as carefully laid, a clear fire glowed in the stove, the cat dozed in its warmth, and Mattie came forward carrying a plate of doughnuts.

She and Ethan looked at each other in silence; then she said, as she had said the night before: "I guess it's about time for supper."

VII

Ethan went out into the passage to hang up his wet garments. He listened for Zeena's step and, not hearing it, called her name up the stairs. She did not answer, and after a moment's hesitation he went up and opened her door. The room was almost dark, but in the obscurity he saw her sitting by the window, bolt upright, and knew by the rigidity of the outline projected against the pane that she had not taken off her traveling dress.

"Well, Zeena," he ventured from the threshold.

She did not move, and he continued: "Supper's about ready. Ain't you coming?"

She replied: "I don't feel as if I could touch a morsel."

It was the consecrated formula, and he expected it to be followed, as usual, by her rising and going down to supper. But she remained seated, and he could think of nothing more felicitous than: "I presume you're tired after the long ride."

Turning her head at this, she answered solemnly: "I'm a great deal sicker than you think."

Her words fell on his ear with a strange shock of wonder. He had often heard her pronounce them before—what if at last they were true?

He advanced a step or two into the dim room. "I hope that's not so, Zeena," he said.

She continued to gaze at him through the twilight with a mien of wan authority, as of one consciously singled out for a great fate. "I've got complications," she said.

Ethan knew the word for one of exceptional import. Almost everybody in the neighborhood had "troubles," frankly localized and specified; but only the chosen had "complications." To have them was in itself a distinction, though it was also, in most cases, a death warrant. People struggled on for years with "troubles," but they almost always succumbed to "complications."

Ethan's heart was jerking to and fro between two extremities of feeling, but for the moment compassion prevailed. His wife looked so hard and lonely, sitting there in the darkness with such thoughts.

"Is that what the new doctor told you?" he asked, instinctively lowering his voice.

"Yes. He says any regular doctor would want me to have an operation."

Ethan was aware that, in regard to the important question of surgical intervention, the female opinion of the neighborhood was divided, some glorying in the prestige conferred by operations while others shunned them as indelicate. Ethan, from motives of economy, had always been glad that Zeena was of the latter faction.

In the agitation caused by the gravity of her announcement he sought a consolatory short cut. "What do you know about this doctor anyway? Nobody ever told you that before."

He saw his blunder before she could take it up: she wanted sympathy, not consolation.

"I didn't need to have anybody tell me I was losing ground every day. Everybody but you could see it. And everybody in Bettsbridge knows about Dr. Buck. He has his office in Worcester, and comes over once a fortnight to Shadd's Falls and Bettsbridge for consultations. Eliza Spears was wasting away with kidney trouble before she went to him, and now she's up and around, and singing in the choir."

"Well, I'm glad of that. You must do just what he tells you," Ethan answered sympathetically.

She was still looking at him. "I mean to," she said. He was struck by a new note in her voice. It was neither whining nor reproachful, but drily resolute.

"What does he want you should do?" he asked, with a mounting vision of fresh expenses.

"He wants I should have a hired girl. He says I oughtn't to have to do a single thing around the house."

"A hired girl?" Ethan stood transfixed.

"Yes. And Aunt Martha found me one right off. Everybody said

I was lucky to get a girl to come away out here, and I agreed to give her a dollar extry to make sure. She'll be over tomorrow afternoon."

Wrath and dismay contended in Ethan. He had foreseen an immediate demand for money, but not a permanent drain on his scant resources. He no longer believed what Zeena had told him of the supposed seriousness of her state: he saw in her expedition to Bettsbridge only a plot hatched between herself and her Pierce relations to foist on him the cost of a servant; and for the moment wrath predominated.

"If you meant to engage a girl you ought to have told me before you started," he said.

"How could I tell you before I started? How did I know what Dr. Buck would say?"

"Oh, Dr. Buck—" Ethan's incredulity escaped in a short laugh. "Did Dr. Buck tell you how I was to pay her wages?"

Her voice rose furiously with his. "No, he didn't. For I'd 'a' been ashamed to tell *him* that you grudged me the money to get back my health, when I lost it nursing your own mother!"

"*You* lost your health nursing mother?"

"Yes; and my folks all told me at the time you couldn't do no less than marry me after—"

"Zeena!"

Through the obscurity which hid their faces their thoughts seemed to dart at each other like serpents shooting venom. Ethan was seized with horror of the scene and shame at his own share in it. It was as senseless and savage as a physical fight between two enemies in the darkness.

He turned to the shelf above the chimney, groped for matches and lit the one candle in the room. At first its weak flame made no impression on the shadows; then Zeena's face stood grimly out against the uncurtained pane, which had turned from gray to black.

It was the first scene of open anger between the couple in their sad seven years together, and Ethan felt as if he had lost an irretrievable advantage in descending to the level of recrimination. But the practical problem was there and had to be dealt with.

"You know I haven't got the money to pay for a girl, Zeena. You'll have to send her back: I can't do it."

"The doctor says it'll be my death if I go on slaving the way I've had to. He doesn't understand how I've stood it as long as I have."

"Slaving!—" He checked himself again, "You sha'n't lift a hand, if he says so. I'll do everything round the house myself—"

She broke in: "You're neglecting the farm enough already," and this being true, he found no answer, and left her time to add ironically: "Better send me over to the almshouse and done with it . . . I guess there's been Fromes there afore now."

The taunt burned into him, but he let it pass. "I haven't got the money. That settles it."

There was a moment's pause in the struggle, as though the combatants were testing their weapons. Then Zeena said in a level voice: "I thought you were to get fifty dollars from Andrew Hale for that lumber."

"Andrew Hale never pays under three months." He had hardly spoken when he remembered the excuse he had made for not accompanying his wife to the station the day before; and the blood rose to his frowning brows.

"Why, you told me yesterday you'd fixed it up with him to pay cash down. You said that was why you couldn't drive me over to the Flats."

Ethan had no suppleness in deceiving. He had never before been convicted of a lie, and all the resources of evasion failed him. "I guess that was a misunderstanding," he stammered.

"You ain't got the money?"

"No."

"And you ain't going to get it?"

"No."

"Well, I couldn't know that when I engaged the girl, could I?"

"No." He paused to control his voice. "But you know it now. I'm sorry, but it can't be helped. You're a poor man's wife, Zeena; but I'll do the best I can for you."

For a while she sat motionless, as if reflecting, her arms stretched along the arms of her chair, her eyes fixed on vacancy. "Oh, I guess we'll make out," she said mildly.

The change in her tone reassured him. "Of course we will! There's a whole lot more I can do for you, and Mattie—"

Zeena, while he spoke, seemed to be following out some elaborate mental calculation. She emerged from it to say: "There'll be Mattie's board less, anyhow—"

Ethan, supposing the discussion to be over, had turned to go down to supper. He stopped short, not grasping what he heard. "Mattie's board less—?" he began.

Zeena laughed. It was an odd unfamiliar sound—he did not remember ever having heard her laugh before. "You didn't suppose I was going to keep two girls, did you? No wonder you were scared at the expense!"

He still had but a confused sense of what she was saying. From the beginning of the discussion he had instinctively avoided the mention of Mattie's name, fearing he hardly knew what: criticism, complaints, or vague allusions to the imminent probability of her marrying. But the thought of a definite rupture had never come to him, and even now could not lodge itself in his mind.

"I don't know what you mean," he said. "Mattie Silver's not a hired girl. She's your relation."

"She's a pauper that's hung onto us all after her father'd done his best to ruin us. I've kep' her here a whole year: it's somebody else's turn now."

As the shrill words shot out Ethan heard a tap on the door, which he had drawn shut when he turned back from the threshold.

"Ethan—Zeena!" Mattie's voice sounded gaily from the landing, "do you know what time it is? Supper's been ready half an hour."

Inside the room there was a moment's silence; then Zeena called out from her seat: "I'm not coming down to supper."

"Oh, I'm sorry! Aren't you well? Sha'n't I bring you up a bite of something?"

Ethan roused himself with an effort and opened the door. "Go along down, Matt. Zeena's just a little tired. I'm coming."

He heard her "All right!" and her quick step on the stairs; then he shut the door and turned back into the room. His wife's attitude was unchanged, her face inexorable, and he was seized with the despairing sense of his helplessness.

"You ain't going to do it, Zeena?"

"Do what?" she emitted between flattened lips.

"Send Mattie away—like this?"

"I never bargained to take her for life!"

He continued with rising vehemence: "You can't put her out of the house like a thief—a poor girl without friends or money. She's done her best for you and she's got no place to go to. You may forget she's your kin but everybody else'll remember it. If you do a thing like that what do you suppose folks'll say of you?"

Zeena waited a moment, as if giving him time to feel the full force of the contrast between his own excitement and her composure. Then she replied in the same smooth voice: "I know well enough what they say of my having kep' her here as long as I have."

Ethan's hand dropped from the doorknob, which he had held clenched since he had drawn the door shut on Mattie. His wife's retort was like a knife-cut across the sinews and he felt suddenly weak and powerless. He had meant to humble himself, to argue that Mattie's keep didn't cost much, after all, that he could make out to buy a stove and fix up a place in the attic for the hired girl—but Zeena's words revealed the peril of such pleadings.

"You mean to tell her she's got to go—at once?" he faltered out, in terror of letting his wife complete her sentence.

As if trying to make him see reason she replied impartially; "The girl will be over from Bettsbridge tomorrow, and I presume she's got to have somewheres to sleep."

Ethan looked at her with loathing. She was no longer the listless creature who had lived at his side in a state of sullen self-absorption, but a mysterious alien presence, an evil energy secreted from the long years of silent brooding. It was the sense of his helplessness that sharpened his antipathy. There had never been anything in her that one could appeal to; but as long as he could ignore and command he had remained indifferent. Now she had mastered him and he abhorred her. Mattie was her relation, not his: there was no means by which he could compel her to keep the girl under her roof. All the long misery of his baffled past, of his youth of failure, hardship and vain effort, rose up in his soul in bitterness and seemed to take shape before him in the woman who at every turn had barred his way. She had taken everything else from him; and now she meant to take the one thing that made up for all the others. For a moment such a flame of hate rose in him that it ran down his arm and clenched his fist against her. He took a wild step forward and then stopped.

"You're—you're not coming down?" he said in a bewildered voice.

"No. I guess I'll lay down on the bed a little while," she answered mildly; and he turned and walked out of the room.

In the kitchen Mattie was sitting by the stove, the cat curled up on her knees. She sprang to her feet as Ethan entered and carried the covered dish of meat-pie to the table.

"I hope Zeena isn't sick?" she asked.

"No."

She shone at him across the table. "Well, sit right down then. You must be starving." She uncovered the pie and pushed it over to him. So they were to have one more evening together, her happy eyes seemed to say!

He helped himself mechanically and began to eat; then disgust took him by the throat and he laid down his fork.

Mattie's tender gaze was on him and she marked the gesture.

"Why, Ethan, what's the matter? Don't it taste right?"

"Yes—it's first-rate. Only I—" He pushed his plate away, rose from his chair, and walked around the table to her side. She started up with frightened eyes.

"Ethan, there's something wrong! I *knew* there was!"

She seemed to melt against him in her terror, and he caught her in his arms, held her fast there, felt her lashes beat his cheek like netted butterflies.

"What is it—what is it?" she stammered; but he had found her lips at last and was drinking unconsciousness of everything but the joy they gave him.

She lingered a moment, caught in the same strong current; then she slipped from him and drew back a step or two, pale and troubled. Her look smote him with compunction, and he cried out, as if he saw her drowning in a dream: "You can't go, Matt! I'll never let you!"

"Go—go?" she stammered. "Must I go?"

The words went on sounding between them as though a torch of warning flew from hand to hand through a black landscape.

Ethan was overcome with shame at his lack of self-control in flinging the news at her so brutally. His head reeled and he had to support himself against the table. All the while he felt as if he were still kissing her, and yet dying of thirst for her lips.

"Ethan, what has happened? Is Zeena mad with me?"

Her cry steadied him, though it deepened his wrath and pity. "No, no," he assured her, "it's not that. But this new doctor has scared her about herself. You know she believes all they say the first time she sees them. And this one's told her she won't get well unless she lays up and don't do a thing about the house—not for months—"

He paused, his eyes wandering from her miserably. She stood silent a moment, drooping before him like a broken branch. She was so small and weak-looking that it wrung his heart; but suddenly she lifted her head and looked straight at him. "And she wants somebody handier in my place? Is that it?"

"That's what she says tonight."

"If she says it tonight she'll say it tomorrow."

Both bowed to the inexorable truth: they knew that Zeena never changed her mind, and that in her case a resolve once taken was equivalent to an act performed.

There was a long silence between them; then Mattie said in a low voice: "Don't be too sorry, Ethan."

"Oh, God—oh, God," he groaned. The glow of passion he had felt for her had melted to an aching tenderness. He saw her quick lids beating back the tears, and longed to take her in his arms and soothe her.

"You're letting your supper get cold," she admonished him with a pale gleam of gaiety.

"Oh, Matt—Matt—where'll you go to?"

Her lids sank and a tremor crossed her face. He saw that for the first time the thought of the future came to her distinctly. "I might get something to do over at Stamford," she faltered, as if knowing that he knew she had no hope.

He dropped back into his seat and hid his face in his hands. Despair seized him at the thought of her setting out alone to renew the weary quest for work. In the only place where she was known she was surrounded by indifference or animosity; and what chance had she, inexperienced and untrained, among the million bread-seekers of the cities? There came back to him miserable tales he had heard at Worcester, and the faces of girls whose lives had begun as hopefully as Mattie's. . . . It was not possible to think of such things without a revolt of his whole being. He sprang up suddenly.

"You can't go, Matt! I won't let you! She's always had her way, but I mean to have mine now—"

Mattie lifted her hand with a quick gesture, and he heard his wife's step behind him.

Zeena came into the room with her dragging down-at-the-heel step, and quietly took her accustomed seat between them.

"I felt a little mite better, and Dr. Buck says I ought to eat all I can to keep my stren'th up, even if I ain't got any appetite," she said in her flat whine, reaching across Mattie for the teapot. Her "good" dress had been replaced by the black calico and brown knitted shawl which formed her daily wear, and with them she had put on her usual face and manner. She poured out her tea, added a great deal of milk to it, helped herself largely to pie and pickles, and made the familiar gesture of adjusting her false teeth before she began to eat. The cat rubbed itself ingratiatingly against her, and she said "Good Pussy," stopped to stroke it and gave it a scrap of meat from her plate.

Ethan sat speechless, not pretending to eat, but Mattie nibbled valiantly at her food and asked Zeena one or two questions about her visit to Bettsbridge. Zeena answered in her everyday tone and, warming to the theme, regaled them with several vivid descriptions of intestinal disturbances among her friends and relatives. She looked straight at Mattie as she spoke, a faint smile deepening the vertical lines between her nose and chin.

When supper was over she rose from her seat and pressed her hand to the flat surface over the region of her heart. "That pie of yours always sets a mite heavy, Matt," she said, not ill-naturedly. She seldom abbreviated the girl's name, and when she did so it was always a sign of affability.

"I've a good mind to go and hunt up those stomach powders I got last year over in Springfield," she continued. "I ain't tried them for quite a while, and maybe they'll help the heartburn."

Mattie lifted her eyes. "Can't I get them for you, Zeena?" she ventured.

"No. They're in a place you don't know about," Zeena answered darkly, with one of her secret looks.

She went out of the kitchen and Mattie, rising, began to clear the dishes from the table. As she passed Ethan's chair their eyes met and clung together desolately. The warm still kitchen looked as peaceful as the night before. The cat had sprung to Zeena's rocking chair, and the heat of the fire was beginning to draw out the faint sharp scent of the geraniums. Ethan dragged himself wearily to his feet.

"I'll go out and take a look round," he said, going toward the passage to get his lantern.

As he reached the door he met Zeena coming back into the room, her lips twitching with anger, a flush of excitement on her sallow face. The shawl had slipped from her shoulders and was dragging at her

down-trodden heels, and in her hands she carried the fragments of
the red glass pickle-dish.

"I'd like to know who done this," she said, looking sternly from
Ethan to Mattie.

There was no answer, and she continued in a trembling voice: "I
went to get those powders I'd put away in father's old spectacle-case,
top of the china closet, where I keep the things I set store by, so's
folks sha'n't meddle with them—" Her voice broke, and two small
tears hung on her lashless lids and ran slowly down her cheeks. "It
takes the stepladder to get at the top shelf, and I put Aunt Philura
Maple's pickle-dish up there o' purpose when we was married, and
it's never been down since, 'cept for the spring cleaning, and then I
always lifted it with my own hands, so's 't it shouldn't get broke."
She laid the fragments reverently on the table. "I want to know who
done this," she quavered.

At the challenge Ethan turned back into the room and faced her.
"I can tell you, then. The cat done it."

"The *cat?*"

"That's what I said."

She looked at him hard, and then turned her eyes to Mattie, who
was carrying the dishpan to the table.

"I'd like to know how the cat got into my china closet," she said.

"Chasin' mice, I guess," Ethan rejoined. "There was a mouse
round the kitchen all last evening."

Zeena continued to look from one to the other; then she emitted
her small strange laugh. "I knew the cat was a smart cat," she said
in a high voice, "but I didn't know he was smart enough to pick up
the pieces of my pickle-dish and lay 'em edge to edge on the very shelf
he knocked 'em off of."

Mattie suddenly drew her arms out of the steaming water. "It
wasn't Ethan's fault, Zeena! The cat *did* break the dish; but I got it
down from the china closet, and I'm the one to blame for its getting
broken."

Zeena stood beside the ruin of her treasure, stiffening into a stony
image of resentment. "*You* got down my pickle-dish—what for?"

A bright flush flew to Mattie's cheeks. "I wanted to make the supper table pretty," she said.

"You wanted to make the supper table pretty; and you waited till
my back was turned, and took the thing I set most store by of any-

thing I've got, and wouldn't never use it, not even when the minister come to dinner, or Aunt Martha Pierce come over from Betts-bridge—" Zeena paused with a gasp, as if terrified by her own evo-cation of the sacrilege. "You're a bad girl, Mattie Silver, and I always known it. It's the way your father begun, and I was warned of it when I took you, and I tried to keep my things where you couldn't get at 'em—and now you've took from me the one I cared for most of all—" She broke off in a short spasm of sobs that passed and left her more than ever like a shape of stone.

"If I'd 'a' listened to folks, you'd 'a' gone before now, and this wouldn't 'a' happened," she said; and gathering up the bits of broken glass she went out of the room as if she carried a dead body . . .

VIII

When Ethan was called back to the farm by his father's illness his mother gave him, for his own use, a small room behind the unten-anted "best parlor." Here he had nailed up shelves for his books, built himself a box-sofa out of boards and a mattress, laid out his papers on a kitchen table, hung on the rough plaster wall an engraving of Abraham Lincoln and a calendar with "Thoughts from the Poets," and tried, with these meager properties to produce some likeness to the study of a "minister" who had been kind to him and lent him books when he was at Worcester. He still took refuge there in sum-mer, but when Mattie came to live at the farm he had had to give her his stove, and consequently the room was uninhabitable for several months of the year.

To this retreat he descended as soon as the house was quiet, and Zeena's steady breathing from the bed had assured him that there was to be no sequel to the scene in the kitchen. After Zeena's depar-ture he and Mattie had stood speechless, neither seeking to approach the other. Then the girl had returned to her task of clearing up the kitchen for the night and he had taken his lantern and gone on his usual round outside the house. The kitchen was empty when he came back to it; but his tobacco pouch and pipe had been laid on the table, and under them was a scrap of paper torn from the back of a seeds-man's catalogue, on which three words were written: "Don't trouble, Ethan."

Going into his cold dark "study" he placed the lantern on the table and, stooping to its light, read the message again and again. It was the first time that Mattie had ever written to him, and the possession of the paper gave him a strange new sense of her nearness; yet it deepened his anguish by reminding him that henceforth they would have no other way of communicating with each other. For the life of her smile, the warmth of her voice, only cold paper and dead words!

Confused motions of rebellion stormed in him. He was too young, too strong, too full of the sap of living, to submit so easily to the destruction of his hopes. Must he wear out all his years at the side of a bitter querulous woman? Other possibilities had been in him, possibilities sacrificed, one by one, to Zeena's narrow-mindedness and ignorance. And what good had come of it? She was a hundred times bitterer and more discontented than when he had married her: the one pleasure left her was to inflict pain on him. All the healthy instincts of self-defense rose up in him against such waste . . .

He bundled himself into his old coonskin coat and lay down on the box-sofa to think. Under his cheek he felt a hard object with strange protuberances. It was a cushion which Zeena had made for him when they were engaged—the only piece of needlework he had ever seen her do. He flung it across the floor and propped his head against the wall . . .

He knew a case of a man over the mountain—a young fellow of about his own age—who had escaped from just such a life of misery by going West with the girl he cared for. His wife had divorced him, and he had married the girl and prospered. Ethan had seen the couple the summer before at Shadd's Falls, where they had come to visit relatives. They had a little girl with fair curls, who wore a gold locket and was dressed like a princess. The deserted wife had not done badly either. Her husband had given her the farm and she had managed to sell it, and with that and the alimony she had started a lunch-room at Bettsbridge and bloomed into activity and importance. Ethan was fired by the thought. Why should he not leave with Mattie the next day, instead of letting her go alone? He would hide his valise under the seat of the sleigh, and Zeena would suspect nothing till she went upstairs for her afternoon nap and found a letter on the bed . . .

His impulses were still near the surface, and he sprang up, re-lit the lantern, and sat down at the table. He rummaged in the drawer for a sheet of paper, found one, and began to write.

"Zeena, I've done all I could for you, and I don't see as it's been any use. I don't blame you, nor I don't blame myself. Maybe both of us will do better separate. I'm going to try my luck West, and you can sell the farm and mill, and keep the money—"

His pen paused on the word, which brought home to him the relentless conditions of his lot. If he gave the farm and mill to Zeena what would be left him to start his own life with? Once in the West he was sure of picking up work—he would not have feared to try his chance alone. But with Mattie depending on him the case was different. And what of Zeena's fate? Farm and mill were mortgaged to the limit of their value, and even if she found a purchaser—in itself an unlikely chance—it was doubtful if she could clear a thousand dollars on the sale. Meanwhile, how could she keep the farm going? It was only by incessant labor and personal supervision that Ethan drew a meager living from his land, and his wife, even if she were in better health than she imagined, could never carry such a burden alone.

Well, she could go back to her people, then, and see what they would do for her. It was the fate she was forcing on Mattie—why not let her try it herself? By the time she had discovered his whereabouts, and brought suit for divorce, he would probably—wherever he was— be earning enough to pay her a sufficient alimony. And the alternative was to let Mattie go forth alone, with far less hope of ultimate provision . . .

He had scattered the contents of the table-drawer in his search for a sheet of paper, and as he took up his pen his eye fell on an old copy of the *Bettsbridge Eagle*. The advertising sheet was folded uppermost, and he read the seductive words: "Trips to the West: Reduced Rates."

He drew the lantern nearer and eagerly scanned the fares; then the paper fell from his hand and he pushed aside his unfinished letter. A moment ago he had wondered what he and Mattie were to live on when they reached the West; now he saw that he had not even the money to take her there. Borrowing was out of the question: six months before he had given his only security to raise funds for necessary repairs to the mill, and he knew that without security no one at Starkfield would lend him ten dollars. The inexorable facts closed in on him like prison-warders handcuffing a convict. There was no way out—none. He was a prisoner for life, and now his one ray of light was to be extinguished.

He crept back heavily to the sofa, stretching himself out with limbs so leaden that he felt as if they would never move again. Tears rose in his throat and slowly burned their way to his lids.

As he lay there, the windowpane that faced him, growing gradually lighter, inlaid upon the darkness a square of moon-suffused sky. A crooked tree-branch crossed it, a branch of the apple tree under which, on summer evenings, he had sometimes found Mattie sitting when he came up from the mill. Slowly the rim of the rainy vapors caught fire and burnt away, and a pure moon swung into the blue. Ethan, rising on his elbow, watched the landscape whiten and shape itself under the sculpture of the moon. This was the night on which he was to have taken Mattie coasting, and there hung the lamp to light them! He looked out at the slopes bathed in luster, the silver-edged darkness of the woods, the spectral purple of the hills against the sky, and it seemed as though all the beauty of the night had been poured out to mock his wretchedness . . .

He fell asleep, and when he woke the chill of the winter dawn was in the room. He felt cold and stiff and hungry, and ashamed of being hungry. He rubbed his eyes and went to the window. A red sun stood over the gray rim of the fields, behind trees that looked black and brittle. He said to himself: "This is Matt's last day," and tried to think what the place would be without her.

As he stood there he heard a step behind him and she entered.

"Oh, Ethan—were you here all night?"

She looked so small and pinched, in her poor dress, with the red scarf wound about her, and the cold light turning her paleness sallow, that Ethan stood before her without speaking.

"You must be frozen," she went on, fixing lusterless eyes on him.

He drew a step nearer. "How did you know I was here?"

"Because I heard you go down stairs again after I went to bed, and I listened all night, and you didn't come up."

All his tenderness rushed to his lips. He looked at her and said: "I'll come right along and make up the kitchen fire."

They went back to the kitchen, and he fetched the coal and kindlings and cleared out the stove for her, while she brought in the milk and the cold remains of the meat-pie. When warmth began to radiate from the stove, and the first ray of sunlight lay on the kitchen floor, Ethan's dark thoughts melted in the mellower air. The sight of Mattie going about her work as he had seen her on so many mornings made it seem impossible that she should ever cease to be a part of the scene. He said to himself that he had doubtless exaggerated the significance of Zeena's threats, and that she too, with the return of daylight, would come to a saner mood.

He went up to Mattie as she bent above the stove, and laid his hand on her arm. "I don't want you should trouble either," he said, looking down into her eyes with a smile.

She flushed up warmly and whispered back: "No, Ethan, I ain't going to trouble."

"I guess things'll straighten out," he added.

There was no answer but a quick throb of her lids, and he went on: "She ain't said anything this morning?"

"No. I haven't seen her yet."

"Don't you take any notice when you do."

With this injunction he left her and went out to the cow-barn. He saw Jotham Powell walking up the hill through the morning mist, and the familiar sight added to his growing conviction of security.

As the two men were clearing out the stalls Jotham rested on his pitchfork to say: "Dan'l Byrne's goin' over to the Flats today noon, an' he c'd take Mattie's trunk along, and make it easier ridin' when I take her over in the sleigh."

Ethan looked at him blankly, and he continued: "Mis' Frome said the new girl'd be at the Flats at five, and I was to take Mattie then, so's 't she could ketch the six o'clock train for Stamford."

Ethan felt the blood drumming in his temples. He had to wait a moment before he could find voice to say: "Oh, it ain't so sure about Mattie's going—"

"That so?" said Jotham indifferently; and they went on with their work.

When they returned to the kitchen the two women were already at breakfast. Zeena had an air of unusual alertness and activity. She drank two cups of coffee and fed the cat with the scraps left in the pie-dish; then she rose from her seat and, walking over to the window, snipped two or three yellow leaves from the geraniums. "Aunt Martha's ain't got a faded leaf on 'em; but they pine away when they ain't cared for," she said reflectively. Then she turned to Jotham and asked: "What time'd you say Dan'l Byrne'd be along?"

The hired man threw a hesitating glance at Ethan. "Round about noon," he said.

Zeena turned to Mattie. "That trunk of yours is too heavy for the sleigh, and Dan'l Byrne'll be round to take it over to the Flats," she said.

"I'm much obliged to you, Zeena," said Mattie.

"I'd like to go over things with you first," Zeena continued in an unperturbed voice. "I know there's a huckabuck towel missing; and I can't make out what you done with that match-safe 't used to stand behind the stuffed owl in the parlor."

She went out, followed by Mattie, and when the men were alone Jotham said to his employer: "I guess I better let Dan'l come round, then."

Ethan finished his usual morning tasks about the house and barn; then he said to Jotham: "I'm going down to Starkfield. Tell them not to wait dinner."

The passion of rebellion had broken out in him again. That which had seemed incredible in the sober light of day had really come to pass, and he was to assist as a helpless spectator at Mattie's banishment. His manhood was humbled by the part he was compelled to play and by the thought of what Mattie must think of him. Confused impulses struggled in him as he strode along to the village. He had made up his mind to do something, but he did not know what it would be.

The early mist had vanished and the fields lay like a silver shield under the sun. It was one of the days when the glitter of winter shines through a pale haze of spring. Every yard of the road was alive with Mattie's presence, and there was hardly a branch against the sky or a tangle of brambles on the bank in which some bright shred of memory was not caught. Once, in the stillness, the call of a bird in a mountain ash was so like her laughter that his heart tightened and then grew large; and all these things made him see that something must be done at once.

Suddenly it occurred to him that Andrew Hale, who was a kind-hearted man, might be induced to reconsider his refusal and advance a small sum on the lumber if he were told that Zeena's ill health made it necessary to hire a servant. Hale, after all, knew enough of Ethan's situation to make it possible for the latter to renew his appeal without too much loss of pride; and, moreover, how much did pride count in the ebullition of passions in his breast?

The more he considered his plan the more hopeful it seemed. If he could get Mrs. Hale's ear he felt certain of success, and with fifty dollars in his pocket nothing could keep him from Mattie . . .

His first object was to reach Starkfield before Hale had started for his work; he knew the carpenter had a job down the Corbury road and was likely to leave his house early. Ethan's long strides grew more rapid with the accelerated beat of his thoughts, and as he reached the foot of School House Hill he caught sight of Hale's sleigh in the distance. He hurried forward to meet it, but as it drew nearer he saw that it was driven by the carpenter's youngest boy and that the figure at his side, looking like a large upright cocoon in spectacles, was that of Mrs. Hale. Ethan signed to them to stop, and Mrs. Hale leaned forward, her pink wrinkles twinkling with benevolence.

"Mr. Hale? Why, yes, you'll find him down home now. He ain't going to his work this forenoon. He woke up with a touch o' lumbago, and I just made him put on one of old Dr. Kidder's plasters and set right up into the fire."

Beaming maternally on Ethan, she bent over to add: "I on'y just heard from Mr. Hale 'bout Zeena's going over to Bettsbridge to see that new doctor. I'm real sorry she's feeling so bad again! I hope he thinks he can do something for her? I don't know anybody round here's had more sickness than Zeena. I always tell Mr. Hale I don't know what she'd 'a' done if she hadn't 'a' had you to look after her; and I used to say the same thing 'bout your mother. You've had an awful mean time, Ethan Frome."

She gave him a last nod of sympathy while her son chirped to the horse; and Ethan, as she drove off, stood in the middle of the road and stared after the retreating sleigh.

It was a long time since anyone had spoken to him as kindly as Mrs. Hale. Most people were either indifferent to his troubles, or disposed to think it natural that a young fellow of his age should have carried without repining the burden of three crippled lives. But Mrs. Hale had said "You've had an awful mean time, Ethan Frome," and he felt less alone with his misery. If the Hales were sorry for him they would surely respond to his appeal . . .

He started down the road toward their house, but at the end of a few yards he pulled up sharply, the blood in his face. For the first time, in the light of the words he had just heard, he saw what he was about to do. He was planning to take advantage of the Hales' sympathy to obtain money from them on false pretenses. That was a plain statement of the cloudy purpose which had driven him in headlong to Starkfield.

With the sudden perception of the point to which his madness had carried him, the madness fell and he saw his life before him as it was. He was a poor man, the husband of a sickly woman, whom his desertion would leave alone and destitute; and even if he had had the heart to desert her he could have done so only by deceiving two kindly people who had pitied him.

He turned and walked slowly back to the farm.

IX

At the kitchen door Daniel Byrne sat in his sleigh behind a big-boned gray who pawed the snow and swung his long head restlessly from side to side.

Ethan went into the kitchen and found his wife by the stove. Her head was wrapped in her shawl, and she was reading a book called *Kidney Troubles and Their Cure* on which he had had to pay extra postage only a few days before.

Zeena did not move or look up when he entered, and after a moment he asked: "Where's Mattie?"

Without lifting her eyes from the page she replied: "I presume she's getting down her trunk."

The blood rushed to his face. "Getting down her trunk—alone?"

"Jotham Powell's down in the woodlot, and Dan'l Byrne says he darsn't leave that horse," she returned.

Her husband, without stopping to hear the end of the phrase, had left the kitchen and sprung up the stairs. The door of Mattie's room was shut, and he wavered a moment on the landing. "Matt," he said in a low voice; but there was no answer, and he put his hand on the doorknob.

He had never been in her room except once, in the early summer, when he had gone there to plaster up a leak in the eaves, but he remembered exactly how everything had looked: the red and white quilt on her narrow bed, the pretty pin cushion on the chest of drawers, and over it the enlarged photograph of her mother, in an oxydized frame, with a bunch of dyed grasses at the back. Now these and all other tokens of her presence had vanished, and the room looked as bare and comfortless as when Zeena had shown her into it on the day of her arrival. In the middle of the floor stood her trunk, and on the trunk she sat in her Sunday dress, her back turned to the door and her face in her hands. She had not heard Ethan's call because she was sobbing; and she did not hear his step till he stood close behind her and laid his hands on her shoulders.

"Matt—oh, don't—oh, *Matt*!"

She started up, lifting her wet face to his. "Ethan—I thought I wasn't ever going to see you again!"

He took her in his arms, pressing her close, and with a trembling hand smoothed away the hair from her forehead.

"Not see me again? What do you mean?"

She sobbed out: "Jotham said you told him we wasn't to wait dinner for you, and I thought—"

"You thought I meant to cut it?" he finished for her grimly.

She clung to him without answering, and he laid his lips on her hair, which was soft yet springy, like certain mosses on warm slopes, and had the faint woody fragrance of fresh sawdust in the sun.

Through the door they heard Zeena's voice calling out from below: "Dan'l Byrne says you better hurry up if you want him to take that trunk."

They drew apart with stricken faces. Words of resistance rushed to Ethan's lips and died there. Mattie found her handkerchief and dried her eyes; then, bending down, she took hold of a handle of the trunk.

Ethan put her aside. "You let go, Matt," he ordered her.

She answered: "It takes two to coax it round the corner"; and submitting to this argument he grasped the other handle, and together they maneuvered the heavy trunk out to the landing.

"Now let go," he repeated; then he shouldered the trunk and carried it down the stairs and across the passage to the kitchen. Zeena, who had gone back to her seat by the stove, did not lift her head from her book as he passed. Mattie followed him out of the door and helped him to lift the trunk into the back of the sleigh. When it was in place they stood side by side on the doorstep, watching Daniel Byrne plunge off behind his fidgety horse.

It seemed to Ethan that his heart was bound with cords which an unseen hand was tightening with every tick of the clock. Twice he opened his lips to speak to Mattie and found no breath. At length, as she turned to re-enter the house, he laid a detaining hand on her.

"I'm going to drive you over, Matt," he whispered.

She murmured back: "I think Zeena wants I should go with Jotham."

"I'm going to drive you over," he repeated; and she went into the kitchen without answering.

At dinner Ethan could not eat. If he lifted his eyes they rested on Zeena's pinched face, and the corners of her straight lips seemed to quiver away into a smile. She ate well, declaring that the mild weather made her feel better, and pressed a second helping of beans on Jotham Powell, whose wants she generally ignored.

Mattie, when the meal was over, went about her usual task of clearing the table and washing up the dishes. Zeena, after feeding the cat, had returned to her rocking chair by the stove, and Jotham Powell, who always lingered last, reluctantly pushed back his chair and moved toward the door.

On the threshold he turned back to say to Ethan: "What time'll I come round for Mattie?"

Ethan was standing near the window, mechanically filling his pipe while he watched Mattie move to and fro. He answered: "You needn't come round; I'm going to drive her over myself."

He saw the rise of the color in Mattie's averted cheek, and the quick lifting of Zeena's head.

"I want you should stay here this afternoon, Ethan," his wife said. "Jotham can drive Mattie over."

Mattie flung an imploring glance at him, but he repeated curtly: "I'm going to drive her over myself."

Zeena continued in the same even tone: "I wanted you should stay and fix up that stove in Mattie's room afore the girl gets here. It ain't been drawing right for nigh on a month now."

Ethan's voice rose indignantly. "If it was good enough for Mattie I guess it's good enough for a hired girl."

"That girl that's coming told me she was used to a house where they had a furnace," Zeena persisted with the same monotonous mildness.

"She'd better ha' stayed there then," he flung back at her; and turning to Mattie he added in a hard voice: "You be ready by three, Matt; I've got business at Corbury."

Jotham Powell had started for the barn, and Ethan strode down after him aflame with anger. The pulses in his temples throbbed and a fog was in his eyes. He went about his task without knowing what force directed him, or whose hands and feet were fulfilling its orders. It was not till he led out the sorrel and backed him between the shafts of the sleigh that he once more became conscious of what he was doing. As he passed the bridle over the horse's head, and wound the traces around the shafts, he remembered the day when he had made the same preparations in order to drive over and meet his wife's cousin at the Flats. It was little more than a year ago, on just such a soft afternoon, with a "feel" of spring in the air. The sorrel, turning the same big ringed eye on him, nuzzled the palm of his hand in the same way; and one by one all the days between rose up and stood before him . . .

He flung the bearskin into the sleigh, climbed to the seat, and drove up to the house. When he entered the kitchen it was empty, but Mattie's bag and shawl lay ready by the door. He went to the foot of the stairs and listened. No sound reached him from above, but presently he thought he heard some one moving about in his deserted study, and pushing open the door he saw Mattie, in her hat and jacket, standing with her back to him near the table.

She started at his approach and turning quickly, said: "Is it time?"

"What are you doing here, Matt?" he asked her.

She looked at him timidly. "I was just taking a look round—that's all," she answered, with a wavering smile.

They went back into the kitchen without speaking, and Ethan picked up her bag and shawl.

"Where's Zeena?" he asked.

"She went upstairs right after dinner. She said she had those shooting pains again, and didn't want to be disturbed."

"Did she say good-bye to you?"

"No. That was all she said."

Ethan, looking slowly about the kitchen, said to himself with a shudder that in a few hours he would be returning to it alone. Then the sense of unreality overcame him once more, and he could not bring himself to believe that Mattie stood there for the last time before him.

"Come on," he said almost gaily, opening the door and putting her bag into the sleigh. He sprang to his seat and bent over to tuck the rug about her as she slipped into the place at his side. "Now then, go 'long," he said, with a shake of the reins that sent the sorrel placidly jogging down the hill.

"We got lots of time for a good ride, Matt!" he cried, seeking her hand beneath the fur and pressing it in his. His face tingled and he felt dizzy, as if he had stopped in at the Starkfield saloon on a zero day for a drink.

At the gate, instead of making for Starkfield, he turned the sorrel to the right, up the Bettsbridge road. Mattie sat silent, giving no sign of surprise; but after a moment she said: "Are you going round by Shadow Pond?"

He laughed and answered: "I knew you'd know!"

She drew closer under the bearskin, so that, looking sideways around his coat sleeve, he could just catch the tip of her nose and a blown brown wave of hair. They drove slowly up the road between fields glistening under the pale sun, and then bent to the right down a lane edged with spruce and larch. Ahead of them, a long way off, a range of hills stained by mottlings of black forest flowed away in round white curves against the sky. The lane passed into a pine wood with boles reddening in the afternoon sun and delicate blue shadows on the snow. As they entered it the breeze fell and a warm stillness seemed to drop from the branches with the dropping needles. Here the snow was so pure that the tiny tracks of wood-animals had left on it intricate lace-like patterns, and the bluish cones caught in its surface stood out like ornaments of bronze.

Ethan drove on in silence till they reached a part of the wood where the pines were more widely spaced: then he drew up and helped Mattie to get out of the sleigh. They passed between the aromatic trunks, the snow breaking crisply under their feet, till they came to a small sheet of water with steep wooded sides. Across its frozen surface, from the farther bank, a single hill rising against the western sun threw the long conical shadow which gave the lake its name. It was a shy secret spot, full of the same dumb melancholy that Ethan felt in his heart.

He looked up and down the little pebbly beach till his eye lit on a fallen tree-trunk half submerged in snow.

"There's where we sat at the picnic," he reminded her.

The entertainment of which he spoke was one of the few that they had taken part in together: a "church picnic" which, on a long afternoon of the preceding summer, had filled the retired place with merrymaking. Mattie had begged him to go with her but he had refused. Then, toward sunset, coming down from the mountain where he had been felling timber, he had been caught by some strayed revelers and drawn into the group by the lake, where Mattie, encircled by facetious youths, and bright as a blackberry under her spreading hat, was brewing coffee over a gypsy fire. He remembered the shyness he had felt at approaching her in his uncouth clothes, and then the lighting up of her face, and the way she had broken through the group to come to him with a cup in her hand. They had sat for a few minutes on the fallen log by the pond, and she had missed her gold locket, and set the young men searching for it; and it was Ethan who had spied it in the moss . . . That was all; but all their intercourse had been made up of just such inarticulate flashes, when they seemed to come suddenly upon happiness as if they had surprised a butterfly in the winter woods . . .

"It was right there I found your locket," he said, pushing his foot into a dense tuft of blueberry bushes.

"I never saw anybody with such sharp eyes!" she answered.

She sat down on the tree trunk in the sun and he sat down beside her.

"You were as pretty as a picture in that pink hat," he said.

She laughed with pleasure. "Oh, I guess it was the hat!" she rejoined.

They had never before avowed their inclination so openly, and Ethan, for a moment, had the illusion that he was a free man, wooing the girl he meant to marry. He looked at her hair and longed to touch it again, and to tell her that it smelt of the woods; but he had never learned to say such things.

Suddenly she rose to her feet and said: "We mustn't stay here any longer."

He continued to gaze at her vaguely, only half-roused from his dream. "There's plenty of time," he answered.

They stood looking at each other as if the eyes of each were straining to absorb and hold fast the other's image. There were things he had to say to her before they parted, but he could not say them in that place of summer memories, and he turned and followed her in silence to the sleigh. As they drove away the sun sank behind the hill and the pine-boles turned from red to gray.

By a devious track between the fields they wound back to the Starkfield road. Under the open sky the light was still clear, with a reflection of cold red on the eastern hills. The clumps of trees in the snow seemed to draw together in ruffled lumps, like birds with their heads under their wings; and the sky, as it paled, rose higher, leaving the earth more alone.

As they turned into the Starkfield road Ethan said: "Matt, what do you mean to do?"

She did not answer at once, but at length she said: "I'll try to get a place in a store."

"You know you can't do it. The bad air and the standing all day nearly killed you before."

"I'm a lot stronger than I was before I came to Starkfield."

"And now you're going to throw away all the good it's done you!"

There seemed to be no answer to this, and again they drove on for a while without speaking. With every yard of the way some spot where they had stood, and laughed together or been silent, clutched at Ethan and dragged him back.

"Isn't there any of your father's folks could help you?"

"There isn't any of 'em I'd ask."

He lowered his voice to say: "You know there's nothing I wouldn't do for you if I could."

"I know there isn't."

"But I can't—"

She was silent, but he felt a slight tremor in the shoulder against his.

"Oh, Matt," he broke out, "if I could ha' gone with you now I'd ha' done it—"

She turned to him, pulling a scrap of paper from her breast. "Ethan—I found this," she stammered. Even in the failing light he saw it was the letter to his wife that he had begun the night before and forgotten to destroy. Through his astonishment there ran a fierce thrill of joy. "Matt—" he cried; "if I could ha' done it, would you?"

"Oh, Ethan, Ethan—what's the use?" With a sudden movement she tore the letter in shreds and sent them fluttering off into the snow.

"Tell me, Matt! Tell me!" he adjured her.

She was silent for a moment; then she said, in such a low tone that he had to stoop his head to hear her: "I used to think of it sometimes, summer nights, when the moon was so bright I couldn't sleep."

His heart reeled with the sweetness of it. "As long ago as that?"

She answered, as if the date had long been fixed for her: "The first time was at Shadow Pond."

"Was that why you gave me my coffee before the others?"

"I don't know. Did I? I was dreadfully put out when you wouldn't go to the picnic with me; and then, when I saw you coming down the road, I thought maybe you'd gone home that way o' purpose; and that made me glad."

They were silent again. They had reached the point where the road dipped to the hollow by Ethan's mill and as they descended the darkness descended with them, dropping down like a black veil from the heavy hemlock boughs.

"I'm tied hand and foot, Matt. There isn't a thing I can do," he began again.

"You must write to me sometimes, Ethan."

"Oh, what good'll writing do? I want to put my hand out and touch you. I want to do for you and care for you. I want to be there when you're sick and when you're lonesome."

"You musn't think but what I'll do all right."

"You won't need me, you mean? I suppose you'll marry!"

"Oh, Ethan!" she cried.

"I don't know how it is you make me feel, Matt. I'd a'most rather have you dead than that!"

"Oh, I wish I was, I wish I was!" she sobbed.

The sound of her weeping shook him out of his dark anger, and he felt ashamed.

"Don't let's talk that way," he whispered.

"Why shouldn't we, when it's true? I've been wishing it every minute of the day."

"Matt! You be quiet! Don't you say it."

"There's never anybody been good to me but you."

"Don't say that either, when I can't lift a hand for you!"

"Yes; but it's true just the same."

They had reached the top of School House Hill and Starkfield lay below them in the twilight. A cutter, mounting the road from the village, passed them by in a joyous flutter of bells, and they straightened themselves and looked ahead with rigid faces. Along the main

street lights had begun to shine from the house fronts and stray figures were turning in here and there at the gates. Ethan, with a touch
of his whip, roused the sorrel to a languid trot.

As they drew near the end of the village the cries of children
reached them, and they saw a knot of boys, with sleds behind them,
scattering across the open space before the church.

"I guess this'll be their last coast for a day or two," Ethan said,
looking up at the mild sky.

Mattie was silent, and he added: "We were to have gone down last
night."

Still she did not speak and, prompted by an obscure desire to help
himself and her through their miserable last hour, he went on dis-
cursively: "Ain't it funny we haven't been down together but just that
once last winter?"

She answered: "It wasn't often I got down to the village."

"That's so," he said.

They had reached the crest of the Corbury road, and between the
indistinct white glimmer of the church and the black curtain of the
Varnum spruces the slope stretched away below them without a sled
on its length. Some erratic impulse prompted Ethan to say: "How'd
you like me to take you down now?"

She forced a laugh. "Why, there isn't time!"

"There's all the time we want. Come along!" His one desire now
was to postpone the moment of turning the sorrel toward the Flats.

"But the girl," she faltered. "The girl'll be waiting at the station."

"Well, let her wait. You'd have to if she didn't. Come!"

The note of authority in his voice seemed to subdue her, and when
he had jumped from the sleigh she let him help her out, saying only,
with a vague feint of reluctance: "But there isn't a sled round any
wheres."

"Yes, there is! Right over there under the spruces."

He threw the bearskin over the sorrel, who stood passively by the
roadside, hanging a meditative head. Then he caught Mattie's hand
and drew her after him toward the sled.

She seated herself obediently and he took his place behind her, so
close that her hair brushed his face. "All right, Matt?" he called out,
as if the width of the road had been between them.

She turned her head to say: "It's dreadfully dark. Are you sure you
can see?"

He laughed contemptuously: "I could go down this coast with my eyes tied!" and she laughed with him, as if she liked his audacity. Nevertheless he sat still a moment, straining his eyes down the long hill, for it was the most confusing hour of the evening, the hour when the last clearness from the upper sky is merged with the rising night in a blur that disguises landmarks and falsifies distances.

"Now!" he cried.

The sled started with a bound, and they flew on through the dusk, gathering smoothness and speed as they went, with the hollow night opening out below them and the air singing by like an organ. Mattie sat perfectly still, but as they reached the bend at the foot of the hill, where the big elm thrust out a deadly elbow, he fancied that she shrank a little closer.

"Don't be scared, Matt!" he cried exultantly, as they spun safely past it and flew down the second slope; and when they reached the level ground beyond, and the speed of the sled began to slacken, he heard her give a little laugh of glee.

They sprang off and started to walk back up the hill. Ethan dragged the sled with one hand and passed the other through Mattie's arm.

"Were you scared I'd run you into the elm?" he asked with a boyish laugh.

"I told you I was never scared with you," she answered.

The strange exaltation of his mood had brought on one of his rare fits of boastfulness. "It *is* a tricky place, though. The least swerve, and we'd never ha' come up again. But I can measure distances to a hair's-breadth—always could."

She murmured: "I always say you've got the surest eye . . ."

Deep silence had fallen with the starless dusk, and they leaned on each other without speaking; but at every step of their climb Ethan said to himself: "It's the last time we'll ever walk together."

They mounted slowly to the top of the hill. When they were abreast of the church he stooped his head to her to ask: "Are you tired?" and she answered, breathing quickly: "It was splendid!"

With a pressure of his arm he guided her toward the Norway spruces. "I guess this sled must be Ned Hale's. Anyhow I'll leave it where I found it." He drew the sled up to the Varnum gate and rested it against the fence. As he raised himself he suddenly felt Mattie close to him among the shadows.

"Is this where Ned and Ruth kissed each other?" she whispered breathlessly, and flung her arms about him. Her lips, groping for his, swept over his face, and he held her fast in a rapture of surprise.

"Good-bye—good-bye," she stammered, and kissed him again.

"Oh, Matt I can't let you go!" broke from him in the same old cry.

She freed herself from his hold and he heard her sobbing. "Oh, I can't go either!" she wailed.

"Matt! What'll we do? What'll we do?"

They clung to each other's hands like children, and her body shook with desperate sobs.

Through the stillness they heard the church clock striking five.

"Oh, Ethan, it's time!" she cried.

He drew her back to him. "Time for what? You don't suppose I'm going to leave you now?"

"If I missed my train where'd I go?"

"Where are you going if you catch it?"

She stood silent, her hands lying cold and relaxed in his.

"What's the good of either of us going anywheres without the other one now?" he said.

She remained motionless, as if she had not heard him. Then she snatched her hands from his, threw her arms about his neck, and pressed a sudden drenched cheek against his face. "Ethan! Ethan! I want you to take me down again!"

"Down where?"

"The coast. Right off," she panted. "So 't we'll never come up any more."

"Matt! What on earth do you mean?"

She put her lips close against his ear to say: "Right into the big elm. You said you could. So 't we'd never have to leave each other any more."

"Why, what are you talking of? You're crazy!"

"I'm not crazy; but I will be if I leave you."

"Oh, Matt, Matt—" he groaned.

She tightened her fierce hold about his neck. Her face lay close to his face.

"Ethan, where'll I go if I leave you? I don't know how to get along alone. You said so yourself just now. Nobody but you was ever good to me. And there'll be that strange girl in the house . . . and she'll sleep in my bed, where I used to lay nights and listen to hear you come up the stairs . . ."

The words were like fragments torn from his heart. With them came the hated vision of the house he was going back to—of the stairs he would have to go up every night, of the woman who would wait for him there. And the sweetness of Mattie's avowal, the wild wonder of knowing at last that all that had happened to him had happened to her too, made the other vision more abhorrent, the other life more intolerable to return to . . .

Her pleadings still came to him between short sobs, but he no longer heard what she was saying. Her hat had slipped back and he was stroking her hair. He wanted to get the feeling of it into his hand, so that it would sleep there like a seed in winter. Once he found her mouth again, and they seemed to be by the pond together in the burning August sun. But his cheek touched hers, and it was cold and full of weeping, and he saw the road to the Flats under the night and heard the whistle of the train up the line.

The spruces swathed them in blackness and silence. They might have been in their coffins underground. He said to himself: "Perhaps it'll feel like this . . ." and then again: "After this I sha'n't feel anything . . ."

Suddenly he heard the old sorrel whinny across the road, and thought: "He's wondering why he doesn't get his supper . . ."

"Come," Mattie whispered, tugging at his hand.

Her somber violence constrained him: she seemed the embodied instrument of fate. He pulled the sled out, blinking like a night-bird as he passed from the shade of the spruces into the transparent dusk of the open. The slope below them was deserted. All Starkfield was at supper, and not a figure crossed the open space before the church. The sky, swollen with the clouds that announce a thaw, hung as low as before a summer storm. He strained his eyes through the dimness, and they seemed less keen, less capable than usual.

He took his seat on the sled and Mattie instantly placed herself in front of him. Her hat had fallen into the snow and his lips were in her hair. He stretched out his legs, drove his heels into the road to keep the sled from slipping forward, and bent her head back between his hands. Then suddenly he sprang up again.

"Get up," he ordered her.

It was the tone she always heeded, but she cowered down in her seat, repeating vehemently: "No, no, no!"

"Get up!"

"Why?"

"I want to sit in front."

"No, no! How can you steer in front?"

"I don't have to. We'll follow the track."

They spoke in smothered whispers, as though the night were listening.

"Get up! Get up!" he urged her; but she kept on repeating: "Why do you want to sit in front?"

"Because I—because I want to feel you holding me," he stammered, and dragged her to her feet.

The answer seemed to satisfy her, or else she yielded to the power of his voice. He bent down, feeling in the obscurity for the glassy slide worn by preceding coasters, and placed the runners carefully between its edges. She waited while he seated himself with crossed legs in the front of the sled; then she crouched quickly down at his back and clasped her arms about him. Her breath in his neck set him shuddering again, and he almost sprang from his seat. But in a flash he remembered the alternative. She was right: this was better than parting. He leaned back and drew her mouth to his . . .

Just as they started he heard the sorrel's whinny again, and the familiar wistful call, and all the confused images it brought with it, went with him down the first reach of the road. Halfway down there was a sudden drop, then a rise, and after that another long delirious descent. As they took wing for this it seemed to him that they were flying indeed, flying far up into the cloudy night, with Starkfield immeasurably below them, falling away like a speck in space . . . Then the big elm shot up ahead, lying in wait for them at the bend of the road, and he said between his teeth: "We can fetch it; I know we can fetch it—"

As they flew toward the tree Mattie pressed her arms tighter, and her blood seemed to be in his veins. Once or twice the sled swerved a little under them. He slanted his body to keep it headed for the elm, repeating to himself again and again: "I know we can fetch it"; and little phrases she had spoken ran through his head and danced before him on the air. The big tree loomed bigger and closer, and as they

bore down on it he thought: "It's waiting for us: it seems to know."
But suddenly his wife's face, with twisted monstrous lineaments,
thrust itself between him and his goal, and he made an instinctive
movement to brush it aside. The sled swerved in response, but he
righted it again, kept it straight, and drove down on the black projecting mass. There was a last instant when the air shot past him like
millions of fiery wires; and then the elm . . .

The sky was still thick, but looking straight up he saw a single star,
and tried vaguely to reckon whether it were Sirius, or—or— The
effort tired him too much, and he closed his heavy lids and thought
that he would sleep . . . The stillness was so profound that he heard
a little animal twittering somewhere near by under the snow. It made
a small frightened *cheep* like a field mouse, and he wondered languidly if it were hurt. Then he understood that it must be in pain:
pain so excruciating that he seemed, mysteriously, to feel it shooting
through his own body. He tried in vain to roll over in the direction
of the sound, and stretched his left arm out across the snow. And
now it was as though he felt rather than heard the twittering; it
seemed to be under his palm, which rested on something soft and
springy. The thought of the animal's suffering was intolerable to him
and he struggled to raise himself, and could not because a rock, or
some huge mass, seemed to be lying on him. But he continued to
finger about cautiously with his left hand, thinking he might get hold
of the little creature and help it; and all at once he knew that the soft
thing he had touched was Mattie's hair and that his hand was on her
face.

He dragged himself to his knees, the monstrous load on him moving with him as he moved, and his hand went over and over her face,
and he felt that the twittering came from her lips . . .

He got his face down close to hers, with his ear to her mouth, and
in the darkness he saw her eyes open and heard her say his name.

"Oh, Matt, I thought we'd fetched it," he moaned; and far off, up
the hill, he heard the sorrel whinny, and thought: "I ought to be getting him his feed"   .   .   .   .

    .   .   .   .

    .   .   .   .

X

The querulous drone ceased as I entered Frome's kitchen, and of the two women sitting there I could not tell which had been the speaker.

One of them, on my appearing, raised her tall bony figure from her seat, not as if to welcome me—for she threw me no more than a brief glance of surprise—but simply to set about preparing the meal which Frome's absence had delayed. A slatternly calico wrapper hung from her shoulders and the wisps of her thin gray hair were drawn away from a high forehead and fastened at the back by a broken comb. She had pale opaque eyes which revealed nothing and reflected nothing, and her narrow lips were of the same sallow color as her face.

The other woman was much smaller and slighter. She sat huddled in an armchair near the stove, and when I came in she turned her head quickly toward me, without the least corresponding movement of her body. Her hair was as gray as her companion's, her face as bloodless and shriveled, but amber-tinted, with swarthy shadows sharpening the nose and hollowing the temples. Under her shapeless dress her body kept its limp immobility, and her dark eyes had the bright witch-like stare that disease of the spine sometimes gives.

Even for that part of the country the kitchen was a poor-looking place. With the exception of the dark-eyed woman's chair, which looked like a soiled relic of luxury bought at a country auction, the furniture was of the roughest kind. Three coarse china plates and a broken-nosed milk jug had been set on a greasy table scored with knife cuts, and a couple of straw-bottomed chairs and a kitchen dresser of unpainted pine stood meagerly against the plaster walls.

"My, it's cold here! The fire must be 'most out," Frome said, glancing about him apologetically as he followed me in.

The tall woman, who had moved away from us toward the dresser, took no notice; but the other, from her cushioned niche, answered complainingly, in a high thin voice: "It's on'y just been made up this very minute. Zeena fell asleep and slep' ever so long, and I thought I'd be frozen stiff before I could wake her up and get her to 'tend to it."

I knew then that it was she who had been speaking when we entered.

Her companion, who was just coming back to the table with the remains of a cold mince-pie in a battered pie-dish, set down her unappetizing burden without appearing to hear the accusation brought against her.

Frome stood hesitatingly before her as she advanced; then he looked at me and said: "This is my wife, Mis' Frome." After another interval he added, turning toward the figure in the armchair: "And this is Miss Mattie Silver . . ."

. . . .

Mrs. Hale, tender soul, had pictured me as lost in the Flats and buried under a snowdrift; and so lively was her satisfaction on seeing me safely restored to her the next morning that I felt my peril had caused me to advance several degrees in her favor.

Great was her amazement, and that of old Mrs. Varnum, on learning that Ethan Frome's old horse had carried me to and from Corbury Junction through the worst blizzard of the winter; greater still their surprise when they heard that his master had taken me in for the night.

Beneath their wondering exclamations I felt a secret curiosity to know what impressions I had received from my night in the Frome household, and divined that the best way of breaking down their reserve was to let them try to penetrate mine. I therefore confined myself to saying, in a matter-of-fact tone, that I had been received with great kindness, and that Frome had made a bed for me in a room on the ground floor which seemed in happier days to have been fitted up as a kind of writing room or study.

"Well," Mrs. Hale mused, "in such a storm I suppose he felt he couldn't do less than take you in—but I guess it went hard with Ethan. I don't believe but what you're the only stranger has set foot in that house for over twenty years. He's that proud he don't even like his oldest friends to go there; and I don't know as any do, any more, except myself and the doctor . . ."

"You still go there, Mrs. Hale?" I ventured.

"I used to go a good deal after the accident, when I was first married; but after awhile I got to think it made 'em feel worse to see us. And then one thing and another came, and my own troubles . . . But I generally make out to drive over there round about New Year's, and once in the summer. Only I always try to pick a day when Ethan's off somewheres. It's bad enough to see the two women sitting there—

but *his* face, when he looks round that bare place, just kills me . . . You see, I can look back and call it up in his mother's day, before their troubles."

Old Mrs. Varnum, by this time, had gone up to bed, and her daughter and I were sitting alone, after supper, in the austere seclusion of the horsehair parlor. Mrs. Hale glanced at me tentatively, as though trying to see how much footing my conjectures gave her; and I guessed that if she had kept silence till now it was because she had been waiting, through all the years, for some one who should see what she alone had seen.

I waited to let her trust in me gather strength before I said: "Yes, it's pretty bad, seeing all three of them there together."

She drew her mild brows into a frown of pain. "It was just awful from the beginning. I was here in the house when they were carried up—they laid Mattie Silver in the room you're in. She and I were great friends, and she was to have been my bridesmaid in the spring . . . When she came to I went up to her and stayed all night. They gave her things to quiet her, and she didn't know much till to'rd morning, and then all of a sudden she woke up just like herself, and looked straight at me out of her big eyes, and said . . . Oh, I don't know why I'm telling you all this," Mrs. Hale broke off, crying.

She took off her spectacles, wiped the moisture from them, and put them on again with an unsteady hand. "It got about the next day," she went on, "that Zeena Frome had sent Mattie off in a hurry because she had a hired girl coming, and the folks here could never rightly tell what she and Ethan were doing that night coasting, when they'd ought to have been on their way to the Flats to ketch the train . . . I never knew myself what Zeena thought—I don't to this day. Nobody knows Zeena's thoughts. Anyhow, when she heard o' the accident she came right in and stayed with Ethan over to the minister's, where they'd carried him. And as soon as the doctors said that Mattie could be moved, Zeena sent for her and took her back to the farm."

"And there she's been ever since?"

Mrs. Hale answered simply: "There was nowhere else for her to go"; and my heart tightened at the thought of the hard compulsions of the poor.

"Yes, there she's been," Mrs. Hale continued, "and Zeena's done for her, and done for Ethan, as good as she could. It was a miracle, considering how sick she was—but she seemed to be raised right up just when the call came to her. Not as she's ever given up doctoring, and she's had sick spells right along; but she's had the strength given her to care for those two for over twenty years, and before the accident came she thought she couldn't even care for herself."

Mrs. Hale paused a moment, and I remained silent, plunged in the vision of what her words evoked. "It's horrible for them all," I murmured.

"Yes: it's pretty bad. And they ain't any of 'em easy people either. Mattie *was,* before the accident; I never knew a sweeter nature. But she's suffered too much—that's what I always say when folks tell me how she's soured. And Zeena, she was always cranky. Not but what she bears with Mattie wonderful—I've seen that myself. But sometimes the two of them get going at each other, and then Ethan's face'd break your heart . . . When I see that, I think it's *him* that suffers most . . . anyhow it ain't Zeena, because she ain't got the time . . . It's a pity, though," Mrs. Hale ended, sighing, "that they're all shut up there'n that one kitchen. In the summertime, on pleasant days, they move Mattie into the parlor, or out in the dooryard, and that makes it easier . . . but winters there's the fires to be thought of; and there ain't a dime to spare up at the Fromes.'"

Mrs. Hale drew a deep breath, as though her memory were eased of its long burden, and she had no more to say: but suddenly an impulse of complete avowal seized her.

She took off her spectacles again, leaned toward me across the beadwork tablecover, and went on with lowered voice: "There was one day, about a week after the accident, when they all thought Mattie couldn't live. Well, I say it's a pity she *did.* I said it right out to our minister once, and he was shocked at me. Only he wasn't with me that morning when she first came to . . . And I say, if she'd ha' died, Ethan might ha' lived; and the way they are now, I don't see's there's much difference between the Fromes up at the farm and the Fromes down in the graveyard; 'cept that down there they're all quiet, and the women have got to hold their tongues."

THE TRIUMPH OF NIGHT

(1914)

Although it was not published until 1914, "The Triumph of Night" was written earlier and belongs with a group of tales from 1910 that share many of the same themes: "Afterward," "The Eyes," and "The Blond Beast." These stories emphasize male characters and experience; most are ghost stories, and most involve a corrupt businessman. The ghosts of "The Triumph of Night" and "The Eyes" share a special affinity: the ghostly visitation in the latter takes the form of a pair of eyes; in "Triumph" the ghostly double of the smiling Mr. Lavington has "eyes of deadly menace."

Wharton believed that a good ghost story should not depend on theme or "moral issue" but on its ability to "send a cold shiver down one's spine" (2:878). In "The Triumph of Night" and related stories, though, social criticism looms large as Wharton exposes the dishonesty of the economic system. She even provides a clear moral to the stories: evil must be confronted quickly to be vanquished. George Faxon delays too long in exposing Mr. Lavington's plan to kill his nephew. If he had summoned the courage, "he might have broken the spell of iniquity."

The protagonist's inability to act may have something to do with a raging snowstorm that attacks him. Wharton's first New England ghost story, "The Triumph of Night" is set in New Hampshire in a "bitter black-and-white landscape" similar to that of Ethan Frome. The storm, with its "blades," "darts," and "knives," seems a sentient and hostile force, perhaps another ghost as it holds Faxon in check with "an invisible hand."

IT WAS CLEAR that the sleigh from Weymore had not come; and the shivering young traveler from Boston, who had counted on jumping into it when he left the train at Northridge Junction, found himself standing alone on the open platform, exposed to the full assault of nightfall and winter.

The blast that swept him came off New Hampshire snowfields and ice-hung forests. It seemed to have traversed interminable leagues of frozen silence, filling them with the same cold roar and sharpening its edge against the same bitter black-and-white landscape. Dark, searching and swordlike, it alternately muffled and harried its victim, like a bullfighter now whirling his cloak and now planting his darts. This analogy brought home to the young man the fact that he himself had no cloak, and that the overcoat in which he had faced the relatively temperate air of Boston seemed no thicker than a sheet of paper on the bleak heights of Northridge. George Faxon said to himself that the place was uncommonly well-named. It clung to an exposed ledge over the valley from which the train had lifted him, and the wind combed it with teeth of steel that he seemed actually to hear scraping against the wooden sides of the station. Other building there was none: the village lay far down the road, and thither—since the Weymore sleigh had not come—Faxon saw himself under the necessity of plodding through several feet of snow.

He understood well enough what had happened: his hostess had forgotten that he was coming. Young as Faxon was, this sad lucidity of soul had been acquired as the result of long experience, and he knew that the visitors who can least afford to hire a carriage are almost always those whom their hosts forget to send for. Yet to say that Mrs. Culme had forgotten him was too crude a way of putting it. Similar incidents led him to think that she had probably told her

maid to tell the butler to telephone the coachman to tell one of the
grooms (if no one else needed him) to drive over to Northridge to
fetch the new secretary; but on a night like this, what groom who
respected his rights would fail to forget the order?

Faxon's obvious course was to struggle through the drifts to the
village, and there rout out a sleigh to convey him to Weymore; but
what if, on his arrival at Mrs. Culme's no one remembered to ask
him what this devotion to duty had cost? That, again, was one of the
contingencies he had expensively learned to look out for, and the per-
spicacity so acquired told him it would be cheaper to spend the night
at the Northridge inn, and advise Mrs. Culme of his presence there
by telephone. He had reached this decision, and was about to entrust
his luggage to a vague man with a lantern, when his hopes were raised
by the sound of bells.

Two sleighs were just dashing up to the station, and from the foremost there sprang a young man muffled in furs.

"Weymore? No, these are not the Weymore sleighs."

The voice was that of the youth who had jumped to the platform—
a voice so agreeable that, in spite of the words, it fell consolingly on
Faxon's ears. At the same moment the wandering station lantern,
casting a transient light on the speaker, showed his features to be in
the pleasantest harmony with his voice. He was very fair and very
young—hardly in the twenties, Faxon thought—but this face, although full of a morning freshness, was a trifle too thin and fine-
drawn, as though a vivid spirit contended in him with a strain of
physical weakness. Faxon was perhaps the quicker to notice such del-
icacies of balance because his own temperament hung on lightly quivering nerves, which yet, as he believed, would never quite swing him
beyond a normal sensibility.

"You expected a sleigh from Weymore?" the newcomer continued, standing beside Faxon like a slender column of fur.

Mrs. Culme's secretary explained his difficulty, and the other
brushed it aside with a contemptuous "Oh, *Mrs. Culme!*" that carried both speakers a long way toward reciprocal understanding.

"But then you must be—" The youth broke off with a smile of
interrogation.

"The new secretary? Yes. But apparently there are no notes to be
answered this evening." Faxon's laugh deepened the sense of soli-
darity which had so promptly established itself between the two.

His friend laughed also. "Mrs. Culme," he explained, "was lunching at my uncle's today, and she said you were due this evening. But seven hours is a long time for Mrs. Culme to remember anything."

"Well," said Faxon philosophically, "I suppose that's one of the reasons why she needs a secretary. And I've always the inn at Northridge," he concluded.

"Oh, but you haven't, though! It burned down last week."

"The deuce it did!" said Faxon; but the humor of the situation struck him before its inconvenience. His life, for years past, had been mainly a succession of resigned adaptations, and he had learned, before dealing practically with his embarrassments, to extract from most of them a small tribute of amusement.

"Oh, well, there's sure to be somebody in the place who can put me up."

"No one *you* could put up with. Besides, Northridge is three miles off, and our place—in the opposite direction—is a little nearer." Through the darkness, Faxon saw his friend sketch a gesture of self-introduction. "My name's Frank Rainer, and I'm staying with my uncle at Overdale. I've driven over to meet two friends of his, who are due in a few minutes from New York. If you don't mind waiting till they arrive I'm sure Overdale can do you better than Northridge. We're only down from town for a few days, but the house is always ready for a lot of people."

"But your uncle—?" Faxon could only object, with the odd sense, through his embarrassment, that it would be magically dispelled by his invisible friend's next words.

"Oh, my uncle—you'll see! I answer for *him!* I dare say you've heard of him—John Lavington?

John Lavington! There was a certain irony in asking if one had heard of John Lavington! Even from a post of observation as obscure as that of Mrs. Culme's secretary the rumor of John Lavington's money, of his pictures, his politics, his charities and his hospitality, was as difficult to escape as the roar of a cataract in a mountain solitude. It might almost have been said that the one place in which one would not have expected to come upon him was in just such a solitude as now surrounded the speakers—at least in this deepest hour of its desertedness. But it was just like Lavington's brilliant ubiquity to put one in the wrong even there.

"Oh, yes, I've heard of your uncle."

"Then you *will* come, won't you? We've only five minutes to wait," young Rainer urged, in the tone that dispels scruples by ignoring them; and Faxon found himself accepting the invitation as simply as it was offered.

A delay in the arrival of the New York train lengthened their five minutes to fifteen; and as they paced the icy platform Faxon began to see why it had seemed the most natural thing in the world to accede to his new acquaintance's suggestion. It was because Frank Rainer was one of the privileged beings who simplify human intercourse by the atmosphere of confidence and good humor they diffuse. He produced this effect, Faxon noted, by the exercise of no gift but his youth, and of no art but his sincerity; and these qualities were revealed in a smile of such sweetness that Faxon felt, as never before, what Nature can achieve when she deigns to match the face with the mind.

He learned that the young man was the ward, and the only nephew, of John Lavington, with whom he had made his home since the death of his mother, the great man's sister. Mr. Lavington, Rainer said, had been "a regular brick" to him—"But then he is to everyone, you know"—and the young fellow's situation seemed in fact to be perfectly in keeping with his person. Apparently the only shade that had ever rested on him was cast by the physical weakness which Faxon had already detected. Young Rainer had been threatened with tuberculosis, and the disease was so far advanced that, according to the highest authorities, banishment to Arizona or New Mexico was inevitable. "But luckily my uncle didn't pack me off, as most people would have done, without getting another opinion. Whose? Oh, an awfully clever chap, a young doctor with a lot of new ideas, who simply laughed at my being sent away, and said I'd do perfectly well in New York if I didn't dine out too much, and if I dashed off occasionally to Northridge for a little fresh air. So it's really my uncle's doing that I'm not in exile—and I feel no end better since the new chap told me I needn't bother." Young Rainer went on to confess that he was extremely fond of dining out, dancing and similar distractions; and Faxon, listening to him, was inclined to think that the physician who had refused to cut him off altogether from these pleasures was probably a better psychologist than his seniors.

"All the same you ought to be careful, you know." The sense of elder-brotherly concern that forced the words from Faxon made him, as he spoke, slip his arm through Frank Rainer's.

The latter met the movement with a responsive pressure. "Oh, I *am;* awfully, awfully. And then my uncle has such an eye on me!"

"But if your uncle has such an eye on you, what does he say to your swallowing knives out here in this Siberian wild?"

Rainer raised his fur collar with a careless gesture. "It's not that that does it—the cold's good for me."

"And it's not the dinners and dances? What is it, then?" Faxon good-humoredly insisted; to which his companion answered with a laugh: "Well, my uncle says it's being bored; and I rather think he's right!"

His laugh ended in a spasm of coughing and a struggle for breath that made Faxon, still holding his arm, guide him hastily into the shelter of the fireless waiting room.

Young Rainer had dropped down on the bench against the wall and pulled off one of his fur gloves to grope for a handkerchief. He tossed aside his cap and drew the handkerchief across his forehead, which was intensely white, and beaded with moisture, though his face retained a healthy glow. But Faxon's gaze remained fastened to the hand he had uncovered: it was so long, so colorless, so wasted, so much older than the brow he passed it over.

"It's queer—a healthy face but dying hands," the secretary mused: he somehow wished young Rainer had kept on his glove.

The whistle of the express drew the young men to their feet, and the next moment two heavily-furred gentlemen had descended to the platform and were breasting the rigor of the night. Frank Rainer introduced them as Mr. Grisben and Mr. Balch, and Faxon, while their luggage was being lifted into the second sleigh, discerned them, by the roving lantern gleam, to be an elderly gray-headed pair, of the average prosperous business cut.

They saluted their host's nephew with friendly familiarity, and Mr. Grisben, who seemed the spokesman of the two, ended his greeting with a genial—"and many many more of them, dear boy!" which suggested to Faxon that their arrival coincided with an anniversary. But he could not press the inquiry, for the seat allotted him was at the coachman's side, while Frank Rainer joined his uncle's guests inside the sleigh.

A swift flight (behind such horses as one could be sure of John Lavington's having) brought them to tall gateposts, an illuminated lodge, and an avenue on which the snow had been leveled to the smoothness of marble. At the end of the avenue the long house loomed up, its principal bulk dark, but one wing sending a ray of welcome; and the next moment Faxon was receiving a violent impression of warmth and light, of hothouse plants, hurrying servants, a vast spectacular oak hall like a stage-setting, and, in its unreal middle distance, a small figure, correctly dressed, conventionally featured, and utterly unlike his rather florid conception of the great John Lavington.

The surprise of the contrast remained with him through his hurried dressing in the large luxurious bedroom to which he had been shown. "I don't see where he comes in," was the only way he could put it, so difficult was it to fit the exuberance of Lavington's public personality into his host's contracted frame and manner. Mr. Lavington, to whom Faxon's case had been rapidly explained by young Rainer, had welcomed him with a sort of dry and stilted cordiality that exactly matched his narrow face, his stiff hand, and the whiff of scent on his evening handkerchief. "Make yourself at home—at home!" he had repeated, in a tone that suggested, on his own part, a complete inability to perform the feat he urged on his visitor. "Any friend of Frank's . . . delighted . . . make yourself thoroughly at home!"

II

In spite of the balmy temperature and complicated conveniences of Faxon's bedroom, the injunction was not easy to obey. It was wonderful luck to have found a night's shelter under the opulent roof of Overdale, and he tasted the physical satisfaction to the full. But the place, for all its ingenuities of comfort, was oddly cold and unwelcoming. He couldn't have said why, and could only suppose that Mr. Lavington's intense personality—intensely negative, but intense all the same—must, in some occult way, have penetrated every corner of his dwelling. Perhaps, though, it was merely that Faxon himself was tired and hungry, more deeply chilled than he had known till he came in from the cold, and unutterably sick of all strange houses, and of the prospect of perpetually treading other people's stairs.

"I hope you're not famished?" Rainer's slim figure was in the doorway. "My uncle has a little business to attend to with Mr. Grisben, and we don't dine for half an hour. Shall I fetch you, or can you find your way down? Come straight to the dining room—the second door on the left of the long gallery."

He disappeared, leaving a ray of warmth behind him, and Faxon, relieved, lit a cigarette and sat down by the fire.

Looking about with less haste, he was struck by a detail that had escaped him. The room was full of flowers—a mere "bachelor's room," in the wing of a house opened only for a few days, in the dead middle of a New Hampshire winter! Flowers were everywhere, not in senseless profusion, but placed with the same conscious art that he had remarked in the grouping of the blossoming shrubs in the hall. A vase of arums stood on the writing table, a cluster of strange-hued carnations on the stand at his elbow, and from bowls of glass and porcelain clumps of freesia bulbs diffused their melting fragrance. The fact implied acres of glass—but that was the least interesting part of it. The flowers themselves, their quality, selection and arrangement, attested on someone's part—and on whose but John Lavington's?—a solicitous and sensitive passion for that particular form of beauty. Well, it simply made the man, as he had appeared to Faxon, all the harder to understand!

The half hour elapsed, and Faxon, rejoicing at the prospect of food, set out to make his way to the dining room. He had not noticed the direction he had followed in going to his room, and was puzzled, when he left it, to find that two staircases, of apparently equal importance, invited him. He chose the one to his right, and reached, at its foot, a long gallery such as Rainer had described. The gallery was empty, the doors down its length were closed; but Rainer had said: "The second to the left," and Faxon, after pausing for some chance enlightenment which did not come, laid his hand on the second knob to the left.

The room he entered was square, with dusky picture-hung walls. In the center, about a table lit by veiled lamps, he fancied Mr. Lavington and his guests to be already seated at dinner; then he perceived that the table was covered not with viands but with papers, and that he had blundered into what seemed to be his host's study. As he paused Frank Rainer looked up.

"Oh, here's Mr. Faxon. Why not ask him—?"

Mr. Lavington, from the end of the table, reflected his nephew's smile in a glance of impartial benevolence.

"Certainly. Come in, Mr. Faxon. If you won't think it a liberty—"

Mr. Grisben, who sat opposite his host, turned his head toward the door. "Of course Mr. Faxon's an American citizen?"

Frank Rainer laughed. "That's all right! . . . Oh, no, not one of your pin-pointed pens, Uncle Jack! Haven't you got a quill somewhere?"

Mr. Balch, spoke slowly and as if reluctantly, in a muffled voice of which there seemed to be very little left, raised his hand to say: "One moment: you acknowledge this to be—?"

"My last will and testament?" Rainer's laugh redoubled. "Well, I won't answer for the 'last.' It's the first, anyway."

"It's a mere formula," Mr. Balch explained.

"Well, here goes." Rainer dipped his quill in the inkstand his uncle had pushed in his direction, and dashed a gallant signature across the document.

Faxon, understanding what was expected of him, and conjecturing that the young man was signing his will on the attainment of his majority, had placed himself behind Mr. Grisben, and stood awaiting his turn to affix his name to the instrument. Rainer, having signed, was about to push the paper across the table to Mr. Balch; but the latter, again raising his hand, said in his sad imprisoned voice: "The seal—?"

"Oh, does there have to be a seal?"

Faxon, looking over Mr. Grisben at John Lavington, saw a faint frown between his impassive eyes. "Really, Frank!" He seemed, Faxon thought, slightly irritated by his nephew's frivolity.

"Who's got a seal?" Frank Rainer continued, glancing about the table. "There doesn't seem to be one here."

Mr. Grisben interposed. "A wafer will do. Lavington, you have a wafer?"

Mr. Lavington had recovered his serenity. "There must be some in one of the drawers. But I'm ashamed to say I don't know where my secretary keeps these things. He ought to have seen to it that a wafer was sent with the document."

"Oh, hang it—" Frank Rainer pushed the paper aside. "It's the hand of God—and I'm as hungry as a wolf. Let's dine first, Uncle Jack."

"I think I've a seal upstairs," said Faxon.

Mr. Lavington sent him a barely perceptible smile. "So sorry to give you the trouble—"

"Oh, I say, don't send him after it now. Let's wait till after dinner!"

Mr. Lavington continued to smile on his guest, and the latter, as if under the faint coercion of the smile, turned from the room and ran upstairs. Having taken the seal from his writing case he came down again, and once more opened the door of the study. No one was speaking when he entered—they were evidently awaiting his return with the mute impatience of hunger, and he put the seal in Rainer's reach, and stood watching while Mr. Grisben struck a match and held it to one of the candles flanking the inkstand. As the wax descended on the paper Faxon remarked again the strange emaciation, the premature physical weariness, of the hand that held it: he wondered if Mr. Lavington had ever noticed his nephew's hand, and if it were not poignantly visible to him now.

With this thought in mind, Faxon raised his eyes to look at Mr. Lavington. The great man's gaze rested on Frank Rainer with an expression of untroubled benevolence; and at the same instant Faxon's attention was attracted by the presence in the room of another person, who must have joined the group while he was upstairs searching for the seal. The newcomer was a man of about Mr. Lavington's age and figure, who stood just behind his chair, and who, at the moment when Faxon first saw him, was gazing at young Rainer with an equal intensity of attention. The likeness between the two men—perhaps increased by the fact that the hooded lamps on the table left the figure behind the chair in shadow—struck Faxon the more because of the contrast in their expression. John Lavington, during his nephew's clumsy attempt to drop the wax and apply the seal, continued to fasten on him a look of half-amused affection; while the man behind the chair, so oddly reduplicating the lines of his features and figure, turned on the boy a face of pale hostility.

The impression was so startling that Faxon forgot what was going on about him. He was just dimly aware of young Rainer's exclaiming: "Your turn, Mr. Grisben!" of Mr. Grisben's protesting: "No—no; Mr. Faxon first," and of the pen's being thereupon transferred to his own hand. He received it with a deadly sense of being unable to move, or even to understand what was expected of him, till he became conscious of Mr. Grisben's paternally pointing out the precise spot on which he was to leave his autograph. The effort to fix his attention and steady his hand prolonged the process of signing, and when he stood up—a strange weight of fatigue on all his limbs—the figure behind Mr. Lavington's chair was gone.

Faxon felt an immediate sense of relief. It was puzzling that the man's exit should have been so rapid and noiseless, but the door behind Mr. Lavington was screened by a tapestry hanging, and Faxon concluded that the unknown looker-on had merely had to raise it to pass out. At any rate he was gone, and with his withdrawal the strange weight was lifted. Young Rainer was lighting a cigarette, Mr. Balch inscribing his name at the foot of the document, Mr. Lavington—his eyes no longer on his nephew—examining a strange white-winged orchid in the vase at his elbow. Everything suddenly seemed to have grown natural and simple again, and Faxon found himself responding with a smile to the affable gesture with which his host declared: "And now, Mr. Faxon, we'll dine."

III

"I wonder how I blundered into the wrong room just now; I thought you told me to take the second door to the left," Faxon said to Frank Rainer as they followed the older men down the gallery.

"So I did; but I probably forgot to tell you which staircase to take. Coming from your bedroom, I ought to have said the fourth door to the right. It's a puzzling house, because my uncle keeps adding to it from year to year. He built this room last summer for his modern pictures."

Young Rainer, pausing to open another door, touched an electric button which sent a circle of light about the walls of a long room hung with canvases of the French Impressionist school.

Faxon advanced, attracted by a shimmering Monet, but Rainer laid a hand on his arm.

"He bought that last week. But come along—I'll show you all this after dinner. Or *he* will, rather—he loves it."

"Does he really love things?"

Rainer stared, clearly perplexed at the question. "Rather! Flowers and pictures especially! Haven't you noticed the flowers? I suppose you think his manner's cold; it seems so at first; but he's really awfully keen about things."

Faxon looked quickly at the speaker. "Has your uncle a brother?"

"Brother? No—never had. He and my mother were the only ones."

"Or any relation who—who looks like him? Who might be mistaken for him?"

"Not that I ever heard of. Does he remind you of someone?"

"Yes."

"That's queer. We'll ask him if he's got a double. Come on!"

But another picture had arrested Faxon, and some minutes elapsed before he and his young host reached the dining room. It was a large room, with the same conventionally handsome furniture and delicately grouped flowers; and Faxon's first glance showed him that only three men were seated about the dining table. The man who had stood behind Mr. Lavington's chair was not present, and no seat awaited him.

When the young men entered, Mr. Grisben was speaking, and his host, who faced the door, sat looking down at his untouched soup plate and turning the spoon about in his small dry hand.

"It's pretty late to call them rumors—they were devilish close to facts when we left town this morning," Mr. Grisben was saying, with an unexpected incisiveness of tone.

Mr. Lavington laid down his spoon and smiled interrogatively. "Oh, facts—what *are* facts? Just the way a thing happens to look at a given minute. . . ."

"You haven't heard anything from town?" Mr. Grisben persisted.

"Not a syllable. So you see. . . . Balch, a little more of that *petite marmite*. Mr. Faxon—between Frank and Mr. Grisben, please."

The dinner progressed through a series of complicated courses, ceremoniously dispensed by a prelatical butler attended by three footmen, and it was evident that Mr. Lavington took a certain satisfaction in the pageant. That, Faxon reflected, was probably the joint in his armor—that and the flowers. He had changed the subject—not abruptly but firmly—when the young men entered, but Faxon perceived that it still possessed the thoughts of the two elderly visitors, and Mr. Balch presently observed, in a voice that seemed to come from the last survivor down a mine shaft: "If it *does* come, it will be the biggest crash since '93."

Mr. Lavington looked bored but polite. "Wall Street can stand crashes better than it could then. It's got a robuster constitution."

"Yes; but—"

"Speaking of constitutions," Mr. Grisben intervened: "Frank, are you taking care of yourself?"

A flush rose to young Rainer's cheeks.

"Why, of course! Isn't that what I'm here for?"

"You're here about three days in the month, aren't you? And the rest of the time it's crowded restaurants and hot ballrooms in town. I thought you were to be shipped off to New Mexico?"

"Oh, I've got a new man who says that's rot."

"Well, you don't look as if your new man were right," said Mr. Grisben bluntly.

Faxon saw the lad's color fade, and the rings of shadow deepen under his gay eyes. At the same moment his uncle turned to him with a renewed intensity of attention. There was such solicitude in Mr. Lavington's gaze that it seemed almost to fling a shield between his nephew and Mr. Grisben's tactless scrutiny.

"We think Frank's a good deal better," he began; "this new doctor—"

The butler, coming up, bent to whisper a word in his ear, and the communication caused a sudden change in Mr. Lavington's expression. His face was naturally so colorless that it seemed not so much to pale as to fade, to dwindle and recede into something blurred and blotted out. He half rose, sat down again and sent a rigid smile about the table.

"Will you excuse me? The telephone. Peters, go on with the dinner." With small precise steps he walked out of the door which one of the footmen had thrown open.

A momentary silence fell on the group; then Mr. Grisben once more addressed himself to Rainer. "You ought to have gone, my boy; you ought to have gone."

The anxious look returned to the youth's eyes. "My uncle doesn't think so, really."

"You're not a baby, to be always governed by your uncle's opinion. You came of age today, didn't you? Your uncle spoils you . . . that's what's the matter. . . ."

The thrust evidently went home, for Rainer laughed and looked down with a slight accession of color.

"But the doctor—"

"Use your common sense, Frank! You had to try twenty doctors to find one to tell you what you wanted to be told."

A look of apprehension overshadowed Rainer's gaiety. "Oh, come—I say! . . . What would *you* do?" he stammered.

"Pack up and jump on the first train." Mr. Grisben leaned forward and laid his hand kindly on the young man's arm. "Look here: my nephew Jim Grisben is out there ranching on a big scale. He'll take you in and be glad to have you. You say your new doctor thinks it won't do you any good; but he doesn't pretend to say it will do you harm, does he? Well, then—give it a trial. It'll take you out of hot theaters and night restaurants, anyhow. . . . And all the rest of it. . . . Eh, Balch?"

"Go!" said Mr. Balch hollowly. "Go *at once*," he added, as if a closer look at the youth's face had impressed on him the need of backing up his friend.

Young Rainer had turned ashy pale. He tried to stiffen his mouth into a smile. "Do I look as bad as all that?"

Mr. Grisben was helping himself to terrapin. "You look like the day after an earthquake," he said.

The terrapin had encircled the table, and been deliberately enjoyed by Mr. Lavington's three visitors (Rainer, Faxon noticed, left his plate untouched) before the door was thrown open to readmit their host.

Mr. Lavington advanced with an air of recovered composure. He seated himself, picked up his napkin and consulted the gold-monogrammed menu. "No, don't bring back the filet. . . . Some terrapin; yes. . . ." He looked affably about the table. "Sorry to have deserted you, but the storm has played the deuce with the wires, and I had to wait a long time before I could get a good connection. It must be blowing up a blizzard."

"Uncle Jack," young Rainer broke out, "Mr. Grisben's been lecturing me."

Mr. Lavington was helping himself to terrapin. "Ah—what about?"

"He thinks I ought to have given New Mexico a show."

"I want him to go straight out to my nephew at Santa Paz and stay there till his next birthday." Mr. Lavington signed to the butler to hand the terrapin to Mr. Grisben, who, as he took a second helping, addressed himself again to Rainer. "Jim's in New York now, and going back the day after tomorrow in Olyphant's private car. I'll ask Olyphant to squeeze you in if you'll go. And when you've been out there a week or two, in the saddle all day and sleeping nine hours a night, I suspect you won't think much of the doctor who prescribed New York."

Faxon spoke up, he knew not why. "I was out there once: it's a splendid life. I saw a fellow—oh, a really *bad* case—who'd been simply made over by it."

"It *does* sound jolly," Rainer laughed, a sudden eagerness in his tone.

His uncle looked at him gently. "Perhaps Grisben's right. It's an opportunity—"

Faxon glanced up with a start: the figure dimly perceived in the study was now more visibly and tangibly planted behind Mr. Lavington's chair.

"That's right, Frank: you see your uncle approves. And the trip out there with Olyphant isn't a thing to be missed. So drop a few dozen dinners and be at the Grand Central the day after tomorrow at five."

Mr. Grisben's pleasant grey eye sought corroboration of his host, and Faxon, in a cold anguish of suspense, continued to watch him as he turned his glance on Mr. Lavington. One could not look at Lavington without seeing the presence at his back, and it was clear that, the next minute, some change in Mr. Grisben's expression must give his watcher a clue.

But Mr. Grisben's expression did not change: the gaze he fixed on his host remained unperturbed, and the clue he gave was the startling one of not seeming to see the other figure.

Faxon's first impulse was to look away, to look anywhere else, to resort again to the champagne glass the watchful butler had already brimmed; but some fatal attraction, at war in him with an overwhelming physical resistance, held his eyes upon the spot they feared.

The figure was still standing, more distinctly, and therefore more resemblingly, at Mr. Lavington's back; and while the latter continued to gaze affectionately at his nephew, his counterpart, as before, fixed young Rainer with eyes of deadly menace.

Faxon, with what felt like an actual wrench of the muscles, dragged his own eyes from the sight to scan the other countenances about the table; but not one revealed the least consciousness of what he saw, and a sense of mortal isolation sank upon him.

"It's worth considering, certainly—" he heard Mr. Lavington continue; and as Rainer's face lit up, the face behind his uncle's chair seemed to gather into its look all the fierce weariness of old unsatisfied hates. That was the thing that, as the minutes labored by, Faxon was becoming most conscious of. The watcher behind the chair was no longer merely malevolent: he had grown suddenly, unutterably tired. His hatred seemed to well up out of the very depths of balked effort and thwarted hopes, and the fact made him more pitiable, and yet more dire.

Faxon's look reverted to Mr. Lavington, as if to surprise in him a corresponding change. At first none was visible: his pinched smile was screwed to his blank face like a gaslight to a whitewashed wall. Then the fixity of the smile became ominous: Faxon saw that its wearer was afraid to let it go. It was evident that Mr. Lavington was unutterably tired too, and the discovery sent a colder current through Faxon's veins. Looking down at his untouched plate, he caught the soliciting twinkle of the champagne glass; but the sight of the wine turned him sick.

"Well, we'll go into the details presently," he heard Mr. Lavington say, still on the question of his nephew's future. "Let's have a cigar first. No—not here, Peters." He turned his smile on Faxon. "When we've had coffee I want to show you my pictures."

"Oh, by the way, Uncle Jack—Mr. Faxon wants to know if you've got a double?"

"A double?" Mr. Lavington, still smiling, continued to address himself to his guest. "Not that I know of. Have you seen one, Mr. Faxon?"

Faxon thought: "My God, if I look up now they'll *both* be looking at me!" To avoid raising his eyes he made as though to lift the glass to his lips; but his hand sank inert, and he looked up. Mr. Lavington's glance was politely bent on him, but with a loosening of the strain about his heart he saw that the figure behind the chair still kept its gaze on Rainer.

"Do you think you've seen my double, Mr. Faxon?"

Would the other face turn if he said yes? Faxon felt a dryness in his throat. "No," he answered.

"Ah? It's possible I've a dozen. I believe I'm extremely usual-looking," Mr. Lavington went on conversationally; and still the other face watched Rainer.

"It was . . . a mistake . . . a confusion of memory. . . ." Faxon

heard himself stammer. Mr. Lavington pushed back his chair, and as
he did so Mr. Grisben suddenly leaned forward.

"Lavington! What have we been thinking of? We haven't drunk
Frank's health!"

Mr. Lavington reseated himself. "My dear boy! . . . Peters, another
bottle. . . ." He turned to his nephew. "After such a sin of omission
I don't presume to propose that toast myself . . . but Frank knows.
. . . Go ahead, Grisben!"

The boy shone on his uncle. "No, no. Uncle Jack! Mr. Grisben
won't mind. Nobody but *you*—today!"

The butler was replenishing the glasses. He filled Mr. Lavington's
last, and Mr. Lavington put out his small hand to raise it. . . . As he
did so, Faxon looked away.

"Well, then—All the good I've wished you in all the past years . . .
I put it into the prayer that the coming ones may be healthy and happy
and many . . . and *many,* dear boy!"

Faxon saw the hands about him reach out for their glasses. Au-
tomatically, he reached for his. His eyes were still on the table, and
he repeated to himself with a trembling vehemence: "I won't look
up! I won't. . . . I won't. . . ."

His fingers clasped the glass and raised it to the level of his lips.
He saw the other hands making the same motion. He heard Mr. Grisben's genial "Hear! Hear!" and Mr. Balch's hollow echo. He said to
himself, as the rim of the glass touched his lips: "I won't look up! I
swear I won't!" and he looked.

The glass was so full that it required an extraordinary effort to
hold it there, brimming and suspended, during the awful interval before he could trust his hand to lower it again, untouched, to the table.
It was this merciful preoccupation which saved him, kept him from
crying out, from losing his hold, from slipping down into the bot-
tomless blackness that gaped for him. As long as the problem of the
glass engaged him he felt able to keep his seat, manage his muscles,
fit unnoticeably into the group; but as the glass touched the table his
last link with safety snapped. He stood up and dashed out of the room.

IV

In the gallery, the instinct of self-preservation helped him to turn back
and sign to young Rainer not to follow. He stammered out something

about a touch of dizziness, and joining them presently; and the boy nodded sympathetically and drew back.

At the foot of the stairs Faxon ran against a servant. "I should like to telephone to Weymore," he said with dry lips.

"Sorry, sir; wires all down. We've been trying the last hour to get New York again for Mr. Lavington."

Faxon shot on to his room, burst into it, and bolted the door. The lamplight lay on furniture, flowers, books; in the ashes a log still glimmered. He dropped down on the sofa and hid his face. The room was profoundly silent, the whole house was still: nothing about him gave a hint of what was going on, darkly and dumbly, in the room he had flown from, and with the covering of his eyes oblivion and reassurance seemed to fall on him. But they fell for a moment only; then his lids opened again to the monstrous vision. There it was, stamped on his pupils, a part of him forever, an indelible horror burnt into his body and brain. But why into his—just his? Why had he alone been chosen to see what he had seen? What business was it of *his*, in God's name? Any one of the others thus enlightened, might have exposed the horror and defeated it; but *he*, the one weaponless and defenceless spectator, the one whom none of the others would believe or understand if he attempted to reveal what he knew—*he* alone had been singled out as the victim of this dreadful initiation!

Suddenly he sat up, listening: he had heard a step on the stairs. Someone, no doubt, was coming to see how he was—to urge him, if he felt better, to go down and join the smokers. Cautiously he opened his door; yes, it was young Rainer's step. Faxon looked down the passage, remembered the other stairway and darted to it. All he wanted was to get out of the house. Not another instant would he breathe its abominable air! What business was it of *his*, in God's name?

He reached the opposite end of the lower gallery, and beyond it saw the hall by which he had entered. It was empty, and on a long table he recognized his coat and cap. He got into his coat, unbolted the door, and plunged into the purifying night.

The darkness was deep, and the cold so intense that for an instant it stopped his breathing. Then he perceived that only a thin snow was falling, and resolutely he set his face for flight. The trees along the avenue marked his way as he hastened with long strides over the beaten snow. Gradually, while he walked, the tumult in his brain subsided. The impulse to fly still drove him forward, but he began to feel that he was flying from a terror of his own creating, and that the most urgent reason for escape was the need of hiding his state, of shunning other eyes till he should regain his balance.

He had spent the long hours in the train in fruitless broodings on a discouraging situation, and he remembered how his bitterness had turned to exasperation when he found that the Weymore sleigh was not awaiting him. It was absurd, of course; but though he had joked with Rainer over Mrs. Culme's forgetfulness, to confess it had cost a pang. That was what his rootless life had brought him to: for lack of a personal stake in things his sensibility was at the mercy of such trifles. . . . Yes; that, and the cold and fatigue, the absence of hope and the haunting sense of starved aptitudes, all these had brought him to the perilous verge over which, once or twice before, his terrified brain had hung.

Why else, in the name of any imaginable logic, human or devilish, should he, a stranger, be singled out for this experience? What could it mean to him, how was he related to it, what bearing had it on his case? . . . Unless, indeed, it was just because he was a stranger—a stranger everywhere—because he had no personal life, no warm screen of private egotisms to shield him from exposure, that he had developed this abnormal sensitiveness to the vicissitudes of others. The thought pulled him up with a shudder. No! Such a fate was too abominable; all that was strong and sound in him rejected it. A thousand times better regard himself as ill, disorganized, deluded, than as the predestined victim of such warnings!

He reached the gates and paused before the darkened lodge. The wind had risen and was sweeping the snow into his face. The cold had him in its grasp again, and he stood uncertain. Should he put his sanity to the test and go back? He turned and looked down the dark drive to the house. A single ray shone through the trees, evoking a picture of the lights, the flowers, the faces grouped about that fatal room. He turned and plunged out into the road. . . .

He remembered that, about a mile from Overdale, the coachman had pointed out the road to Northridge; and he began to walk in that direction. Once in the road he had the gale in his face, and the wet snow on his moustache and eyelashes instantly hardened to ice. The same ice seemed to be driving a million blades into his throat and lungs, but he pushed on, the vision of the warm room pursuing him.

The snow in the road was deep and uneven. He stumbled across ruts and sank into drifts, and the wind drove against him like a granite cliff. Now and then he stopped, gasping, as if an invisible hand had tightened an iron band about his body; then he started again, stiffening himself against the stealthy penetration of the cold. The snow continued to descend out of a pall of inscrutable darkness, and once or twice he paused, fearing he had missed the road to Northridge; but, seeing no sign of a turn, he ploughed on.

At last, feeling sure that he had walked for more than a mile, he halted and looked back. The act of turning brought immediate relief, first because it put his back to the wind, and then because, far down the road, it showed him the gleam of a lantern. A sleigh was coming—a sleigh that might perhaps give him a lift to the village! Fortified by the hope, he began to walk back toward the light. It came forward very slowly, with unaccountable zigzags and waverings; and even when he was within a few yards of it he could catch no sound of sleigh bells. Then it paused and became stationary by the roadside, as though carried by a pedestrian who had stopped, exhausted by the cold. The thought made Faxon hasten on, and a moment later he was stooping over a motionless figure huddled against the snowbank. The lantern had dropped from its bearer's hand, and Faxon, fearfully raising it, threw its light into the face of Frank Rainer.

"Rainer! What on earth are you doing here?"

The boy smiled back through his pallor. "What are *you*, I'd like to know?" he retorted; and, scrambling to his feet with a clutch on Faxon's arm, he added gaily: "Well, I've run you down!"

Faxon stood confounded, his heart sinking. The lad's face was grey.

"What madness—" he began.

"Yes, it *is*. What on earth did you do it for?"

"I? Do what? . . . Why I. . . . I was just taking a walk. . . . I often walk at night. . . ."

Frank Rainer burst into a laugh. "On such nights? Then you hadn't bolted?"

"Bolted?"

"Because I'd done something to offend you? My uncle thought you had."

Faxon grasped his arm. "Did your uncle send you after me?"

"Well, he gave me an awful rowing for not going up to your room

with you when you said you were ill. And when we found you'd gone
we were frightened—and he was awfully upset—so I said I'd catch
you. . . . You're *not* ill, are you?

"Ill? No. Never better." Faxon picked up the lantern. "Come; let's
go back. It was awfully hot in that dining room."

"Yes; I hoped it was only that."

They trudged on in silence for a few minutes; then Faxon questioned: "You're not too done up?"

"Oh, no. It's a lot easier with the wind behind us."

"All right. Don't talk any more."

They pushed ahead, walking, in spite of the light that guided them,
more slowly than Faxon had walked alone into the gale. The fact of
his companion's stumbling against a drift gave Faxon a pretext for
saying: "Take hold of my arm," and Rainer, obeying, gasped out:
"I'm blown!"

"So am I. Who wouldn't be?"

"What a dance you led me! If it hadn't been for one of the servants
happening to see you—"

"Yes; all right. And now, won't you kindly shut up?"

Rainer laughed and hung on him. "Oh, the cold doesn't hurt
me. . . ."

For the first few minutes after Rainer had overtaken him, anxiety
for the lad had been Faxon's only thought. But as each laboring step
carried them nearer to the spot he had been fleeing, the reasons for
his flight grew more ominous and more insistent. No, he was not ill,
he was not distraught and deluded—he was the instrument singled
out to warn and save; and here he was, irresistibly driven, dragging
the victim back to his doom!

The intensity of the conviction had almost checked his steps. But
what could he do or say? At all costs he must get Rainer out of the
cold, into the house and into his bed. After that he would act.

The snowfall was thickening, and as they reached a stretch of the
road between open fields the wind took them at an angle, lashing
their faces with barbed thongs. Rainer stopped to take breath and
Faxon felt the heavier pressure of his arm.

"When we get to the lodge, can't we telephone to the stable for a
sleigh?"

"If they're not all asleep at the lodge."

"Oh, I'll manage. Don't talk!" Faxon ordered; and they plodded
on. . . .

At length the lantern ray showed ruts that curved away from the road under tree darkness.

Faxon's spirits rose. "There's the gate! We'll be there in five minutes."

As he spoke he caught, above the boundary hedge, the gleam of a light at the farther end of the dark avenue. It was the same light that had shone on the scene of which every detail was burnt into his brain; and he felt again its overpowering reality. No—he couldn't let the boy go back!

They were at the lodge at last, and Faxon was hammering on the door. He said to himself: "I'll get him inside first, and make them give him a hot drink. Then I'll see—I'll find an argument. . . ."

There was no answer to his knocking, and after an interval Rainer said: "Look here—we'd better go on."

"No!"

"I can, perfectly—"

"You shan't go to the house, I say!" Faxon redoubled his blows, and at length steps sounded on the stairs. Rainer was leaning against the lintel, and as the door opened the light from the hall flashed on his pale face and fixed eyes. Faxon caught him by the arm and drew him in.

"It *was* cold out there," he sighed; and then, abruptly, as if invisible shears at a single stroke had cut every muscle in his body, he swerved, drooped on Faxon's arm, and seemed to sink into nothing at his feet.

The lodgekeeper and Faxon bent over him, and somehow, between them lifted him into the kitchen and laid him on a sofa by the stove.

The lodgekeeper, stammering: "I'll ring up the house," dashed out of the room. But Faxon heard the words without heeding them: omens mattered nothing now, beside this woe fulfilled. He knelt down to undo the fur collar about Rainer's throat, and as he did so he felt a warm moisture on his hands. He held them up, and they were red. . . .

V

The palms threaded their endless line along the yellow river. The little steamer lay at the wharf, and George Faxon, sitting on the verandah of the wooden hotel, idly watched the coolies carrying the freight across the gangplank.

He had been looking at such scenes for two months. Nearly five had elapsed since he had descended from the train at Northridge and strained his eyes for the sleigh that was to take him to Weymore: Weymore, which he was never to behold! . . . Part of the interval—the first part—was still a great grey blur. Even now he could not be quite sure how he had got back to Boston, reached the house of a cousin, and been thence transferred to a quiet room looking out on snow under bare trees. He looked out a long time at the same scene, and finally one day a man he had known at Harvard came to see him and invited him to go out on a business trip to the Malay Peninsula.

"You've had a bad shake-up, and it'll do you no end of good to get away from things."

When the doctor came the next day it turned out that he knew of the plan and approved it. "You ought to be quiet for a year. Just loaf and look at the landscape," he advised.

Faxon felt the first faint stirring of curiosity.

"What's been the matter with me, anyway?"

"Well, overwork, I suppose. You must have been bottling up for a bad breakdown before you started for New Hampshire last December. And the shock of that poor boy's death did the rest."

Ah, yes—Rainer had died. He remembered. . . .

He started for the East, and gradually, by imperceptible degrees, life crept back into his weary bones and leaden brain. His friend was patient and considerate, and they traveled slowly and talked little. At first Faxon had felt a great shrinking from whatever touched on familiar things. He seldom looked at a newspaper and he never opened a letter without a contraction of the heart. It was not that he had any special cause for apprehension, but merely that a great trail of darkness lay on everything. He had looked too deep down into the abyss. . . . But little by little health and energy returned to him, and with them the common promptings of curiosity. He was beginning to wonder how the world was going, and when, presently, the hotel-keeper told him there were no letters for him in the steamer's mailbag, he felt a distinct sense of disappointment. His friend had gone into the jungle on a long excursion, and he was lonely, unoccupied and wholesomely bored. He got up and strolled into the stuffy reading room.

There he found a game of dominoes, a mutilated picture puzzle, some copies of *Zion's Herald* and a pile of New York and London newspapers.

He began to glance through the papers, and was disappointed to find that they were less recent than he had hoped. Evidently the last numbers had been carried off by luckier travelers. He continued to turn them over, picking out the American ones first. These, as it happened, were the oldest: they dated back to December and January. To Faxon, however, they had all the flavor of novelty, since they covered the precise period during which he had virtually cased to exist. It had never before occurred to him to wonder what had happened in the world during that interval of obliteration; but now he felt a sudden desire to know.

To prolong the pleasure, he began by sorting the papers chronologically, and as he found and spread out the earliest number, the date at the top of the page entered into his consciousness like a key slipping into a lock. It was the seventeenth of December: the date of the day after his arrival at Northridge. He glanced at the first page and read in blazing characters: "Reported Failure of Opal Cement Company. Lavington's name involved. Gigantic Exposure of Corruption Shakes Wall Street to Its Foundations."

He read on, and when he had finished the first paper he turned to the next. There was a gap of three days, but the Opal Cement "Investigation" still held the center of the stage. From its complex revelations of greed and ruin his eye wandered to the death notices, and he read: "Rainer. Suddenly, at Northridge, New Hampshire, Francis John, only son of the late . . ."

His eyes clouded, and he dropped the newspaper and sat for a long time with his face in his hands. When he looked up again he noticed that his gesture had pushed the other papers from the table and scattered them at his feet. The uppermost lay spread out before him, and heavily his eyes began their search again. "John Lavington comes forward with plan for reconstructing company. Offers to put in ten millions of his own—The proposal under consideration by the District Attorney."

Ten millions . . . ten millions of his own. But if John Lavington was ruined? . . . Faxon stood up with a cry. That was it, then—that was what the warning meant! And if he had not fled from it, dashed wildly away from it into the night, he might have broken the spell of iniquity, the powers of darkness might not have prevailed! He caught up the pile of newspapers and began to glance through each in turn for the headline: "Wills Admitted to Probate." In the last of all he found the paragraph he sought, and it stared up at him as if with Rainer's dying eyes.

That—*that* was what he had done! The powers of pity had singled him out to warn and save, and he had closed his ears to their call, and washed his hands of it, and fled. Washed his hands of it! That was the word. It caught him back to the dreadful moment in the lodge, when, raising himself up from Rainer's side, he had looked at his hands and seen that they were red. . . .

BEWITCHED

(1925)

"Bewitched" appeared in a popular magazine in 1925 and was collected the next year in Here and Beyond, whose title reflects Wharton's growing fascination with ghost stories. Most reviewers selected "Bewitched" as the best tale in the volume.

The story is told by an Ethan Frome-type narrator and takes place in the same area. Starkfield is even mentioned as south of Ashmore, the site of the Rutledge farm. Significantly, the summer home of Wharton's friends the Nortons—Charles Eliot, the Harvard professor, and his daughter Sally, the original "angel at the grave"—was in Ashfield, forty miles from the Mount. Wharton may have gotten from the Nortons the pedigree of Ashmore: it is supposedly the ruin of a royalist colony that was burned. Wharton thus has her pun, ash more, and the suggestion that the Rutledge farm lies on top of a cemetery and is haunted by the past. Prudence Rutledge looks like a marble statue, Saul has a "spectral smile," and their tomblike home boasts "fluted urns." As the snow falls, the characters feel "as if a winding sheet were descending from the sky to envelop them all in a common grave."

What this death-in-life atmosphere might mean is left up to the reader. In a story so filled with ambiguities that it is hard to figure out what happens, Wharton suggests alternative supernatural and natural explanations of events. Does Mr. Brand shoot the ghost of his daughter Ora or does he kill the living Venny, who has been Mr. Rutledge's lover? At any rate, the witchlike Mrs. Rutledge, a relative of Zeena and Mattie, feels herself avenged.

THE SNOW was still falling thickly when Orrin Bosworth, who farmed the land south of Lonetop, drove up in his cutter to Saul Rutledge's gate. He was surprised to see two other cutters ahead of him. From them descended two muffled figures. Bosworth, with increasing surprise, recognized Deacon Hibben, from North Ashmore, and Sylvester Brand, the widower, from the old Bearcliff farm on the way to Lonetop.

It was not often that anybody in Hemlock County entered Saul Rutledge's gate; least of all in the dead of winter, and summoned (as Bosworth, at any rate, had been) by Mrs. Rutledge, who passed, even in that unsocial region, for a woman of cold manners and solitary character. The situation was enough to excite the curiosity of a less imaginative man than Orrin Bosworth.

As he drove in between the broken-down white gateposts topped by fluted urns the two men ahead of him were leading their horses to the adjoining shed. Bosworth followed, and hitched his horse to a post. Then the three tossed off the snow from their shoulders, clapped their numb hands together, and greeted each other.

"Hallo, Deacon."

"Well, well, Orrin—" They shook hands.

"'Day, Bosworth," said Sylvester Brand, with a brief nod. He seldom put any cordiality into his manner, and on this occasion he was still busy about his horse's bridle and blanket.

Orrin Bosworth, the youngest and most communicative of the three, turned back to Deacon Hibben, whose long face, queerly blotched and moldy-looking, with blinking peering eyes, was yet less forbidding than Brand's heavily-hewn countenance.

"Queer, our all meeting here this way. Mrs. Rutledge sent me a message to come," Bosworth volunteered.

The Deacon nodded. "I got a word from her too—Andy Pond come with it yesterday noon. I hope there's no trouble here—"

He glanced through the thickening fall of snow at the desolate front of the Rutledge house, the more melancholy in its present neglected state because, like the gateposts, it kept traces of former elegance. Bosworth had often wondered how such a house had come to be built in that lonely stretch between North Ashmore and Cold Corners. People said there had once been other houses like it, forming a little township called Ashmore, a sort of mountain colony created by the caprice of an English Royalist officer, one Colonel Ashmore, who had been murdered by the Indians, with all his family, long before the Revolution. This tale was confirmed by the fact that the ruined cellars of several smaller houses were still to be discovered under the wild growth of the adjoining slopes, and that the Communion plate of the moribund Episcopal church of Cold Corners was engraved with the name of Colonel Ashmore, who had given it to the church of Ashmore in the year 1723. Of the church itself no traces remained. Doubtless it had been a modest wooden edifice, built on piles, and the conflagration which had burnt the other houses to the ground's edge had reduced it utterly to ashes. The whole place, even in summer, wore a mournful solitary air, and people wondered why Saul Rutledge's father had gone there to settle.

"I never knew a place," Deacon Hibben said, "as seemed as far away from humanity. And yet it ain't so in miles."

"Miles ain't the only distance," Orrin Bosworth answered; and the two men, followed by Sylvester Brand, walked across the drive to the front door. People in Hemlock County did not usually come and go by their front doors, but all three men seemed to feel that, on an occasion which appeared to be so exceptional, the usual and more familiar approach by the kitchen would not be suitable.

They had judged rightly; the Deacon had hardly lifted the knocker when the door opened and Mrs. Rutledge stood before them.

"Walk right in," she said in her usual dead-level tone; and Bosworth, as he followed the others, thought to himself: "Whatever's happened, she's not going to let it show in her face."

It was doubtful, indeed, if anything unwonted could be made to show in Prudence Rutledge's face, so limited was its scope, so fixed were its features. She was dressed for the occasion in a black calico with white spots, a collar of crochet lace fastened by a gold brooch, and a gray woolen shawl, crossed under her arms and tied at the back. In her small narrow head the only marked prominence was that of the brow projecting roundly over pale spectacled eyes. Her dark hair, parted above this prominence, passed tight and flat over the tops of her ears into a small braided coil at the nape; and her contracted head looked still narrower from being perched on a long hollow neck with cord-like throat muscles. Her eyes were of a pale cold gray, her complexion was an even white. Her age might have been anywhere from thirty-five to sixty.

The room into which she led the three men had probably been the dining room of the Ashmore house. It was now used as a front parlor, and a black stove planted on a sheet of zinc stuck out from the delicately fluted panels of an old wooden mantel. A newly-lit fire smoldered reluctantly, and the room was at once close and bitterly cold.

"Andy Pond," Mrs. Rutledge cried to some one at the back of the house, "Step out and call Mr. Rutledge. You'll likely find him in the woodshed, or round the barn somewhere." She rejoined her visitors. "Please suit yourselves to seats," she said.

The three men, with an increasing air of constraint, took the chairs she pointed out, and Mrs. Rutledge sat stiffly down upon a fourth, behind a rickety beadwork table. She glanced from one to the other of her visitors.

"I presume you folks are wondering what it is I asked you to come here for," she said in her dead-level voice. Orrin Bosworth and Deacon Hibben murmured an assent; Sylvester Brand sat silent, his eyes, under their great thicket of eyebrows, fixed on the huge boot tip swinging before him.

"Well, I allow you didn't expect it was for a party," continued Mrs. Rutledge.

No one ventured to respond to this chill pleasantry, and she continued: "We're in trouble here, and that's the fact. And we need advice—Mr. Rutledge and myself do." She cleared her throat, and added in a lower tone, her pitilessly clear eyes looking straight before her: "There's a spell been cast over Mr. Rutledge."

The Deacon looked up sharply, an incredulous smile pinching his thin lips. "A spell?"

"That's what I said: he's bewitched."

Again the three visitors were silent; then Bosworth, more at ease or less tongue-tied than the others, asked with an attempt at humor: "Do you use the word in the strict Scripture sense, Mrs. Rutledge?"

She glanced at him before replying: "That's how *he* uses it."

The Deacon coughed and cleared his long rattling throat: "Do you care to give us more particulars before your husband joins us?"

Mrs. Rutledge looked down at her clasped hands, as if considering the question. Bosworth noticed that the inner fold of her lids was of the same uniform white as the rest of her skin, so that when she drooped them her rather prominent eyes looked like the sightless orbs of a marble statue. The impression was unpleasing, and he glanced away at the text over the mantelpiece, which read:

.*The Soul That Sinneth It Shall Die.*

"No," she said at length, "I'll wait."

At this moment Sylvester Brand suddenly stood up and pushed back his chair. "I don't know," he said, in his rough bass voice, "as I've got any particular light on Bible mysteries; and this happens to be the day I was to go down to Starkfield to close a deal with a man."

Mrs. Rutledge lifted one of her long thin hands. Withered and wrinkled by hard work and cold, it was nevertheless of the same leaden white as her face. "You won't be kept long," she said. "Won't you be seated?"

Farmer Brand stood irresolute, his purplish underlip twitching. "The Deacon here—such things is more in his line. . . ."

"I want you should stay," said Mrs. Rutledge quietly; and Brand sat down again.

A silence fell, during which the four persons presented seemed all to be listening for the sound of a step; but none was heard, and after a minute or two Mrs. Rutledge began to speak again.

"It's down by that old shack on Lamer's pond; that's where they meet," she said suddenly.

Bosworth, whose eyes were on Sylvester Brand's face, fancied he saw a sort of inner flush darken the farmer's heavy leathern skin. Deacon Hibben leaned forward, a glitter of curiosity in his eyes.

"They—*who*, Mrs. Rutledge?"

"My husband, Saul Rutledge . . . and her. . . ."

Sylvester Brand again stirred in his seat. "Who do you mean by *her*?" he asked abruptly, as if roused out of some far-off musing.

Mrs. Rutledge's body did not move; she simply revolved her head on her long neck and looked at him.

"Your daughter, Sylvester Brand."

The man staggered to his feet with an explosion of inarticulate sounds. "My—my daughter? What the hell are you talking about? My daughter? It's a damned lie . . . it's . . . it's. . . ."

"Your daughter *Ora*, Mr. Brand," said Mrs. Rutledge slowly.

Bosworth felt an icy chill down his spine. Instinctively he turned his eyes away from Brand, and they rested on the mildewed countenance of Deacon Hibben. Between the blotches it had become as white as Mrs. Rutledge's and the Deacon's eyes burned in the whiteness like live embers among ashes.

Brand gave a laugh: the rusty creaking laugh of one whose springs of mirth are never moved by gaiety. "My daughter *Ora?*" he repeated.

"Yes."

"My *dead* daughter?"

"That's what he says."

"Your husband?"

"That's what Mr. Rutledge says."

Orrin Bosworth listened with a sense of suffocation; he felt as if he were wrestling with long-armed horrors in a dream. He could no longer resist letting his eyes turn to Sylvester Brand's face. To his surprise it had resumed a natural imperturbable expression. Brand rose to his feet. "Is that all?" he queried contemptuously.

"All? Ain't it enough? How long is it since you folks seen Saul Rutledge, any of you?" Mrs. Rutledge flew out at them.

Bosworth, it appeared, had not seen him for nearly a year; the Deacon had only run across him once, for a minute, at the North Ashmore post office, the previous autumn, and acknowledged that he wasn't looking any too good then. Brand said nothing, but stood irresolute.

"Well, if you wait a minute you'll see with your own eyes; and he'll tell you with his own words. That's what I've got you here for— to see for yourselves what's come over him. Then you'll talk different," she added, twisting her head abruptly toward Sylvester Brand.

The Deacon raised a lean hand of interrogation.

"Does your husband know we've been sent for on this business, Mrs. Rutledge?

Mrs. Rutledge signed assent.

"It was with his consent, then—?"

She looked coldly at her questioner. "I guess it had to be," she said. Again Bosworth felt the chill down his spine. He tried to dissipate the sensation by speaking with an affectation of energy.

"Can you tell us, Mrs. Rutledge, how this trouble you speak of shows itself . . . what makes you think . . . ?"

She looked at him for a moment; then she leaned forward across the rickety beadwork table. A thin smile of disdain narrowed her colorless lips. "I don't think—I know."

"Well—but how?"

She leaned closer, both elbows on the table, her voice dropping. "I seen 'em."

In the ashen light from the veiling of snow beyond the windows the Deacon's little screwed-up eyes seemed to give out red sparks. "Him and the dead?"

"Him and the dead."

"Saul Rutledge and—and Ora Brand?"

"That's so."

Sylvester Brand's chair fell backward with a crash. He was on his feet again, crimson and cursing. "It's a God-damned fiend-begotten lie. . . ."

"Friend Brand . . . friend Brand . . ." the Deacon protested.

"Here, let me get out of this. I want to see Saul Rutledge himself, and tell him—"

"Well, here he is," said Mrs. Rutledge.

The outer door had opened; they heard the familiar stamping and shaking of a man who rids his garments of their last snowflakes before penetrating to the sacred precincts of the best parlor. Then Saul Rutledge entered.

II

As he came in he faced the light from the north window, and Bosworth's first thought was that he looked like a drowned man fished out from under the ice—"self-drowned," he added. But the snow light plays cruel tricks with a man's color, and even with the shape of his features; it must have been partly that, Bosworth reflected, which transformed Saul Rutledge from the straight muscular fellow he had been a year before into the haggard wretch now before them.

The Deacon sought for a word to ease the horror. "Well, now, Saul—you look's if you'd ought to set right up to the stove. Had a touch of ague, maybe?"

The feeble attempt was unavailing. Rutledge neither moved nor answered. He stood among them silent, incommunicable, like one risen from the dead.

Brand grasped him roughly by the shoulder. "See here, Saul Rutledge, what's this dirty lie your wife tells us you've been putting about?"

Still Rutledge did not move. "It's no lie," he said.

Brand's hand dropped from his shoulder. In spite of the man's rough bullying power he seemed to be undefinably awed by Rutledge's look and tone.

"No lie? You've gone plumb crazy, then, have you?"

Mrs. Rutledge spoke. "My husband's not lying, nor he ain't gone crazy. Don't I tell you I seen 'em?"

Brand laughed again. "Him and the dead?"

"Yes."

"Down by the Lamer pond, you say?"

"Yes."

"And when was that, if I might ask?"

"Day before yesterday."

A silence fell on the strangely assembled group. The Deacon at length broke it to say to Mr. Brand: "Brand, in my opinion we've got to see this thing through."

Brand stood for a moment in speechless contemplation: there was something animal and primitive about him, Bosworth thought, as he hung thus, lowering and dumb, a little foam beading the corners of that heavy purplish underlip. He let himself slowly down into his chair. "I'll see it through."

The two other men and Mrs. Rutledge had remained seated. Saul Rutledge stood before them, like a prisoner at the bar, or rather like a sick man before the physicians who were to heal him. As Bosworth scrutinized that hollow face, so wan under the dark sunburn, so sucked inward and consumed by some hidden fever, there stole over the sound healthy man the thought that perhaps, after all, husband and wife spoke the truth, and that they were all at that moment really standing on the edge of some forbidden mystery. Things that the rational mind would reject without a thought seemed no longer so easy to dispose of as one looked at the actual Saul Rutledge and remembered the man he had been a year before. Yes; as the Deacon said, they would have to see it through. . . .

"Sit down then, Saul; draw up to us, won't you?" the Deacon suggested, trying again for a natural tone.

Mrs. Rutledge pushed a chair forward, and her husband sat down on it. He stretched out his arms and grasped his knees in his brown bony fingers; in that attitude he remained, turning neither his head nor his eyes.

"Well, Saul," the Deacon continued, "your wife says you thought mebbe we could do something to help you through this trouble, whatever it is."

Rutledge's gray eyes widened a little. "No; I didn't think that. It was her idea to try what could be done."

"I presume, though, since you've agreed to our coming, that you don't object to our putting a few questions?"

Rutledge was silent for a moment; then he said with a visible effort: "No; I don't object."

"Well—you've heard what your wife says?"

Rutledge made a slight motion of assent.

"And—what have you got to answer? How do you explain . . . ?"

Mrs. Rutledge intervened. "How can he explain? I seen 'em."

There was a silence; then Bosworth, trying to speak in an easy reassuring tone, queried: "That so, Saul?"

"That's so."

Brand lifted up his brooding head. "You mean to say you . . . you sit here before us all and say. . . ."

The Deacon's hand again checked him. "Hold on, friend Brand. We're all of us trying for the facts, ain't we?" He turned to Rutledge. "We've heard what Mrs. Rutledge says. What's your answer?"

"I don't know as there's any answer. She found us."

"And you mean to tell me the person with you was . . . was what you took to be . . ." the Deacon's thin voice grew thinner, "Ora Brand?"

Saul Rutledge nodded.

"You knew . . . or thought you knew . . . you were meeting with the dead?"

Rutledge bent his head again. The snow continued to fall in a steady unwavering sheet against the window, and Bosworth felt as if a winding sheet were descending from the sky to envelop them all in a common grave.

"Think what you're saying! It's against our religion! Ora . . . poor child! . . . died over a year ago. I saw you at her funeral, Saul. How can you make such a statement?"

"What else can he do?" thrust in Mrs. Rutledge.

There was another pause. Bosworth's resources had failed him, and Brand once more sat plunged in dark meditation. The Deacon laid his quivering finger tips together, and moistened his lips.

"Was the day before yesterday the first time?" he asked.

The movement of Rutledge's head was negative.

"Not the first? Then when . . . ?"

"Nigh on a year ago, I reckon."

"God! And you mean to tell us that ever since—?"

"Well . . . look at him," said his wife. The three men lowered their eyes.

After a moment Bosworth, trying to collect himself, glanced at the Deacon. "Why not ask Saul to make his own statement, if that's what we're here for?"

"That's so," the Deacon assented. He turned to Rutledge. "Will you try and give us your idea . . . of . . . of how it began?"

There was another silence. Then Rutledge tightened his grasp on his gaunt knees, and still looking straight ahead, with his curiously clear unseeing gaze: "Well," he said, "I guess it begun away back, afore even I was married to Mrs. Rutledge. . . ." He spoke in a low automatic tone, as if some invisible agent were dictating his words, or even uttering them for him. "You know," he added, "Ora and me was to have been married."

Sylvester Brand lifted his head. "Straighten that statement out first, please," he interjected.

"What I mean is, we kept company. But Ora she was very young. Mr. Brand here he sent her away. She was gone nigh to three years, I guess. When she come back I was married."

"That's right," Brand said, relapsing once more into his sunken attitude.

"And after she came back did you meet her again?" the Deacon continued.

"Alive?" Rutledge questioned.

A perceptible shudder ran through the room.

"Well—of course," said the Deacon nervously.

Rutledge seemed to consider. "Once I did—only once. There was a lot of other people round. At Cold Corners Fair it was."

"Did you talk with her then?"

"Only a minute."

"What did she say?"

His voice dropped. "She said she was sick and knew she was going to die, and when she was dead she'd come back to me."

"And what did you answer?"

"Nothing."

"Did you think anything of it at the time?"

"Well, no. Not till I heard she was dead I didn't. After that I thought of it—and I guess she drew me." He moistened his lips.

"Drew you down to that abandoned house by the pond?"

Rutledge made a faint motion of assent, and the Deacon added: "How did you know it was there she wanted you to come?"

"She . . . just drew me. . . ."

There was a long pause. Bosworth felt, on himself and the other two men, the oppressive weight of the next question to be asked. Mrs. Rutledge opened and closed her narrow lips once or twice, like some beached shellfish gasping for the tide. Rutledge waited.

"Well, now, Saul, won't you go on with what you was telling us?" the Deacon at length suggested.

"That's all. There's nothing else."

The Deacon lowered his voice. "She just draws you?"

"Yes."

"Often?"

"That's as it happens. . . ."

"But if it's always there she draws you, man, haven't you the strength to keep away from the place?"

For the first time, Rutledge wearily turned his head toward his questioner. A spectral smile narrowed his colorless lips. "Ain't any use. She follers after me. . . ."

There was another silence. What more could they ask, then and there? Mrs. Rutledge's presence checked the next question. The Deacon seemed hopelessly to revolve the matter. At length he spoke in a more authoritative tone. "These are forbidden things. You know that, Saul. Have you tried prayer?"

Rutledge shook his head.

"Will you pray with us now?"

Rutledge cast a glance of freezing indifference on his spiritual adviser. "If you folks want to pray, I'm agreeable," he said. But Mrs. Rutledge intervened.

"Prayer ain't any good. In this kind of thing it ain't no manner of use; you know it ain't. I called you here, Deacon, because you remember the last case in this parish. Thirty years ago it was, I guess; but you remember. Lefferts Nash—did praying help *him*? I was a little girl then, but I used to hear my folks talk of it winter nights. Lefferts Nash and Hannah Cory. They drove a stake through her breast. That's what cured him."

"Oh—" Orrin Bosworth exclaimed.

Sylvester Brand raised his head. "You've speaking of that old story as if this was the same sort of thing?"

"Ain't it? Ain't my husband pining away the same as Lefferts Nash did? The Deacon here knows—"

The Deacon stirred anxiously in his chair. "These are forbidden things," he repeated. "Supposing your husband is quite sincere in thinking himself haunted, as you might say. Well, even then, what proof have we that the . . . the dead woman . . . is the specter of that poor girl?"

"Proof? Don't he say so? Didn't she tell him? Ain't I seen 'em?" Mrs. Rutledge almost screamed.

The three men sat silent, and suddenly the wife burst out: "A stake through the breast! That's the old way; and it's the only way. The Deacon knows it!"

"It's against our religion to disturb the dead."

"Ain't it against your religion to let the living perish as my husband is perishing?" She sprang up with one of her abrupt movements and took the family Bible from the whatnot in a corner of the parlor. Putting the book on the table, and moistening a livid fingertip, she turned the pages rapidly, till she came to one on which she laid her hand like a stony paperweight. "See here," she said, and read out in her level chanting voice:

"'*Thou shalt not suffer a witch to live.*'

"That's in Exodus, that's where it is," she added, leaving the book open as if to confirm the statement.

Bosworth continued to glance anxiously from one to the other of the four people about the table. He was younger than any of them, and had had more contact with the modern world; down in Starkfield, in the bar of the Fielding House, he could hear himself laughing with the rest of the men at such old wives' tales. But it was not for nothing that he had been born under the icy shadow of Lonetop, and had shivered and hungered as a lad through the bitter Hemlock County winters. After his parents died, and he had taken hold of the farm himself, he had got more out of it by using improved methods, and by supplying the increasing throng of summer boarders over Stotesbury way with milk and vegetables. He had been made a Selectman of North Ashmore; for so young a man he had a standing in the county. But the roots of the old life were still in him. He could remember, as a little boy, going twice a year with his mother to that bleak hill farm out beyond Sylvester Brand's, where Mrs. Bosworth's aunt, Cressidora Cheney, had been shut up for years in a cold clean room with iron bars in the windows. When little Orrin first saw Aunt Cressidora she was a small white old woman, whom her sisters used to "make decent" for visitors the day that Orrin and his mother were expected. The child wondered why there were bars to the window. "Like a canary bird," he said to his mother. The phrase made Mrs. Bosworth reflect. "I do believe they keep Aunt Cressidora too lonesome," she said; and the next time she went up the mountain with the little boy he carried to his great-aunt a canary in a little wooden cage. It was a great excitement; he knew it would make her happy.

The old woman's motionless face lit up when she saw the bird, and her eyes began to glitter. "It belongs to me," she said instantly, stretching her soft bony hand over the cage.

"Of course it does, Aunt Cressy," said Mrs. Bosworth, her eyes filling.

But the bird, startled by the shadow of the old woman's hand, began to flutter and beat its wings distractedly. At the sight, Aunt Cressidora's calm face suddenly became a coil of twitching features. "You she-devil, you!" she cried in a high squealing voice; and thrusting her hand into the cage she dragged out the terrified bird and wrung its neck. She was plucking the hot body, and squealing "she-devil, she-devil!" as they drew little Orrin from the room. On the way down the mountain his mother wept a great deal, and said: "You must never tell anybody that poor Auntie's crazy, or the men would come and take her down to the asylum at Starkfield, and the shame of it would kill us all. Now promise." The child promised.

He remembered the scene now, with its deep fringe of mystery, secrecy and rumor. It seemed related to a great many other things below the surface of his thoughts, things which stole up anew, making him feel that all the old people he had known, and who "believed in these things," might after all be right. Hadn't a witch been burned at North Ashmore? Didn't the summer folk still drive over in jolly buckboard loads to see the meetinghouse where the trial had been held, the pond where they had ducked her and she had floated? . . . Deacon Hibben believed; Bosworth was sure of it. If he didn't, why did people from all over the place come to him when their animals had queer sicknesses, or when there was a child in the family that had to be kept shut up because it fell down flat and foamed? Yes, in spite of his religion, Deacon Hibben *knew*. . . .

And Brand? Well, it came to Bosworth in a flash: that North Ashmore woman who was burned had the name of Brand. The same stock, no doubt; there had been Brands in Hemlock County ever since the white men had come here. And Orrin, when he was a child, remembered hearing his parents say that Sylvester Brand hadn't ever oughter married his own cousin, because of the blood. Yet the couple had had two healthy girls, and when Mrs. Brand pined away and died nobody suggested that anything had been wrong with her mind. And Vanessa and Ora were the handsomest girls anywhere round. Brand knew it, and scrimped and saved all he could to send Ora, the eldest, down to Starkfield to learn bookkeeping. "When she's married I'll send you," he used to say to little Venny, who was his favorite. But Ora never married. She was away three years, during which Venny ran wild on the slopes of Lonetop; and when Ora came back she sickened and died—poor girl! Since then Brand had grown more savage and morose. He was a hard-working farmer, but there wasn't much to be got out of those barren Bearcliff acres. He was said to have taken to drink since his wife's death; now and then men ran across him in the "dives" of Stotesbury. But not often. And between times he labored hard on his stony acres and did his best for his daughters. In the neglected graveyard of Cold Corners there was a slanting headstone marked with his wife's name; near it, a year since, he had laid his eldest daughter. And sometimes, at dusk, in the autumn, the village people saw him walk slowly by, turn in between the graves, and stand looking down on the two stones. But he never brought a flower there, or planted a bush; nor Venny either. She was too wild and ignorant. . . .

Mrs. Rutledge repeated: "That's in Exodus."

The three visitors remained silent, turning about their hats in reluctant hands. Rutledge faced them, still with that empty pellucid gaze which frightened Bosworth. What was he seeing?

"Ain't any of you folks got the grit—?" his wife burst out again, half hysterically.

Deacon Hibben held up his hand. "That's no way, Mrs. Rutledge. This ain't a question of having grit. What we want first of all is . . . proof . . ."

"That's so," said Bosworth, with an explosion of relief, as if the words had lifted something black and crouching from his breast. Involuntarily the eyes of both men had turned to Brand. He stood there smiling grimly, but did not speak.

"Ain't it so, Brand?" the Deacon prompted him.

"Proof that spooks walk?" the other sneered.

"Well—I presume you want this business settled too?"

The old farmer squared his shoulders. "Yes—I do. But I ain't a sperritualist. How the hell are you going to settle it?"

Deacon Hibben hesitated; then he said, in a low incisive tone: "I don't see but one way—Mrs. Rutledge's."

There was a silence.

"What?" Brand sneered again. "Spying?"

The Deacon's voice sank lower. "If the poor girl *does* walk . . . her that's your child . . . wouldn't you be the first to want her laid quiet? We all know there've been such cases . . . mysterious visitations. . . . Can any one of us here deny it?"

"I seen 'em," Mrs. Rutledge interjected.

There was another heavy pause. Suddenly Brand fixed his gaze on Rutledge. "See here, Saul Rutledge, you've got to clear up this damned calumny, or I'll know why. You say my dead girl comes to you." He labored with his breath, and then jerked out: "When? You tell me that, and I'll be there."

Rutledge's head drooped a little, and his eyes wandered to the window. "Round about sunset, mostly."

"You know beforehand?"

Rutledge made a sign of assent.

"Well, then—tomorrow, will it be?"

Rutledge made the same sign.

Brand turned to the door. "I'll be there." That was all he said. He strode out between them without another glance or word. Deacon Hibben looked at Mrs. Rutledge. "We'll be there too," he said, as if she had asked him; but she had not spoken, and Bosworth saw that her thin body was trembling all over. He was glad when he and Hibben were out again in the snow.

III

They thought that Brand wanted to be left to himself, and to give him time to unhitch his horse they made a pretense of hanging about in the doorway while Bosworth searched his pockets for a pipe he had no mind to light.

But Brand turned back to them as they lingered. "You'll meet me down by Lamer's pond tomorrow?" he suggested. "I want witnesses. Round about sunset."

They nodded their acquiescence, and he got into his sleigh, gave the horse a cut across the flanks, and drove off under the snow-smothered hemlocks. The other two men went to the shed.

"What do you make of this business, Deacon?" Bosworth asked, to break the silence.

The Deacon shook his head. "The man's a sick man—that's sure. Something's sucking the life clean out of him."

But already, in the biting outer air, Bosworth was getting himself under better control. "Looks to me like a bad case of the ague, as you said."

"Well—ague of the mind, then. It's his brain that's sick."

Bosworth shrugged. "He ain't the first in Hemlock County."

"That's so," the Deacon agreed. "It's a worm in the brain, solitude is."

"Well, we'll know this time tomorrow, maybe," said Bosworth. He scrambled into his sleigh, and was driving off in his turn when he heard his companion calling after him. The Deacon explained that his horse had cast a shoe; would Bosworth drive him down to the forge near North Ashmore, if it wasn't too much out of his way? He didn't want the mare slipping about on the freezing snow, and he could probably get the blacksmith to drive him back and shoe her in Rutledge's shed. Bosworth made room for him under the bearskin, and the two men drove off, pursued by a puzzled whinny from the Deacon's old mare.

The road they took was not the one that Bosworth would have followed to reach his own house. But he did not mind that. The shortest way to the forge passed close by Lamer's pond, and Bosworth, since he was in for the business, was not sorry to look the ground over. They drove on in silence.

The snow had ceased, and a green sunset was spreading upward into the crystal sky. A stinging wind barbed with ice flakes caught them in the face on the open ridges, but when they dropped down into the hollow by Lamer's pond the air was as soundless and empty as an unswung bell. They jogged along slowly, each thinking his own thoughts.

"That's the house . . . that tumble-down shack over there, I suppose?" the Deacon said, as the road drew near the edge of the frozen pond.

"Yes: that's the house. A queer hermit fellow built it years ago, my father used to tell me. Since then I don't believe it's ever been used but by the gypsies."

Bosworth had reined in his horse, and sat looking through pine trunks purpled by the sunset at the crumbling structure. Twilight already lay under the trees, though day lingered in the open. Between two sharply patterned pine boughs he saw the evening star, like a white boat in a sea of green.

His gaze dropped from that fathomless sky and followed the blue-white undulations of the snow. It gave him a curious agitated feeling to think that here, in this icy solitude, in the tumble-down house he had so often passed without heeding it, a dark mystery, too deep for thought, was being enacted. Down that very slope, coming from the graveyard at Cold Corners, the being they called "Ora" must pass toward the pond. His heart began to beat stiflingly. Suddenly he gave an exclamation: "Look!"

He had jumped out of the cutter and was stumbling up the bank toward the slope of snow. On it, turned in the direction of the house by the pond, he had detected a woman's footprints; two; then three; then more. The Deacon scrambled out after him, and they stood and stared.

"God—barefoot!" Hibben gasped. "Then it *is* . . . the dead. . . ."

Bosworth said nothing. But he knew that no live woman would travel with naked feet across that freezing wilderness. Here, then, was the proof the Deacon had asked for—they held it. What should they do with it?

"Supposing we was to drive up nearer—round the turn of the pond, till we get close to the house," the Deacon proposed in a colorless voice. "Mebbe then. . . ."

Postponement was a relief. They got into the sleigh and drove on. Two or three hundred yards farther the road, a mere lane under steep bushy banks, turned sharply to the right, following the bend of the pond. As they rounded the turn they saw Brand's cutter ahead of them. It was empty, the horse tied to a treetrunk. The two men looked at each other again. This was not Brand's nearest way home.

Evidently he had been actuated by the same impulse which had made them rein in their horse by the pondside, and then hasten on to the deserted hovel. Had he too discovered those spectral footprints? Perhaps it was for that very reason that he had left his cutter and vanished in the direction of the house. Bosworth found himself shivering all over under his bearskin. "I wish to God the dark wasn't coming on," he muttered. He tethered his own horse near Brand's, and without a word he and the Deacon ploughed through the snow, in the track of Brand's huge feet. They had only a few yards to walk to overtake him. He did not hear them following him, and when Bosworth spoke his name, and he stopped short and turned, his heavy face was dim and confused, like a darker blot on the dusk. He looked at them dully, but without surprise.

"I wanted to see the place," he merely said.

The Deacon cleared his throat. "Just take a look . . . yes . . . we thought so. . . . But I guess there won't be anything to *see*. . . ." he attempted a chuckle.

The other did not seem to hear him, but labored on ahead through the pines. The three men came out together in the cleared space before the house. As they emerged from beneath the trees they seemed to have left night behind. The evening star shed a luster on the speckless snow, and Brand, in that lucid circle, stopped with a jerk, and pointed to the same light footprints turned toward the house—the track of a woman in the snow. He stood still, his face working. "Bare feet. . . ." he said.

The Deacon piped up in a quavering voice: "The feet of the dead." Brand remained motionless. "The feet of the dead," he echoed.

Deacon Hibben laid a frightened hand on his arm. "Come away now, Brand; for the love of God come away."

The father hung there, gazing down at those light tracks on the snow—light as fox or squirrel trails they seemed, on the white immensity. Bosworth thought to himself: "The living couldn't walk so light—not even Ora Brand couldn't have, when she lived. . . ." The cold seemed to have entered into his very marrow. His teeth were chattering.

Brand swung about on them abruptly. "*Now!*" he said, moving on as if to an assault, his head bowed forward on his bull neck.

"Now—now? Not in there?" gasped the Deacon. "What's the use? It was tomorrow he said—" He shook like a leaf.

"It's now," said Brand. He went up to the door of the crazy house, pushed it inward, and meeting with an unexpected resistance, thrust his heavy shoulder against the panel. The door collapsed like a playing card, and Brand stumbled after it into the darkness of the hut. The others, after a moment's hesitation, followed.

Bosworth was never quite sure in what order the events that succeeded took place. Coming in out of the snow dazzle, he seemed to be plunging into total blackness. He groped his way across the threshold, caught a sharp splinter of the fallen door in his palm, seemed to see something white and wraithlike surge up out of the darkest corner of the hut, and then heard a revolver shot at his elbow, and a cry—

Brand had turned back, and was staggering past him out into the lingering daylight. The sunset, suddenly flushing through the trees, crimsoned his face like blood. He held a revolver in his hand and looked about him in his stupid way.

"They *do* walk, then," he said and began to laugh. He bent his head to examine his weapon. "Better here than in the churchyard. They shan't dig her up *now*," he shouted out. The two men caught him by the arms, and Bosworth got the revolver away from him.

IV

The next day Bosworth's sister Loretta, who kept house for him, asked him, when he came in for his midday dinner, if he had heard the news.

Bosworth had been sawing wood all the morning, and in spite of the cold and the driving snow, which had begun again in the night, he was covered with an icy sweat, like a man getting over a fever.

"What news?"

"Venny Brand's down sick with pneumonia. The Deacon's been there. I guess she's dying."

Bosworth looked at her with listless eyes. She seemed far off from him, miles away. "Venny Brand?" he echoed.

"You never liked her, Orrin."

"She's a child. I never knew much about her."

"Well," repeated his sister, with the guileless relish of the unimaginative for bad news, "I guess she's dying." After a pause she added: "It'll kill Sylvester Brand, all alone up there."

Bosworth got up and said: "I've got to see to poulticing the gray's fetlock." He walked out into the steadily falling snow.

Venny Brand was buried three days later. The Deacon read the service; Bosworth was one of the pallbearers. The whole countryside turned out, for the snow had stopped falling, and at any season a funeral offered an opportunity for an outing that was not to be missed. Besides, Venny Brand was young and handsome—at least some people thought her handsome, though she was so swarthy— and her dying like that, so suddenly, had the fascination of tragedy.

"They say her lungs filled right up. . . . Seems she'd had bronchial troubles before . . . I always said both them girls was frail. . . . Look at Ora, how she took and wasted away! And it's colder'n all outdoors up there to Brand's. . . . Their mother, too, *she* pined away just the same. They don't ever make old bones on the mother's side of the family. . . . There's that young Bedlow over there; they say Venny was engaged to him. . . . Oh, Mrs. Rutledge, excuse *me*. . . . Step right into the pew; there's a seat for you alongside of grandma. . . ."

Mrs. Rutledge was advancing with deliberate step down the narrow aisle of the bleak wooden church. She had on her best bonnet, a monumental structure which no one had seen out of her trunk since old Mrs. Silsee's funeral, three years before. All the women remembered it. Under its perpendicular pile her narrow face, swaying on the long thin neck, seemed whiter than ever; but her air of fretfulness had been composed into a suitable expression of mournful immobility.

"Looks as if the stonemason had carved her to put atop of Venny's grave," Bosworth thought as she glided past him; and then shivered at his own sepulchral fancy. When she bent over her hymn book her lowered lids reminded him again of marble eyeballs; the bony hands clasping the book were bloodless. Bosworth had never seen such hands since he had seen old Aunt Cressidora Cheney strangle the canary bird because it fluttered.

The service was over, the coffin of Venny Brand had been lowered into her sister's grave, and the neighbors were slowly dispersing. Bosworth, as pallbearer, felt obliged to linger and say a word to the stricken father. He waited till Brand had turned from the grave with the Deacon at his side. The three men stood together for a moment; but not one of them spoke. Brand's face was the closed door of a vault, barred with wrinkles like bands of iron.

Finally the Deacon took his hand and said: "The Lord gave—"

Brand nodded and turned away toward the shed where the horses were hitched. Bosworth followed him. "Let me drive along home with you," he suggested.

Brand did not so much as turn his head. "Home? What home?" he said; and the other fell back.

Loretta Bosworth was talking with the other women while the men unblanketed their horses and backed the cutters out into the heavy snow. As Bosworth waited for her, a few feet off, he saw Mrs. Rutledge's tall bonnet lording it above the group. And Pond, the Rutledge farm hand, was backing out the sleigh.

"Saul ain't here today, Mrs. Rutledge, is he?" one of the village elders piped, turning a benevolent old tortoise head about on a loose neck, and blinking up into Mrs. Rutledge's marble face.

Bosworth heard her measure out her answer in slow incisive words. "No. Mr. Rutledge he ain't here. He would 'a' come for certain, but his aunt Minorca Cummins is being buried down to Stotesbury this very day and he had to go down there. Don't it sometimes seem zif we was all walking right in the Shadow of Death?"

As she walked toward the cutter, in which Andy Pond was already seated, the Deacon went up to her with visible hesitation. Involuntarily Bosworth also moved nearer. He heard the Deacon say: "I'm glad to hear that Saul is able to be up and around."

She turned her small head on her rigid neck, and lifted the lids of marble.

"Yes, I guess he'll sleep quieter now. And *her* too, maybe, now she don't lay there alone any longer," she added in a low voice, with a sudden twist of her chin toward the fresh black stain in the graveyard snow. She got into the cutter, and said in a clear tone to Andy Pond: "'S long as we're down here I don't know but what I'll just call round and get a box of soap at Hiram Pringle's."

ALL SOULS'

(1937)

"All Souls'," Wharton's last completed story, was finished about six months before her death in 1937. The narrator claims it isn't "exactly" a ghost story (because there are only suspected witches and no actual apparitions), but the tale was published posthumously in the collection Ghosts (1937).

Wharton seems to have eerily anticipated her own death, for the protagonist lies disabled in a cold, empty, silent house which is named Whitegates and suggests the grave. Mrs. Clayburn resembles Wharton more than any of her previous New England characters. An upper-class, elderly, childless woman living alone and dependent on servants, she seems at the least to act out Wharton's deep-seated fear that her servants might leave her to die. One critic notes that the story "dramatizes the psychic deformation entailed by Mrs. Claymore's [sic] inheritance of an authoritarian male position in relation to the house and servants" (Allan Gardner Smith, "Edith Wharton and the Ghost Story," in Edith Wharton, ed. Harold Bloom [New York: Chelsea House, 1986], 91). Although on the surface the character accepts her class position, her terror shows that underneath she recognizes its injustice and arbitrary nature. What if the servants exacted their revenge? What if they were in league with the devil—or, in the case of New England, witches?

The triumph of the servants in "All Souls'" reenacts the major theme of Wharton's stories in her final decade, the revenge of the least powerful in society. Usually the least powerful person is a woman who bests a man, such as Prudence Rutledge in "Bewitched," but on All Souls' Eve three "old stand-bys" walk.

QUEER AND INEXPLICABLE as the business was, on the surface it
appeared fairly simple—at the time, at least; but with the passing of
years, and owing to there not having been a single witness of what
happened except Sara Clayburn herself, the stories about it have become so exaggerated, and often so ridiculously inaccurate, that it
seems necessary that someone connected with the affair, though not
actually present—I repeat that when it happened my cousin was (or
thought she was) quite alone in her house—should record the few
facts actually known.

In those days I was often at Whitegates (as the place had always
been called)—I was there, in fact, not long before, and almost immediately after, the strange happenings of those thirty-six hours. Jim
Clayburn and his widow were both my cousins, and because of that,
and of my intimacy with them, both families think I am more likely
than anybody else to be able to get at the facts, as far as they can be
called facts, and as anybody can get at them. So I have written down,
as clearly as I could, the gist of the various talks I had with cousin
Sara, when she could be got to talk—it wasn't often—about what
occurred during that mysterious weekend.

I read the other day in a book by a fashionable essayist that ghosts
went out when electric light came in. What nonsense! The writer,
though he is fond of dabbling, in a literary way, in the supernatural,
hasn't even reached the threshold of his subject. As between turreted
castles patrolled by headless victims with clanking chains, and the
comfortable suburban house with a refrigerator and central heating
where you feel, as soon as you're in it, *that there's something wrong*,
give me the latter for sending a chill down the spine! And, by the way,
haven't you noticed that it's generally not the high-strung and imag-

inative who see ghosts, but the calm matter-of-fact people who don't believe in them, and are sure they wouldn't mind if they did see one? Well, that was the case with Sara Clayburn and her house. The house, in spite of its age—it was built, I believe, about 1780—was open, airy, high-ceilinged, with electricity, central heating and all the modern appliances: and its mistress was—well, very much like her house. And, anyhow, this isn't exactly a ghost story and I've dragged in the analogy only as a way of showing you what kind of woman my cousin was, and how unlikely it would have seemed that what happened at Whitegates should have happened just there—or to her.

When Jim Clayburn died the family all thought that, as the couple had no children, his widow would give up Whitegates and move either to New York or Boston—for being of good Colonial stock, with many relatives and friends, she would have found a place ready for her in either. But Sally Clayburn seldom did what other people expected, and in this case she did exactly the contrary; she stayed at Whitegates.

"What, turn my back on the old house—tear up all the family roots, and go and hang myself in a bird-cage flat in one of those new skyscrapers in Lexington Avenue, with a bunch of chickweed and a cuttlefish to replace my good Connecticut mutton? No, thank you. Here I belong, and here I stay till my executors hand the place over to Jim's next-of-kin—that stupid fat Presley boy. . . . Well, don't let's talk about him. But I tell you what—I'll keep him out of here as long as I can." And she did—for being still in the early fifties when her husband died, and a muscular, resolute figure of a woman, she was more than a match for the fat Presley boy, and attended his funeral a few years ago, in correct mourning, with a faint smile under her veil.

Whitegates was a pleasant hospitable-looking house, on a height overlooking the stately windings of the Connecticut River; but it was five or six miles from Norrington, the nearest town, and its situation would certainly have seemed remote and lonely to modern servants. Luckily, however, Sara Clayburn had inherited from her mother-in-law two or three old stand-bys who seemed as much a part of the family tradition as the roof they lived under; and I never heard of her having any trouble in her domestic arrangements.

The house, in Colonial days, had been foursquare, with four spacious rooms on the ground floor, an oak-floored hall dividing them, the usual kitchen extension at the back, and a good attic under the roof. But Jim's grandparents, when interest in the "Colonial" began to revive, in the early eighties, had added two wings, at right angles to the south front, so that the old "circle" before the front door became a grassy court, enclosed on three sides, with a big elm in the middle. Thus the house was turned into a roomy dwelling, in which the last three generations of Clayburns had exercised a large hospitality; but the architect had respected the character of the old house, and the enlargement made it more comfortable without lessening its simplicity. There was a lot of land about it, and Jim Clayburn, like his fathers before him, farmed it, not without profit, and played a considerable and respected part in state politics. The Clayburns were always spoken of as a "good influence" in the county, and the townspeople were glad when they learned that Sara did not mean to desert the place—"though it must be lonesome, winters, living all alone up there atop of that hill"—they remarked as the days shortened, and the first snow began to pile up under the quadruple row of elms along the common.

Well, if I've given you a sufficiently clear idea of Whitegates and the Clayburns—who shared with their old house a sort of reassuring orderliness and dignity—I'll efface myself, and tell the tale, not in my cousin's words, for they were too confused and fragmentary, but as I built it up gradually out of her half-avowals and nervous reticences. If the thing happened at all—and I must leave you to judge of that—I think it must have happened in this way. . . .

I

The morning had been bitter, with a driving sleet—though it was only the last day of October—but after lunch a watery sun showed for a while through banked-up woolly clouds, and tempted Sara Clayburn out. She was an energetic walker, and given, at that season, to tramping three or four miles along the valley road, and coming back by way of Shaker's wood. She had made her usual round, and was following the main drive to the house when she overtook a plainly-dressed woman walking in the same direction. If the scene had not been so lonely—the way to Whitegates at the end of an autumn day was not a frequented one—Mrs. Clayburn might not have paid any attention to the woman, for she was in no way noticeable; but when she caught up with the intruder my cousin was surprised to find that she was a stranger—for the mistress of Whitegates prided herself on knowing, at least by sight, most of her country neighbors. It was almost dark, and the woman's face was hardly visible, but Mrs. Clayburn told me she recalled her as middle-aged, plain and rather pale.

Mrs. Clayburn greeted her, and then added: "You're going to the house?"

"Yes, ma'am," the woman answered, in a voice that the Connecticut Valley in old days would have called "foreign," but that would have been unnoticed by ears used to the modern multiplicity of tongues. "No, I couldn't say where she came from," Sara always said. "What struck me as queer was that I didn't know her."

She asked the woman, politely, what she wanted, and the woman answered: "Only to see one of the girls." The answer was natural enough, and Mrs. Clayburn nodded and turned off from the drive to the lower part of the gardens, so that she saw no more of the visitor then or afterward. And, in fact, a half hour later something happened which put the stranger entirely out of her mind. The brisk and light-footed Mrs. Clayburn, as she approached the house, slipped on a frozen puddle, turned her ankle and lay suddenly helpless.

Price, the butler, and Agnes, the dour old Scottish maid whom Sara had inherited from her mother-in-law, of course knew exactly what to do. In no time they had their mistress stretched out on a lounge, and Dr. Selgrove had been called up from Norrington. When he arrived, he ordered Mrs. Clayburn to bed, did the necessary examining and bandaging, and shook his head over her ankle, which he feared was fractured. He thought, however, that if she would swear not to get up, or even shift the position of her leg, he could spare her the discomfort of putting it in plaster. Mrs. Clayburn agreed, the more promptly as the doctor warned her that any rash movement would prolong her immobility. Her quick imperious nature made the prospect trying, and she was annoyed with herself for having been so clumsy. But the mischief was done, and she immediately thought what an opportunity she would have for going over her accounts and catching up with her correspondence. So she settled down resignedly in her bed.

"And you won't miss much, you know, if you have to stay there a few days. It's beginning to snow, and it looks as if we were in for a good spell of it," the doctor remarked, glancing through the window as he gathered up his implements. "Well, we don't often get snow here as early as this; but winter's got to begin sometime," he concluded philosophically. At the door he stopped to add: "You don't want me to send up a nurse from Norrington? Not to nurse you, you know; there's nothing much to do till I see you again. But this is a pretty lonely place when the snow begins, and I thought maybe—"

Sara Clayburn laughed. "Lonely? With my old servants? You forget how many winters I've spent here alone with them. Two of them were with me in my mother-in-law's time."

"That's so," Dr. Selgrove agreed. "You're a good deal luckier than most people, that way. Well, let me see; this is Saturday. We'll have to let the inflammation go down before we can X-ray you. Monday morning, first thing, I'll be here with the X-ray man. If you want me sooner, call me up." And he was gone.

II

The foot at first, had not been very painful; but toward the small hours Mrs. Clayburn began to suffer. She was a bad patient, like most healthy and active people. Not being used to pain she did not know how to bear it, and the hours of wakefulness and immobility seemed endless. Agnes, before leaving her, had made everything as comfortable as possible. She had put a jug of lemonade within reach, and had even (Mrs. Clayburn thought it odd afterward) insisted on bringing in a tray with sandwiches and a thermos of tea. "In case you're hungry in the night, madam."

"Thank you; but I'm never hungry in the night. And I certainly shan't be tonight—only thirsty. I think I'm feverish."

"Well, there's the lemonade, madam."

"That will do. Take the other things away, please." (Sara had always hated the sight of unwanted food "messing about" in her room.)

"Very well, madam. Only you might—"

"Please take it away," Mrs. Clayburn repeated irritably.

"Very good, madam." But as Agnes went out, her mistress heard her set the tray down softly on a table behind the screen which shut off the door.

"Obstinate old goose!" she thought, rather touched by the old woman's insistence.

Sleep, once it had gone, would not return, and the long black hours moved more and more slowly. How late the dawn came in November! "If only I could move my leg," she grumbled.

She lay still and strained her ears for the first steps of the servants. Whitegates was an early house, its mistress setting the example; it would surely not be long now before one of the women came. She was tempted to ring for Agnes, but refrained. The woman had been up late, and this was Sunday morning, when the household was always allowed a little extra time. Mrs. Clayburn reflected restlessly: "I was a fool not to let her leave the tea beside the bed, as she wanted to. I wonder if I could get up and get it?" But she remembered the doctor's warning, and dared not move. Anything rather than risk prolonging her imprisonment. . . .

Ah, there was the stable clock striking. How loud it sounded in the snowy stillness! One—two—three—four—five. . . .

What? Only five? Three hours and a quarter more before she could hope to hear the door handle turned. . . . After a while she dozed off again, uncomfortably.

Another sound aroused her. Again the stable clock. She listened. But the room was still in deep darkness, and only six strokes fell. . . . She thought of reciting something to put her to sleep; but she seldom read poetry, and being naturally a good sleeper, she could not remember any of the usual devices against insomnia. The whole of her leg felt like lead now. The bandages had grown terribly tight—her ankle must have swollen. . . . She lay staring at the dark windows, watching for the first glimmer of dawn. At last she saw a pale filter of daylight through the shutters. One by one the objects between the bed and the window recovered first their outline, then their bulk, and seemed to be stealthily regrouping themselves, after goodness knows what secret displacements during the night. Who that has lived in an old house could possibly believe that the furniture in its stays still all night? Mrs. Clayburn almost fancied she saw one little slender-legged table slipping hastily back into its place.

"It knows Agnes is coming, and it's afraid," she thought whimsically. Her bad night must have made her imaginative for such non-sense as that about the furniture had never occurred to her before. . . .

At length, after hours more, as it seemed, the stable clock struck eight. Only another quarter of an hour. She watched the hand moving slowly across the face of the little clock beside her bed . . . ten minutes . . . five . . . only five! Agnes was as punctual as destiny . . . in two minutes now she would come. The two minutes passed, and she did not come. Poor Agnes—she had looked pale and tired the night before. She had overslept herself, no doubt—or perhaps she felt ill, and would send the housemaid to replace her. Mrs. Clayburn waited.

She waited half an hour; then she reached up to the bell at the head of the bed. Poor old Agnes—her mistress felt guilty about waking her. But Agnes did not appear—and after a considerable interval Mrs. Clayburn, now with a certain impatience, rang again. She rang once; twice; three times—but still no one came.

Once more she waited; then she said to herself: "There must be something wrong with the electricity." Well—she could find out by switching on the bed lamp at her elbow (how admirably the room was equipped with every practical appliance!). She switched it on— but no light came. Electric current cut off; and it was Sunday, and nothing could be done about it till the next morning. Unless it turned out to be just a burnt-out fuse, which Price could remedy. Well, in a moment now some one would surely come to her door.

It was nine o'clock before she admitted to herself that something uncommonly strange must have happened in the house. She began to feel a nervous apprehension; but she was not the woman to encourage it. If only she had had the telephone put in her room, instead of out on the landing! She measured mentally the distance to be traveled, remembered Dr. Selgrove's admonition, and wondered if her broken ankle would carry her there. She dreaded the prospect of being put in plaster, but she had to get to the telephone, whatever happened.

She wrapped herself in her dressing gown, found a walking stick, and, resting heavily on it, dragged herself to the door. In her bedroom the careful Agnes had closed and fastened the shutters, so that it was not much lighter there than at dawn; but outside in the corridor the cold whiteness of the snowy morning seemed almost reassuring. Mysterious things—dreadful things—were associated with darkness; and here was the wholesome prosaic daylight come again to banish them. Mrs. Clayburn looked about her and listened. Silence. A deep nocturnal silence in that day-lit house, in which five people were presumably coming and going about their work. It was certainly strange. . . . She looked out of the window, hoping to see someone crossing the court or coming along the drive. But no one was in sight, and the snow seemed to have the place to itself: a quiet steady snow. It was still falling, with a business-like regularity, muffling the outer world in layers on layers of thick white velvet, and intensifying the silence within. A noiseless world—were people so sure that absence of noise was what they wanted? Let them first try a lonely country house in a November snowstorm!

She dragged herself along the passage to the telephone. When she unhooked the receiver she noticed that her hand trembled.

She rang up the pantry—no answer. She rang again. Silence—more silence! It seemed to be piling itself up like the snow on the roof and in the gutters. Silence. How many people that she knew had any idea what silence was—and how loud it sounded when you really listened to it?

Again she waited: then she rang up "Central." No answer. She tried three times. After that she tried the pantry again. . . . The telephone was cut off, then; like the electric current. Who was at work downstairs, isolating her thus from the world? Her heart began to hammer. Luckily there was a chair near the telephone, and she sat down to recover her strength—or was it her courage?

Agnes and the housemaid slept in the nearest wing. She would certainly get as far as that when she had pulled herself together. Had she the courage—? Yes, of course she had. She had always been regarded as a plucky woman; and had so regarded herself. But this silence—

It occurred to her that by looking from the window of a neighboring bathroom she could see the kitchen chimney. There ought to be smoke coming from it at that hour; and if there were she thought she would be less afraid to go on. She got as far as the bathroom and looking through the window saw that no smoke came from the chimney. Her sense of loneliness grew more acute. Whatever had happened belowstairs must have happened before the morning's work had begun. The cook had not had time to light the fire, the other servants had not yet begun their round. She sank down on the nearest chair, struggling against her fears. What next would she discover if she carried on her investigations?

The pain in her ankle made progress difficult; but she was aware of it now only as an obstacle to haste. No matter what it cost her in physical suffering, she must find out what was happening below-stairs—or had happened. But first she would go to the maid's room. And if that were empty—well, somehow she would have to get herself downstairs.

She limped along the passage, and on the way steadied herself by resting her hand on a radiator. It was stone-cold. Yet in that well-ordered house in winter the central heating, though damped down at night, was never allowed to go out, and by eight in the morning a mellow warmth pervaded the rooms. The icy chill of the pipes startled her. It was the chauffeur who looked after the heating—so he too was involved in the mystery, whatever it was, as well as the house servants. But this only deepened the problem.

III

At Agnes's door Mrs. Clayburn paused and knocked. She expected no answer, and there was none. She opened the door and went in. The room was dark and very cold. She went to the window and flung back the shutters; then she looked slowly around, vaguely apprehensive of what she might see. The room was empty but what frightened her was not so much its emptiness as its air of scrupulous and undisturbed order. There was no sign of anyone having lately dressed in it—or undressed the night before. And the bed had not been slept in.

Mrs. Clayburn leaned against the wall for a moment; then she crossed the floor and opened the cupboard. That was where Agnes kept her dresses; and the dresses were there, neatly hanging in a row. On the shelf above were Agnes's few and unfashionable hats, rearrangements of her mistress's old ones. Mrs. Clayburn, who knew them all, looked at the shelf, and saw that one was missing. And so was also the warm winter coat she had given to Agnes the previous winter.

The woman was out, then; had gone out, no doubt, the night before, since the bed was unslept in, the dressing and washing appliances untouched. Agnes, who never set foot out of the house after dark, who despised the movies as much as she did the wireless, and could never be persuaded that a little innocent amusement was a necessary element in life, had deserted the house on a snowy winter night, while her mistress lay upstairs, suffering and helpless! Why had she gone, and where had she gone? When she was undressing Mrs. Clayburn the night before, taking her orders, trying to make her more comfortable, was she already planning this mysterious nocturnal escape? Or had something—the mysterious and dreadful Something for the clue of which Mrs. Clayburn was still groping—occurred later in the evening, sending the maid downstairs and out of doors into the bitter night? Perhaps one of the men at the garage—where the chauffeur and gardener lived—had been suddenly taken ill, and someone had run up to the house for Agnes. Yes—that must be the explanation. . . . Yet how much it left unexplained.

Next to Agnes's room was the linen room; beyond that was the housemaid's door. Mrs. Clayburn went to it and knocked. "Mary!" No one answered, and she went in. The room was in the same immaculate order as her maid's, and here too the bed was unslept in, and there were no signs of dressing or undressing. The two women had no doubt gone out together—gone where?

More and more the cold unanswering silence of the house weighed down on Mrs. Clayburn. She had never thought of it as a big house, but now, in this snowy winter light, it seemed immense, and full of ominous corners around which one dared not look.

Beyond the housemaid's room were the back stairs. It was the nearest way down, and every step that Mrs. Clayburn took was increasingly painful; but she decided to walk slowly back, the whole length of the passage, and go down by the front stairs. She did not know why she did this; but she felt that at the moment she was past reasoning, and had better obey her instinct.

More than once she had explored the ground floor alone in the small hours, in search of unwonted midnight noises; but now it was not the idea of noises that frightened her, but that inexorable and hostile silence, the sense that the house had retained in full daylight its nocturnal mystery, and was watching her as she was watching it; that in entering those empty orderly rooms she might be disturbing some unseen confabulation on which beings of flesh-and-blood had better not intrude.

The broad oak stairs were beautifully polished, and so slippery that she had to cling to the rail and let herself down tread by tread. And as she descended, the silence descended with her—heavier, denser, more absolute. She seemed to feel its steps just behind her, softly keeping time with hers. It had a quality she had never been aware of in any other silence, as though it were not merely an absence of sound, a thin barrier between the car and the surging murmur of life just beyond, but an impenetrable substance made out of the world-wide cessation of all life and all movement.

Yes, that was what laid a chill on her: the feeling that there was no limit to this silence, no outer margin, nothing beyond it. By this time she had reached the foot of the stairs and was limping across the hall to the drawing room. Whatever she found there, she was sure, would be mute and lifeless; but what would it be? The bodies of her dead servants, mown down by some homicidal maniac? And what if it were her turn next—if he were waiting for her behind the heavy curtains of the room she was about to enter? Well, she must find out—she must face whatever lay in wait. Not impelled by bravery—the last drop of courage had oozed out of her—but because anything, anything was better than to remain shut up in that snowbound house without knowing whether she was alone in it or not, "I must find that out, I must find that out," she repeated to herself in a sort of meaningless sing-song.

The cold outer light flooded the drawing room. The shutters had not been closed, nor the curtains drawn. She looked about her. The room was empty, and every chair in its usual place. Her armchair was pushed up by the chimney and the cold hearth was piled with the ashes of the fire at which she had warmed herself before starting on her ill-fated walk. Even her empty coffee cup stood on a table near the armchair. It was evident that the servants had not been in the room since she had left it the day before after luncheon. And suddenly the conviction entered into her that, as she found the drawing room, so she would find the rest of the house; cold, orderly—and empty. She would find nothing, she would find no one. She no longer felt any dread of ordinary human dangers lurking in those dumb spaces ahead of her. She knew she was utterly alone under her own roof. She sat down to rest her aching ankle, and looked slowly about her.

There were the other rooms to be visited, and she was determined to go through them all—but she knew in advance that they would give no answer to her question. She knew it, seemingly, from the qual-ity of the silence which enveloped her. There was no break, no thin-nest crack in it anywhere. It had the cold continuity of the snow which was still falling steadily outside.

She had no idea how long she waited before nerving herself to con-tinue her inspection. She no longer felt the pain in her ankle, but was only conscious that she must not bear her weight on it, and therefore moved very slowly, supporting herself on each piece of furniture in her path. On the ground floor no shutter had been closed, no curtain drawn, and she progressed without difficulty from room to room: the library, her morning room, the dining room. In each of them, every piece of furniture was in its usual place. In the dining room, the table had been laid for her dinner of the previous evening, and the candelabra, with candles unlit, stood reflected in the dark ma-hogany. She was not the kind of woman to nibble a poached egg on a tray when she was alone, but always came down to the dining room, and had what she called a civilized meal.

The back premises remained to be visited. From the dining room she entered the pantry, and there too everything was in irreproachable order. She opened the door and looked down the back passage with its neat linoleum floor covering. The deep silence accompanied her; she still felt it moving watchfully at her side, as though she were its prisoner and it might throw itself upon her if she attempted to escape. She limped on toward the kitchen. That of course would be empty too, and immaculate. But she must see it.

She leaned a minute in the embrasure of a window in the passage. "It's like the 'Mary Celeste'—a 'Mary Celeste' on *terra firma*," she thought, recalling the unsolved sea mystery of her childhood. "No one ever knew what happened on board the 'Mary Celeste.' And per-haps no one will ever know what has happened here. Even I shan't know."

At the thought her latent fear seemed to take on a new quality. It was like an icy liquid running through every vein, and lying in a pool about her heart. She understood now that she had never before known what fear was, and that most of the people she had met had probably never known either. For this sensation was something quite different. . . .

It absorbed her so completely that she was not aware how long she remained leaning there. But suddenly a new impulse pushed her forward, and she walked on toward the scullery. She went there first because there was a service slide in the wall, through which she might peep into the kitchen without being seen; and some indefinable instinct told her that the kitchen held the clue to the mystery. She still felt strongly that whatever had happened in the house must have its source and center in the kitchen.

In the scullery, as she had expected, everything was clean and tidy. Whatever had happened, no one in the house appeared to have been taken by surprise; there was nowhere any sign of confusion or disorder. "It looks as if they'd known beforehand, and put everything straight," she thought. She glanced at the wall facing the door, and saw that the slide was open. And then, as she was approaching it, the silence was broken. A voice was speaking in the kitchen—a man's voice, low but emphatic, and which she had never heard before.

She stood still, cold with fear. But this fear was again a different one. Her previous terrors had been speculative, conjectural, a ghostly emanation of the surrounding silence. This was a plain everyday dread of evildoers. Oh, God, why had she not remembered her husband's revolver, which ever since his death had lain in a drawer in her room?

She turned to retreat across the smooth slippery floor but halfway her stick slipped from her, and crashed down on the tiles. The noise seemed to echo on and on through the emptiness, and she stood still, aghast. Now that she had betrayed her presence, flight was useless. Whoever was beyond the kitchen door would be upon her in a second. . . .

But to her astonishment the voice went on speaking. It was as though neither the speaker nor his listeners had heard her. The invisible stranger spoke so low that she could not make out what he was saying, but the tone was passionately earnest, almost threatening. The next moment she realized that he was speaking in a foreign language, a language unknown to her. Once more her terror was surmounted by the urgent desire to know what was going on, so close to her yet unseen. She crept to the slide, peered cautiously through into the kitchen, and saw that it was as orderly and empty as the other rooms. But in the middle of the carefully scoured table stood a portable wireless, and the voice she heard came out of it. . . .

She must have fainted then, she supposed; at any rate she felt so weak and dizzy that her memory of what next happened remained indistinct. But in the course of time she groped her way back to the pantry, and there found a bottle of spirits—brandy or whisky, she could not remember which. She found a glass, poured herself a stiff drink, and while it was flushing through her veins, managed, she never knew with how many shuddering delays, to drag herself through the deserted ground floor, up the stairs, and down the corridor to her own room. There, apparently, she fell across the threshold, again unconscious. . . .

When she came to, she remembered, her first care had been to lock herself in; then to recover her husband's revolver. It was not loaded, but she found some cartridges, and succeeded in loading it. Then she remembered that Agnes, on leaving her the evening before, had refused to carry away the tray with the tea and sandwiches, and she fell on them with a sudden hunger. She recalled also noticing that a flask of brandy had been put beside the thermos, and being vaguely surprised. Agnes's departure, then, had been deliberately planned, and she had known that her mistress, who never touched spirits, might have need of a stimulant before she returned. Mrs. Clayburn poured some of the brandy into her tea, and swallowed it greedily.

After that (she told me later) she remembered that she had managed to start a fire in her grate, and after warming herself, had got back into her bed, piling on it all the coverings she could find. The afternoon passed in a haze of pain, out of which there emerged now and then a dim shape of fear—the fear that she might lie there alone and untended till she died of cold, and of the terror of her solitude. For she was sure by this time that the house was empty—completely empty, from garret to cellar. She knew it was so, she could not tell why; but again she felt that it must be because of the peculiar quality of the silence—the silence which had dogged her steps wherever she went, and was now folded down on her like a pall. She was sure that the nearness of any other human being, however dumb and secret, would have made a faint crack in the texture of that silence, flawed it as a sheet of glass is flawed by a pebble thrown against it. . . .

IV

Is that easier? the doctor asked, lifting himself from bending over her ankle. He shook his head disapprovingly. "Looks to me as if you'd disobeyed orders—eh? Been moving about, haven't you? And I guess Dr. Selgrove told you to keep quiet till he saw you again, didn't he?"

The speaker was a stranger, whom Mrs. Clayburn knew only by name. Her own doctor had been called away that morning to the bedside of an old patient in Baltimore, and had asked this young man, who was beginning to be known at Norrington, to replace him. The newcomer was shy, and somewhat familiar, as the shy often are, and Mrs. Clayburn decided that she did not much like him. But before she could convey this by the tone of her reply (and she was past mistress of the shades of disapproval) she heard Agnes speaking—yes, Agnes, the same, the usual Agnes, standing behind the doctor, neat and stern-looking as ever. "Mrs. Clayburn must have got up and walked about in the night instead of ringing for me, as she'd ought to," Agnes intervened severely.

This was too much! In spite of the pain, which was now exquisite, Mrs. Clayburn laughed. "Ringing for you? How could I, with the electricity cut off?"

"The electricity cut off?" Agnes's surprise was masterly. "Why, when was it cut off?" She pressed her finger on the bell beside the bed, and the call tinkled through the quiet room. "I tried that bell before I left you last night, madam, because if there'd been anything wrong with it I'd have come and slept in the dressing room sooner than leave you here alone."

Mrs. Clayburn lay speechless, staring up at her. "Last night? But last night I was all alone in the house."

Agnes's firm features did not alter. She folded her hands resignedly across her trim apron. "Perhaps the pain's made you a little confused, madam." She looked at the doctor, who nodded.

"The pain in your foot must have been pretty bad," he said.

"It was," Mrs. Clayburn replied. "But it was nothing to the horror of being left alone in this empty house since the day before yesterday, with the heat and the electricity cut off, and the telephone not working."

The doctor was looking at her in evident wonder. Agnes's sallow face flushed slightly, but only as if in indignation at an unjust charge. "But, madam, I made up your fire with my own hands last night—and look, it's smoldering still. I was getting ready to start it again just now, when the doctor came."

"That's so. She was down on her knees before it," the doctor corroborated.

Again Mrs. Clayburn laughed. Ingeniously as the tissue of lies was being woven about her, she felt she could still break through it. "I made up the fire myself yesterday—there was no one else to do it," she said, addressing the doctor, but keeping her eyes on her maid. "I got up twice to put on more coal, because the house was like a sepulcher. The central heating must have been out since Saturday afternoon."

At this incredible statement Agnes's face expressed only a polite distress; but the new doctor was evidently embarrassed at being drawn into an unintelligible controversy with which he had no time to deal. He said he had brought the X-ray photographer with him, but that the ankle was too much swollen to be photographed at present. He asked Mrs. Clayburn to excuse his haste, as he had all Dr. Selgrove's patients to visit besides his own, and promised to come back that evening to decide whether she could be X-rayed then, and whether, as he evidently feared, the ankle would have to be put in plaster. Then, handing his prescriptions to Agnes, he departed.

Mrs. Clayburn spent a feverish and suffering day. She did not feel well enough to carry on the discussion with Agnes; she did not ask to see the other servants. She grew drowsy, and understood that her mind was confused with fever. Agnes and the housemaid waited on her as attentively as usual, and by the time the doctor returned in the evening her temperature had fallen; but she decided not to speak of what was on her mind until Dr. Selgrove reappeared. He was to be back the following evening; and the new doctor preferred to wait for him before deciding to put the ankle in plaster—though he feared this was now inevitable.

v

That afternoon Mrs. Clayburn had me summoned by telephone, and I arrived at Whitegates the following day. My cousin, who looked pale and nervous, merely pointed to her foot, which had been put in plaster, and thanked me for coming to keep her company. She explained that Dr. Selgrove had been taken suddenly ill in Baltimore, and would not be back for several days, but that the young man who replaced him seemed fairly competent. She made no allusion to the strange incidents I have set down, but I felt at once that she had received a shock which her accident, however painful, could not explain.

Finally, one evening, she told me the story of her strange weekend, as it had presented itself to her unusually clear and accurate mind, and as I have recorded it above. She did not tell me this till several weeks after my arrival; but she was still upstairs at the time, and obliged to divide her days between her bed and a lounge. During those endless intervening weeks, she told me, she had thought the whole matter over: and though the events of the mysterious thirty-six hours were still vivid to her, they had already lost something of their haunting terror, and she finally decided not to reopen the question with Agnes, or to touch on it in speaking to the other servants. Dr. Selgrove's illness had been not only serious but prolonged. He had not yet returned, and it was reported that as soon as he was well enough he would go on a West Indian cruise, and not resume his practice at Norrington till the spring. Dr. Selgrove, as my cousin was perfectly aware, was the only person who could prove that thirty-six hours had elapsed between his visit and that of his successor; and the latter, a shy young man, burdened by the heavy additional practice suddenly thrown on his shoulders, told me (when I risked a little private talk with him) that in the haste of Dr. Selgrove's departure the only instructions he had given about Mrs. Clayburn were summed up on the brief memorandum: "Broken ankle. Have X-rayed."

Knowing my cousin's authoritative character, I was surprised at her decision not to speak to the servants of what had happened; but on thinking it over I concluded she was right. They were all exactly as they had been before that unexplained episode: efficient, devoted, respectful and respectable. She was dependent on them and felt at home with them, and she evidently preferred to put the whole matter out of her mind, as far as she could. She was absolutely certain that something strange had happened in her house, and I was more than ever convinced that she had received a shock which the accident of a broken ankle was not sufficient to account for; but in the end I agreed that nothing was to be gained by cross-questioning the servants or the new doctor.

I was at Whitegates off and on that winter and during the following summer, and when I went home to New York for good early in

October I left my cousin in her old health and spirits. Dr. Selgrove had been ordered to Switzerland for the summer, and this further postponement of his return to his practice seemed to have put the happenings of the strange weekend out of her mind. Her life was going on as peacefully and normally as usual, and I left her without anxiety, and indeed without a thought of the mystery, which was now nearly a year old.

I was living then in a small flat in New York by myself, and I had hardly settled into it when, very late one evening—on the last day of October—I heard my bell ring. As it was my maid's evening out, and I was alone, I went to the door myself, and on the threshold, to my amazement, I saw Sara Clayburn. She was wrapped in a fur cloak, with a hat drawn down over her forehead, and a face so pale and haggard that I saw something dreadful must have happened to her. "Sara," I gasped, not knowing what I was saying, "where in the world have you come from at this hour?"

"From Whitegates. I missed the last train and came by car." She came in and sat down on the bench near the door. I saw that she could hardly stand, and sat down beside her, putting my arm about her. "For heaven's sake, tell me what's happened."

She looked at me without seeming to see me. "I telephoned to Nixon's and hired a car. It took me five hours and a quarter to get here." She looked about her. "Can you take me in for the night? I've left my luggage downstairs."

"For as many nights as you like. But you look so ill—"

She shook her head. "No; I'm not ill. I'm only frightened—deathly frightened," she repeated in a whisper.

Her voice was so strange, and the hands I was pressing between mine were so cold, that I drew her to her feet and led her straight to my little guest room. My flat was in an old-fashioned building, not many stories high, and I was on more human terms with the staff than is possible in one of the modern babels. I telephoned down to have my cousin's bags brought up, and meanwhile I filled a hot water bottle, warmed the bed, and got her into it as quickly as I could. I had never seen her as unquestioning and submissive, and that alarmed me even more than her pallor. She was not the woman to let herself be undressed and put to bed like a baby; but she submitted without a word, as though aware that she had reached the end of her tether.

"It's good to be here," she said in a quieter tone, as I tucked her up and smoothed the pillows. "Don't leave me yet, will you—not just yet."

"I'm not going to leave you for more than a minute—just to get you a cup of tea," I reassured her; and she lay still. I left the door open, so that she could hear me stirring about in the little pantry across the passage, and when I brought her the tea she swallowed it gratefully, and a little color came into her face. I sat with her in silence for some time; but at last she began: "You see it's exactly a year—"

I should have preferred to have her put off till the next morning whatever she had to tell me; but I saw from her burning eyes that she was determined to rid her mind of what was burdening it, and that until she had done so it would be useless to proffer the sleeping draft I had ready.

"A year since what?" I asked stupidly, not yet associating her precipitate arrival with the mysterious occurrences of the previous year at Whitegates.

She looked at me in surprise. "A year since I met that woman. Don't you remember—the strange woman who was coming up the drive the afternoon when I broke my ankle? I didn't think of it at the time, but it was on All Souls' eve that I met her."

Yes, I said, I remembered that it was.

"Well—and this is All Souls' eve, isn't it? I'm not as good as you are on Church dates, but I thought it was."

"Yes. This is All Souls' eve."

"I thought so. . . . Well, this afternoon I went out for my usual walk. I'd been writing letters, and paying bills, and didn't start till late; not till it was nearly dusk. But it was a lovely clear evening. And as I got near the gate, there was the woman coming in—the same woman . . . going toward the house. . . ."

I pressed my cousin's hand, which was hot and feverish now. "If it was dusk, could you be perfectly sure it was the same woman?" I asked.

"Oh, perfectly sure, the evening was so clear. I knew her and she knew me; and I could see she was angry at meeting me. I stopped her and asked: 'Where are you going?' just as I had asked her last year. And she said, in the same queer half-foreign voice: 'Only to see one of the girls,' as she had before. Then I felt angry all of a sudden, and I said: 'You shan't set foot in my house again. Do you hear me? I order you to leave.' And she laughed; yes, she laughed—very low, but distinctly. By that time it had got quite dark, as if a sudden storm was sweeping up over the sky, so that though she was so near me I could hardly see her. We were standing by the clump of hemlocks at the turn of the drive, and as I went up to her, furious at her impertinence, she passed behind the hemlocks, and when I followed her she wasn't there. . . . No; I swear to you she wasn't there. . . . And in the darkness I hurried back to the house, afraid that she would slip by me and get there first. And the queer thing was that as I reached the door the black cloud vanished, and there was the transparent twilight again. In the house everything seemed as usual, and the servants were busy about their work; but I couldn't get it out of my head that the woman, under the shadow of that cloud, had somehow got there before me." She paused for breath, and began again. "In the hall I stopped at the telephone and rang up Nixon, and told him to send me a car at once to go to New York, with a man he knew to drive me. And Nixon came with the car himself. . . ."

Her head sank back on the pillow and she looked at me like a frightened child. "It was good of Nixon," she said.

"Yes; it was very good of him. But when they saw you leaving— the servants, I mean. . . ."

"Yes. Well, when I got upstairs to my room I rang for Agnes. She came, looking just as cool and quiet as usual. And when I told her I was starting for New York in half an hour—I said it was on account of a sudden business call—well, then her presence of mind failed her for the first time. She forgot to look surprised, she even forgot to make an objection—and you know what an objector Agnes is. And as I watched her I could see a little secret spark of relief in her eyes, though she was so on her guard. And she just said: 'Very well, madam,' and asked me what I wanted to take with me. Just as if I were in the habit of dashing off to New York after dark on an autumn night to meet a business engagement! No, she made a mistake not to show any surprise—and not even to ask me why I didn't take my own car. And her losing her head in that way frightened me more than anything else. For I saw she was so thankful I was going that she hardly dared speak, for fear she should betray herself, or I should change my mind."

After that Mrs. Clayburn lay a long while silent, breathing less unrestfully; and at last she closed her eyes, as though she felt more at ease now that she had spoken, and wanted to sleep. As I got up quietly to leave her, she turned her head a little and murmured: "I shall never go back to Whitegates again." Then she shut her eyes and I saw that she was falling asleep.

I have set down above, I hope without omitting anything essential, the record of my cousin's strange experience as she told it to me. Of what happened at Whitegates that is all I can personally vouch for. The rest—and of course there is a rest—is pure conjecture; and I give it only as such.

My cousin's maid, Agnes, was from the isle of Skye, and the Hebrides, as everyone knows, are full of the supernatural—whether in the shape of ghostly presences, or the almost ghostlier sense of unseen watchers peopling the long nights of those stormy solitudes. My cousin, at any rate, always regarded Agnes as the—perhaps unconscious, at any rate irresponsible—channel through which communications from the other side of the veil reached the submissive household at Whitegates. Though Agnes had been with Mrs. Clayburn for a long time without any peculiar incident revealing this affinity with the unknown forces, the power to communicate with them may all the while have been latent in the woman, only awaiting a kindred touch; and that touch may have been given by the unknown visitor whom my cousin, two years in succession, had met coming up the drive at Whitegates on the eve of All Souls'. Certainly the date bears out my hypothesis; for I suppose that, even in this unimaginative age, a few people still remember that All Souls' eve is the night when the dead can walk—and when, by the same token, other spirits, piteous or malevolent, are also freed from the restrictions which secure the earth to the living on the other days of the year.

If the recurrence of this date is more than a coincidence—and for my part I think it is—then I take it that the strange woman who twice came up the drive at Whitegates on All Souls' eve was either a "fetch," or else, more probably, and more alarmingly, a living woman inhabited by a witch. The history of witchcraft, as is well known, abounds in such cases, and such a messenger might well have been delegated by the powers who rule in these matters to summon Agnes and her fellow servants to a midnight "Coven" in some neighboring solitude. To learn what happens at Covens, and the reason of the irresistible fascination they exercise over the timorous and superstitious, one need only address oneself to the immense body of literature dealing with these mysterious rites. Anyone who has once felt the faintest curiosity to assist at a Coven apparently soon finds the curiosity increase to desire, the desire to an uncontrollable longing, which, when the opportunity presents itself, breaks down all inhibitions; for those who have once taken part in a Coven will move heaven and earth to take part again.

Such is my—conjectural—explanation of the strange happening at Whitegates. My cousin always said she could not believe that incidents which might fit into the desolate landscape of the Hebrides could occur in the cheerful and populous Connecticut Valley; but if she did not believe, she at least feared—such moral paradoxes are not uncommon—and though she insisted that there must be some natural explanation of the mystery, she never returned to investigate it.

"No, no," she said with a little shiver, whenever I touched on the subject of her going back to Whitegates, "I don't want ever to risk seeing that woman again. . . ." And she never went back.